CURRENTS OF WAR

BY ZOE SAADIA

At Road's End
The Young Jaguar
The Jaguar Warrior
The Warrior's Way

The Highlander
Crossing Worlds
The Emperor's Second Wife
Currents of War
The Fall of the Empire
The Sword
The Triple Alliance

Two Rivers
Across the Great Sparkling Water
The Great Law of Peace
The Peacekeeper

Beyond the Great River
The Foreigner
Troubled Waters
The Warpath
Echoes of the Past

CURRENTS OF WAR

The Rise of the Aztecs, Book 4

ZOE SAADIA

ISBN: 1537358553
ISBN-13: 978-1537358550

CHAPTER 1

Tenochtitlan
1427

Pushing his way through the crowds, Tlacaelel cursed. People shouted and gestured, pressing against each other, trying to get closer. The hum of their voices carried down the alley and into the marketplace, drawing more onlookers.

"Shove off!" he shouted, pushing them roughly. "Move. Go away." Out of the corner of his eye, he saw his warriors following briskly, not waiting for his orders.

Pleased with their quick reactions, he went on. His closest guards had been handpicked and trained by him personally. He expected them to understand what he wanted without the necessity to explain.

People around him murmured but moved obediently, not daring to anger a warrior, let alone a person of his status. Not yet officially the Chief Warlord, he had acted like such for more than a few market intervals. The whole of Tenochtitlan knew it was just a matter of time before he'd be allowed to don the exquisite headdress and the regalia of this highest military office.

With the crowds parting reluctantly, it took him time to reach the low wall, and the bodies scattered alongside it. Frowning, he studied the bloody mess. He should not have been summoned here he knew, and if he hadn't already been close by, attending a ceremony in the nearby temple, he would never have come. People got killed on the marketplace, in some alleys more than in others. There was nothing out of the ordinary in that. Nothing worth bothering the warriors' leader.

His eyes picked out a group of richly decorated cloaks. "Where is your headman?" he asked curtly, bearing down on them.

"Oh, Honorable Leader!" A short, thickset man knelt hastily, then sprang to his feet. "I am the Second Scribe of the Honorable Judge. I was honored to be entrusted with making inquiries."

"So you were the one who sent for me?"

"Oh, no!" The man flopped his arms in the air, as if trying to push the accusation away. "This was the decision of the Honorable Judge of this district."

Tlacaelel let out a sigh of exasperation. "Tell me what happened, and do it fast. I have *important* matters to attend to."

Like making sure that the party of engineers, sent to the mainland in order to commence yet another repair of the water construction had an adequate amount of escorting warriors, not too little, but not too many either, he thought grimly. Tenochtitlan had, once again, been left with no fresh water. He stifled a curse. The damn water, and the damn Tepanecs.

"Two of the murdered people were Tepanec merchants," he heard the thickset man saying. "It complicates the matter, but not as much as the identity of the man they had, probably, come to meet here."

"No filthy trader can be important enough to justify dragging me here." Turning abruptly, Tlacaelel headed toward the bloody mess lining the wall of the warehouse.

Whoever had killed these men had definitely known how to do the job. No, these traders had not been murdered by simple marketplace robbers, but had been cut neatly and efficiently, with a few clean strikes of the sharpest obsidian. He shrugged, mildly curious now.

"Was there a fight reported in this part of the marketplace?" he asked without turning his head, knowing that the city official would be following.

"No, Honorable Leader. No fights were reported. This part of the marketplace is quite abandoned these days, used mainly for storing goods." The man hesitated. "Even the pleasure women are not frequenting this alley anymore."

"Then what were the stupid Tepanecs doing here?"

The man raised his arms in a helpless gesture, but his gaze lingered, holding Tlacaelel's eyes, pregnant with meaning. *Oh, so some filthy traders were having a clandestine meeting,* he thought grimly. *Is that what the Chief Warlord's duties were coming to?*

"Who are the other two?" he asked, turning one of the bodies with the tip of his sandal.

The chubby man hesitated. "There seem to be two warriors and, well, you may wish to take a look, Honorable Leader." The man's voice trailed off.

Ignoring the obvious fear of the petty official, Tlacaelel knelt, studying the cut.

"Quite a blow," he muttered, appreciating the gash that had almost severed the man's head, cutting deeply into the depths of his neck.

He studied the victim's face, twisted and caked with a mixture of dust and blood.

"I've seen this man in the Palace," he said, still talking to himself. He tried to remember. Yes, definitely, and more than a few times during the past few moons. But as a trader bringing goods? No, this man mingled in higher circles.

"He is no trader," he said, getting up. "But whoever he was, he had no business wandering these parts of the marketplace, and his death still doesn't warrant you interrupting my duties." Not bothering to frighten the official with yet another of his direful glances, he moved toward the other pile.

Oh, those were warriors, indeed, and of the royal guard. He frowned. So that's why he was called? He paid no attention to arrows sticking out of their sides, now anxious to know whom those two had been escorting.

Walking toward the last body, crumbled under the wall, he felt his interest piquing. But for the unnaturally twisted limbs, one might have thought that the man was taking a nap, resting his head against his knees. Tlacaelel kicked it lightly, to make it tip, watching the richly embroidered gown rustling, revealing the man's upper parts, fat and undeveloped. No, this one was no warrior, and he hadn't been cut with a sword either. The beefy arms spread, revealing a gash in the man's padded chest, made by a single thrust from a large knife. As though its victim did not deserve an honorable death by a sword.

Another careful kick, and the dead face was staring into the clearness of the midmorning sky, making Tlacaelel gasp. Wide-eyed, he studied the twisted features of Ikintzin, one of the minor advisers. Unbelievable! An adviser killed in the marketplace. This was the sort of event Tenochtitlan was not accustomed to.

"Get a litter," he said to the stocky official, who by now seemed to be holding his breath, agog with excitement. "Quick. If a litter in not here in a few hundred heartbeats you will be fined, but not before you lose your position."

The man scampered away, terrified.

"Check the warriors," said Tlacaelel curtly, addressing his men. "See if you can identify them. If not, put them in the litter." He hesitated. "Tell the officials to get another one for the warriors."

What a mess, he thought. A minor adviser, damn his eyes. Why would the man run in dubious alleys, holding clandestine meetings with the shady Tepanecs? And why would someone go to such lengths as ambushing and killing them all?

The people who had done this clearly had to spend an effort organizing it, shooting the warriors, then slaying the other three. It had to be done swiftly and efficiently, as too much fuss would bring marketplace frequenters, or even city officials, before the deed was done. Ikintzin was just a minor adviser, and he had fallen out of the Emperor's grace anyway; still, the man's blood was noble and his connections – important.

"Honorable Leader." One of his warriors lingered beside a nearby shed, studying the base of the wide beam. "I think you may want to see this."

Taking a last glance at the lifeless face of the adviser, Tlacaelel got to his feet, remembering the embarrassing incident upon which the Empress had lost her temper, throwing this same minor adviser out of the main hall almost physically. She was not hot-tempered, Tenochtitlan's Empress, and unlike her predecessor, she did not interrupt the Emperor's policies. Not openly, anyway.

Tlacaelel shrugged. That woman had a great influence on her husband. No sensible man had made the mistake of assuming the opposite. Yet, her advice was sound and wise, and if this *altepetl* had to make do with so young an Emperor, it was good to know that he was under the spell of a wise person of enough years and experience.

"What is it?"

He studied the pole the warrior was pointing at, blinking. The face of a carved jaguar stared back at him, glaring from the wooden base, wonderfully detailed and alarmingly real, its eyes round and hallow, teeth bared.

Fighting the urge to take a step back, Tlacaelel muttered a curse. But, of course! He should have guessed without this obvious clue. Glancing at the crumbled face of the murdered adviser, he remembered the last time he had seen the man in the Palace, dressed more richly than ever, sparkling jewelry, his cotton garments of the best quality, making everyone wonder at its owner's sudden riches. Had it something to do with the Tepanec traders that the man had been seen with on many occasions?

The Tepanecs! He stifled another curse. Would his *altepetl* ever be free of their dangerous, intimidating presence? During the past seven summers, since Chimalpopoca, the young Emperor, had let his engineers build the water construction, everything seemed to be quiet, even promising. The Tepanecs remained friendly, despite the death of the previous Empress, Tenochtitlan's main connection to the Tepanec royal house. Even when, over the summers, the matters began to deteriorate as the water pipes, made out of clay, broke again and again, causing much tension between the island nation and their overlords, who were not very prompt at granting permissions to rebuild, or providing the required materials, it didn't come to an outright confrontation, not yet.

However, before the tension reached its peak, Tezozomoc, the Tepanec Emperor, had finally died, leaving his throne to one of his sons, Tayatzin, a quiet, pleasant, reasonable man; a man who didn't seem as though bent on expanding the already too vast empire.

Yes, Tayatzin was a reasonable man and an able ruler, reflected Tlacaelel, having met the man personally. The tension began wearing down again, with Tenochtitlan receiving the needed materials and the permission to use more of the mainland springs. Yet, not everyone had been happy. Maxtla-tzin, one of Tezozomoc's other sons, now the ruler of Coyoacan, had clearly coveted Azcapotzalco's throne, speaking openly against the policies of his brother, stirring up trouble. His people, all sorts of doubtful types, traders and scribes and what-not, now frequented Tenochtitlan's plazas and markets, as they were reported to do through the other city-states and provinces, talking to people, promising things.

Well, this was the company the now-murdered adviser had kept through the past few seasons, getting richer and fatter with each passing moon, while his attempts to convince Tenochtitlan's Emperor to support Maxtla against this lawful brother-ruler grew more and more shameless. But that was not why the Emperor's Chief Wife had lost her temper, ordering the man out of the main hall and the Palace's grounds, looking as though she might throw him out with her own pretty, well groomed hands.

Tlacaelel shook his head, remembering the afternoon, two dawns ago, when he had been almost as enraged as the Empress at the audacious suggestion of the man who, without further ado, had demanded that Nezahualcoyotl, the displaced heir to the Texcoco throne, and brother to the Empress, should not only be thrown out of Tenochtitlan, but actually put to death.

Coyotl was not in the city at the time, having gone to Texcoco, being permitted to do so by Tezozomoc himself. Not as a ruler or citizen, but as a visitor. Apparently, Tezozomoc hadn't seen the threat the young man might have presented, or his plans were subtler than this. So for the past two summers, Coyotl had been traveling between both *altepetls*, detouring from time to time, so it would take him some market intervals to complete a journey of a few days. If he was traveling through his former provinces or even venturing into the Highlands, he didn't share this information with Tenochtitlan's royal family, and Tlacaelel had preferred it this way. He was too busy with his own mounting duties as the Leader of the Warriors, and the water troubles provided enough distraction. He wasn't sure he wanted to know what the Acolhua provinces were up to, not yet.

"It is an omen," muttered the warrior beside him, bringing Tlacaelel back from his reverie. "It's the ocelot's spirit. The only one capable of slaying six people in one single blow, so no one would know or hear."

Tlacaelel tore his eyes off the staring jaguar. The emptiness of the round, carved orbs made his stomach flutter.

"Stop talking nonsense," he said rudely, angered by the shiver that went down his own spine. "They were killed by different weapons. Two of the warriors were shot, and both, the adviser and the filthy trader, were fat, useless pieces of meat, anyway. A child could have slain them with no trouble, and without making too much noise."

"But it's a marketplace, Honorable Leader," insisted the warrior, while two of his peers nodded, their gazes firm upon the ground. "Always full of gossipy people. How could—"

"It happened at night, for gods' sake!" Angered by his own lack of control, Tlacaelel made an effort to calm down. "Make sure the adviser is taken back in a closed litter, then dispose of the Tepanec traders. They were just traders, so there is no need to notify the Tepanec authorities." He stared the paunchy official down. "Whatever their connections were, they were just traders. So they are your responsibility now." Turning back to his followers, he frowned. "Take care of the warriors who were killed. Notify priests. They will decide which rites are the most appropriate."

He glanced at the carved jaguar once again, his skin prickling. Through the past seven summers he had happened to see those hollow eyes and the bared teeth, only two or three times, but always when someone of importance had died. The jaguar was a harbinger of violent, political deaths. And, come to think of it, the deaths were always of people who would go against the Emperor's policies concerning Texcoco and the Acolhua provinces.

He narrowed his eyes. "You two, come with me," he said curtly, addressing a pair of warriors. "The rest of you take care of this mess, then meet me in the Palace when the sun will be at its highest."

"But Honorable Leader," exclaimed the tall warrior, the head of his personal guard. "It is not appropriate for a person of your importance to walk the city with such a small entourage. Allow me to send for your litter, and allocate at least half of twenty men to accompany you, and—"

"Take care of this mess, then meet me in the Palace at the time I said," Tlacaelel cut him off impatiently. "You are overstepping your authority, warrior!"

After the reprimand the man's objections were subdued, but the tension was there in the air, making it denser, more difficult to breath. He glanced at the jaguar once again. "Leave the carving alone for now. I'll see what can be done with it."

The sun bounced prettily off the polished stone walls as the roads became wider, cleaner, and better swept. Tlacaelel felt his anger evaporating. It was such a rare pleasure these days, to just walk, barely attended, not hindered by the bumping palanquin or too many followers.

Feeling like a *calmecac* boy again, he looked around, enjoying the sight of his beloved *altepetl*. He remembered the city when it was smaller and dirtier, too busy to pay attention to impractical elegance and luxury. It was changing rapidly now.

Now the streets of Tenochtitlan were cleaner and wider, consisting of two-story buildings made out of adobe or solid, thoroughly polished stone. Well, at least, this is how the neighborhoods around the Plaza looked, the ones that housed minor leaders of warriors and other prominent citizens of the city. Not like the best aristocratic parts near the Palace and the Great Pyramid, but better than anything that was closer to the marketplace and the wharves.

A group of children, playing along the road, stared at him as he turned into a small, but well groomed, garden, crossing it as he headed toward the wide, perfectly clean patio.

"Is the master of the house here?" he asked a slave who had rushed toward him, wide-eyed.

"Oh, yes, Honorable Warlord," mumbled the man, sinking onto his knees in order to prostrate himself. "The Master did not leave the city as he was supposed to."

"Let him know that I'm here."

"Oh, Honorable Leader, the Master went out to visit the baths."

"Then send for him," growled Tlacaelel, resuming his walk toward the house.

Another slave came out, taller and surer of himself than the one who was still trembling on the ground.

"Please, Honorable Leader," said the second man smoothly. "Allow me to escort you in while the word is being sent to the Master."

Inside the relatively spacious hall, Tlacaelel blinked, having difficulty adjusting to the semidarkness after the brilliant light outside.

A woman rushed toward him. Small and a little too thin, she looked very appealing, nevertheless, wearing a pretty turquoise blouse and skirt, her hair pulled high, her slender arms sporting matching bracelets. A child, sitting on her hip, nestled safely against the curve of her arm, contributed to the cozy, domestic picture the woman presented.

"Please, come on in," she said smiling, stopping a few paces short of the entrance. "It is a great honor." Hesitating, she shifted her gaze toward the low tables scattered in the far corner. "The refreshments! Let me make sure the refreshments are on their way." The child in her arms went absolutely still, afraid and expectant at the same time, sensing its mother's tension.

"Just send word to your man. I need to talk to him urgently," said Tlacaelel, smiling back, liking her, remembering this *cihua* as a young, frightened, and later on, very determined, girl. Just a slave girl, really, but not a slave nevertheless. A little savage who had cared nothing for Tenochtitlan's nobility or appropriate behavior, concerned with her Highlander only, oblivious of anything else.

Oh, she had stalked him carefully, the canny little thing, he reflected. Always around, blending into the background, but usually there, sometimes catching the Highlander's attention, sometimes holding it even for a little while. Acutely aware of his surroundings, used to noticing little details, to mark them for a possible future use, Tlacaelel had noticed that, too, without paying it much attention. Just a funny little detail about the wild foreigner who had fascinated him from the very beginning. The girl was just one more thing in the strange, intriguing world of the two youths who had come out of nowhere, determined to play their part in making Tenochtitlan's history.

"Please, make yourself comfortable, Warlord," the woman repeated, gesturing toward the pretty arrangement of mats. Everything in this room looked cozy and inviting.

He squatted upon the mat and watched the maid coming in, carrying a tray.

"I'm not the Chief Warlord yet," he said, winking at the child. "When you see me wearing the headdress you can call me that."

The fleeting smile transformed her face, making it look girlish and irresistibly attractive.

"Oh, I apologize," she said, suddenly at ease, almost teasing. "I should not have listened to the people, but, rather, trusted my eyes." The child moved, trying to reach for her mother's hair.

"So you keep giving him a child every summer, don't you?" His eyes slid down her gown. In such a slender woman it was easy to see that her belly looked rounder than it should be.

Her eyes danced. "He is a vigorous man."

"Yes, I see he is not wasting his time each time he comes back to Tenochtitlan. No wonder he takes no additional wife."

"Yes, he is too busy for that." Frowning, she watched the maid arranging plates and cups, then bent to put the child down. "You are useless, Nakaztli," she said, addressing the woman. "You can serve your friends from the marketplace this way, but not the Honorable Warlord."

Kneeling beside the table, she shot the maid a direful glance, then began rearranging the plates, turning the low table into a beautiful affair, while Tlacaelel let his gaze wander, liking this house, so elegant and cozy, so invitingly warm. An island of peacefulness and tranquility, to relax and to put one's worries aside. Even the sword upon the wide podium did not interfere with the warm serenity of the place, looking less ominous than when in its owner's hands.

Glad for the rare opportunity, he let his gaze dwell on the most famous weapon in the city, and even beyond it. Oh, the whole of Tenochtitlan talked about this sword, wondering at this unique affair of beautiful carvings covering it almost entirely, not only the handle, but the wooden shaft as well, running forcefully between the obsidian spikes. Some carvings were fresh, added more recently. Others looked shadowed, disturbingly real, their cuts brownish with the old, congealed blood, enhancing the threatening images.

Many believed that this sword held magical qualities, doubling its owner's power or keeping him from harm. Sometimes, Tlacaelel tended to believe that himself. The Highlander had survived many battles, but this happened to veteran warriors, and he had his share of wounds like anybody else. Yet, there were occasions upon which even this fierce, resourceful warrior should not have survived. Like that evening, seven summers ago, when the Highlander should have died for certain. His sword has been only half covered with carvings back in those days, but what it had was obviously more than enough. Shivering, he forced his attention back to the table and the pretty woman kneeling beside it.

"Why didn't he leave for Texcoco with the Acolhua heir this time?" he asked, enjoying the sight of her small, slender hands moving busily as she made sure everything had been set in a perfect balance against each other.

Her face darkened. "I'm sorry. I don't know."

The child, who had, in the meanwhile, crawled toward the table, reached for a plate, clearly more out of curiosity than from actually coveting the piles of rolled tortillas. The woman jumped to her feet and picked the protesting baby up.

"Where are his boys?"

Not put out with this domestic scene, Tlacaelel remembered his friend's older sons. His own children were smaller, and his spacious set of rooms in the main wing of the Palace never enjoyed a quarter of this peace, with both of his wives canceling each other's orders, struggling for dominance. Amused, he had let them be, too busy to interfere.

She smiled again. "They ran ahead of the servant in order to fetch their father. The fiercest creatures of the Underworld would not be able to prevent them from doing so."

At her last words, they could hear the clamor on the patio.

"That'll be enough. Off with you two," he heard the Highlander's voice, as a shadow fell across the room. His wide shoulders blocking the light for a moment, the man turned back toward the patio. "No, you are not getting in."

The children's voices rang in protest, but drew away eventually.

"What an honor!" Paces wide, the Highlander crossed the room in what seemed like a single leap, dropping to the opposite side of the table, eyes twinkling. "The whole neighborhood went into frenzy. Even before those two wild ocelots reached me, beating the panting slave to the baths, I heard everyone talking about the Chief Warlord coming here on foot, and with no entourage, like the last of the commoners."

"Oh, yes, I couldn't drag my palanquin bearers and the more respectable of my warriors into such a dismal neighborhood." Reaching for another tortilla, Tlacaelel laughed. "They would complain to our current Chief Warlord, asking him to choose another man in my stead."

"Oh, no! That might have changed Tenochtitlan's future. But whether for the best or for the worst..." Hungrily, the Highlander reached for food, then looked up at his wife, who still stood there, expectant, clutching the struggling child. "Off with you, woman," he said, flashing at her an affectionate smile. "And make sure we are not disturbed, even by the servants. Oh, and send here a flask of *octli*."

"*Octli*? At this time of the day?" Tlacaelel grinned, watching her as she frowned. He tried to remember her name, something outlandish but pretty, rolling off one's tongue.

"Why not?"

"Well, your type can slumber in baths and drink *octli* in the morning, but a busy leader needs to keep his wits sharp during the day."

"Oh, for gods' sake, what can a cup of *octli* do to your ever-busy head?" The Highlander leaned against the wall, devouring another tortilla. "I'm famished. The baths always do this to me. If not for you, I would slumber there for a whole day." He grinned. "I wish I could live in my uncle's mansion, with that bathhouse in the middle of his gardens, his and his alone."

"Oh, yes, I would take his house, too. I hate living in the Palace. It's a pain unless you are the emperor." Tlacaelel shrugged. "And maybe even then."

He saw the shadow crossing the Highlander's face and thought about what he'd seen on the marketplace. Yes, there were dark rings around the widely spaced eyes, and one could see more signs of the obvious lack of sleep.

Another maid brought a tray with a flask and two cups, then scampered away hurriedly. They could hear his wife outside, raising her voice, admonishing the boys.

"An unruly lot," said Kuini, pouring from the flask, his grin one of the widest. "Only their mother can tell them from each other, and they like nothing better than to confuse everyone. A wild pair who behave as alike as they look. I can't wait to ship them to *calmecac*, but I pity the place."

"Two boys born together is an omen. The gods were kind to you, more than once, through that particular span of seasons." Frowning, he remembered that turbulent night seven summers ago, when the whole Palace had held its breath as the Warlord and the Tepanec Empress were ready to go for each other's throat, throwing all their power and influence into the deadly lock of wills. He still wished to know what had happened, under which circumstances the Empress had died and how it all was connected to his friend, the unpredictable Highlander, who had also come oh-so-very-close to death on that night. "You didn't finish your

Path of the Dead seven summers ago, because the gods had decided to save you for their own purpose. And just a few seasons later, they sent you the twins. It might be an omen. Maybe you, or those boys, are destined to help Mexica people to take their real path."

But the Highlander just laughed. "Oh, spare me the story of the eagle and the prophecy. I know you, people, want to rule the world, but I'm no Mexica Aztec, and neither are my boys. I'm helping you against the Tepanecs only because my people are threatened by them, and also because of Coyotl. I don't want to see the Aztecs ruling the world. I think you may prove worse than the Tepanecs." He poured more *octli* into their cups, then smiled widely. "Don't turn all red on me, old friend. I know you take your destiny seriously, but I'm not with you in this. Also," he laughed and drained his cup in almost one gulp, "the twins must have already been there, in her belly, when those events took place. They were born only two and a half seasons later. If the gods really interfered, I suppose they just wanted to get a good laugh at my expense. I bet it was Huitzilopochtli, that strange Mexica god of yours. He doesn't like foreigners."

"Or maybe some of your wild highlander gods," grunted Tlacaelel, not pacified in the least. "A deity with the face of a jaguar, eh? Bared teeth, round eyes. Anything of that kind."

The amusement on his host's face drained off at once. "We have no such deities," he said stonily, staring into his cup. "Camaxtli has nothing to do with jaguars."

"Interesting, because this ominous deity keeps haunting Tenochtitlan every time something in the Palace goes wrong." Still seething, Tlacaelel enjoyed watching the broad face turning angrier by the heartbeat. "The Empress, that paragon of virtue, losing her temper only two dawns ago, and here we have that strange foreign god dealing with those who made her angry."

"This is a farfetched conclusion." The Highlander's voice had a growling sound to it.

"Not that farfetched. You see, this thing catches the eye. It makes people uneasy, makes them remember. It makes them scared. Today, I saw this jaguar again, and it made me nervous, although I knew better than the simple warriors. Not to mention the stupid marketplace lot." He caught the stormy eyes and held it. "This time the priests might be involved, and they are wise, canny people with sharp eyes. They have time and resources to investigate, to go around and ask people, to come to all sorts of conclusions." Watching the dark, haunted face, he felt an unusual wave of compassion. "I'm not telling you to stop guarding the interests of our royal family, or the Acolhua parts of it. We are friends of many summers, and as long as you do not go against my policies, I will not tell you what to do. But as a friend, I want to warn you. Stop doing things in your peculiar way. Stop leaving such obvious marks. It works. It scares people. But it can also work against you. I would hate to see the authorities going after you. Like you said, you are no Mexica Aztec, and, although your connections in Tenochtitlan are exceptional, they may still execute you, leader of warriors or not."

"They can try!" The eyes peering at him softened as a surprisingly unguarded smile stretched the man's lips. "You are a great friend, Chief Warlord." The smile widened. "For an Aztec, you are a truly good man."

"And you are everything they say about the Highlanders, but twenty times worse." Picking up his cup, Tlacaelel studied the milky liquid, then drank it in one gulp. "Why didn't you go with Coyotl this time?"

Kuini's cup made a hollow sound, banging against the polished wood. "Itzcoatl, curse his damn squinted eyes into the deepest parts of the Underworld." He filled the cup once again, shaking the flask to get the last of the liquid. "The damn manure-eater wouldn't listen. He wanted me to take my warriors on another raid, against the stupid Amecameca, or what was left of them. As though no one could take a pitiful amount of three times twenty warriors over Lake Chalco but me." He drained his cup once again, then looked up, eyes troubled and dark. "And I'm telling you, I worry about Coyotl. Something isn't right this time. This man, the one who tried to make the Emperor throw Coyotl out, or even execute him, is backed by more than just a few filthy traders. There are plenty of those types all over the towns of the valley, you know? They are going around, spreading rumors, trying to get people to side with that discontented frog-eater, the other Tepanec heir. They are up to something, I'm telling you. And it's nothing good."

Tlacaelel felt his stomach tightening. "What do you know?"

"All sorts of things. I talked to my uncle the other day, after what happened in the Palace. Well, he thinks this Maxtla is a dangerous bastard. He thinks this manure-eater may get to Azcapotzalco's throne after all. He thinks Tenochtitlan is not ready to rebel, not yet, and, therefore, the Emperor should not take sides, but that he should let the Tepanec royal house sort out its differences all by itself."

"Oh, I know all that! I told the Emperor as much, but he wouldn't listen. That boy can get stubborn from time to time, and his pretty Empress is not always as smart as she looks."

The Highlander's face closed. "She is smart, but maybe she didn't think of it yet. Maybe you should talk to her."

"Or maybe you should. She likes talking to you, one can see that." Tlacaelel ducked out of range as a fist shot at the direction of his elbow, halfheartedly so. "Oh, the haughty Empress's honor is safe with her guarding spirit never asleep." He began getting up. "Get some sleep, guarding spirit. You look horrible, and Itzcoatl will not like it. Especially if he is planning to send you to take those Chalcoans all by yourself."

"Listen," the Highlander sprang to his feet too, swaying a little. "I want you to have something." He caught the nearby pole to steady himself, then shook his head. "Stupid tiredness."

"That's no tiredness, man. That's a whole flask of *octli* consumed in the middle of the morning."

"No, it's the baths and the tiredness." Kuini shook his head once again, as if trying to clear it, then reached for his girdle. "I want you to have this. That filthy adviser who got himself killed by the marketplace robbers, guided by the outlandish jaguar spirit that scares stupid people, well, he received this note from the Tepanec trader, who was not really a trader. You remember this man, right? Hanging around the Palace in the company of the adviser, sparkling with nice jewelry."

"Yes, I remember him. He got himself killed by the same bunch of robbers." Tlacaelel took the piece of *amate*-paper, making an effort not to unfold it right away. "I wonder how many robbers there were. They must have been well organized. If it were possible, I would think it was only one robber."

The Highlander's eyes sparkled. "You have too much faith in the abilities of some robbers. One man can't dispose of so many people quickly and soundlessly unless aided."

"Oh, that's a relief." Shrugging, Tlacaelel headed for the doorway. "I hope he can trust the people he used. This was a very dangerous robbery."

"Yes, his aid was trustworthy and just as involved. Let me know what's in the note. I couldn't decipher it myself, and I tried."

Outside, the boys, two half naked affairs of uncut hair and fit, brown bodies, were busy digging a ditch around the pole supporting the gate.

"Stop doing what you are doing, you two rascals," shouted Kuini, laughing. He leaped forward to catch the offenders, but the boys just giggled and bolted away, as swift as two rodents, their round, foreign-looking faces glimmering, their mirth spilling.

He had no chance of reaching them, reflected Tlacaelel, amused. Maybe while at his best, but not now, drunk and swaying with exhaustion.

"See what one has to put up with?" gasped the Highlander, leaning against the sabotaged pole. "It's safer out there, with the warriors."

"You should discipline them, you know."

But Kuini just shrugged. "They'll be all right." He straightened up with an effort. "I like them that way. I'm not going to be the one trying to break their spirits." Shielding his eyes against the glow of the midday sun, he peered into the distance. "I wish I knew what's going on in Texcoco."

CHAPTER 2

Texcoco was in decline. One could feel that even with one's eyes shut, reflected Coyotl, suppressing a shudder. There was a smell of neglect along the broad roads and the narrow alleys alike, with garbage piled in some corners and an occasional rat sneaking between one's feet.

Once a great *altepetl*, clean and groomed to perfection, after eight summers of foreign occupation, Texcoco had been turned into just another province, a large city of no importance. The Great Pyramid was still there, and the broad avenue with the multitude of temples, and the Palace with gardens and artificial groves, yet they looked pitifully neglected now, unheeded, their walls cracking, their plaster peeling off. Just another provincial city belonging to the Tepanecs, but paying its tribute to the Aztecs.

Clenching his teeth, Coyotl pushed away the familiar wave of despondency. *One thing at a time. First, you fight and survive, so you can get your* altepetl *back. Then, you think of its troubles, of the ways to return it to its previous glory.*

Impossible? Maybe. But he had nothing to lose by now. Eight summers of waiting had taught him patience. Shrugging, he straightened his gaze, facing his companions.

"We will pay our respects to the governor in the Palace, but we will not stay for more than a day or two," he said lightly, returning their worried glances. "I would rather see us heading out tonight, but it won't be possible. The governor may insist, overwhelmed by the honor of receiving guests of our status." He grinned. "I hope he doesn't."

"Why don't we just leave the city now, Honorable Leader?"

asked one of the warriors. "In this time of the cycle of seasons we can spend the most pleasant night camping outside. It will also spare us time on our way to the mountains, the way you planned."

"No. We have to show our faces here in Texcoco, as we were supposed to do. Our official destination is here, not in the south or in the Highlands." He smiled at them, pleased to be surrounded by the people he trusted. "We can detour without drawing too much attention, but we cannot *not* show our faces in Texcoco at all."

Sure enough, a group of officials were already bearing down on them, descending the broad road from the direction of the Plaza. Again, his gaze lingered, remembering this road, always perfectly swept and teeming with busy, dignified Texcocans, well fed and well groomed, the aristocrats of the Great Lake. Oh, he had traveled this road countless times, always running and in a hurry, in summers and in winters, as a boy and then a youth, a *calmecac* student and then the imperial heir, sure of himself and his future, knowing that some things would never change.

Oh, how little had he known! The road was still clean, but the signs of dilapidation and neglect showed in the peeling walls of the temples, in the fresh grass sprouting through the cracked pavement, in the simple looking people rushing about their business, silent and in a hurry, their heads down. He ground his teeth and forced his mind to concentrate on the greetings of the new masters of Texcoco.

"What a rare honor, oh Noble Nezahualcoyotl!" The head of the delegation was saying, his smile unnaturally wide, his tension as obvious as that of the passersby. "Our governor was delighted to learn of your arrival. The preparations for the welcoming feast are at their highest. Oh, Noble Nezahualcoyotl, you grace this city with your presence!"

Not a difficult feat these days, reflected Coyotl gloomily, forcing a smile.

"The honor is all mine," he said. "However, I wouldn't want to interfere with the busy day of the Honorable Governor. Please, don't let him put himself to any trouble on my account. My men will find an appropriate accommodation in the city, while I will be honored to pay my respects to the governor in the Palace."

The man's face broke into a smile of obeisance. "Oh, Noble Nezahualcoyotl, the Palace will not be the same without you gracing it with your presence. Your men, your followers, will be accommodated and entertained most lavishly. The Honorable Governor is awaiting you."

A litter swept by, carried by sturdy slaves, and followed by a small army of maids. He watched it absently, but as the curtains moved, he caught a glimpse of a young, round face and a pair of huge, liquid eyes peering at him, wide open and as if dazed. Struggling to keep his attention on the flowery pleasantries of the petty official, he followed the girl with his gaze, strangely curious, watching the gentle palm sneaking out, the long bejeweled fingers lifting the curtain, rewarding him with a more generous view of her prettily round face.

"The baths are awaiting you, and the best set of rooms for you and your men," went on the official. "Please, Noble Nezahualcoyotl, please, let us escort you to the Palace."

"Of course."

Forcing another smile, Coyotl signed to his men, avoiding their troubled glances. There was no way of escaping the Palace, as unpleasant and as unnecessary as this experience might be. They had no choice. The new Tepanec ruler should hear about his visit in Texcoco, which was officially planned and approved beforehand. But they better not learn of the places he had visited on his way here, or the places he had planned to visit while heading back to Tenochtitlan.

He suppressed his elation, remembering the eagerness with which the Acolhua towns had greeted him. For two summers, since being allowed to visit his former *altepetl*, he had made a point of traveling through his former provinces, visiting towns and villages, talking to prominent people, listening to their complaints, like a governor would. Not bringing up any troublesome issues, oh, no. Let them arrive at all sort of conclusions by themselves, he thought, remembering his first conversation with Kuini's father, that wise Highlander leader, who, thanks to Coyotl, was not the Warriors' Leader anymore, but who still wielded much influence among his fierce country folk.

With an effort, he hide his grin, watching the Palace's walls towering ahead. Oh but he would detour by way of the Highlands before heading back to Tenochtitlan, like he always did, and he would spend more than a few dawns in the company of this remarkable man.

The word to Huexotzinco had already been sent through the pool of shady individuals the First Warlord of Tenochtitlan still had at his disposal. They would always do that, send word so the old Highlander would wait by the first pass of the high ridges separating the mountains from the coastal towns. Seven summers had passed, yet Coyotl did not dare to show his face in Huexotzinco itself, having fled this town in the most shameful of ways once upon a time.

He shrugged. He had been very young and very stupid back then, but Kuini's father had believed in him nevertheless, going to great lengths to save his, Coyotl's, life. Oh, what would he do without this formidable man and his calm advice, given always in light, amused, unobtrusive ways? Through the past seven summers, he and Kuini would sneak to the Highlands from time to time, once or twice through every span of seasons, with the former Warriors' Leader waiting in relatively neutral areas where they would camp for days, talking and hunting, and then talking some more.

Of late, Kuini was too busy to join him, and so Coyotl would go alone, in the hidden parts of his heart welcoming the chance to have the impressive man's company all for himself. Oh, it was such a pleasure to sit beside the crackling fire, with the tranquility of the night surrounding them, at peace and not in a hurry, talking history and politics and laughing, making jokes. It was impossible to have a long, serious conversation with Kuini's father. The man's acute sense of humor lightened every subject, no matter how serious or hopeless the matter looked.

Taking life as lightly as possible, the old man would say, one spares himself a whole deal of troubled thoughts and sleepless nights. There were no problems that could not be dealt with, and there was no sense in trying to solve any of them before they had pressed themselves upon you. One thing at a time, he would say, one thing at a time. And so they would talk history and joke about it, the Tepanecs and the Aztecs and the Lowlanders and the Highlanders, while Coyotl had learned a thousand fold more from this wise man than he had learned in all his summers in *calmecac*, discovering how great empires were governed and what the mistakes of many prominent rulers were.

"Tezozomoc is a very able man," the old Highlander would say. "But at some point, he lost control over his ever-growing empire. It got out of his hands and began rolling down the hill, the way a snowball does. It grew and gained power, assuming life of its own. It went out of control, running its course toward the inevitable crash. And it will happen soon, Nezahualcoyotl. It will. It has reached the flat land now, and it's still rolling, thanks to the accumulated force behind it." The man's eyes glimmered in the flickering light of the small fire, surrounded by the tranquility of the night. "Great empires can do this to people. You have to be very able and very farsighted in order to not let it rule you, to retain control of your realm. Usually, pure greediness blinds a person, a ruler. It makes him see only the power and the impressive size of this snowball, but what he fails to see is the fact that this magnificent thing has far since escaped, running wild, dragging him along, unruly and out of control."

Shivering, Coyotl would tuck the rims of his cloak around his limbs. The nights were still cold in the high ridges of the First Pass. "How can one prevent this from happening? How can one retain control of his empire?"

"Oh, this is a tricky matter. How can one keep from allowing his greediness to get the better of him?" The old Highlander's grin was wide. "Great rulers are not the only people who are forced to face this particular danger. Anyone could lose control over his life, not noticing that he has let it go in favor of some benefits." The large eyes sparkled, amused. "How can you avoid this? I don't know. You just try to be true to yourself, to see the general picture, to remember what you wanted in the first place." A light shrug. "Anyway, I don't think you will be in any danger of your future empire growing too large. The Aztecs will be there, making sure you, the Acolhua people, don't grow too powerful. And the Tepanecs, too. You will be forced to guard your realm's independence most of your life, spending a lot of effort on doing this, I'm afraid."

Coyotl stared into the fire. "Kuini thinks the Aztecs will prove worse than the Tepanecs one day."

"Yes, I remember him harping on this idea more than once." The older man threw another bunch of sticks into the fire, then began stirring the embers, deep in thought. "Well, he may be right, but we can do nothing about it, can we? You need the Aztecs. You can't throw off the Tepanecs' yoke without their aid. So, like I said – one problem at a time. First the Tepanecs, then the Aztecs."

"I hope I live long enough, as this undertaking will take a lifetime, or maybe more."

"Oh, yes, you will have to leave a firm legacy for your descendants to follow." The old Highlander shook his head. "I'm tempted to visit Tenochtitlan, you know. This *altepetl* must have a certain magic to it. Every member of my family who has gone there stayed. My brother, and now my son, with all his litany for the overlooked danger of the Aztecs. It seems like he's staying there for good, doesn't it? Leading warriors, growing family. I wonder why he didn't make an effort to find himself a local *cihua* of noble blood, to establish a dynasty. The way he breeds with his Highland girl, he really should take care of his Aztec progeny."

"His wife is all right. She is a good woman."

He knew it was ridiculous, but it hurt to hear even this man talking about Kuini's wife in such a dismissive way. Enough that the Highlander himself never saw the treasure behind the small, pretty thing, taking everything she had done for him for granted. As if there were nothing outstanding in the way this woman had always been there, doing everything for him, from saving his life to running his household in the most perfect of manners, making his place warm and cozy and safe to come back and relax, giving him good, healthy children. Not to mention the miracle of the twins, born shortly after she had brought him back from the first pass of the Underworld realm.

"She is a good woman," he repeated. "Kuini is lucky to have her."

"Oh," the old man nodded lightly, his smile quivering. "I'm glad my son is that well settled. But how about you?"

"Me?" Coyotl shrugged, unsettled. "When I have my Texcoco back, I will take plenty of wives, and I will start a dynasty. But not before that."

The smile of the old leader was wide. "You've made a long way toward this goal, and you will not have to wait much longer. You worked very hard through the past half twenty of summers, and you did better than I expected." The proud smile bestowed on him had made Coyotl's heart swell, and now, preparing for the welcoming feast, a guest in the Palace that had once belonged to him, he thought that so far he did, indeed, seem to be living up to this great man's expectations.

He did everything according to the complicated plan that the two brothers, two former Tepanecs, had concocted. He had made friends with Tenochtitlan's young Emperor, who had promptly intercepted on his, Coyotl's, behalf before the mighty Tezozomoc, until Coyotl was allowed to live in Tenochtitlan openly, without the need to hide his identity. He fought in the Mexica campaigns at Zacatlan, learning to be a good warrior and a leader, growing closer with Itzcoatl and Tlacaelel, and many other influential people, who had seen his potential and had appreciated him for what he was, and not only for his blood ties. He had turned into a man, learning patience and subtlety, along with other helpful skills a ruler might need one day.

So now, allowed to visit his former lands, he felt that he was ready. Tezozomoc had been dead for more than two seasons, and the Acolhua people began to arrive at all sorts of conclusions. They were ready to fight for their independence, but they still needed their former allies.

"The Great Capital is not the same since the death of the mighty Emperor." Reclining upon his cushioned mat, the paunchy governor sighed, reaching for a plate of tomatoes. "I wish the gods would have granted this glorious man an eternal life."

"Yes, the mighty Tezozomoc was an outstanding ruler," agreed Coyotl politely, picking a tomato from the same plate. Absently, he watched the spacious hall, remembering the receptions his father used to throw there for the benefit of his Acolhua subjects, between the first and the second of the Tepanecs' invasions.

You don't think of it now, he ordered himself, pursing his lips. *You don't think of the times when this Palace was yours. You control yourself, and you concentrate on the more immediate problems. Like the necessity of not touching any food, even though you are so damn hungry. Like the urgency to leave, to escape this trap you have been so stupid as to put yourself into.*

"So sad that his successor is not living up to his great father's expectations," the beefy man went on, devouring tomatoes one after another, the folds of his gown falling around his impressively large belly.

"Revered Tayatzin had proven himself a good ruler," said Coyotl, wondering if it was safe to sample food off the same plate. "I'm sure he will carry on his father's legacy well."

But the governor shook his head vigorously. "Oh, no, Honorable Nezahualcoyotl." Leaning forward as if about to share something personal, the man knitted his forehead, his eyebrows threatening to create a single line. "His brother, the Revered Maxtla-tzin, would prove a better ruler to the Great Capital. It's a shame such a man is wasting his skills ruling a meaningless province while his brother is ruining everything the Great Emperor has achieved through the decades of his remarkable reign."

Coyotl shifted uneasily, unsettled by the unexpected passion in the man's voice. Had the governor just shared his thoughts with his questionable guest, incautiously at that?

He studied the round, puffy face of the new Texcoco governor, appointed by the Tepanec royal house. The Acolhua Capital could pay its tribute to Tenochtitlan, but everyone knew who ruled this *altepetl.* The dark eyes returned his gaze, seemingly sincere, but their depths were sealed, impossible to read.

"I trust Azcapotzalco's royal house to sort out its differences," said Coyotl, non-committal.

He watched the maid pouring into his cup and fought the urge to pick it up. He would have to remain thirsty for just a little more time, he promised himself. Until the feast thrown in his honor was over, and he could fill his cup from a water source he could trust, preferably on his way out of this accursed place.

He pressed his lips tight. What a mess. How did it come to this? He had traveled his former lands, visiting his *altepetl* openly and officially. Tezozomoc himself declared him trustworthy, with Tayatzin, his successor, abiding to the legacies of his father, confirming Coyotl's right to visit Texcoco, and even to live here. How could he have guessed that this time entering the Palace, he would put his life in danger?

Yes, he had told his warriors he would rather avoid spending his time here, yet, when pressed he didn't try to get away. How could he have guessed?

Toying with the tomato from the governor's plate, he recalled the hot, early afternoon, when he had finished loitering in the steam baths and was sprawling in the coolness of the guests' suite of rooms, drifting into the peacefulness of a well deserved nap. About to fall asleep, he had seen the girl slipped in, startling him. She had carried a pile of cushions, but she looked too uncomfortable to be just a maid. Her troubled eyes kept darting around as he stared at her, very put out. His warriors should not have let anyone in, even a harmless maid, he thought, enraged. His rest was important. Having spent too long a time in the baths, he needed to gather his strength to share the governor's evening without raising any suspicions of this yet another Tepanec puppet. He would need his wits sharp and his senses alert. They'd have to head back toward Tenochtitlan, making their detour through Huexotla and Coatlinchan as unnoticeable as possible.

"Go away," he told her, disliking her frightened looks. "Put those cushions wherever they belong, and go away. Don't you see that you are disturbing me?"

"Oh, but I have to..." The color left the girl's face, and she looked as if she was about to faint. "Oh, please, Honorable Master, please. You have to come..."

"What?" He stared at her in disbelief, raising his head but still hoping to return to the restful position. "To come where? Who sent you?"

"My Mistress... she told me... she said... she is waiting for you by the pond." The maid swallowed, her voice dropping to a whisper. "There is a pond, beside the small back gate, right behind—"

"I know where the pond is, and where the back gate is, too!" he called out, exasperated. Oh, he knew those Palace's gardens better than any of them, the filthy invaders. "Who is your mistress? What does she want with me?"

The girl took a step back, bumping her head against the wall.

"Oh, don't get that scared," he said. "Just tell me who your mistress is and what does she want."

"She is... she is waiting for you by the pond." The girl's voice trembled so badly, he had difficulty understanding her words.

Sighing, he contemplated his next move. He wanted to go back to sleep, but the girl, as scared as she looked, seemed as if she would not give up. And maybe it was something important. Maybe some of his Acolhua contacts needed to send him an urgent message.

"Lead me to your mistress," he said, snatching up his cloak. "But be quick about it. And it better be something of importance."

The quiet gardens swept by, deserted in the heat of such early afternoon time, when the decent people were resting, gathering their strength for the evening. He made his way beneath the trees, avoiding broad alleys, choosing smaller paths in their stead. The maid panted behind, clearly not familiar with the gardens at all. As were the two warriors, who had insisted on accompanying him, although he wanted to go alone. Those men had been handpicked by Kuini, instructed to guard him, Coyotl, with their very lives, clearly determined to do just that.

Coyotl grinned. As he had expected all along, the Highlander turned out to be a stern leader of the warriors, good and quick, and usually just, but his men were afraid of angering him. For all his impulsiveness and his irregular thinking, Kuini was a born leader, and he was in his element now. If only his friend were less fond of *octli*, drinking this spicy beverage at all times of the day.

The pond's waters flickered invitingly, reflecting the rays of the high noon sun, reminding him of the times he had been running around or sneaking between the trees as a child, with Iztac Ayotl by his side, up to their usual mischief.

Iztac Ayotl, the Empress of Tenochtitlan!

He had seen her quite a lot through the past seven summers, being a frequent guest in the Mexica Palace. However, it was never the same. The playmate of his childhood was gone, replaced by the serene, aloof, beautiful woman; the reserved, preoccupied empress. Her conversations were friendly, her smile held affection, but her eyes never sparkled, and there was no emotion behind the perfect facade.

Even though it was clear that she didn't lack any feelings at all. She clearly liked the young Emperor, her husband, who had relied on her entirely and who had worshipped the ground she stepped on. She had also, most obviously, disliked Itzcoatl, the Warlord and the main adviser of the Emperor. If she could get rid of the man, she would, reflected Coyotl, uncomfortably aware that somehow he felt she was capable of doing something like that.

And there was only one man who could banish the coldness out of the dark, indifferent eyes, who would make them sparkle like polished obsidian put into too strong of a light. Every time the Highlander would visit the Palace under this or that pretext, usually coming to report to Itzcoatl, the Empress's eyes would light with a deep glow, bringing the golden mask of her face to life, to shine with an almost indecent beauty.

Oh, something had gone on between these two, something worse than a simple indiscretion, something that made people wonder and shake their heads, forcing their minds to arrive at all sorts of conclusions, none of them good. It was too obvious to miss, and he, Coyotl, her only brother, a person she had been only nice and friendly to now, as though their past had never existed, was worried. Worried about her and worried about his friend, whose status of the promising leader of the warriors was solid, but not solid enough. The Emperor, for one, hated the Highlander openly, and Coyotl had heard him complaining more than once, telling the Warlord that he should not let foreigners lead contingents of his Mexica warriors.

Sighing, he forced his thoughts off Tenochtitlan's Palace, concentrating on the deserted pond.

"Where is that mistress of yours?" he asked the sweaty maid rudely, whirling at her.

"Behind the pond, Revered Master." The girl stumbled over her words. "She is waiting, waiting over there."

He strained his eyes, until able to pick out the small, hooded figure out of the surrounding green. The woman's gown was almost of the same color, a bright shade of green with streaks of bright blue, as though she were a part of the gardens. Coming closer, he saw that she was young, curvy if not plump, very unsure of herself, although on her wrists sparkled bracelets of topaz, and her blouse was cotton and richly embroidered, covering her chest up to her neck, demurely at that. A noble lady.

Her gaze flew to him, startled, and his breath caught. The same huge, liquid eyes looked at him, the way they had peered at him this morning upon the Plaza as her litter swept by. Yet if the first time her eyes held a shy curiosity, now they were full of fear and uncertainty, peering at him, afraid even to blink, as it seemed.

He knew he should say something, but the words stuck, refusing to come out, so the girl was the one to break the awkward silence.

"I... I wish to apologize for bringing you here at such an unusual time of the day, oh Noble Nezahualcoyotl," she said in a surprisingly steady voice that did not match her frightened expression.

As if it would have been more natural had she summoned him here in any other time of the day, he thought randomly.

"Oh, no, there is no need to apologize," he said, still at a loss, having difficulty tearing his eyes off the generous curve of her mouth.

"I..." She seemed to grow more uncertain under his gaze. "I

sent my maid, and I hope she didn't disturb you. You must have been resting after your journey."

Fascinated, he watched her high cheekbones taking a darker shade. "Oh, no, not at all. I was not disturbed."

"Yet, I shouldn't have..." Her voice trailed off as her fingers seemed to be making a mess of the decorations adorning her blouse.

It was a funny sight, and it made his head clear. "Please, Noble Lady, do not concern yourself with such meaningless matters." He smiled broadly in order to reassure her. "How can I be of service to you?"

It should have worked, but, instead, she grew more frightened. He glanced at his warriors, who kept a respectable distance. Were they the ones frightening her?

"I assure you, your maid did not disturb me, and I'm delighted and honored to meet you." Not daring to come closer, he extended his hand in a reassuring gesture. "What can I do for you?"

"Oh, well." She was the one to take a step forward, as though attempting to close the distance between them. "I needed to tell you something important..." Frowning, she took a deep breath, some determination creeping into the darkness of her troubled eyes. "You have to be careful. When you are here in the Palace, and outside, too. You are not safe in Texcoco."

"What?" He gaped at her, taken completely by surprise.

The girl licked her lips, her gaze tense but not afraid anymore. "You are not safe here, in the Palace," she repeated. "You need to leave as soon as you can."

He stared at her, still finding it difficult to understand. She seemed so young and so innocent, and her accent was not of the Acolhua people.

"Who are you?" he asked finally, feeling compelled to say something.

"My name is Azcal-Xochitl," said the girl composedly, not averting her eyes. Over her initial fright, she seemed in perfect control now, innocent and serene. "I am the First Daughter of the honorable Temictzin, the noble of Tenochtitlan."

Oh, that would account for her accent, he reflected randomly.

"What are you doing here in Texcoco?"

A tiny crease crossed her forehead as she frowned. "I live here."

"In the Palace?"

"Yes, of course." Her frown deepened. "My father is the leading member of the council. The former governor trusted his advice, and so does the new one."

"What council?"

She peered at him, puzzled. "The council that is dealing with Texcoco affairs."

"Oh." He fought his sudden irritation, unwilling to learn how the filthy invaders governed *his* Texcoco. Yes, of course they would need to form a council, to make the tribute collection easier. He pursed his lips. Of course, it would be comprised of Tenochtitlan's noblemen, the ones whom the emperor would want to reward or encourage, putting them closer to the source of the riches.

"Well, what did you want to tell me?" he said finally, irritated by the way her bottomless eyes studied him, too openly and with no shame. She was just a daughter of some filthy Aztec noble, busy robbing his, Coyotl's, subjects of the last of their possessions.

"I told you already," she said, not taken aback by his rudeness. "I told you that you are in danger and need to go away."

"What kind of danger?"

This time her gaze dropped, and for a while she studied her palms, her elegant fingers motionless in her lap. He listened to the breeze murmuring in the bushes.

"They are planning to kill you," she said finally, her voice hardly audible, difficult to hear over the rustling leafs.

"Who?"

She kept studying her hands.

"You have to tell me," he said, fighting the urge to look around. The trees surrounding the small pond stood suddenly dark, ominously tall, threatening. "You can't tell me only half of it."

Now even the breeze stopped whispering. The trees went still, and the air froze.

"Who is planning to kill me?" He felt his voice rising and made an effort to keep it down, mainly because of her frightened state. She might turn and run away, and he would never know what these people were planning before they made the first move.

"Don't be afraid. If it'll get you into trouble, I will protect you."

Her gaze flew to him, surprised and expectant. "You won't be able to protect me, not from them." She frowned, then straightened her shoulders resolutely. "The new governor, and some of the people of the council. They think you are dangerous. They think you are planning something. They know you are detouring while coming to Texcoco. They know you never go straight back to Tenochtitlan." The tip of her tongue came out, licking her lips. "The Tepanec ruler, the one who went to govern Coyoacan, thinks your very existence is a problem that should be corrected. He thinks his father's policy toward you was a mistake. He asked them to correct it."

Oh, he should have guessed, he should have thought about it all by himself. But then, why should he be concerned with that petty, discontented Maxtla, a son of a dead Emperor? The dirty piece of excrement was nothing.

"That petty son of a rat is nothing," he growled finally. "He is nothing but an unimportant ruler of an unimportant province."

"He is going to be the next Tepanec Emperor." The girl's eyes peered at him, very dark and very serene.

"He is not! His brother is the Tepanec Emperor. That useless lump of meat won't live long enough to inherit his brother." Her eyes held his, and he knew he sounded silly and out of control. He took a deep breath. "Why do you tell me all this?"

"Oh, I don't... I don't know." Her gaze dropped all of a sudden, as her exquisite cheekbones took on an even darker shade. "I thought you needed to be warned, so you could try to be careful." At that her words trailed off for good.

He took another deep breath, looking around.

"Thank you for letting me know. I will not forget what you did."

She looked up. "How will you escape?"

"Escape? I'll just leave. They would never dare to hold me here by force."

"Wouldn't they?" A broad crease crossed her forehead as she frowned, but still her eyes were upon him, so incredibly serene.

"Oh, may they all stay in the worst parts of the Underworld for all eternity!" He clenched his teeth against more cursing, aware of the girl's presence, and her uneasiness, part of his mind noticing the way the gold of her skin shone through the brightness of her blouse, where the light material creased. He tried to collect his thoughts. "You took a great risk."

"No, I did not." Her lips quivered shyly. "I just thought you should know. I'm not in any danger. My maid is trustworthy."

It made him think of Iztac Ayotl and her wild excursions into the city. This girl looked not much older than Iztac had been back in those days. "Do you do this often? Sneak out like that?"

She backed away as if struck. "I've never done this before. I am of a noble family!" He watched the enormous eyes filling with tears. "I don't sneak out. I never do this. I just went for a walk now, and I stopped to tell you, to warn you..." She took a convulsive breath.

He stared at her, at a loss. "Of course. I didn't mean to imply anything." Oh, he really hadn't, and worst of all, his hands were already full, so he had no desire, or need, to deal with a woman's crisis. "I'm grateful to you for going to all this trouble to tell me."

"It is no trouble," she repeated, blinking away the tears. "I just thought you should know. They say Revered Maxtla-tzin is going to be the new emperor, and very soon. Maybe this market interval, maybe the next."

"How?"

The look in her eyes made him want to bite his tongue. What silly question.

"And he wants to kill me so he won't have to deal with me later?"

She frowned. "Yes, I gather that it is so. The governor told my father that it is very important, to get rid of you now, before you can get away. He seems to be afraid of you and your connections. He thinks you are stirring up trouble, here and in Tenochtitlan."

She hesitated, and her voice dropped even lower, although she had almost been whispering before. "Maxtla-tzin, he may want to get rid of Tenochtitlan's Emperor, too. I happened to overhear, unintentionally. I didn't mean to eavesdrop. I promise you I didn't." She peered at him, very troubled now. "I didn't mean to get into any of this."

"I know. I'm sure of that." He wanted to touch her arm, to reassure her, a part of his mind wondering how her smooth skin would feel against his palm. "But please, tell me what you heard. It's very important."

Would dirty Maxtla try to kill Chimal? No, it was impossible. Who would try to do this, and how? And why?

"I don't know why they think you are so dangerous, but they do. They didn't talk about their reasons."

"But what about Tenochtitlan's Emperor? Do they think he is dangerous, too?"

"No, they don't." Her eyes grew calmer. "But he was rude to the ruler of Coyoacan and his delegations, on more than one occasion. He is a great friend of Tayatzin, the official Emperor, and Maxtla-tzin knows that he even advised the Emperor to execute him, his own brother."

Oh, thought Coyotl, frustrated. How unwise. Chimal was so impulsive at times. Yes, he liked the new Tepanec Emperor, foreseeing good, fruitful decades for Tenochtitlan to grow and develop and prosper with such a reasonable, well disposed ruler of the great Tepanec Empire. But he gambled, and a wise ruler shouldn't do such things.

He watched her dark eyes, so large, so wide open and sincere, peering at him with shameless innocence. "Thank you for letting me know, Noble Azcal-Xochitl. You are a very brave woman." Enjoying the sight of her darkening cheeks, he smiled, anxious to go back, to think it all over, yet also wishing to stay, to prolong this conversation. "So whom else is he wishing to help embark upon their journey through the Underworld?"

"The ruler of Tlatelolco," said the girl readily, startling him once again. He didn't expect her to answer his last question. Tlatelolco was a sister-city of Tenochtitlan, located on the nearby island, small and unimportant, its ruler not worthy of the trouble disposing of him would take.

"I can't believe it. The dirty piece of a rat is insane!"

"Yes, it doesn't make sense," agreed the girl. "He can't just go and kill all the rulers of his allied and subjected provinces."

He winced at the mention of the subjected provinces. "Some subjected nations should not stay subject, so I can understand him wishing to kill me. But Chimal? Or the ruler of Tlatelolco? Or even his own brother? How would he go about killing the Tepanec Emperor? It shouldn't be easy."

The girl shrugged, curiously unperturbed with this strange conversation concerning so many killings. "They didn't say that, but the way they talked it sounded like it will happen, and soon." He liked the way her slender eyebrows moved to meet each other as she frowned. "They sounded very sure of themselves about you, too. You should go away." She hesitated. "And you should not touch any food that is served to you at the celebratory evening meal."

The way she said that sent a shiver down his spine, taking his attention away from the generous curve of her mouth.

"I will not touch any food, and I will leave as soon as I can." He smiled at her, sorry to leave. "I thank you most sincerely. I will never forget what you've done for me." Unable to fight his urge, he touched her palm lightly. "I will find you, Noble Azcal-Xochitl. As soon as this matter is settled." Her golden cheeks glowed red, and he could feel her shivering under his touch, not attempting to take her hand away. "And it will happen soon, sooner than they all may think."

And now, back in the Palace, Coyotl forced his thoughts away from the afternoon meeting, concentrating on the sweaty face of the governor.

"I trust Revered Tayatzin to rule his vast empire well," he said lightly, toying with the tomato, but not eating it, just in case. "His revered father left the Tepanec Empire well organized, encompassing so many lands, ruling so many peoples. I'm sure the new Emperor will manage."

The governor's face twisted as though the tomato he had just eaten was unripe and bitter. "Oh, Noble Nezahualcoyotl, I wish it were that simple. The Great Empire is in turmoil, bubbling in discontent. If you traveled the countryside, visiting the provinces, you would know."

This time there was an unmistakable glint in the man's eyes. He thought about what the girl had said. They knew he was traveling in too leisurely a fashion, spending too much time in places like Coatlinchan and Huexotla, stopping to rest often, staying in small towns and villages. He suppressed a shiver. They knew he was up to something, and they wanted to get rid of him.

"It's difficult to imagine," he said, toying with his cup. "Revered Tezozomoc left a firm legacy. Nothing can happen to the empire he carved as expertly as the best of the figurine-makers, sculpturing wonderful statues out of simple stone."

"Oh, yes, Revered Tezozomoc was a great ruler, inspired by gods." The chubby man smiled politely. "Aren't you hungry, Honorable Nezahualcoyotl? You haven't touched the food on your plate or the drink in your cup."

"I'm replete with food, thank you. But your *octli* is of the best quality." He picked up a cup and pretended to drink, not allowing the milky liquid to penetrate the insides of his mouth, blocking the flow with his tongue. "I will regret leaving your hospitality."

"Oh, but you will surely stay to share more than a few meals." The man shifted, making himself more comfortable against his numerous cushions. "You honor this Palace with your presence."

Coyotl stood the man's gaze. "Regretfully, I will have to leave with dawn." *Preferably tonight,* he thought, his stomach churning with hunger.

"Oh, no, Honorable Nezahualcoyotl, you can't leave us so soon. This Palace will not be the same without you. You have just arrived, and you will have to grace us with your delightful presence for a little longer."

Where had he heard that before? wondered Coyotl, not wasting his time on arguing, letting the man talk, answering absently, his thoughts elsewhere Someone had said it before. Here in the Texcoco Palace, under similar circumstances. Someone, sometime, a long time ago.

"Yes, of course, it would be my honor," he heard himself saying. "Although, I planned to be on my way no later than the next day. The Honorable Chief Warlord of Tenochtitlan will be expecting me, to take a part in yet another raid against the insolent Chalcoans. But, of course, it would be a pleasure..."

And then he remembered. The Aztec Warlord! It was the morning meal, a few market intervals before the first Tepanec invasion, with his, Coyotl's father, the mighty Emperor of the influential Acolhua Capital, telling his arrogant visitor that he would have to enjoy Texcoco's hospitality for a little longer, letting the man know that he wouldn't be allowed to leave the city unless permitted, the meaning perfectly obvious under the thin coating of the polite words. Oh, he remembered listening to his father, delighted to think that the cheeky Aztec would have to learn a lesson, paying with his life, probably, for his presumptuous arrogance.

He also remembered how the man's strong, broad face closed, how he didn't bother to argue, answering politely, but how his concentration seemed to wander. Oh, the remarkable man had known what to do. Not bothering with his high, dignified status, he had slunk away under the cover of the night, leading his warriors through the back gate, killing the guards, not deterred by the fact that the unusual journey was beneath the dignity of the powerful war leader of many summers.

Well, thought Coyotl, pretending to drink once again. There was no reason he should not follow the example of Kuini's uncle. He was capable of doing exactly the same, and he knew this Palace, better than its unwelcome current dwellers did.

CHAPTER 3

Iztac Ayotl stormed through the corridors, seething. Servants scattered out of her way, and the thumping of her steps resounded against the walls, signaling alarm down the spacious corridors.

A maid leaped aside so hurriedly, the tray in her hands toppled, then went crashing around her feet. The woman gasped, terrified, clasping her mouth with her hands, and the two of her companions froze, but Iztac paid them no attention, too angry to focus on anything save her furious thoughts.

Oh, no, she thought bursting into her richly decorated set of rooms. *He could not be that careless, that arrogant, that sure of himself. It had to be someone else.*

"Prepare my litter," she told the maid curtly. "I want to go to the marketplace, and I want to do it now!"

Chiko, her main maid, hesitated, but only for a heartbeat.

"Of course, Revered Mistress," she said placidly. "But won't the Revered Emperor require your presence through his afternoon meetings?"

"I'll be back by the afternoon." Tearing the embroidered diadem off her head, Iztac hurled it into the far corner. "The stupid thing is too tight!" she complained. "It makes my head ache. Get the servants to loosen it some."

"Of course, Mistress."

A curt gesture of the woman's hand caused another girl to rush toward the discarded regalia, to pick it up hastily.

"Get the Revered Empress her chocolate drink and some refreshments," she added, addressing a group of frightened maids, sounding almost imperious all of a sudden. "And be quick about it."

Unable to relax, Iztac began pacing, counting the polished tiles in the stone floor. "I don't want refreshments or chocolate. Just bring me my fan, the one with the large feathers, and send me the girl who does my hair."

"But your hair is perfect, Revered Mistress," called out the woman, now clearly unsettled. "Why don't you rest a little? It is high noon. Time to rest, to hide from the heat, to gather your strength for the evening."

"I don't want to rest! Just do as I asked. Ready my litter, send me that girl, and you may go. I don't need you to fuss over me. I'm not a child. I can decide for myself when I need a rest and when my hair is a mess. You are forgetting your place!" Aware that she was taking her frustrations out on an undeserving object, Iztac took a deep breath.

Control yourself, she thought. *Angry people make mistakes, and you can't afford one, not today. Not with all the troubles looming.*

The memory of the meeting in the main hall earlier this morning, when Chimal had been rude to the representative of Coyoacan, a province governed by Tezozomoc's discontented son, Maxtla, made her shiver. Chimal liked the current Azcapotzalco ruler, who was a quiet, reasonable man. They had met twice, once upon Tezozomoc's death, when no ruler of any *altepetl* could spare himself a pilgrimage to pay his respects to the most famous emperor of the Great Lake's Valley.

She remembered accompanying Chimal on this long, tiresome journey, nauseated by the swings of the large boat, and then tossed for what seemed like an eternity in the decorated litter, reluctant, and even afraid to enter the Tepanec capital.

However, the Highlander was there, among the warriors guarding the royal procession, walking with his long, sure-footed paces only some distance away. Tlacaelel, a very promising young man, Chimal's half-brother and Itzcoatl's half-nephew, the man who had obviously been groomed to be the next Chief Warlord, was the one who had insisted on bringing the Highlander along. If he had not, she, Iztac, would have been the one insisting, she knew. She wouldn't enter her former enemies' city without adequate protection, and he was the only one capable of protecting her, really protecting her.

Also, she wanted to show him Azcapotzalco, remembering the way he had talked about this *altepetl* once, when they had met after a long time, while the matters in Tenochtitlan's Palace were boiling. She had wanted him to tell her how ugly Azcapotzalco was, but he had just laughed and told her that this *altepetl* looked beautiful from the nearby hills, regretting his inability to enter it.

And it, indeed, was a magnificent city, she was forced to admit, looking for signs of it being tasteless and pretentious, but finding only the elegance and the beauty, and the enormous, unsettling riches. Oh, the Tepanec Empire would be impossible to beat. Why, why had her father, the Texcoco Emperor, had to anger the mighty beast, robbing his heir of his throne, and his people of their rightful rulers? Coyotl, of course, had found plenty of excuses not to come. He was in a passable stance with the intimidating Tepanecs, allowed to live in Tenochtitlan, and, recently, to visit his former Acolhua lands. Still, it wouldn't be wise to tempt the gods.

She shook her head, banishing the unwelcome memories. The second time Chimal had met Tayatzin, Tezozomoc's heir, was during the festivities that anointed this man and confirmed his right to sit on the magnificent throne of the mighty Capital. At almost twenty, Chimal was not a boy anymore, and he possessed enough personal charm and a certain authority that made people trust him.

Oh, yes, he was not a bad Emperor, and he listened to her, Iztac, his Chief Wife's opinions, prizing her advice ahead of this of Itzcoatl's. Which was a good thing. She had never trusted the dangerous, grim-looking man who might have been aspiring to a higher position, having a necessary amount of royal blood and much more influence and power than she felt comfortable with.

Well, this morning, the Chief Adviser did not argue with his Emperor, for a change. He just watched Chimal getting angry with the delegation from Coyoacan, his eyes dark and unreadable, flickering with what looked like satisfaction. But wasn't he the one who had tried to make Chimal stay neutral, to keep away from the struggle for the Tepanec throne?

She frowned. No, it was Tlacaelel who had carried on and on, trying to convince Chimal not to take sides. Well, Tlacaelel was extremely wise and far-sighted, yet she didn't feel like taking his side this time. The current Emperor of Azcapotzalco was a promising ruler, and there was no harm in making friends with him. He would remember Chimal's support and reward Tenochtitlan when the time came. And anyway, that was not what had made her so angry.

She ground her teeth, remembering that when Coyoacan's delegation went away, offended and seething, Chimal had dismissed some of the advisers, asking Itzcoatl to stay.

"I've asked the priests to make inquiries," he said frowning. "Regarding the despicable murder on the marketplace, when one of my advisers was killed, along with many more people, and even a group of warriors."

"I see," said Itzcoatl calmly. "But why the priests, Revered Emperor?"

"Because for days the marketplace has been buzzing, talking of omens and foreign gods," said Chimal, narrowing his eyes, his tone almost challenging. "People, who had seen the place, went away frightened, thinking that the murdered persons had angered a powerful, foreign deity with a frightening jaguar-like face. Market frequenters went on muttering that Tenochtitlan had angered this ominous deity, too. The priests wanted to make inquiries, and I authorized them to do so."

"Well, what did they find out?" The former Warlord didn't move, but his gaze turned blank, unreadable, and Iztac clasped her palms tight, remembering how she had felt upon hearing the news of the murdered adviser, the despicable man whom she had wished to murder with her own hands. Oh, she knew very well who had done this, and she had applauded his alertness and skill.

Chimal's frown deepened. "The strange carving has nothing to do with any gods familiar to our priests. Yet, there was one connection." The young man paused, and his troubled gaze shot toward her, then returned to his Chief Adviser. It was an involuntary gesture, she was sure of that, yet her back was suddenly covered with sweat despite the efforts of the maids waving large fans, struggling to banish the heat.

"I saw this carving," she heard Itzcoatl saying, unperturbed. "It's unsettling, but only a superstitious market lot would take it as far as the angry deities. It's just a carving, and it should be scratched off." He shrugged. "I'll see to it."

Chimal drew his breath angrily. "Your man is responsible for this deed, isn't he? That same insolent foreigner, whom you trust to lead larger and larger groups of warriors!"

The eyebrows of the former Chief Warlord climbed high, arrogantly at that. "My people are warriors, not murderers. I do not resort to such means. The murdered adviser had a clandestine meeting with dubious foreigners in the middle of the night. He was killed by the marketplace robbers. If I had decided the adviser was guilty of treason, I would have suggested you try this man properly, to execute him according to the law. I do not resort to such means, and neither do my men, whatever their origins."

But Chimal refused to be put back in his place this time. "This highlander warrior has a sword full of similar looking carvings. The whole of Tenochtitlan is talking about this infamous weapon, so the priests told me. This man is connected to this murder, and if he acted without your knowledge, without your approval, you should punish him most severely."

Iztac watched him taking a deep breath, standing the Warlord's glare bravely. Under different circumstances she would have been very proud of him, yet now... She felt her own breaths coming in gasps, the suddenly diluted air giving no relief to the suffocating sensation.

"I punish my warriors when they deserve punishments, and I promote my warriors when they deserve promotions." The Warlord's voice was calm, unbearably condescending, yet Iztac welcomed this man's impudence this time. "You should not concern yourself with such meaningless matters, oh Revered Nephew. You should trust your faithful servants and advisers. We are guarding your interests, your safety, your realm, day and night. Let the experienced war leaders take care of the matters that concern your warriors' forces."

But Chimal's eyes glowered unpleasantly, and his lips were pressed into a thin line. "You are forgetting your place, Honorable Uncle! I'm grateful for your help and your most highly prized advice, but I am not a child anymore. I don't need to be reminded of my place. I am Tenochtitlan's Emperor. I am the ruler of this *altepetl*. I am the one to make the final decisions."

Now Itzcoatl's eyes blazed murder, and Iztac shivered, suddenly cold in the suffocating heat of the main hall. No, the former Chief Warlord and the current Main Adviser was not the man to anger in such a way. He had attempted changing governments once upon a time, and he very well might try to do this again.

"Of course, Revered Nephew," she heard the man saying, his voice cold, cutting like the sharpest obsidian. "But even great emperors are forced to listen to the advice of their elders. You are still very young, Nephew. You still need the support of your family."

The glaring gaze of the Warlord was difficult to bear. Ashamed of a certain sensation of relief that she was not the one required to stand this glare, Iztac watched Chimal's pleasant face twisting, fighting for control.

"Yes, of course, Honorable Uncle. I didn't mean to sound harsh, or unappreciative of your help. I'm very lucky to have you by my side." He frowned, gathering the remnants of his courage. "It's just that I don't want this man leading Mexica warriors. He can fight for Tenochtitlan, if you feel he is good enough to do so, but I don't want to see this foreigner in any leading position, and I don't want him visiting my Palace. I will entrust you with making your own inquiries regarding dubious activities of this warrior, and I will trust your judgment." He rose to his feet, his lips clasped tight, eyes dark. "This afternoon we will meet to discuss the shameless proposals of those people from Coyoacan. Please come to share my evening meal, and if my honorable half-brother is still in Tenochtitlan, I would be delighted if he joined us." Making a visible effort to lighten the atmosphere, he turned to face her. "I wish your brother would return to Tenochtitlan soon.

His presence is missed in this Palace."

Oh, but it did not help, thought Iztac, pacing her rooms angrily. The former Warlord, this dangerous, powerful man was enraged now at being challenged, and she, the Empress, was scared. What if the priests were allowed to go after Kuini? Because yes, oh yes, he *was* a foreigner. With exceptionally good connections in Tenochtitlan, but still a foreigner, a highlander, a savage. He was a minor leader of the warriors, a nephew of Tenochtitlan's First Chief Warlord, a good friend of Tlacaelel, the next warriors' leader. Even Itzcoatl had evidently prized his abilities. Although he had not grown any fonder of the insolent Highlander during the past seven summers, the Warlord had, nevertheless, advanced the young man, using him in all sorts of leading capacities, according to his talents and skills. Maybe he had done so because of his friendship with the young man's uncle, yet Iztac was sure that the vile man had his own, not very pure, reasons for promoting the Highlander.

The maid's footsteps broke into her reverie, and she whirled around the see the insistent women coming in, carrying trays with drinks and refreshments. About to scold them for not following her orders, she saw another slender figure sliding in.

"Revered Empress?" The girl hesitated at the doorway.

"Come on in," said Iztac, relieved. "This diadem messed up my hair. I need you to fix it." Kneeling upon the cluster of mats, she gave the puzzled girl a meaningful look.

"Oh, of course, Revered Mistress," cried out the maid. "Those tresses, oh yes, I'll have to retie them. Let me just loose this thread." She knelt beside Iztac gracefully, busy with the colorful bunch of strings.

"I need you to deliver a message, as fast as you can," whispered Iztac, turning her face away from the entrance and the women who seemed to be busy arranging the plates.

"What am I to say?" The girl's voice barely reached her, her gaze firm on her strings and combs.

"Marketplace, the small temple belonging to Tlaloc, beside the colorful wall. And he needs to be there right away. Make sure he understands. He is to leave everything and rush there the moment he hears you."

"And if he is elsewhere?"

"Try to find him. If you can't, rush to the temple yourself and tell me."

For some time, the girl fussed with the numerous tresses, tying them together, her fingers experienced and nimble. Then she was gone.

Good, thought Iztac in relief. *So now you go and make sure you bring along no more than two maids.* The two Mayans who could barely speak any Nahuatl and who were too afraid of her to say anything or ask questions.

Shifting upon her cushioned seat, Iztac eyed the colorful cloths absently.

"Yes, this one is pretty," she said, liking the feel of the exquisite cotton. "I'll take this, and the blue one, too. It will go nicely with my favorite topaz girdle."

"Yes, Revered Mistress." The maid smiled shyly and rushed toward the stall to pick up the indicated material.

Her fellow maids hesitated, clutching onto their loaded baskets and other goods. It was not often that the Empress would go on such a wild shopping trip, buying everything her eyes brushed past.

Iztac smiled to herself. Oh, yes, now they were too busy to be interested in her activities. All they wanted was to reach the Palace with their expensive cargo unharmed.

She gestured to Chiko, who was loaded with goods now as well.

"Take all this to the Palace, and make sure it is stored properly or put to use with no delay. Leave a maid or two to escort me. I wish to visit a temple on my way back." She frowned. "And take the Palace's guards, too. I don't need any warriors. The slaves who are clearing my way will be more than enough."

The woman stared at her in disbelief. "Oh, Revered Mistress, you can't travel around the city unprotected!"

"Of course, I can. I am the Empress of Tenochtitlan, not its visitor. Who would dare to harm me?" She glared at the woman, enraged. *Why did she have to argue all the time, watching her, Iztac, with the eyes of a hawk?* "Do as I say! Make my maids bring everything I chose to my rooms, and take the warriors with you. I will visit the temple and will come back in time to share the Emperor's afternoon meal. I will be perfectly safe, and I will not be late." She narrowed her eyes. "If I hear one more word from you, I will have you thrown out of the Palace! Don't you ever think I will not."

As the roly-poly woman scampered away, genuinely afraid now, Iztac pursed her lips. Damn slaves. Why couldn't they leave a person alone from time to time?

"Take me to the temple of Tlaloc, beside the colorful wall," she called to her litter bearers.

Yes, she thought, leaning back and closing the curtains. It was also the time to make an offering to the benevolent deity.

The swaying of the litter made her nauseous, reminding her of that terrible evening which was carved into her memory and which would stay there for as long as she lived. Seven summers had passed and many things had changed, yet the memories were always there, frequenting her dreams, dreadful memories accompanied by that slight feeling of being sick.

She had never been ill before, but since then she would feel it every time she remembered, because even when those dreadful days have passed and she didn't die, becoming the Empress of Tenochtitlan instead, the nausea didn't go away, haunting her for days, making her hate the thought of food, making her stop consuming her chocolate drink in the mornings. And then, a moon or so later, she knew she was with a child.

Already a Chief Wife to the young Emperor, she did the only sensible thing. She had admitted Chimal to her bed. He was very young, but very eager, and so all was well. Even the nausea had passed as she grew in proportions, but this child was not Chimal's, she knew, and dreaded the day when it would be born. What would it look like? Would it turn out to be a boy, as impressively tall and wide shouldered, as wild and hot-tempered as his father? Well, it should not raise any suspicions. She was half Tepanec herself, and so her child could look like a Tepanec.

But then, she had almost died trying to bring her child into the world, and so she forgot the rest of her fears. Bleeding and twisting in pain, just like *him* when he was supposed to die, but for so, so much longer. A whole day, and a night, and then another day of agony and suffering and fear and exhaustion, wishing for this to be over, one way or another, the healers rushing about, and the midwives, and all sorts of slaves, and some of the noblewomen, yet no one she loved or trusted.

If only Ihuitl were alive, or even her own mother, or anyone, really. She wanted to see Coyotl, too, but most of all she craved to feel *him*, the Highlander, but they were away, of course, and also they were men, not interested in this women's business. Chimal would be sad when she died, she knew, although he wasn't allowed to enter the pavilion allocated to the sacred process of giving birth even had he wanted to.

Swaying with the wavering of the palanquin, she shivered. She hadn't died, mostly because, at some point, she had decided that it wasn't her time. She hang on, making great efforts to keep awake and to drink all the potions they had made for her to drink, while they sewed everything that had been torn. Her child had been long since taken out of her, given to a suitable wet nurse with plenty of breast milk, while she, Iztac, had been fighting to stay alive, too busy to think of its looks or origins. She hadn't even known that it was a girl, a small, wrinkled affair with a scant amount of hair and huge, bright, cat-like yellowish eyes. She didn't care. She was just glad to be alive, and also grateful to hear that she wasn't likely to bear any more children.

However, since then her nightmares were over. He was cut badly and he suffered, but not like her, never like her. It was not as dreadful as she'd thought. What she'd gone through was dreadful. He had suffered for a short time, and she was alongside him, and also the annoying *cihua* that he had later taken to be his woman was there, taking care of him. While she had suffered for so long, dying and alone.

The palanquin stopped, and she rushed out, breathing with relief, her nausea fading. It had all happened almost six summers ago. It was in the past, and Citlalli, the cute little thing with her yellow eyes and her outlandish looks, was worth all of it and more. She may not have looked like Chimal or her mother, but she didn't look like the Highlander either, so it was a relief.

Mounting the steps of the temple, which was abandoned at this time of the day, Iztac smiled to herself. Chimal loved his firstborn daughter, but he had two sons by now, born to him by two of his minor wives. He had no time for the girl, and it was a good thing. He had no leisure to start wondering. But he did hate the Highlander all the same. This was not the first time he had expressed a wish to be rid of the man, as though the Emperor should be concerned with the minor leaders of his multitude of warriors.

"Wait for me at the head of the alley," she tossed over her shoulder without looking at the two troubled maids and her litter bearers. "Don't enter the temple even if it takes me a long time to come out."

The dimly lit hall swallowed her, enveloping in its coolness and the heavy smell. She made her way hurriedly, her paces resounding against the stone walls, eyes struggling to adjust after the brilliance of the daylight. Oh yes, she was alone in the eerie semidarkness. But for the faint buzz of the outside she might have thought she was all alone in the whole world.

It took her an effort to pull the curtain aside, her hands trembling, as always when in the temple of the wrong god. Mighty Tlaloc was not the deity she was supposed to worship, to offer of her flesh. Tenochtitlan had different customs. However, she was Texcocan. She grew up in the shade of the Tlaloc Hill, and she would always pray to the Rain and Earth Deity, whether it was appropriate or not. The mighty Tlaloc was the one who had spared her life, she knew. And he was the one who had left her her child, instead of collecting the yellow-eyed girl with the other dying children into his distant realm, to sit under the tree with its branches dripping nourishing milk, to feed and gain strength while awaiting the end of this World of the Fifth Sun. These children were destined to populate the next world when it was created. Their mission was important, their destiny exciting. Still, she had prayed and asked the god to choose another child in her stead, and the mighty Tlaloc had listened.

Pulling a large maguey thorn from the pile beside the altar, she concentrated her thoughts, addressing the benevolent deity and not thinking of the pain. She had never done this while still a young girl, afraid of the pain and the bleeding, but since her child was born she had offered of her flesh quite often. This pain was nothing compared to the other, real pain.

She winced as the thorn pierced her tongue, but her hands did not shake, and her tongue did not try to sneak back into the safety of her mouth. Pushing the spike all the way through, she let it soak with the warm, salty flow, then pulled it back as slowly as she could, letting it gather the life-giving liquid.

Hands steady, she placed the glittering thorn upon the altar, in the small, special niche, peering at the round orbs of the stony deity, praying and asking for nothing in return. The mighty god knew what she wanted. She didn't need to tell him.

Licking the blood off her lips, she opened her eyes and turned around, all of a sudden knowing that she was not alone in the temple, not anymore. Her eyes narrowed and she peered at him as he stood there, leaning against a wide column, watching her solemnly, motionless, just another statue of the temple. Typical of him, he just appeared out of nowhere. If he had entered the temple through either of the two entrances, he had made no sound. But, of course! He was a Jaguar, she thought, sucking the blood, her tongue numb and swelling. How else should he move if not quietly and by stealth?

As always, her legs lost some of their strength, and her thoughts refused to organize properly as she watched him, taking in his strong, broad face and the wideness of his shoulders, and the intensity behind the darkness of his eyes. It had only been a moon or so since she'd seen him, but it seemed like an eternity, to grow accustomed to his presence anew every time they had met.

He watched her for a few more heartbeats, then smiled broadly, mischievously, breaking the spell.

"The Revered Empress is offering of her flesh," he said loudly, spoiling the solemnity of her offering.

"It is nothing to laugh about," she said sharply, her tongue difficult to move.

His smile disappeared. "No, of course not. But you do look funny with this blood all over your mouth. Like an ocelot after a good meal." His eyes stood her glare, challenging. "A beautiful, dangerous, breathtaking female jaguar."

"You and your animal references," she said, refusing to be pacified. "From the moon goddess through serpents and lizards, to jaguars, I find it difficult to follow my switching forms." She wiped her mouth with the back of her palm. "Do your highland gods receive no offering of your flesh?"

"No." He shrugged, his grin light. "My gods seem to be satisfied with the offerings of the priests."

"Then there is no wonder they are not truly happy."

He raised his eyebrows. "How would you know if they are happy or not?"

"If they were happy, they would help your people achieve great victories."

His eyes narrowed as his gaze grew colder. "It doesn't seem as if your people's offerings were very helpful, either."

"Oh, you are impossible!" She jumped onto her feet, wishing to smash something. "You just ruined my offering, and you keep insulting me. Forget it, forget that I sent for you. Go away."

For a heartbeat he watched her, his eyes dark and stormy. "With all due respect to the mighty empress, I'm not one of your slaves. You sent for me. You took me away from my duties. You made me come here in a hurry. So no, you won't send me off like one of your slaves."

She just stared at him, unable to talk, the salty taste in her mouth revolting.

"Why did you make me come here in such a hurry?" he asked finally, making a visible effort to calm down. "And why here?"

"I needed to talk to you urgently." She drew a deep breath, finding it difficult to unclench her teeth. "And this temple was the only place I thought we could be alone on such short notice."

"What happened?" He didn't move, didn't change his position, still leaning casually against the column, but something had changed nevertheless. His whole body seemed alerted, ready to move, to pounce, to attack the danger with a powerful leap, or to avoid it. A jaguar!

"Your arrogant self-assurance, that's what happened," she said tersely. "Your annoying self-confidence, your way of doing things like there is no one in the world to tell you not to do them."

His eyes were now two slits in the stony broadness of his face. "Oh, so now we are unhappy with my way of doing things. Is there anything in particular?"

"Yes, there is!" She felt like screaming or breaking something. How did it come to them being angry with each other? She had come here so expectant, excited to see him again, anxious for him and his safety. "Your way of leaving marks after disposing of people. Those strange, outlandish marks which are difficult to miss, or to pay no attention to. Marks that scare people." She watched his eyes turning blank. "Speaking of gods, a certain carved deity received an impressive offering. You truly have no need of piercing your body parts."

His glare burned her skin. "What about those marks?"

"The priests talked to the Emperor, and he is mighty angry with you now. With you in particular, Kuini! Not just generally displeased, but very, very angry. He went as far as offending your precious commander-in-chief, Itzcoatl, by demanding to deal with you urgently, to bring you to justice."

His face remained motionless, as if carved out of stone, yet an obvious air of danger surrounded him now, radiating from every pour of his skin, as it seemed. "What did Itzcoatl say?"

"Well, he was angry with Chimal, of course. He is not used to being argued with or receiving orders." She frowned, her anger cooling rapidly, her heart squeezing with worry for him. "Chimal was unusually insistent. He truly hates you, and I can't understand why." Coming closer, not angry anymore, she peered into the darkness of his eyes. "You have to be more careful. You should not make such obvious deeds, leave such obvious marks. I can handle Chimal, but still, he is the Emperor. He has the ultimate power. And for some reason, he hates you, you out of all people."

"For some reason?" A flicker of grim amusement crossed his face. "Isn't it obvious why the mighty emperor would stop to hate a warrior of no consequence? The little bastard is jealous."

"He is no little bastard," she said, aware of a twinge of anxiety rolling down her spine. "And he doesn't know about us."

"Of course he does, Iztac Ayotl." He towered above her, not angry anymore, either. "He is no fool, that mighty husband of yours. And you are right, he is no little bastard anymore. He is a clever young man, patient and keen, fit to rule this large *altepetl*, believing that he is prepared and knows how to do it. He doesn't want Itzcoatl ruling in his stead, he doesn't want his guidance anymore; he detests the way he tells him what to do. He doesn't want his Chief Wife to do that, either. That's why he is being so stubborn, balking up against every good advice, especially in the affair of the Tepanec heirs. He wants to start ruling all by himself." The dark eyes sparkled with a familiar glint, the one that made her limbs weak. "He knows about us. I suppose that he has no evidence. He can't be sure if the filthy foreigner is actually laying his filthy hands on the deeply admired, greatly loved Chief Wife of his, but his instincts are telling him that it doesn't matter, that there is something deeper in there than a simple laying around, if something like that is actually happening." She felt his arms lifting, taking hold of her shoulders, squeezing them firmly, lovingly. "He is not to blame. He doesn't know that the filthy foreigner has more rights on this woman, that he had known her before, that she had given herself to him when Tenochtitlan was nothing but a strange, misty island for her." His arms pulled her closer, pressed her tightly against his chest as his lips sought hers, forceful as always, not asking for permission. "He doesn't know that she is not just a woman but a goddess, whom this pushy foreigner has worshipped for half of twenty summers. He is the mighty Emperor, but he can do nothing about it. Nothing at all."

She wanted him to go on, telling her his version of *their* story. Inhaling his smell, this clean, masculine smell of his, and some sweat mixed with a distinct aroma of *octli*, she melted against his body, listening to his murmuring, enchanted. However, his lips were now busy parting hers, and her mind went blank, powerless against his will, and against her desire.

The stone wall cut into her back, but she didn't pay it any attention, clinging to him, clutching his body with her limbs, helping him find his way into her, their bodies familiar, fitting each other perfectly.

Oh, it was a homecoming. A wonderful, blissful sensation of returning from a long journey. She spent so much time doing silly things, running an empire, listening to advisers and engineers with their endlessly breaking water pipes, making sure the scribes wrote down the letters correctly. Yet, her home was here, inside his arms, curled around his body, inhaling his smell, letting him take her to places where nothing mattered save the touch of their skins and their lips whispering, exchanging their warmth.

Breathing heavily, he tried to protect her back, taking her weight and doing his best to pleasure her at the same time, until they did a sensible thing, sliding down, putting their bodies against the coldness of the stone floor.

"I'm sorry," he whispered as she wriggled, trying to find a better position. "It's not the best of places. Maybe we should stop."

But she clutched him tighter, making it impossible for his body to escape her grip. "No, don't stop. I need you. I need you here or anywhere. I need you inside me."

Later, they lay upon the cold floor, spent, regaining their breath.

"I'm sorry," he repeated, propped on his arm, towering above her. "It couldn't have been pleasant for you. I know it was not."

She smiled. "Of course, it was! It wasn't as perfect as on the grass around the pond, or in this strange warehouse you smuggled me in the last time, but I loved it all the same. I love your way of worshipping the Moon Goddess, no matter where you do it."

His eyes glowed. "I do worship her, I do! It has never faded, through all these long summers."

"We were such silly children back then," she said dreamily.

"But even then we knew."

He helped her up and watched her as she smoothed her clothes, trying to bring her tresses into some sort of an order.

"Luckily, this girl, whom I've been sending to fetch you every time I need to be worshipped, can take care of my hair." She looked up at him. "She is outside, isn't she?"

"Yes, she is guarding the entrance."

"Is it late in the afternoon? The priests will be coming soon."

"Yes, I suppose we had better be leaving, before your maids at the other entrance and your guards and the palanquin bearers begin to worry that you bled yourself to death on the altar of mighty Tlaloc." He straightened his cloak and began retying his loincloth. "I missed you, Revered Empress. I'm glad the Emperor grew angry with me this morning."

She winced, her peacefulness gone. "Don't take it lightly. Chimal can be vengeful, and he is not always open to my advice. If you are right and he suspects the truth about us, he will try to harm you." Seeing the challenging flicker returning into his eyes, she caught his arm. "The priests were the ones to report the carving to him, and when he demanded from the Chief Warlord to punish you, he mentioned your sword and similar carvings upon it. Everyone in Tenochtitlan knows about your sword. The priests are not the only ones to think of the connection. And they are powerful, Kuini! They have enough clout to go even against the warlord. And anyway, Itzcoatl cannot be trusted. He will abandon you the moment he thinks he doesn't need you."

"But he still needs me. So as long as he does, we have nothing to worry about." His smile widened, filled with affection, taking her breath away. "And I have the mighty Empress, the Goddess of the Moon, to protect me." He laughed, breaking the spell. "Also Tlacaelel will be the Chief Warlord soon. And he is a friend, a real friend. So you don't need to worry about me, but you can go on sending me warnings just like you did today. I'd appreciate it if you did this more often, every market interval or so."

She slapped his hand, laughing. "You are impossible! But I do thank you for killing that worm, the filthy, stinking adviser. How dared he demand that Coyotl should be thrown out, or even put to death. What a fat, stupid rat this man was!"

But his face darkened again. "This killing solved nothing. Your dear husband should know better than to meddle in the Tepanec affairs. He should not side with Tayatzin so openly. He should stay neutral and let the Tepanecs sort out their own problems. He is trying to prove his independence, but does so in the worst of timings. He should listen to Itzcoatl. He is acting like a spoiled little brat."

"Since when do you care for Tenochtitlan's policies?" she retorted, offended on Chimal's behalf. "It's deeper and more intricate than you think. Tayatzin is the official heir, anointed to be the Emperor of Azcapotzalco and the ruler of the Tepanec Empire. He is a reasonable man, and he will remember Tenochtitlan's support. We still have troubles with the water construction. We will need better building materials, and we will need to use more of the Chapultepec Hill's springs. He'll give us all this, when his troubles are over."

"Unless he is out of the game, probably dead, and Maxtla is in. Then your Chimal will face a bitter enemy instead of a grateful friend. It's a bean game, and the chances that Chimal will win are no better than the chances of a man whose figurines are only halfway up the board. He can win, he can lose, but whatever he thinks may happen, he is gambling all he has, and it's not the wise thing for a ruler to do."

"Oh, please, Kuini, go back to organizing and leading your warriors and your raids. Politics are more complicated than this!"

But he just laughed. "Oh, how haughty you are at times, mighty Empress." He caught her shoulders, peering into her eyes, his mirth spilling. "You are refusing to see the truth only because you hate Itzcoatl, and you like to see your husband going against his wishes. But in this case, you should know better. Tlacaelel thinks it is disastrous, too, and he would know. He is smarter than you and your Emperor and Itzcoatl all put together."

"Oh, that one!" she cried out, frustrated, in the corner of her mind suspecting that he might be correct, even if only partly. "This man is not as pure as he wants us to think he is. He is coveting the throne. I know he is. Mark my words. He is the First

Son, and he never forgets that fact. Chimal cannot be safe with this man around."

But the Highlander's eyes lost their amusement. "He is not, Iztac. Believe me on that. Tlacaelel is a good man, and he is to be trusted. He doesn't covet your husband's position, but he wants to be listened to. He deserves that." He peered into her eyes. "Think about it, think about what I said when you are not so angry with us all. Think about it, then talk to your husband. He will listen to you."

There was a rustling beside the doorway, and they turned around, tensing.

"Honorable Mistress." The girl's voice was hardly audible, seeping in from the brightness of the outside. "The priests will be coming soon."

She clutched his arm tight. "You have to go now," she said, refusing to loosen her grip. "I don't want you to go."

He released his arm gently, then pulled her into his embrace. "I may stay in Tenochtitlan for another market interval. Send your girl whenever you can, by day or by night. I will leave whatever I'm doing, and I will come running all the way." Snug in his arms, she heard more than saw the grin in his voice. "After all, I owe you a better lovemaking than this quick thing on the stone floor."

"I will. I'll arrange for us to meet in a better place."

They walked the hall toward the side entrance, together and as though having every right to do this, but her nerves were taut, and she knew he would dash for one of the darker corners should a priest appear all of a sudden.

"How are your boys?" she asked, still holding him tight.

His smile turned so wide and unguarded, it made her jealous. "Wonderful, brilliant, invincible. An unruly lot."

"Still can't tell them apart?"

"Well, I can. Most of the time. When they don't make an effort to confuse me on purpose. Their mother is the only one who never fails to catch them on all their tricks."

The familiar feeling was back, making her stomach tighten. "How is she?"

"She is good. With child again."

"For such a small, skinny thing, she is a breeder."

"She is not. She is just a good girl, who is doing her best and excelling at it." He grinned. "My household is easier to manage than yours, you have to admit that. So she does have time to bear healthy children. She hasn't had an empire to run."

"She would never have managed that!"

But he shrugged, unperturbed. "Who knows? She runs my household like a leader of the warriors. The slaves are afraid of her, and everything is always cozy, perfectly clean, and in place. It's nice to live in such a dwelling, to come back to this house. Coyotl spends more time in my house than anywhere else when he is in Tenochtitlan, and Tlacaelel comes to share my meals whenever he can. Both of them admire her so greatly, I wonder if I should get jealous."

"I'm very happy for you," she said stiffly, unable to even force a smile.

He beamed at her. "Are you jealous, Iztac Ayotl? You?" She felt his palm sneaking under her chin, trying to force her face upwards. "What do you do with the other wives of the emperor, eh? Women do have to share their men."

"I'm not jealous. I was the one to convince Chimal to take more wives when I knew I couldn't bear more children. I choose them for him. And I don't care a bit about your breeder. She can bear you a new child every summer as far as I'm concerned. You should take more wives, too, you know? You will father half of Tenochtitlan one day."

But his amusement faded. "How is she?"

"Who?"

"The princess. Your daughter."

"Oh, the Emperor's First Daughter, you mean? She is good. She is a good girl. She is wonderful, brilliant, invincible, and she makes no mischief and gives no trouble."

He pursed his lips. "Not like her mother at all."

"And not like her father." She hesitated. "And she looks like neither of them. Nothing Tepanec about her. An outlandish creature."

"I wish I could meet her."

She glanced at his darkening face, satisfied with him feeling so bad. "Maybe one day. When she is older and allowed to go into the city."

The maid slipped inside, her face troubled. "Please, follow," she whispered, gesturing urgently. And then he was gone, as nimbly and soundlessly as he had appeared.

The Jaguar, she thought, walking the hall toward the main entrance. Still an untamed beast, after almost half twenty of summers. No wonder his boys were wild and unruly.

Oh, I hope they give much trouble to that filthy cihua of his, she thought, walking into the brightness of the outside, a respectable Empress who had spent her time praying to Tenochtitlan's God of Rain.

CHAPTER 4

"No, I still can't believe it. Those filthy bastards, curse their stinking, rotting eyes into the worst parts of the Underworld!"

Tlacaelel looked around, feeling like crushing something, finding no suitable objects to break, or to throw against the wall. The guard house was empty, save for a few warriors and piles of mats thrown around.

"I told him, oh gods, how many times I kept telling him, over and over. Oh, what a filthy, stinking, gods-cursed mess!" He felt the heavy gaze of Itzcoatl's brother upon him and made an effort to control his temper. It was neither the time, nor the place to let out his frustrations or to be too open about it. "What else is happening in Azcapotzalco?"

"What else should happen?" asked the former Warlord's brother grimly. "One emperor dead, the other takes his place. Like here, or anywhere else."

"And the new emperor is Maxtla, of course."

"Oh, yes, who else?"

"Who else? Tezozomoc left hundreds of sons, most of them legitimate and fitting. It doesn't have to be this filthy, gods-cursed, stupid son of a whore."

"Oh, yes, of course, Tlacaelel. Go to Azcapotzalco and tell them that. I'll be more than happy to provide you with a long boat and a proper entourage." The heavyset man pulled a face. "Although, I won't bother to send many warriors to accompany you. I don't want to throw the lives of my men away for no reason."

"But mine you'll be too happy to throw away, eh? One warlord dead, the other takes his place."

The large eyes stood his glare, narrowing slightly, their expression challenging. "I'd make a good warlord, yes." Shrugging, the man grinned, the intensity of his gaze lessening. "But I'm not going to hasten your death, if that's what you worry about. You'll do it all by yourself, with your wild escapades and your far-fetched plans and ideas. I don't know why my brother values your advice, and I don't understand what he sees in you to make you his successor. You are too young, too arrogant, and you think your opinions are the only ones that matter."

"Oh, spare me your jealousy-filled litany!" Clenching his fists, Tlacaelel turned to the doorway. "My opinions are too good not to listen to, and you may now make yourself comfortable while watching what happens when they are not listened to. I told the Emperor to take no sides, but he jumped into Azcapotzalco's mess with relish, gambling it all on one man, the man who is now dead and forgotten." The old wood screeched as he pushed the screen aside forcefully. "So now let us see what happens when Azcapotzalco is being ruled by the man our Emperor was rude and offensive to." He narrowed his eyes at the still strong afternoon sun. "I'm off to see your brother. He is at the old Tepanec's, isn't he?"

A grunt was his answer.

His paces resounded angrily against the stone pavement of the main road as he stormed out of the Palace's gates, heading down the broad path, surrounded by colorful buildings, seeing none of their beauty.

He couldn't even begin to think of the complications. The fact that Maxtla had just murdered his own brother, the lawful Tepanec Emperor, was obvious. No one in his right mind would assume otherwise. A healthy, middle-aged man dying all of a sudden, without being ill or wounded. What a coincidence!

He snorted. His own father had died the same way, relatively young and healthy, in the prime of his life, and just when he had been about to change his policies in the Acolhua War. How convenient for those who had disagreed with him.

A palanquin with royal symbols swept by, and, momentarily interested, he glanced at the drawn curtains, picking out the elegant silhouette of the Emperor's Chief Wife as she sat there, leaning against the cushions. A very pretty sight, even though hardly visible behind the swaying material. What was the highborn *cihua* doing outside the Palace at such an unusual time of the day? he wondered absently, rushing on, oblivious of his warriors, who had a difficult time keeping up.

The high walls of the spacious dwelling belonging to Tenochtitlan's First Warlord towered ahead, bright and newly plastered. The old Tepanec lived in a grand style. Very old now, having seen close to seventy summers, the man seemed to be one of the city's monuments, like the first causeway or the Great Pyramid, an inseparable part of it, its history and its present alike. When he finally died, the whole part of Tenochtitlan would go away with him, melting into the mist of the past, thought Tlacaelel, following the main servant who had rushed to show him in personally, not summoning the relevant slave, paying due respect to the newly appointed Chief Warlord.

Making his way along the familiar halls, passing the spaciousness of the main chambers, Tlacaelel grinned. No, this man would not go away any time soon. He was as solid as the Great Pyramid, and as impressive, the wide cracks in the formidable blocks of stones notwithstanding.

"Well, well, if it's not our Honorable Chief Warlord!"

The two leaders squatted on the patio, comfortable, surrounded by clouds of smoke. The Tepanec was the one enjoying his long, elaborately carved pipe, while his guest reclined leisurely, sipping from his cup.

"It's a pleasure to see you." The old man smiled widely, his eyes twinkling in a familiar way. "You grace my poor dwelling with your presence."

Tlacaelel returned the grin, imagining this man making his way through the Underworld, still amused, making jokes and laughing, challenging the bloodthirsty beasts and the clashing obsidian rocks.

"It took you some time to arrive," grunted Itzcoatl, not changing his position. "Or have you received the news only now?"

"Yes, the news reached me with a considerable delay," said Tlacaelel, squatting upon the vacant mat. He accepted a cup from a slave and studied the milky liquid. "I spent my morning by the wharves, preparing the boats. We'll be taking half twenty of the long ones, and two times twenty of the regular canoes."

"I'm not sure you'll be going anywhere now," said Itzcoatl, giving him a gloomy look.

"Yes, I suppose we may need to readjust some of our plans." Sipping from his cup, Tlacaelel made sure his voice didn't change. "Yet, it doesn't mean I will be canceling the upcoming campaign. The next few dawns will allow us to learn of the developments in Azcapotzalco."

He saw the narrowing eyes and stood the glare of the former War Leader, seething. *I am the Warlord now*, he thought, furious. *You will not tell me what to do, certainly not in the way leaders speak to inferiors.*

"Azcapotzalco is certainly boiling." The words of the old Tepanec interrupted the heavy silence, spoken placidly, as though not noticing the tension. "Such outright taking of power cannot go down well, not in the Great Capital." The man inhaled from his pipe, allowing the smoke to come out slowly, prettily. "Maxtla will need to divert the attention from what he has done. And what better way is there to do that than by creating trouble in the provinces?" The red-rimmed eyes looked up, suddenly dark and full of meaning. "Provinces, or troublesome allies."

Tlacaelel felt the taste of the *octli* losing its spiciness. "Tenochtitlan is not a troublesome ally."

"If the new Tepanec ruler is prepared to forget the offensive behavior of our Emperor, then yes, Tenochtitlan is not a troublesome ally." Lowering his pipe, the man shook his head. "It happened too soon," he muttered, as though talking to himself. "We are not ready yet."

"We may be able to deal with it," said Itzcoatl, glancing up from under his eyebrows. "The causeways can be blocked on a short notice, and our superiority on the water is undeniable these days."

The old warrior grunted. "Oh, so we can withstand a siege.

Good for us. But is this the height of our inspirations? Not to be conquered? Is that what we planned for?" The gaze he shot at the former Warlord was dark and heavy with meaning. "The foolish escapades of our Emperor could have been prevented easily, remember that."

Tlacaelel watched the two men glaring at each other, their nostrils widening with every breath taken. Oh, those two were up to something, but he had known this for more than a few moons, since the death of Tezozomoc. He'd had inkling as soon as Itzcoatl had stopped backing him, Tlacaelel, in his attempts to convince the Emperor to behave sensibly by keeping away from the Tepanec royal family's quarrel. Suddenly, the oh-so-very-opinionated Adviser, the man who before had patronized poor Chimal to the point of being outright disrespectful, had nothing to say, watching impassively, doing nothing, letting the young Emperor choose sides in the most careless, foolish manner fitting only to a boy. Hiding his curiosity, he watched the two leaders, aware that because of him they hadn't been able to converse as freely as they may have wished to.

"Well, Old Friend," said Itzcoatl finally, his tone startling in its sudden lightness. "I wasn't the one to dispose of the Tepanec Emperor too soon. It happened, and we'll just have to deal with it."

The older man shook his head, his grin flashing out, reluctant to a degree. "You'll be the one expected to deal with it. But I daresay you'll manage. So, Warlord," the old eyes turned to Tlacaelel, glimmering with their usual mischief. "How do you propose to deal with the situation? Are we ready for a possible conflict with our worthwhile allies and overlords?"

"Well, as the Honorable Adviser said, we can withstand a siege, and we can repulse any water-born attack." He paused, choosing his words carefully. "Yet, as you so wisely stated, to repulse the attack may not be enough. In order to war on Azcapotzalco we will need allies, trustworthy, committed allies and friends."

The man nodded. "Where is the Acolhua heir? Running all over his former provinces again?"

"Yes, he left a few market intervals ago, in order to visit Texcoco. I predict it'll take him another market interval or two to make his journey back."

"He is traveling at a slow pace."

"Yes, he does that."

The old warrior's grin widened. "He is a good man."

"Yet, he should have postponed his journey this time," said Itzcoatl. "With Maxtla hurrying up the events, the Acolhua heir is not safe traveling his former lands. The new Tepanec Emperor hates him openly, making no secret of it."

Tlacaelel felt like cursing. "Maxtla is not an emperor yet!"

"He will be." Unperturbed, Itzcoatl reached for his cup. "How many warriors accompanied him?"

"Half of twenty."

"Hopelessly not enough."

"Well, yes, but he couldn't have taken more, or he would have made the governor of Texcoco and some of the provinces uneasy. He is just a visitor there, with no aspirations." Watching the frown upon the broad, wrinkled face of their host, Tlacaelel felt his own uneasiness welling. "The Highlander picked those men personally, so this party is worth two, even three times that of a larger group."

The older man nodded, his face softening, as it always did when discussing his favorite nephew, but Itzcoatl just frowned. "The Highlander is in trouble himself." He shrugged. "But isn't he always?"

"What happened now?" asked the old Tepanec a little too hastily.

"Meddling in politics, this one. Trying to protect his Acolhua friend. Or the Acolhua Chief Wife. Thinking that without his push Tenochtitlan will not be able to go downhill as fast as it can."

"What did he do?" The grin of the older man was wide, laced with generous amount of pride.

But Itzcoatl grunted, not amused. "He killed that filthy manure-eating adviser, the one who had tried to make our Emperor side with Maxtla, while throwing the Acolhua guest out, or better yet, putting him to death."

Tlacaelel pursed his lips, remembering the bodies, and the bared fangs of the carved jaguar.

The old Tepanec shrugged. "I remember this manure-eater. My nephew did a sensible thing."

"But he acted less sensibly by leaving clear marks, leading this murder straight back to him. The Emperor is furious."

"What obvious marks can a warrior leave while killing someone?" cried out the old leader. "A too neatly cut throat? Too deeply opened stomach? The Emperor should concentrate on his own blunders instead of trying to take his frustrations out on his warriors or their leaders."

"Unless those particular leaders bother to carve those marks, making it difficult to miss, tossing the marketplace of Tenochtitlan into a superstitious fit of fear. Pushing the priests into making inquiries."

The wooden shaft of the pipe creaked under their host's tightening fingers, as the broad face lost some color and the widely spaced eyes grew alarmingly dark. "Stupid hothead."

"Yes, he is." Itzcoatl shrugged. "I told the Emperor to leave it to me, and I ordered the carving to be scratched off."

The older warrior nodded. "Thank you, Old Friend." Inhaling from his pipe deeply, he seemed to sink into his thoughts. "We need the Acolhua provinces rallied and ready, and we need the people of Tlatelolco committed, too. They have been too vague, promising help but doing nothing to fortify their flowery speeches."

"I'll go to Tlatelolco at once," said Tlacaelel.

"No, I'll pay them a visit." Itzcoatl frowned. "They deserve this honor, and it may also serve to remind them that we are near and not to be angered."

"Yes, do that, Old Friend. Your visit may impress or intimidate them, which will work for us either way." The old eyes sparkled. "And your family connections would warrant such a visit."

Relieved to be free of such mundane mission, Tlacaelel grinned, remembering that Itzcoatl's Chief Wife was born to the ruler of Tlatelolco.

"What about Tlacopan?" he asked.

"Tlacopan?" The old Tepanec grinned, while Itzcoatl shook his head. "I wish this dung-infested place could be intimidated as easily."

"They were favorably inclined toward us when I last heard of them. They are Tepanecs, but they do not like to be ruled by Azcapotzalco."

"Yes, they may betray their own Emperor. But they must be pushed there subtly and carefully. I suppose you were planning to pay them a visit yourself, weren't you?"

Tlacaelel just nodded, not put out with the fact that the old man should read him so easily. He would be furious if it happened with anyone but the First Warlord of Tenochtitlan.

"Their ruler is fat and timid. I believe I'll be able to convey our message to him in a way that will cause it to sink in."

Their host nodded in his turn. "Like I said, we need more time, and the Acolhua provinces need to be organized, possibly backed by some of their neighbors, or their old enemies."

"The highlanders, eh?" Itzcoatl's grin was untypically wide.

"Well, yes, why not?"

"Judging by your nephew, this lot won't be easy to handle."

The old leader's grin matched that of his friend. "My nephew is a law unto himself. I certainly hope they have more warriors like him."

"Oh, please," said Itzcoatl, then fell silent as the slaves brought in plates with refreshments, and two more flasks of *octli*. "Come to think of it, your nephew can be useful in more ways than just leading warriors and killing useless advisers," he muttered, almost to himself.

Something in the former Warlord's voice startled Tlacaelel, and he concentrated, trying to read through the dark, closed up face of his superior.

"What ways?" asked the Tepanec suspiciously, obviously as alerted.

"He can rid us of some people who are rapidly becoming a nuisance."

"No!" called the old leader sharply. His pipe made a screeching sound, banging against the side of the table. "He is not to be involved in any of *this*."

Itzcoatl looked up, unperturbed. "Why not?"

"There are twenty reasons and more, and I won't go into any of them." The Tepanec's voice rose. "We are not ready for that move either, and when we are, my nephew is to be left out of it."

"The wild beast has a mind of his own, you know. And a great will into the bargain." Itzcoatl's eyes glimmered, the way they always did when he was pleased with himself for having thought of a way to solve his problems. After so many summers, fighting under this man's personal command, Tlacaelel had learned to read his moods as if they were written on a bark paper. "You tried to keep him away from the Palace's troubles seven summers ago, Old Friend, and he just pushed himself more forcefully into the middle of the maelstrom. He is a law unto himself, indeed, and a priceless asset, if used correctly." A shrug. "And anyway, he never has kept away from our politics."

"He gets involved when his Acolhua friend is involved. But this time, the Texcocan has nothing to do with it."

Itzcoatl's lips were pressed thinly, his grin – a mirthless affair. "He guards the interests of more than one highborn Acolhua. The Emperor's Chief Wife is involved in this, even if not directly."

Tlacaelel watched the weathered face of their host twisting as though the man had eaten something incredibly bitter.

"Leave my nephew out of it," he repeated stonily. "You can use his warriors' skills all you like, but don't make him cause any more trouble in the Palace. What happened seven summers ago was more than enough." He picked up his pipe, concentrating on the beautifully decorated wood, running his fingers along the carvings, deep in thought. The Highlander must have made this thing for his uncle, thought Tlacaelel, recognizing the patterns. "It may be too soon to do the deed, anyway" he said finally. "We should wait and see what happens in Azcapotzalco, what their new Emperor is up to."

And this was be the wisest thing to do, reflected Tlacaelel after some time, when the meeting had broken up and Itzcoatl began bidding his farewells. They could do nothing but wait to see what the next step of the dangerous, power-hungry Maxtla would be.

The clamor of the broad avenue burst upon them, along with the soft light of the afternoon sun. Welcoming the fact that Itzcoatl had sent his warriors and his palanquin bearers ahead, Tlacaelel went alongside the man unhurriedly, enjoying the opportunity to walk. Elevated into the position of the Chief Warlord, he was haunted by his own palanquin bearers more often than he cared to appreciate.

"I need your advice," said Itzcoatl, his voice low, eyes still on the road.

"Yes, Honorable Uncle?"

"You are close with the Highlander. If I find a way to force him into solving our problem, will he be able to do this? The Emperor is never alone, and this annoying *cihua*, his Chief Wife, is studying me with the eyes of a hawk, afraid I might decide her husband has ruled for enough summers already." The man snorted derisively. "She watches over him as though he were her child. But she is not his mother. Wives should keep to the wives' quarters, even the chief ones. Not spending their time in the main hall, listening to the matters of the government, not above offering advice, as if she understands any of it." He flopped his arms in the air angrily. "Why is it that these highborn Tepanec *cihuas* never know their place?"

Because that's what they are, thought Tlacaelel, secretly sympathizing with his half-brother's First Wife. She was a wise woman, he reflected, having encountered her often. Not bad and not spiteful, unless provoked, and this happened rarely and usually with a good reason. Also she had good cause to be suspicious, too. Wasn't the Honorable Adviser planning to do just that, to get rid of her husband in order to take the burden of the government upon his own shoulders?

Tlacaelel shrugged. Chimalpopoca was a nice young man, and he had tried very hard. Yet, at such difficult times Tenochtitlan needed a strong ruler of enough years, a dedicated man of great abilities and, most importantly, a man of immense willpower and no fear.

Glancing at Itzcoatl, he took in the wide shoulders, the forceful gait, the broad, set face. Yes, he thought calmly. His half uncle was the right person to stand up to the Tepanecs. Therefore Chimalpopoca would have to go.

"The Highlander would be a perfect person, but I don't believe he'll be willing to do this."

"Why ever not? His Acolhua friend would benefit from Tenochtitlan taking the action, at long last. Hasn't the wily Texcocan been waiting for just that opportunity?"

"Yes, he has. But the Highlander is also unusually fond of the Emperor's Chief Wife. He would do nothing to hurt her."

"Oh, yes, that he is." Itzcoatl snorted again. "I'm telling you, this woman has no shame!"

"We don't even know if anything is happening between those two," said Tlacaelel, feeling ridiculous but somehow obliged to defend his friend's honor.

"Don't we?"

For a few heartbeats they proceeded in silence.

"I don't want him to get hurt." Feeling even more foolish, Tlacaelel shrugged. "He is a good warrior and a good man."

"No one is wishing to hurt this collection of admirable qualities, Nephew," said Itzcoatl tersely. "I want to use some of those qualities, that's all." A brief piercing glance brushed past his face. "He may be able to accomplish this task more swiftly and efficiently than anyone else."

CHAPTER 5

The sun broke through the clouds as the high-noon humidity began to recede. Coyotl ground his teeth, watching the pine trees covering yet another slope. They were lost, desperately lost, and he was to blame.

He cursed. Since entering Texcoco on the previous dawn, things had gone downhill. But how had it come to this? Hadn't he come to visit his former *altepetl* openly and officially, the way he had done half twenty of times through the past two summers? What was different this time? Why had the dirty son of a rat, Maxtla, felt confident enough to try and kill a noble person of his, Coyotl's, status? Openly and unashamedly at that, too!

He frowned. The girl had said that the filthy manure-eating would-be-emperor was planning to rid himself of many more influential persons around the Great Lake. Also that he would be the Tepanec emperor soon. Which, of course, meant only one thing – the hastened death of the current Azcapotzalco ruler.

He peered at the narrow trail they had been following since crossing the low pass in the first ridge of the mountains. "If it doesn't turn eastward soon, we'll have to go back," he said firmly.

The warriors grunted in consent.

"We'll find our way back toward the Lowlands, and we will take our chances proceeding alongside the coastal towns."

The tall leader of his warriors nodded thoughtfully. "I'm sure we'll be able to find a way to sail back to Tenochtitlan from this or that village. All we need is a few canoes, four or five at the most, and we can do with even less, given the circumstances. They are after you, Honorable Leader, so all we need is to get you back to

Tenochtitlan safely. The rest of us can stay and wait until you send more boats to pick us up."

"Yes, it's a good plan," said Coyotl, kicking at a pine cone, sending it rolling down the hill. "But you will be the ones sailing to Tenochtitlan. I have other things to do."

His tall escort stopped dead in his tracks. "What do you mean, Honorable Leader?"

Coyotl shrugged. "I will re-enter the Highlands, but in the places I know well."

"Alone?"

"Yes, alone. Or maybe with a few of you. But not all. Ten warriors is a raiding party. The Highlanders won't take it well."

The tall man frowned. "I can't let you do this, Honorable Leader. I am entrusted with your life. I was asked specifically to bring you back to Tenochtitlan, safe and sound. It is my duty to do so."

Coyotl grinned, not put out with the decisive words thanks to the deference in the man's tone. "I appreciate your devotion, but the circumstances have changed. I need to visit the Highlands, and I need to go to Huexotzinco." He watched the forested hill ahead of them. "It is time I do this."

The wind grew colder, and he knew they should go back. Their hurried flight into unfamiliar parts of the Highlands was a mistake. They should have proceeded along the regular routes, southward, down the coast; to sail to Tenochtitlan or to enter the Highlands through the passes and trails he knew well.

He shrugged. The previous night had begun as an easy adventure, sneaking out of the Palace in the dead of night, passing through the gardens he had known by heart, every trail, every alley, every mosaic-covered pond. Unguarded and empty, the back gates welcomed him and his people, the dark trees surrounding it, swaying in the night breeze, wishing him well. A quick dash down the dark alleys, also familiar from his childhood, and they were crossing the Plaza, heading southward, leaving his favorite Tlaloc Hill behind.

The Tlaloc Hill! So many memories. He wished Kuini had come with him, this time more than ever.

By dawn break they were well on their way toward Coatlinchan, but the roads became more and more crowded, teeming with flustered travelers. Traders and peasants, women with baskets and children, and warriors, many warriors, with their cloaks embroidered with the symbol of Azcapotzalco's giant ant. Their agitated voices filled the morning air, disturbing the peacefulness of the countryside, bringing back the dreadful memories of refugees flooding the roads that led out of burning Huexotla, more than seven summers ago.

Shivering, he exchanged glances with the leader of his warriors and, not wishing to draw attention, they left the main road, steering deeper into the countryside, leaving the bubbling coastal areas behind. Which was a relief in the beginning, as the clamor of the towns receded and the serenity of the towering cliffs, covered with the deep, late-spring forest, enveloped them. However, as the day progressed and the sun began its journey toward its resting place, Coyotl's worry began to mount. He did not know these parts of the Highlands, and his surroundings did not become anymore recognizable as they kept plodding southward and eastward.

The trail twisted, wide enough to suggest that people may be using it, yet he began doubting it would bring him to the vicinity of Huexotzinco. Also, now he remembered that his entourage, comprised of purely Aztec warriors, would not be welcomed anywhere around the prominent town. He doubted his own welcome would be much warmer than that. Seven summers had passed, but ugly incidents tended to stay in people's memories. More so than the good ones.

"We go back the way we came," he said resolutely, ignoring his companions' frowns. "We should be able to reach the pass before darkness falls."

The forest rustled with the straightening breeze, not happy with the careless invaders. He felt it watching him with invisible eyes. Taking a deep breath, he tried to understand the strange sensation. *Were* they being observed? His warrior's senses probed the surroundings, telling him that no, no one followed them. Still, his skin crawled, and he wished Kuini were there, with his sword covered with carvings, ready to fight anything that may attack them, humans or spirits alike.

The thought of the Highlander's sword brought the memory of the carved jaguar with the hollow eyes and the bared teeth, the likeness of which he had seen a few times through the past summers, every time he had sensed trouble looming. He shivered. In places like this, in the deepening shadows, it was easy to imagine what had inspired the Highlander to carve this particular image while dealing with despicable people.

He remembered the last time, close to three summers ago, when he had seen those intimidating, bared teeth, and the hollow eyes staring at him, along with the other onlookers, from the wall of a warehouse located in the area of the wharves. It had happened after some dirty killers, despised, lowly types, had tried to murder him while he had been busy with Tenochtitlan's engineers, measuring the banks of one of the shores.

Oh, he had not come close to death on that day. The killers' attempt was weak and ill prepared, easy for a warrior like him to avoid and then to chase the filthy commoners down, to kill them one by one.

Yet, a few days later, a prominent Tepanec trader and some other shady types had died, their bodies thrown on display beside the same wharf, with the jaguar staring eerily, guarding, ominous and threatening, sending shivers down everyone's spine, Coyotl's included. Although he knew who had committed the murders. As well as who had drawn the carving. Having his guesses, he could never bring himself to ask about it openly. The people who had arranged the attempt on his life had paid with their own lives. Justice had been served, and he had made sure to accompany the engineers as though nothing happened. To do otherwise was to admit a weakness.

He shook his head. It had been an interesting pastime, the one he had enjoyed wholeheartedly. Planning the improvements of water construction made the moons of idleness, when he couldn't go to Texcoco yet, bearable. Chimal was curious, eager to know how things worked, so together they would pore over the engineers' bark sheets, and Coyotl would explain the drawings and how they should be read. He even devised a way to build a huge duke, to keep the Great Lake's annually rising water at bay. Tenochtitlan suffered from frequent flooding, and Chimal was all shining, telling his Acolhua guest how they would commence this project, together, after the Tepanecs left Tenochtitlan alone, and after Coyotl regained control of his Texcoco and Acolhua provinces.

The clearing burst upon them, bathed in the soft afternoon sun, teeming with people. Clearly hunters, the men were busy cutting deer carcasses, their hair tied, their faces sweaty, smeared with blood and meat juices. Springing to their feet, they stared at the intruders, clearly just as surprised as Coyotl's warriors were.

"Wait," called Coyotl as the squat, fairly decorated man, obviously a leader, grabbed his club. "We no harm. No war." He tried to remember what little he knew of the Highlanders' tongue.

The hunters' leader frowned, while the rest stirred uneasily.

"Who are you?" asked the man. "What are those warriors doing here?"

"We no harm," repeated Coyotl, searching frantically for better words. "We lost, we not know the way."

"Lowlanders?"

"Yes, but no Tepanecs."

"Who then?"

He hesitated and the eyes of the man in front of him narrowed.

"Listen, we go, go back Lowlands, no disturb people Highlanders. We go back now."

The stony gaze bore at him. "Good," said the man finally. "Go back."

So very generous of you, thought Coyotl, his anger rising. *With us almost the same number of people, but warriors, with a fair chance of killing you all.*

"Let us go," he said to his men quietly, turning away, his eyes on the hunters.

"Honorable Leader." His leading warrior came closer, talking in a quiet, urgent voice. "We should kill them. They'll notify their warriors before we are able to reach the pass."

"I know, but I need these people to fight for me in the near future. I won't get their cooperation if I kill their hunters."

The Highlanders kept staring at them, but he could see in their faces the realization now. They knew they had no chance.

He stood their leader's piercing gaze. "Remember, I can kill, but I no, not kill. I want friends your people, not enemies."

The man's eyes flashed. "You would be trapped here, anyway. Our warriors are nearby."

He felt those words cascading down his spine in a freezing wave. "Where?"

"Near." The man grinned mirthlessly. "Otherwise we would be more careful, wouldn't be surprised by you, filthy Lowlanders, who are crashing through the woods like a pack of deer, careless and making so much noise."

"We no raiding, no fight party," replied Coyotl, ridiculously offended. "We move quiet, when need."

"And so are they," said the man, motioning with his head.

Heart falling, Coyotl turned to watch, expecting to see the long-haired warriors before he actually did see their unpainted faces, sunburned and glittering with sweat. He felt his men tensing beside him.

Taking a step forward, he stood next to his warriors' leader. "We keep each other's backs," he whispered. "Keep very close. Make sure no one gets captured."

The veteran's nod was barely imperceptible.

As the warriors poured into the clearing, not very numerous, probably about two times twenty of them, he watched them. Just a regular raiding party, nothing more. He measured them with his gaze. No, they had no chance against so many seasoned Highlander fighters, but they would have to do their best, he decided. He wouldn't go down in shame.

The hunters were talking rapidly, but he didn't try to follow their conversation, his eyes remaining glued to the man who was clearing his way through the crowd, his imposing height and wide shoulders making his progress easy.

Ice filled his stomach, making it difficult to breath. If he could have entertained any idea of trying to talk his way out of it, to reach some sort of an understanding, he knew now that they were lost beyond any hope. The hatred in the broad, painfully familiar face was impossible to mistake, twisting the strong features, making it look ugly.

"So, Lowlander, you have dared to come here again," cried out Nihi, crossing the clearing in a few long paces. Like the Highlander, he seemed to move with the same catlike grace and swiftness, surprising in such a large man. Coyotl just stared."You are going to die, you know that?"

Fighting the urge to take a step back, Coyotl did not move, almost pressed against the taller man as his assailant stopped with only a pace separating them.

"I'll thank mighty Camaxtli for sending you here, for me to take your life personally. I never hoped for such luck."

Coyotl glared at the broad face. There was no point trying to talk, to bring up his connection with this man's father. He wouldn't listen.

"You tell men kill, or you fight like a man?" he asked, strangely relieved, anticipating the fight now.

"Oh, I will kill you all by myself."

The club came out, looking smaller than it actually was in the man's large, brown hands. Coyotl hurried to untie his sword. His mind numb, he worried that his fingers would move clumsily, but the sword was out quickly, and his hands did not tremble, which pleased him.

Taking a step back, he brought his weapon up, staring at the strong, weathered face, recognizing familiar traits. Kuini did not look much like his brother, but there were similarities.

He felt his warriors moving closer.

"Don't," he said curtly, not turning his head. "Stay where you are."

His adversary's eyes were narrow slits, blazing with hatred. "You should never have returned."

The club pounced so suddenly, he almost missed its movement, having hardly enough time to leap aside. Wavering, he stabilized himself in time to meet the next onslaught, his hands trembling, making it difficult to hold out against the pressure. The man *was* strong.

The blazing eyes were close now, and he could smell spicy food on his adversary's breath.

"You should have stayed in your Lowlands." This time the man spoke Nahuatl.

His whole body trembling with the effort, Coyotl held out under the mighty pressure, surprised with his own ability to do so. "I came to talk... peacefully. I want our people to stop fighting."

The pressure of the club grew. "You only want that because your people lost and need our help."

Unable to hold on, Coyotl disengaged, leaping aside and thus avoiding the crushing touch of the heavily weighted club. His sword was about to pounce, seeing the opportunity of the momentarily exposed torso. Instead, he waited, ready to avoid another attack.

The eyes of his rival narrowed, but again, he attacked fiercely. His blow made Coyotl's sword crack, shattering one of the obsidian spikes.

He held on stubbornly, having the opportunity to disengage. "My people need help, yes... But your people need it now, too." He felt the bones in his arms straining as though about to crack. "We should fight together... not against each other."

With the last of his strength, he threw his body aside, panting, regaining his breath. Yet the club was swishing toward him again.

"You should have looked for other allies," gasped the man, when another attack was avoided, but barely. "Go to Lake Chalco, go to Xochimilco, go back to Tenochtitlan, maybe those traitors will deign to help." The club descended again. "With leaders like that stupid brother of mine, they may very well be that irrational."

This time he blocked the blow, seeing another opportunity to attack but missing it deliberately. "He is not stupid. He is a great leader."

The sweaty face was so close, burning his skin with the fierce, hate-filled glare. "Oh, yes! A great leader, living among his people's enemies, leading them..."

"Our people don't have to be enemies." He clenched his teeth in desperation, determined to hold on. "He saw it... your father saw it—"

"Don't talk about my father! You ruined him, you and no one else. For this alone you deserve to die."

Too enraged now, the man attacked fiercely, his club swishing, crushing against obstacles where Coyotl might have stood a moment before. Fighting the rising wave of panic, he concentrated on the ensuing storm of blows, pleased with his own quick reactions. When the opportunity presented itself after yet another wild leap, with his rival wavering, his hands still high, his unprotected ribs exposed, he had had enough presence of mind to make sure the flat side of his sword was the one to land against it.

The broad man wavered, stifling a gasp but recovering fast. If Coyotl had entertained an idea of pressing the attack, it was too late now. People around them held their breath. He could feel their awed silence. The club was high in the man's large hands, yet they were trembling now.

"Why don't you fight properly? Why don't you attack?" he hissed, refusing to move this time.

"I can't..." He could not feel his fingers anymore, his grip on his sword handle crushing. "Can't do this... to your father, to your brother. I can't."

"So you will die!" Still the man made no movement, his hands wrapped so tightly against the base of his club, his knuckles turned white.

"I know." His voice rang in his own ears as though belonging to someone else. "What can a warrior ask for, if not for that sort of a honorable death?"

The eyes of his rival narrowed again, this time with an open resentment rather than hatred.

"Oh, you dirty son of a rat," he exclaimed, shaking his head violently.

The club came down slowly, reluctantly. Breathing heavily, he stared at Coyotl, sweat pouring down his face.

"I'm going to take you to Huexotzinco." The words came out, seeping through the clenched teeth. "But should you even think of making any trouble... Just a passing thought of doing so, and I'll kill you with relish. I can't believe I'm giving you this opportunity now. I don't want to fight alongside your people. I want to fight against them. And I still hate you personally. Is that clear to you?"

Coyotl licked his lips, his palms locked around his sword, impossible to unclench. "Yes, I understand that. And I thank you for doing this." He brought his sword down with an effort, then remembered his warriors. "Will you let my people leave now? I wish to accompany you alone."

Kuini's brother's broad shoulders lifted in a shrug. "They may leave. Until nightfall, they are safe. But with dawn they should be deep in the coastal areas, away from our mountains. Otherwise, they are dead."

"But, Honorable Leader," cried out the leader of his warriors, aghast. "It's impossible! We can't leave you—"

"Do as you are told, warrior!" Coyotl cut him off with more authority than he had ever used with his personal guards. "I order you to go back to Tenochtitlan at once. Notify your leader. Tell him where I am. This is your mission now." The man seemed as though about to argue still, so he silenced him with the fierce glare. "Go now!" Still tense, he turned back to Kuini's brother, who was conversing with his own people, seemingly arguing, too. "Let us proceed."

The large man whirled at him. "Shut up and wait! You are our prisoner—"

"I'm not a prisoner!"

They glared at each other, and then the dark eyes twinkled, suddenly reminding him of Kuini. "You were not appointed to lead us, either."

"I'm coming with you to talk to your leaders, to offer them my people's help, and to ask for theirs." Feeling the reaction, he clenched his palms tight, afraid that the trembling would show. His whole body felt weak, drained of strength, making him yearn to sit, or to lean against something. He was still alive, although he wasn't supposed to be. He took a deep breath. "I'm coming to negotiate, and I'm grateful and appreciative of your willingness to help, even if it goes against your better judgment."

The thin lips twisted into a hint of a derisive grin. "You talk well, Emperor's Heir. I wonder if it'll help you with our town's elders and the clans' councils this time. You came a long way since your last visit in Huexotzinco, didn't you?" A curt nod invited Coyotl to come along as the man began walking the trail, with his warriors and hunters organizing hastily. "Two stupid hotheads. Oh, how I itched to kill both of you back then, you and this troublesome brother of mine. But for Father, I would have strangled the two of you with my bare hands. You were still too young to resist me, although you managed to kill Yoho."

He remembered the rude hunter, the angry husband of that Iso-girl. "I didn't want to kill that man. He left me with no choice."

"Oh, I suppose taking his woman was also something you'd been forced into."

He sighed. "No. It was stupid of me to do that."

The broad man's sudden grin was wide, strangely open. "Well, youths do these things. But you were very lucky my father believed in you and was ready to go to great lengths in order to save your stupid life." The grin disappeared. "You had better not disappoint him, do you hear me?"

"I will not. I'm trying to do all I can. I've been following his advice for long summers now. I will not disappoint him." He paused. "I know he believes in me, and I'm honored by his trust. He is an outstanding man, and I will do everything I can to bring his vision to life. Even if it goes against my own goals."

"But it does not."

"No, it does not."

The broad man sighed. "There is something about you, Lowlander, something that makes me want to put you in your place time after time. I don't know what it is. Maybe you talk too smoothly. Maybe you are too self-assured for the mere fugitive that you are." He shrugged. "Maybe you'll make a good emperor with those qualities. But you had better keep your promise to my father. I swear, I'll find a way to harm you if you don't."

Coyotl did not fight his anger this time. "Your threats are meaningless to me. I do what I do for my reasons, and what is between me and your father stays between us!"

"Oh, but you will need my cooperation as well, Lowlander,"

said his companion unperturbed. "You are talking to the Leader of Huexotzinco's Warriors, the man allowed to speak in the clans' council, the man who is asked to do so. The man whose cooperation you will need to ensure."

A Warriors' Leader? Coyotl glanced at the imposing figure and the proudly held head.

"I'm pleased to hear that," he said, striving to be polite. *Oh, why him, of all people?* "You have my best wishes and my praise."

"I'm sure I have those." The arrogant chuckle made Coyotl yet angrier. "So, how is that troublesome brother of mine?"

Coyotl made an effort to relax. "Kuini is doing well. He is much appreciated, entrusted with larger and larger groups of warriors to lead. He is a born leader."

His companion's bushy eyebrows climbed up. "I would love to see that, the unruly bastard turning into an impeccable leader."

Coyotl fought his smile from showing. "He is still what he is. The former Warlord hates his unruliness, and the current one appreciates it mainly because he is extremely wise and farsighted." He shrugged. "But your brother is a good leader all the same. His warriors admire him, because they know they can trust him. He plans his raids carefully, and he is never wild or unpredictable about his missions. Only with private things, when he is responsible for no one but himself, he still behaves like there are no laws but his own."

"Oh, that's my wild little brother!" But there was a glint of satisfaction in the man's voice now. "The unruly bastard was always like that, even when still toddling. Keeping to himself, doing whatever he liked, impossible to intimidate or be beaten into obedience. An annoying type."

"Many important people appreciate him for what he is," said Coyotl, feeling obliged to defend his friend's honor. "One day he'll be the Chief Warlord of Texcoco."

"I'll make offerings for this day to come," said Nihi, but his voice was openly mocking. "Although, those offerings will be the Lowlanders' hearts, unless you are successful."

Coyotl said nothing, hating every moment of this conversation, wishing to reach Huexotzinco already.

I will be successful, you arrogant, bad-tempered bastard, he thought. *And it'll happen sooner than you think, with or without your cooperation.*

CHAPTER 6

"Your brother fled Texcoco, and no one knows where he is."

She felt it like a punch in her stomach, a hit that made her insides shrink, leaving her feeling as though she did not have enough air to breathe. She had expected all sorts of bad news since that day, some dawns ago, when Chimal had grown angry over the marketplace murder.

Her worry mounting, she was not reassured by the fleeting meeting with the Highlander, fearing for him, and for Chimal too, but never for her brother. She thought that of all people, Coyotl was too careful, too thoughtful, too wise to get into trouble. The new Tepanec emperor, that dirty, sleazy, despicable Maxtla, who had not been above murdering his own brother, could hate Coyotl all he liked, but she knew her brother could deal with it, just as he dealt with the rest of the troubles, working hard to get his Texcoco back.

"What happened?" she asked weakly, hardly hearing her own voice.

Chimal gestured the servants out, then came toward her, his slender, pleasant looking face twisted with compassion.

"No one knows, Iztac Ayotl." He squatted beside her, taking her hand between his palms. "But I'm sure he is all right. Nezahualcoyotl is a great warrior and a resourceful man. He won't allow himself to be lured into a trap." Squeezing her hand, he smiled, seeking her gaze. "It's not his first time fleeing Texcoco, and I have a fair guess where he has gone."

"But what happened? Why did he have to flee?" She forced a reluctant grin, her heart still fluttering.

His face darkened, losing its perpetual pleasantness.

"Maxtla, of course! Who else would dare to try to kill the highborn Acolhua?" His lips were now just a thin line, quivering with disdain. "Oh, this man is despicable! Tayatzin should have executed him, officially, accusing this lowly person of treason, judging him in his royal court. I told him to do so! He should have done it with no hesitation instead of allowing his misgivings, his doubts, his good nature to get the better of him. And so now, here we are, with this wonderful man dead. Poisoned, Iztac Ayotl! Poisoned by his own despicable, lowly brother." Jumping to his feet, he began pacing the room, shooting angry glances at the elegant furniture that hindered his progress. "How foolish, how useless, how ridiculous! The dirty murderer is ruling the Tepanec Capital, feeling invincible, capable of anything." He stopped and peered at her, eyes flashing. "And why shouldn't he, I ask you. Why shouldn't he feel invincible? He has found a perfect way of ridding himself of his enemies, or anyone whom he considers to be standing in his way. People like your brother. Good, decent people."

She tried to control her panic, striving to keep her presence of mind. For his sake. He needed her strength. He always came to her when troubled.

"Did he try to kill Coyotl?" she asked, pleased to hear her voice ringing steadily.

"Yes, he did! The despicable good-for-nothing tried to kill your brother when Nezahualcoyotl came to Texcoco, on an official, completely innocent and agreed upon visit."

"How?" She heard a snap and felt the delicate wood of her fan breaking under her fingers. Absently, she watched it, finding it difficult to unclench her palm.

"My advisers don't know yet. All we heard was the rumor about the attempt on the life of the Acolhua heir and that he had fled the city." He stopped pacing and stood in front of her, shoulders sagging. "I'm sorry, Iztac Ayotl. I should have sent more warriors to accompany him. Maybe I should have tried to convince him to give up on his journey this time. But he went away before we heard of Tayatzin's death, you see?" Squatting again beside her, he sought her gaze. "He will be all right. I'm sure he fled into the Highlands once again."

"His friend is not with him this time," she said, without thinking. "I'm not sure the Highlanders will receive him kindly without his friend's presence and protection."

Chimal's face lost some of its affectionate affability. "How do you know that the notorious Highlander didn't accompany your brother this time?"

Her stomach tightened. "You talked about this man with Itzcoatl, only a few dawns ago. You accused him of things, ridiculous things."

He looked at her hard and said nothing, the cozy atmosphere gone.

"Well, let us get back to Coyotl. How do you know he fled Texcoco?" She made an effort to keep her voice calm and indifferent

Frowning, Chimal shrugged and refused to say anything, reminding her of the boy from her first summer in Tenochtitlan, when they would play around and she would say things that would hurt his pride.

"The rumor says he sneaked out of the Palace in the middle of the night and then disappeared."

"Why didn't he sail back to Tenochtitlan?"

"How could he, with the Tepanecs controlling the coastal towns?" There was a victorious spark to Chimal's eyes now. "Come on, Iztac Ayotl, think sensibly."

She glared at him, her anger helping her to overcome her worry. "I am thinking sensibly, Chimalpopoca. I always think sensibly. You have been coming here to consult me every time something happens, or inviting me to attend your morning meetings, *because* I think sensibly!"

He glared at her, bringing back the memories of the boy in the Palace's gardens in force now, until she felt like laughing.

"You are such a child sometimes, Chimal. Such a spoiled, petulant, angry baby!" Getting to her feet, she came closer, placed her palms on his shoulders, almost the same height as he was. "But I do love you for that, you know? You never change, and I love that."

Scowling, he peered at her, his lips twisting, evidently fighting a smile. "You have never changed either, Iztac Ayotl. You are as wild as you've always been. You do things your way, and you never bother with customs or appearances. You have no respect for traditional ways."

She laughed into his eyes. "Are you complaining, Revered Emperor? Does your faithful First Wife displease you?"

His arms encircled her, pulling her closer gently, with much consideration. "No, Chief Wife. You please me greatly, but you *are* impossible."

"Well, you have more wives now. You can always put me aside, advance one of the other two in my stead." She kissed his lightly, teasingly.

"I may do that," he said, laughing now. "Just to see what you would do. It would be quite a scene, I'm sure."

"Oh, don't you mess with me, Chimalpopoca."

But his kisses grew more ardent, and she knew her maids would be slipping quietly out of her rooms now. Didn't he have any meetings or cases to judge? No. It was high noon, and the Palace was getting ready for the midday rest.

Fighting the urge to find yet another excuse, she forced herself to answer his kisses. He was her lawful husband, and she did love him, in her way.

"I love you, Iztac Ayotl," he murmured after the lovemaking, lying beside her, spent.

She caressed his slender shoulder, its skin smooth and pleasing to touch. Nothing rough about it, and no scar tissue. "I love you too, Chimal."

"Did you enjoy it?"

"Yes, of course."

"Sometimes I'm not sure." He rose on his elbow, peering at her.

"You please me, husband, if that's what you want to know. I love when you make love to me." She smiled, not wishing to get into this particular discussion. "I hope I please you too, Mighty Emperor."

He grinned. "You please me greatly, Chief Wife. You don't

have to worry about that. You will please me even when we are as old as those trees outside your window."

She laughed. "I see you are planning to live longer than Tezozomoc himself."

"Oh, yes, I do. I will turn Tenochtitlan into the mightiest city around our Great Lake, and I will leave a firm legacy for my descendants to follow." He hugged her. "We will do it together, Iztac Ayotl, you and me."

"Yes, we will."

She laid her head on his shoulder, uncomfortable with the awareness that none of what he said would happen. None of it. They wouldn't grow old together, and he would not leave a great legacy for the future generations to follow. Somehow she knew it now, though never having experienced any premonition, any foresight, before.

Her sadness welled. "I wish the Tepanecs would leave us alone," she murmured into his shoulder, swallowing her tears. "I wish my brother would get his Texcoco back. I wish I could help you both, could influence the events, could change something for real."

His voice was soft, caressing, just as his hands that were stroking her hair. "There is no need to be sad, Iztac Ayotl. It will happen. It will. You'll see."

"I wish I believed it as firmly as you do." Angry with herself for those silly, whiny tears, she clasped her lips tight. "We have been struggling against the Tepanecs for so many summers, yet nothing happens. They are still there, controlling our every movement, menacing, wishing us harm. My father rebelled, and he paid with his life and his lands, his *altepetl* and his provinces. Yet, our wise, careful behavior seems to bear no fruit, either. We are struggling for every little bit of freedom, and we feel victorious with every tiny success. Yet, when you think about the situation in general, nothing has changed, nothing! The Tepanecs are still here, watching us and the rest of the peoples around the Great Lake, mean, invincible. Sometimes I think they will always be there, like the bad, evil presence of some Underworld spirit. They will go nowhere, and we will keep growing excited and happy over small things like being granted permission to fix our water construction after it breaks for the hundredth of twenty times."

She fought his hands when they pulled her face up, gently but firmly, his eyes large and beautiful, beaming at her.

"Come on, Iztac Ayotl, stop being so gloomy. Stop looking at small, unimportant details. See the general picture, the entirety of the drawing. In the times of my grandfather, Revered Acamapichtli, Tenochtitlan was not even allowed to campaign on its own. They had no fresh water and hardly any trade. The city was full of reed-and-cane houses, so the elders say. People wore maguey clothes, and the Great Pyramid was small and simple. It was not so very long time ago. Ask our First Chief Warlord, he is still alive. But you see, hardly two times twenty summers later, we are a strong, fairly rich, independent *altepetl*. Yes, we still have to please the Tepanecs, but we are working to change that, too, remember? Your brother and I, along with my faithful advisers, we'll change it. Trust us!"

He beamed at her, excited, oh-so-very-young and pleasant looking, still just a boy. He had seen twenty summers, but she had seen close to thirty, she thought. Yet, maybe he was right, maybe his enthusiasm, his naive trust in himself and his destiny would achieve the results where the other experienced, crafty politicians seemed to have failed.

She smiled reluctantly. "Yes, you may be right. I should trust you more. I shouldn't allow my impatience to get the better of me. It's just..." Shrugging, she raised her head, propping her chin against her palm. "It's just that I worry about my brother. Why can't he receive what was rightfully his? Why does he have to plot and scheme and risk his life over and over again. What if he's been hurt? What if he didn't reach the Highlands?"

She saw her maid lingering at the doorway, at a respectable distance, her whole posture radiating a careful message.

"Your brother is one of the most patient, courageous, resourceful men I have ever met," she heard Chimal saying. "He won't be trapped, and he won't be hurt."

Gesturing for the maid to come in, Iztac began to get up. "I hope you are right," she said. "I hope he'll come back to Tenochtitlan unharmed."

"Revered Emperor," murmured the maid, her eyes firmly upon the floor. "The messenger from the Chief Adviser is waiting in the main hall. Your main servant insisted I should let you know."

"Oh, the messenger from Itzcoatl," called out Chimal, jumping to his feet. "Good!" He beamed at her, his happiness spilling. "He is so efficient. It's been only one dawn since he left for Tlatelolco, and here he is, sending a messenger, a bearer of good news, I'm sure."

Signaling for her maid to bring her new clothes, Iztac looked up at him. "Why did he go to Tlatelolco?"

"To make sure of their continued loyalty, of course." He gestured to the other two maids and watched them rushing forward, picking up his loincloth and his girdle, both still on the floor where he had dropped them earlier.

"Tlatelolco can't do anything else but remain loyal. They are too close to us to try playing games."

"Oh, yes, of course, but with the upheavals of the Tepanec royal house, one can't be too careful." Dressed again in his imperial regalia, Chimal looked older and surer of himself. "And the Chief Adviser is just the man to convey our message to them most clearly."

"Oh, yes, the Chief Adviser will scare the life out of them." She tilted her head and let the young maid slip a pretty, honey-colored gown over her shoulders. "I don't envy the ruler of Tlatelolco, torn between Itzcoatl and the envoys of the new Tepanec Emperor. They are not so dissimilar, your Adviser and the Tepanec Emperor, come to think of it."

Busy adjusting his girdle, Chimal looked up. "Now you are not being fair, Iztac. My uncle, my Chief Adviser, is a good man. There is nothing in common between him and that filthy, despicable, lowly Maxtla!" He glared at her, half amused, half put out. "I know you don't like Itzcoatl, but he is a good man. He has the best interests of Tenochtitlan in his heart."

Involuntarily, she rolled her eyes. "I don't doubt his loyalty to Tenochtitlan, but I do doubt his loyalty to you. And anyway, he still doesn't pay you enough respect."

"Oh, he does, Iztac Ayotl, he does. More than once, recently, he admitted that I was right and he was wrong."

"Oh, that would be a novelty! On what occasions?" She didn't want to offend him, but her eyebrows climbed high of their own accord.

"On the day before he left, he admitted I might have been right involving the priests in the case of the dead adviser."

He said it so casually she didn't react at first, watching the maids as the women smoothed the rims of her gown. Then his words sank in.

"What?" She straightened up abruptly, causing one of the women drop the pretty string she had been about to tie around Iztac's waist. "What do you mean?"

Chimal's expression did not change, but the look in his eyes hardened, lost some of its affability. "Yes, my adviser makes mistakes from time to time," he said noncommittally, but his lips were pressed tight.

"But this case, the case of the murdered adviser, Itzcoatl said it was nothing. He said he would erase the carving; he said this whole affair was nothing."

"Well, he admitted that he was wrong and I was right. The man who did this deed will be brought to justice."

"In what court? Under what accusation?" She knew she should calm down, should talk him out of it carefully and thoughtfully, as though interested in this affair only mildly, as the Empress should be, but her thoughts whirled around like panicked squirrels. *Itzcoatl had betrayed him, but why? Why would he do this?*

"The murder of the adviser cannot go unpunished," said Chimal stubbornly, standing her glare.

"This adviser was thrown out of your Palace in disgrace. He was the man who had tried to betray Tenochtitlan by going openly against its Emperor's policies. He was murdered holding a clandestine meeting with Maxtla's shady people. You should have executed this man yourself or, at least, you should be thankful to those who have done this for you."

"The adviser was not disgraced officially, and he was not

accused of treason, so his murder was not warranted." Chimal's eyes narrowed. "He was thrown out of the Palace mainly by you, Iztac Ayotl! You were the one to accuse this man of all sorts of things, behaving in a manner unfitting the Empress."

She clenched her palms tight. "He wanted you to support filthy Maxtla, and he wanted you to execute my brother, the *lawful* heir to the Texcoco throne. You should have been busy yelling at him, instead of me."

He tore his cloak off the frightened slave's hands, striving to appear calm, but she saw his hands were trembling.

"You are forgetting your place, woman," he said, his voice low. "I didn't ask for your advice on this matter."

"Then why don't you send someone to murder this leader of the warriors right away?" She heard herself shouting, but she didn't care, too frightened to think straight. "Why bother bringing him to the Imperial Court, if you have already found him guilty?"

"Tenochtitlan is a civilized *altepetl* with laws and traditional ways," he said, giving her a frustrated look. "You may be fascinated with the way of the savages, Iztac Ayotl, but you are the Empress of a civilized city. Now, please, stop making a scene. Your screaming is disturbing the harmony of this Palace."

"I'll scream all I like," she shouted into his face, glad to be able to lose her temper. "Because under all those pretty words about the civilized laws, you are just trying to avenge yourself against this man instead of acting decently, like a civilized person would."

His eyes grew very dark. "And why would I want to avenge myself against this man?"

"I don't know. You tell me!"

She saw him clenching and unclenching his hands, his nostrils widening with every breath.

"I'm not accusing you of anything, Iztac Ayotl," he said finally. "I don't know why this man's fate makes you so upset. But it doesn't change anything. He will be held accountable for what he has done." He shifted his weight from one foot to another, giving her another painfully frustrated look. "You should forget this incident and behave like the Empress of a great *altepetl*."

The pain in his eyes brought some of her sanity back. She was there to protect him, wasn't she? Not to make him feel bad.

"Listen, Chimal," she said, taking a deep breath, although it came out convulsive, almost a sob. "This whole incident doesn't make any sense. Your Chief Adviser should have taken care of it, or maybe your Chief Warlord." The thought of Tlacaelel gave her a spark of hope. "Let your Chief Warlord make the inquiries. This matter concerns one of his warriors, after all."

He narrowed his eyes suspiciously. "My Chief Warlord is away now. He went to Tlacopan."

"But he will be back soon. He is not on one of his campaigns." Trying to control her voice, she clasped her palms, clinging to this only hope. "It can wait until then, can't it?"

Chimal's face darkened. "It *will* have to wait until then, because I suspect he has taken that warrior with him. They were always thick together, those two. Yet, I shall talk to my half brother about it." His lips clasped tight, he gave her an offended look. "But I will not consult you about any of that anymore, Iztac Ayotl."

Her breath caught, she watched him going away, her gaze following the swirls of his beautifully embroidered cloak. *What happened? Why had Itzcoatl betrayed him?*

The horrified maids stood around her, trembling.

"Out, all of you!" said Iztac curtly, repulsed by their open fear.

Lingering by the reed podium, she picked up one of the pretty figurines upon it, her fingers running along the smooth surface, eyes seeing nothing. Oh, he should be warned. He should be warned urgently. He might need to flee the city. Like Coyotl did, disappearing into the mists of the Highlands once again.

She bit her lower lip until it hurt. Would they never know any peace? She, her brother, the Highlander, all people connected to Texcoco, they were always wandering, always living on the edge. Since her beautiful *altepetl* had been conquered, none of them had known any peace. There had to be a way to influence the events, to change them, to make everything right again.

Her fingers slid over the object in her hand, squeezing the figurine, painful against the sharp edges. She must find a way, she must. She was the Empress of Tenochtitlan, not an insignificant princess. But first things first.

"Send me the girl who does my hair," she called out loudly enough for the maids to hear, sure they would be cowering just outside the entrance.

According to Chimal, he was not in the city, but she could send him a warning in an even better way.

"Go to the usual place," she told the girl when this one arrived, hurried and out of breath. "But this time, talk to the mistress of the house. Bring her here." She peered at the slave, her gaze heavy with meaning. "Whatever she does, whatever she says, tell her to leave everything and come here, because the Empress of Tenochtitlan wishes to see her. Take no refusal for an answer." Frowning, she thought about an appropriate place for such a meeting. Not here, in her suite of rooms, surely, although it would have a better effect. "The maids will serve the refreshments by the pond, the one with the mosaic. Bring her there, and don't make me wait."

She did not recognize the woman who had followed her maid, walking briskly and confidently, her head held high. But for the smallness of the woman's form, and the slightly familiar large, oval, peculiarly tilted eyes, she might have thought that her slave had been mistaken, bringing along someone else.

Narrowing her eyes, she watched them nearing, remembering the slim, wild-looking *cihua*, with huge eyes and too much hair, pale and disheveled, frightened and then oh-so-very-determined, offensively unafraid. Well, the lack of fear was still there, written across the beautiful face of the well-dressed, confident woman, with her set face and unreadable eyes.

"Honorable Mistress," muttered the slave, halting at a respectable distance. This one looked frightened. Unduly so. She was Iztac's confidant and usually much surer of herself. Iztac moderated her gaze.

"Thank you, Xochitl," she said as calmly as she could, although she wanted to growl, or maybe hiss something frightening and offensive. This woman had no right to come here so calmly and placidly, as though belonging here in the Palace. "You may go."

The servant scampered off.

"Sit there, upon this mat," said Iztac coldly, not trying to conceal her enmity. She had not intended to harm this woman, but now she felt that she might. The filthy *cihua* had no right to stand there, returning the gaze of Tenochtitlan's Empress as though she were her equal. And she certainly had no right to look that good, with her skin so golden and smooth, and her figure curving in all the right places.

Gracefully, the woman knelt across the low table.

"Well," Iztac let the silence hang for another heartbeat, seeing the slender jaw hardening and the generous lips pressing thinner. "It's been a long time since we've meet."

For a moment the woman said nothing, seemingly as occupied with the staring contest.

"Yes, it's been a while." Her voice was still husky, strangely low for such a small creature.

"Revered Empress!" said Iztac, barely holding onto her temper now.

"Revered Empress," repeated the woman calmly, her lips nothing but a thin line..

Another heartbeat of staring and the intensity of her rival's gaze lessened. Feeling victorious, Iztac took a deep breath, trying to calm herself.

"You haven't changed."

A light shrug was her answer.

"Still dealing with herbs?"

"Sometimes."

"Selling on the marketplace, I presume." Picking up her cup, Iztac allowed the smile of contempt to show.

The woman frowned. "No, not really." She hesitated, and her eyes grew darker, the challenge sparking in them once again. "But I do help my friend when I have time. She is a great healer, and I wish I had more time to do that. I loved being a healer. I was good at it."

Iztac felt the taste of the sweetened water growing bitter. "Oh, yes, you *were* good. I happened to taste one of your brews." She felt her fingers tightening around the beautiful pottery and half-wished it would crack, breaking into many little pieces.

This time the woman dropped her gaze, peering at the low table as though trying to memorize the carvings upon it.

"I'm sorry about that," she said quietly.

Iztac's fingers kept pressing into her cup, as though trying to leave a print. "Only about that?"

"Yes," said the woman firmly, still immersed in studying the carvings. "Only about that."

She found it difficult to control her voice now. "Do you know why I summoned you here?"

"No."

"What do you think?"

"You need some help, some potion or medicine."

"What?" Gasping, Iztac stared at the dark, wary eyes, which again met hers, firm and unwavering. "I don't need your stupid brews. I had one too many once upon a time. You are nothing but a filthy commoner. How dare you presume I would need anything from you?"

The eyes gazing at her grew flinty. "Then why *did* you bring me here?" The woman's lips hardly moved, and her voice seeped out with difficulty through her clenched teeth.

"I can have you killed, you know." Making an effort to keep her voice quiet, Iztac pressed her cup again. "Your insolence would warrant this. You are talking to the Empress of Tenochtitlan as if she is nothing more than another filthy commoner from the marketplace. I can send you to the courts for that, or I can just have you put to dead here and now."

She glared at the woman, taking in the slender, heart-shaped face, thinking how it would feel to sink her nails into it. Would it wipe the unspoken challenge out of the depths of those eyes?

"Why now?" asked the woman stonily.

"What?"

"Why did you wait all these summers to have me killed?" The full lips quivered, stretching into a contemptuous grin. "He is not on one of his campaigns, you know. He'll be back in the city soon." The grin disappeared. "He won't take it kindly."

Iztac gasped again, breathless at so much effrontery. "I did not bring you here to have you killed either! I have better, more important, things to do. You think too highly of yourself, woman."

Something flickered through the dark eyes, but this time her adversary kept quiet. Iztac put her cup down carefully, making sure her hands didn't tremble.

"I did not bring you here to argue or to threaten," she repeated, taking a deep breath. "I never intended to seek your company. You are not important enough to warrant my attention." Glancing at the surrounding trees and the flowerbeds, she made sure no servants lingered nearby. "I will not bother to have you killed, although you do deserve that for what you did seven summers ago. You deserved to be flayed for that, and not only for what you did to me. You killed Ihuitl, my best friend, and I will never forgive you for that." The wave of anger welled anew, and she made another effort to control herself. "But I will not have you killed. It's in the past now, and you saved his life." She watched the set, stony face, uncomfortable with the knowledge that this woman was anything but an insignificant breeder. The annoying *cihua* was pretty and sure of herself. And she wasn't afraid. She was angry and strong, and maybe even dangerous. "I have brought you here for another reason."

The frown crossed the woman's face, as Iztac shrugged, reaching for her cup once again. It was empty, and she gestured for the maid, who watched them from a respectable distance.

"Bring us a flask of sweetened water and tortillas with avocado, then leave. Don't stand there and watch us. This is not a ceremony."

The maid winced and rushed off.

"I wish to apologize for what I did seven summers ago," said the woman, eyes reserved but not stony anymore. "I was young and stupid. And scared. I wish I had known better than to act the way I acted." Her teeth came out, biting her lips savagely. "I knew better when he almost died. I grew up through that evening. I'm sorry it took me so much time, and I'm sorry it cost your friend her life."

Fascinated, Iztac watched the slender face twisting, the small teeth making a mess out of the full lips.

"Yes, I understand," she said, uncomfortable with the sudden wave of compassion. *She hated this woman, didn't she?* "I did many stupid things back then, too. I felt bad, trapped, pushed around." Wincing at the unpleasant memories, she bit her lips in her turn. "That evening made me grow up, too." She grinned without humor. "And I wasn't even as young as you were. I should have known better."

The smile transformed the woman's face, making it look even prettier. "I wasn't that young. They all kept assuming I was a child, but I was not. I'd seen fifteen summers, back then. I was not a child."

"You looked like one." Iztac watched the maids bringing trays with flasks and plates. "He is in danger," she said, when the drinks had been poured and the maids melted into the midday heat.

The woman's face paled. "What danger?"

"He may need to flee the city. Tell him exactly that when he comes back. Tell him the Emperor is going to let the priests make their inquiries. Tell him Itzcoatl will not interfere." She watched the large eyes widening to enormous proportions. "Over the marketplace incident."

"What incident?"

Iztac picked a tortilla. "I see he doesn't share his activities with you." Sinking her teeth into a crispy pastry, she felt better by the moment. "But it doesn't matter. Just tell him exactly what I told you, word for word." Allowing some of her contentment to show, she smiled, a perfect hostess. "It's all right. Regular women are not for this. They are to bear children and to watch over the servants."

The woman's lips tightened again and her eyes flashed. "Yes, regular women do that. And they get to enjoy their men, too. They get to *live* with them."

Grinding her teeth, Iztac picked another tortilla. "They are still nothing but meaningless breeders. And they don't see their warriors that often."

"More than some others," muttered the woman, her eyes upon the table once again.

Iztac forced the tortilla into her mouth, her appetite gone. She eyed her rival who sat there, still graceful but tense, ill at ease.

"Why don't you drink or eat something?" she asked sweetly. "Are you afraid? I promise this drink is innocent. It will not make you dizzy, and you won't have to vomit for the next half of evening."

The woman said nothing, but her lips were now a thin split in the paleness of her face.

Satisfied, Iztac allowed a cold smile to show. "Well, as I said, it's all in the past now. So just deliver my message as soon as you see him." She frowned. "If only we had a way of sending word to him…"

"I can try to send him word."

"You? You can't possibly have a way of contacting him."

The large eyes flashed somewhat victoriously. "You may be surprised."

The urge to throw the tortilla into the delicate, self-assured face welled. "Oh, yes, I forgot how surprising you can be. One day you may try to behave normally, like a civilized woman would. One who knows her place, especially when speaking to the Empress."

"I'm sorry," said the woman, her gaze hard and unwavering. She picked up her cup and drank from it briefly. "What else should I tell him?"

"Just what I told you before. He'll find a way of contacting me, so I'll be able to explain better."

"Will he have to leave Tenochtitlan?"

"Yes, it may happen."

"Good!"

Iztac wanted to curse aloud. She hadn't thought of that aspect, not yet.

"Don't start gathering your belongings, and don't prepare any celebrations yet," she said through her clenched teeth. "It may not happen, and if it does, he will find a way. He always has. You will never have him the way you want to."

The dark eyes blazed now, losing any trace of their previous reserved defensiveness. "And neither will you!"

Iztac was afraid her cup would crack under her rigid fingers.

"You are pushing it again, woman," she growled. "You are nothing but a *cihua*, a breeder, to bear his children and to take care of his basic needs. There is nothing common between the two of us, and don't you ever dare to presume it so! You are just a filthy forest rat that was lucky to catch his attention, to save him once upon a time. But you have no idea what his love can be. You will never feel that. You will just go on bearing his children, nothing more."

The woman's face was stark now, a mask chiseled out of lifeless stone.

"You know what, Revered Empress?" she said, her hands, still clutching the cup, trembling, but her voice steady, cutting, dripping with disdain. "You are jealous. You are jealous of me and of what I have. He loves me, and he loves his children. He cherishes us more than you would care to hear about. He would do anything for us. Maybe he would do the same for you, too, but you are alone, and I am not. I do have him, and I do have his children, and I did save his life, more than once, just to let you know. I saved the life of your brother, too. And he appreciates that. Your brother is a great man, and he thinks highly of me, he even confides in me sometimes. I am anything but the meaningless *cihua* you would love to believe I am!" The generous lips quivered. "And I'm not stupid, either. I know your secret, too, oh mighty Empress. I know who fathered your only child. No one knows better."

Feeling the air leaving her lungs at once, Iztac stared into the blazing eyes, mesmerized, taking in the straying tendril of silky hair that fell upon the high forehead, escaping the elaborately pulled tresses. She tried to react, but her thoughts rushed about, and her chest could not get enough air. How had it come to this?

"You are talking nonsense," she said hoarsely. "Spreading stupid rumors, like the marketplace rat that you really are. You can chatter and blabber and gossip all you like, but it won't make any difference." She took a deep breath, trying to find an appropriate thing to say. "You cannot know, and you cannot prove anything."

But the generous lips in front of her stretched into a vicious smile. "Oh, you think simply, Acolhua princess. It suits you to think this way. But I'm none of what you think I am. I don't talk and I don't gossip, but if you ever try to hurt me or my children, or *my* man, I will find a way to get back at you, and it will be anything but pleasant." The large eyes peered at her, ablaze with passion. "I am not the simple *cihua* from the marketplace, and you better not try to cross my path anymore than I will try to cross yours." Nimbly, the woman rose to her feet, as gracious as before, but different, taller and more impressive, as though the fury had made her grow in stature.

"I will give him your message, and I thank you for your warning. Now, with your permission, I will leave."

Iztac's feet pushed her up as though of their own accord. One moment she was sitting, gaping. The next she was up, facing the furious woman, towering, almost a head taller than her rival.

"You will leave, when I give you my permission to leave!"

"Why do you need me to stay for?" The woman glared at Iztac, not wavering, not taking a step back, not intimidated by her physical disadvantage. "To try to convince yourself that I'm nothing, not a worthy rival? It won't work."

"I want to know how you know. I want to know what made you say what you said, what made you think something that stupid, aside from your silly suspicions, originated in jealousy."

The smile was back, stretching the full lips, the smile of a female, smug and victorious. "But it is so easy, Revered Empress. The Princess's eyes are of the most unusual color. There are no people in Tenochtitlan or its provinces with such strikingly strange, yellow eyes. There are not many such people anywhere around our Great Lake. I'm sure if you look through the whole Tepanec Empire you will find none, or very few, of those ocelot-eyed people." The woman's own dark brown eyes narrowed, sparkling, relishing her victory. "I know only one person with such eyes."

"Who is it?" asked Iztac, her limbs going numb.

"The Highlander Priestess of the Obsidian Butterfly Goddess. My husband's mother. She is a very revered person, and a real witch with the gift of foresight and all. You would find it interesting to meet her, I'm sure of that."

CHAPTER 7

Tlacaelel shifted in his reed chair, longing to get up and stretch his cramped muscles. It had been a long afternoon, with much humidity and a heavy heath, an afternoon that could be better spent outside, by a lake shore or in Tenochtitlan, in the Palace's groves, enjoying the breeze. Or, maybe, slumbering in the coolness of his suite of rooms, in the arms of that pretty new concubine he had acquired before the events in the Tepanec Capital began to take most of his time.

He shifted again, wishing the slaves would get enough sense to open more shutters. The Tlacopan Palace was wide and spacious, but dim, lacking the sunlight, strangled with no air.

"We are living in foul times," the ruler of Tlacopan, a paunchy, pleasant-looking man was saying. "Oh, how I wish that the eternal peace would rule the Great Lake and its valleys. Our people are brothers, Honorable Chief Warlord. They would not war against each other. You should put your worries to rest." The man raised his palm, his beefy arm sparkling with jewelry. "Azcapotzalco would not take arms against Tenochtitlan, against our most faithful friends and allies. Revered Maxtla-tzin, our new beloved Emperor, would wish to preserve the warm friendship and brotherhood that has existed between our nations for, oh twenty, two times twenty of summers. Since your wise first Emperor, your grandfather Acamapichtli, oh Honorable Tlacaelel, who had seen the futility of the struggle against the mighty Tepanec Empire."

And here ends your friendship and brotherhood, thought Tlacaelel, bored. *If we behave, we are allies and friends, if we don't, then we get admonished like children, and it all boils and spills again and again, every time the water construction breaks or someone decides to revolt against the Tepanec rule. Like the stupid Acolhua, damn their eyes into the lifeless spaces of the Underworld's second part of the journey.*

He watched the man's round face, trying to read through it, to see what the dark eyes held, what was beneath the polite words and meaningless promises. Would Tlacopan rise against Azcapotzalco if prompted? Would they be tempted to support their Mexica so-called allies in the hope of rich pickings and a considerable amount of promises?

"Of course, oh Honorable Totoquihuaztli," he said when it was his time to respond. "Our nations should never war on each other. In those foul, difficult times, we should remember the value of a good partnership, of a strong, firm alliance. The memory of loyal friendship, of timely received aid, will last generations." He paused, letting the words sink in. "We should not forsake each other in our mutual struggle against the enemy that should decide to take up arms against us."

It came out well, he thought, satisfied, watching the ruler's face twisting as though the man had just bitten into an unripe fruit.

"Oh, we do cherish your people's friendship. We always enjoy helping our neighbors." The heavyset nobleman was sweating, profusely at that, although the slaves waved their feathered fans vigorously, moving the otherwise motionless air.

We need more than this, thought Tlacaelel, only part of his mind on the exchange of meaningless pleasantries and subtle messages. He needed to meet this man, or one of his representatives, privately, if he wished to make any progress. Otherwise, he would return with his hands empty, having spent his time on this journey to the mainland in vain.

"Would you grace our Palace with your presence for more than just a brief visit, Honorable Warlord?" the fleshy man asked, clearly as anxious to finish the fruitless meeting. "Would you stay to share our afternoon meal?"

Tlacaelel concentrated. "I would be honored," he said, sensing the message behind the man's words. "Although my Emperor will expect me to return promptly on the morrow."

Welcoming the opportunity to escape the airless hall, he rose to his feet, forcing himself to move slowly, with much dignity. He was Tenochtitlan's Chief Warlord and the Second Emperor's First Son. He was honoring this Palace and its governor if he decided to stay for a feast.

"Where is your leader?" he asked his warriors curtly as they greeted him outside the doorway, falling in step with him, ready to accompany him wherever he went.

The tall, broad-faced man cleared his throat. "He went into the city, Honorable Leader. He appointed me to lead our men in his stead, until he comes back."

Tlacaelel had a hard time suppressing his irritation. "Oh, the dirty troublemaker," he muttered, controlling his temper with difficulty. "I swear I will not honor him with leading my warriors anymore! Or maybe I'll just throw him out of my warriors' forces for good." He took a deep breath. "I'll be dining here, in the Palace. But send a messenger to our people that are guarding the boats. We'll be sailing back to Tenochtitlan this evening."

Unruly bastard, he thought, storming down the hall. The damn Highlander had no right taking a walk around the city as though he were a stupid tourist. The man could be his enterprising, independent self as long as he was just a junior warrior, doing whatever he felt was right, risking those frequent punishments. However, now, when he had been entrusted with leading warriors more and more often, his independent behavior could not be tolerated. Charged with the safety of the Chief Warlord himself, the Highlander should have known better. And if he returned having so much as the slightest odor of *octli* around him… Tlacaelel clenched his fists. The dirty piece of dung would be done for. He would see to that.

However, his mood began to improve when he saw the arrangement of the mats and the low tables, which promised nearly perfect privacy for him and the Tlacopan's ruler. Oh, the Tepanec certainly *did* wish to talk.

"Revered Chimalpopoca should not do anything rash," said his host carefully, as they reclined upon their mats, served course after course of delicious food. Even the meat of the mainland tasted differently, having a richer, tender taste to it! "Azcapotzalco is not pleased with Tenochtitlan and its unwillingness to accept the lawful ruler of the Tepanec Empire."

"Oh, Tenochtitlan would never presume to interfere with the Great Empire's affairs." Tlacaelel wiped his fingers to remove the juices of the rabbit meat, then accepted the bowl of water from a groveling servant's hands. "Our people were grieved and shattered by the sequence of deaths in the Tepanec royal house. We were still mourning the passing of Revered Tezozomoc, when his chosen successor had hurried to join his great father in the perilous Underworld journey. It happened too soon, and our Emperor, being a great friend of Revered Tayatzin, grieved deeply." He peered at the pudgy man, allowing his gaze to reflect some of his feelings. "I hope you will relate this message to your new Emperor. I hope he'll understand."

But the ruler of Tlacopan shrugged and his eyes clouded. "It will take more than that to please our new Emperor," he muttered, reaching for his cup. He peered into the thick, milky liquid. "He will not let the offenses of the past go unnoticed. You may need to adjust to another ruler."

Tlacaelel felt the meat sticking halfway down his throat. "It would be unwarranted interference in our policies. We are not a subjected nation. We are an independent *altepetl*."

"And yet..." The pudgy man shrugged. "Your Emperor interfered in our politics, too. He was the one to advise the deceased ruler to execute his brother, our current Emperor." The narrowing eyes rested on Tlacaelel, sealed, unreadable. "Revered Maxtla-tzin cannot let the offense pass. He would be a happier man if Tenochtitlan was ruled by a more reasonable person." The man's gaze deepened. "Tenochtitlan's royal house has many suitable heirs."

Fighting his rising anger, Tlacaelel stood the piercing gaze. "Our *altepetl* has a lawful ruler. Our Emperor was anointed according to our customs, and the omens were favorable. His claim to the throne is legitimate beyond any doubt. No one can request of us to change our ruler because another ruler is unhappy with him. We are not a subjected nation!"

The pudgy man's face fell. "Then it may come to trouble, Honorable Warlord," he said quietly, his voice trembling.

"Mexica people are ready to defend their independence, their right to decide what is best for them." Placing his cup upon the table, Tlacaelel let his gaze dwell upon the man, this time heavy, ominous, deliberately threatening. "Should it come to an open conflict, we expect Tlacopan to stay neutral. We will not ask you to join our rightful case, although we should. The relationship between Tenochtitlan and Tlacopan would warrant that. Yet, while not expecting you to join our struggle, we will not tolerate any interference against us." He saw the man leaning backward as though trying to escape, and he let his gaze turn even more menacing. "We will not go down. We will win, and then we will turn on those who betrayed us, and our revenge will be worse than the wrath of the gods."

It came out well. The man in front of him seemed to be shrinking in size.

Tlacaelel moderated his tone. "I regret my harsh words, but what was said had to be said." He allowed a small, mirthless smile to show. "We do trust our old friends and allies. We know we will never be forced to send you neither *tizatl* nor a shield and arrows to prepare for the war and the honorable, but inevitable, death. I know we will not be forced to use our arms against Tlacopan."

And this was the afternoon well spent, he decided, saying polite farewells to the subdued ruler of Tlacopan at the end of the meal. This man was timid and fearful, caught between the mighty Tepanecs of the Capital and the fierce rising Aztecs of Tenochtitlan.

Yet, he needed to be reminded, decided Tlacaelel, making his way out of the main hall, followed by the nervous noblemen and the cowering servants. *We are strong and we are fierce and we have nothing to lose, nowhere to go but up. And up we will go. Not down, never down.*

His warriors waited outside, squatting comfortably beside the local guards, drinking and laughing, playing beans. He glanced at the board drawn upon the earth, the main squares crossing each other in the form of a pair of spears, wonderfully detailed. There was only one man who could draw such an elaborate thing for a meaningless temporary use. He sought the wide shoulders of the Highlander, clearly visible in the darkening air, holding his cup, laughing too loudly.

He pursed his lips. "What's that?"

The warriors jumped to their feet, looking guilty, his men and the local guards alike.

"Who said you could drink and eat and feel at home?"

"I did," said the Highlander, rising to his feet slowly, still steady, although there was a glint to his large, widely spaced eyes. "I assumed you would be staying for a longer span of time, and I thought there would be no harm in serving refreshments to our people."

"Well, you assumed wrong," said Tlacaelel tersely. "We are moving, and your men better be in a fitting condition to do that."

"May I have a word with you, Honorable Leader?"

"Now?" Tlacaelel felt like striking the man, or maybe making his threat true by turning his old friend into a simple warrior right there on the spot.

Yet, something in the tone of the Highlander made him pause. The man was too polite, too formal, too well spoken, unusually so. *An 'honorable leader,' coming from this one?*

"You have no more than a few heartbeats," he said curtly.

The large eyes held his. "Over there, by the flowerbeds."

They made their way in silence, with Tlacaelel's anger rising higher and higher. They should be on their way now, hurrying back to Tenochtitlan. He had many interesting things to report to Itzcoatl.

"What do you want?" he asked more rudely than he had intended. "We have no time for this. No more than for your tours around the city or for stupid bean games."

The Highlander halted abruptly. "Oh, then you can run straight away for your boats."

Tlacaelel just stared. "You are a cheeky bastard, you know that? And this time you've really been pushing it. Who gave you permission to go into the city, leaving your warriors to take care of themselves; leaving me, your leader, Tenochtitlan's Chief Warlord, unattended? Or was it that you couldn't do without a whole flask of *octli* for more than half a day?"

The Highlander's eyes were now two narrow slits in the broadness of his face. "I left neither you nor my warriors unattended. I made Ehekatl responsible, and he is a good choice, a brave man and a responsible leader. You can spill your foul mood on someone else." The typical amused, challenging smile flashed. "Did it go that badly with the Tepanec ruler?"

"It went well enough." Tlacaelel narrowed his eyes against the glow of the setting sun. "But it could go badly when my warriors, or their leaders, are behaving as though they are in our Palace's guards' quarters. I will not bring you along next time. You are good for campaigns, so back to campaigns you will go."

"Suit yourself." The Highlander shrugged, unimpressed. "But, if I'm still leading your warriors now, we will detour through the back alleys of this town. We are not leaving Tlacopan by the main road."

"What are you talking about?

A mirthless half grin stretched the generous lips. "I'll explain it all to you on our way. I think we had better leave now." The smile widened. "You still trust me, don't you, Honorable Warlord?"

"Oh, shut up!" Aware of the stares all around them, Tlacaelel shook his head. "We will go the way you chose, but you better have a good explanation for all of this." Coldly, he gestured to his palanquin bearers. "Let us be on our way."

The alleys of the town swept by, with the sways of the litter making him sleepy. Leaning against the wooden partition, Tlacaelel drew the curtain and allowed himself to sink into his thoughts, not bothering to wonder as to the nature of the unexpected detour. For all his shortcomings, his unruliness, his utter lack of respect for any sort of authority, the Highlander was a born leader, quick and enterprising, having the sharp senses and admirable reactions of a forest beast, but the keen mind of a cunning human being, able to analyze situations, reaching right decisions on the spur of a moment. Oh but he had grown to rely on this man's judgment entirely, and so, he knew, had Itzcoatl, with all his continuous dislike for the insolent foreigner. The Highlander was a deep one, deeper than he cared to display.

Itzcoatl, he thought. Oh, what would the wily adviser have to say about this latest development? The dirty Maxtla's wishes were going along with those of Tenochtitlan's Chief Adviser, for a change. Interesting.

He pressed his lips tight. Itzcoatl would prove to be a more fitting Emperor for Tenochtitlan, especially in these difficult times. But would he be able to beat the Tepanecs, still invincible, spreading everywhere, enormously strong, enormously rich. And yet...

The palanquin slowed down, and he drew the curtain to see the Highlander's broad face peeking in.

"Time to walk, Revered Emperor," said the man, eyes twinkling, bright and unconcerned. "With your permission I'll send those manure-eaters with their palanquin off."

"Where are we?" asked Tlacaelel, stepping out, glad for the opportunity to stretch his legs.

"Somewhere on the outskirts of the city." The Highlander waved his hand noncommittally. "This road should lead us out, eventually. Or so I was told. Traders use it. Those who are going to Azcapotzalco."

"Planning to conquer the Tepanec Capital on your way?"

The Highlander laughed. "Why not? I participated in the siege laid on this *altepetl*, and I'm still hopeful. Would love to finish that particular undertaking."

"But not tonight." Hastening his step, Tlacaelel frowned. "Now tell me what happened. Why do we detour?"

"Our Tepanec hosts thought it might be entertaining to kill you on your way out. Many warriors are waiting by the guard house, on the main road leading out of the city."

"What?" Unable to control the suddenness of his fury, Tlacaelel stopped dead in his tracks. "The dirty Totoquihuaztli would never dare!"

"Oh, it's not him," said the Highlander, unconcerned, walking on in a regular pace, his eyes scanning the road. "Those are direct orders from the Great Capital. Our dear friend Maxtla has some interesting ideas. Planning to switch the whole leading class around the Great Lake as it seems. A fascinating type."

Not amused in the least, Tlacaelel hastened his step, catching up with his companion. "How do you know all that?"

"Drinking *octli* on the marketplace while looking like a Tepanec has its benefits."

"I daresay so!" But his direful glance was wasted, as the Highlander turned to watch the cluster of warehouses. "Tell me everything you have heard."

"Well, it seems that the dirty Tepanec really wants to rid himself of all sorts of important people around his precious empire. They say that the ruler of Tlatelolco died this morning. No one knows why or how, but here you have another dead ruler, to join Tayatzin on his Underworld journey." For a moment they proceeded in silence. "Also, I heard that our own Emperor may be in danger. I didn't understand what sort of danger, but people say he may not be destined to walk our Fifth World for much longer." He took a deep breath. "I fear for Coyotl. The dirty Tepanec may wish to get rid of him, too. And what better opportunity would there be than now, while he is running around his provinces, alone and unprotected."

"Coyotl can take care of himself." Narrowing his eyes, Tlacaelel watched the warehouses and the simple-looking constructions as they passed by them, his senses honed, probing the surroundings. "They might have a guarding post in this part of the city, too."

"Yes, of course. But they weren't expecting us to detour, so they might be less prepared by the back gates." The Highlander shrugged. "I hope they won't have enough sense to send a group of warriors to the Lake's shore, to sabotage our boats. That would be a smart move on their part."

"They won't."

"Why? I would have done this."

"They want to kill me here, in Tlacopan. To do it anywhere else would defeat their purpose."

"How so?"

"By killing me here, Maxtla would create an incident, which would ruin the relationship of Tenochtitlan and Tlacopan." He grinned as his friend's handsome face lost its usual challenging twinkle, concentrating most visibly. "Tlacopan would be blamed for the incident, of course. And it would bring the immediate declaration of war, with all the *tizatl* and the symbolic weapons hitting the road faster than you could say Zacatlan. And here they'll have us warring against a Tepanec province, giving the dirty manure-eating Maxtla his perfect chance to attack us, while we are alone, with no allies at all. No Acolhua, no Highlanders, and not even the people of Tlatelolco, who, if the rumors you heard are true, would be now grief stricken and at a loss, useless to us." He ground his teeth. "And all this, after I spent a whole afternoon trying to scare Tlacopan's ruler into taking our side when the time comes, or, at the very least, into staying neutral."

The houses became scarcer, and the wide fields began to peek through the opening view. A few passersby scattered out of their way, wide eyed.

"You are a deep one," said the Highlander, eyes scanning the surroundings. "I thought they would like to kill you mainly because you may be the next one to take the throne."

"Oh, no! Maxtla is stupid, but he is not that stupid. He knows who the next in line is."

The wide shoulders tensed. "Is that a sure thing?"

"Oh, yes." Tlacaelel watched the group of warriors, standing beside a low tent, clearly on duty, their backs straight, their cloaks embroidered with Tlacopan's royal house symbols. "And take this advice from me. Keep away from this man for the next market interval or so. It would do you nothing but good."

The warriors, busy letting a group of traders pass, straightened up, watching the procession nearing. Tlacaelel's eyes counted no more than half of twenty. Less than his entourage. Good. They'd dispose of them easily, if the need should arise.

If?

His anger kept mounting, difficult to control. How dared they? He was the Chief Warlord of Tenochtitlan, he was the First Son of the previous Emperor, and half-brother of the current one. He came here on an official visit. How dare they make him leave by running away like an outlaw?

"Honorable Warlord," muttered one of the warriors, stepping onto the road, blocking his way.

"Who is your leader?" asked Tlacaelel curtly, ignoring the man in front of him.

"I am, Honorable Warlord," said another warrior, stepping forward. He was a tall, formidably broad man, with a richly decorated girdle and a wide scar crossing his chest.

"You are here to detain me." He made it a statement, his gaze boring into the man's face, making his adversary drop his.

"Oh, Honorable Warlord," muttered the man. "We would never... it is not our intention... It's just that you are leaving in the most unusual way."

"Larger forces are waiting for me on the usual way out of the city." Stepping forward, Tlacaelel forced the man in front of him to retreat a step. "Well, go ahead. Stop me from leaving."

The rest of the warriors shifted uneasily, while the tall man took another step back.

"Oh, no, Honorable Leader, we would not dare to stop you."

"Oh, yes, you will." Tlacaelel's tore his sword from the ties of his girdle, bringing it up with both hands, ready to attack. "Follow your orders, warrior. Fight me. Stop me from leaving your filthy town."

Behind his back, he could feel the Highlander gesturing to his men, sensing them moving closer, forming half a circle, protecting his sides.

The tall man hesitated for only a heartbeat, his honor of a leading warrior demanding him to stand up to this challenge, unusual as it was. Sweating and obviously out of his depth, he untied his sword hurriedly, glancing at his companions.

Hesitating for another heartbeat, he looked at the Aztec warriors, frowning.

Tlacaelel let out a humorless chuckle. "Yes, we outnumber you. But I will not ask my warriors to clear my way. I will do my own dirty work. I will kill all of you one by one, and then I will leave this cowardly place." He brought his sword higher. "And now fight. Don't let me slaughter you like the last of the peasants."

He saw the man's knuckles whitening as his grip around the

sword's hilt tightened. It rose swiftly, but Tlacaelel attacked before it reached its peak. His own sword made a beautiful half circle, pouncing toward the man's momentarily exposed torso, not disappointed with meeting the solid wood of his opponent's sword, instead.

A few more thrusts were delivered and parried, before the man gathered enough confidence to attack back. Circling, attacking and leaping aside, Tlacaelel took his time, not hurrying to finish his rival off, enjoying a good hand-to-hand. The man was a worthy opponent, strong and swift, obviously having had enough fighting experience. And yet, they needed to hurry. The word must have gotten around that they didn't leave by the usual way, and so all the warriors congregating around the main roads would be flowing back into the city, seeking the sight of their escaping prey.

With obsidian blades slicing some flesh off his shoulder, Tlacaelel decided he'd had enough. His next thrust was planned most carefully, making his adversary raise his arms in order to stop the blow, yet his wrists twisted in the last second, sending his sword sideways, toward the unprotected side of the man's neck.

It landed with such a force he winced, his arms absorbing the suddenness of the impact. Clutching at his sword, he tried not to let it slip out of his sweaty palms as the body of his rival shot sideways, hitting the ground while the blood spouted in a powerful surge, in a fountain, where the half-severed head tilted unnaturally, like a broken doll.

The silence was deep, encompassing. Breathing heavily, Tlacaelel stretched his shoulders, forcing his own body to relax, his palms numb from the force with which they had clutched his sword. No one dared to move. Mesmerized, they watched the pulsating flow weakening gradually, losing its crimson powerfulness.

"I will fight you one by one, until no one is left to stand in my way," growled Tlacaelel, hardly recognizing his own voice, so hoarse, so raspy it sounded. "Who is next?"

They shifted uneasily, nine warriors from the Palace's guard, none of them as elite, or as battle-experienced as he and his men were.

"I will be honored to face you in a battle," said a slender young man, stepping forward. His sword was already out.

Tlacaelel measured him with a glance. "I recognize your bravery, warrior. It's my honor to fight you."

But this hand-to-hand was finished even quicker, with the young man twisting in the dust, trying to suppress his screams of agony. Tlacaelel hurried to finish him off, nodding to the brave youth solemnly and delivering him a clean, honorable death.

He watched the warriors, now pressing against the wall, not fleeing but not daring to meet his gaze.

"Who is next? Are you all just dirty manure-eating peasants?"

The Highlander's arm touched his shoulder, startling him. "It's getting late, and I think you made your point perfectly." The large glimmering eyes met his. "You are an impressive man, Chief Warlord."

Watching the smile quivering around the generous lips, Tlacaelel wanted to curse aloud. Oh, the dirty savage. Was there nothing sacred that would make this man appreciate the solemnity of the moment?

With an effort, he took his gaze off the cowed warriors. "You've seen nothing yet! What happened here today does not even begin to show you what the Aztec warriors can do. Let your people know. Make them understand that Tlacopan would do better to have Mexica people as your allies and not your enemies. Should Tlacopan raise its arms against Tenochtitlan, it will be destroyed, not only conquered, but destroyed, until nothing will be left to remind you that there was a city here once upon a time."

Turning abruptly, he began walking the road, still not fully aware of his movements, feeling the elation, the excitement pumping, circulating through his body, making it light, weightless, invincible. Oh, but for more of those moments.

The fields swept by and, gradually, he became more aware of his surroundings. He could hear the steady slam of his warriors' sandals against the dusted ground. They followed him, keeping a fitting distance, not interfering, respecting his need to be alone now, to bask in the glorious feeling, to come to grips with the deaths. Even the Highlander was quiet, walking ahead of the warriors, deep in thought.

"Do you know this terrain well?" Slowing down, Tlacaelel fell into his friend's step.

"No, not really. But I think we will manage to reach the Great Lake if we keep to this road. Upon the shores it will be easier to determine our direction." He shrugged. "I've been here only once, with the Acolhua forces, when the siege on Azcapotzalco was lifted, and we were heading back home. I think I remember this road, but I may be wrong." A slight grin dawned. "Such long forgotten memories."

"Ten summers," said Tlacaelel. "Ten summers have passed. I remember this time well. My father was still alive, although the Tepanec woman was ruling the Palace unashamedly already. Oh, how I hated her!" He grinned. "I was busy doing my shield-bearing duties, happy to be done with *calmecac*. But those raids against unimportant towns around Lake Chalco were annoying. Every time I heard of Acolhua exploits on the Tepanec side of the lake, I wanted to scream and hit something. I would have killed for the opportunity to join *that* war. Your siege on Azcapotzalco cost me many sleepless nights. I wanted to be there badly." Shrugging, he turned his head and watched the road as it twisted between the hills. "One day I'll walk it, leading ten times, two, three ten times twenty of warriors. And our siege on Azcapotzalco will not end in defeat."

The Highlander's smile was wide, back to his light, unconcerned, slightly provoking self. "I like that vision of yours, Chief Warlord. I'll join you in this undertaking, too." His grin widened. "That is, if you still want me among your forces."

"You? You will take Azcapotzalco single-handedly. Of course, I will bring you along."

"Back in that dung-filled Palace, you promised this would be the last time you would trust me."

Tlacaelel frowned, the thought of Tlacopan's Palace spoiling his mood. "Back in that stinking, manure-infested place, I was angry with you for going into the city without permission. I thought you were after a flask of *octli*."

The Highlander's eyes sparkled. "I did get this thing. More than a pitiful flask, too. Their *octli* is nice, more delicate tasting than Tenochtitlan's brews." He pitted his face against the wind, smiling happily. "People talk more readily when you buy them a round of drinks. I found this out some time ago, when finally managing to lay my hands on reasonable amounts of cocoa beans and such."

"You are a hopeless drunkard. What else did you hear?"

"I told you everything already. Plenty of changes our dear friend Maxtla is planning, plenty of changes."

"Maxtla is stupid. He is nothing but a dirty son of the cheapest whore from the filthiest corner of the marketplace!" Tlacaelel clenched his teeth. "And what he doesn't understand – but why should he, when all he knows is how to poison people or try to trap them otherwise? – is that with Itzcoatl for an Emperor he'll have a more difficult time. He hates Chimalpopoca, because Chimal was rude to him, and because Chimal supported his brother too openly. Stupidly at that, if you ask me, but they did not bother to ask me, or to listen to my advice." He took a deep breath, trying to calm himself, watching the hills sweeping by. "But what ruler, what leader, would allow his personal passion of revenge to cloud his judgment? Only a stupid manure-eater like him."

"So Itzcoatl is the sure thing? No chance of you taking Chimal's place?"

"No. I don't want any of this. Even if Itzcoatl drops dead the moment he gets rid of Chimal, I won't take the throne."

"Does he plan to get rid of Chimal?"

Tlacaelel glanced at the suddenly guarded face of his friend. "Who knows?"

"You, for sure." The Highlander wiped his brow, then waved away an insistent fly. "Well, it's too much politics for one evening. There is only a certain amount of the Lowlanders' devious activity that I can take in one day."

"One good turn deserves another." Making sure no one was within hearing range, Tlacaelel touched his friend's arm. "Keep away from the politics for some time. Don't come near the Palace, or near Itzcoatl, if you can help it."

The glance that was shot at him was quick and guarded. "Why?"

"All sorts of reasons. Just take my word for it. It's for your good alone. I gain or lose nothing from those particular politics."

"He will want something from me." It came out as a statement.

Tlacaelel shrugged. "I can't go into any of this. I can only tell you to keep away, maybe leave the capital for some time." The idea struck, and he brightened, thinking it over hurriedly. "He is not your leader anymore. But I am. So I'll send you to look the Texcocan up. It'll do you good to tour those places, and it'll serve Tenochtitlan as well. We need your Acolhua friend back, safe and sound."

The Highlander stopped abruptly. "What do you mean 'look him up'? Is he not in Texcoco? What do you know?"

Tlacaelel did not slow his pace. "He fled that city some time ago. Like you said, our dear Maxtla is up to serious changes."

"Where is he?"

"No one knows, but a fair guess is that he may be touring your homeland at these very moments. Your mountains are the only place he would be out of the Tepanecs' reach."

"Why didn't you tell me before?"

"I thought your drunken friends from Tlacopan had told you everything."

"Stop joking about it." The broad face turned to him, stony and strained. "What exactly happened? How did he flee?"

"No one knows, so don't look at me as though you would rather kill me right now. I only heard about it in Tlacopan, and I was busy with more important matters." He squinted against the thickening darkness. "Get the men to prepare torches. We will walk for half of the night, and we'll need some light. I want to be beside my boats before the dawn breaks."

"Will you give me one of the smaller boats to sail on when we arrive? We'll reach Tenochtitlan somewhere around midmorning, so if I sailed on I'd reach the other side toward the high noon."

"Can't do this. The warriors need their rest. You may be determined enough to row on and on, hopping from mission to mission, but they are not you."

"I don't need your warriors. I need a boat!"

"Will you be going all by yourself?"

"Yes, *Chief Warlord*." The slightest grin brought back the Highlander he knew. "You don't want me to roam the Highlands with a bunch of Aztec warriors. You may need those men one day, when filthy Maxtla decides to take Tenochtitlan by force."

"Won't you check the towns around Texcoco first?"

"I will, but I won't need your Aztecs there, either. It'll draw the attention of the Tepanecs in no way you would want to."

"Well, we'll see about that when we reach Tenochtitlan. Stay for a day or so, spend time with your family. Don't come near the Palace. After I contact you, you sail."

The Highlander's smile flashed, open and unguarded. "Thank you. You are a great friend."

Warmed by this smile, Tlacaelel frowned, uncomfortable with feeling so close, so friendly toward this man. Friendships were for lesser beings. A person of his abilities and ambitions should be above making close contacts, unless it served his goals. To sympathize with someone, a man or a woman, would leave him vulnerable, would cloud his judgment, would influence his decisions.

He shrugged. "You saved my life once again. It accounts for something."

The Highlander's grin twisted crookedly. "I never meant to save your precious life. It just happened. All I wanted was a good gulp of *octli*, and I got that. The rest was just a coincidence." The unconcerned laughter began melting in the darkness. "I'm off to take care of the torches."

And that was that, realized Tlacaelel, relieved. No gratitude required. No acknowledgment. The wild Highlander *was* a law unto himself, he thought grinning. And that was probably why he was so valuable. Exceptionally able, unruly, but smart and resourceful, the Highlander was loyal to those whom he cherished. A perfect tool.

Shaking his head, Tlacaelel slowed his steps, waiting for his warriors to catch up. *Make this man respect you, and he would move mountains for your benefit, would achieve the impossible. Such a useful partner.*

No, not a partner. Nezahualcoyotl was a partner, Itzcoatl was a partner. But the Highlander, oh this man was something out of any regular definition of roles. Not noble in the slightest, but not a commoner, either.

He squinted his eyes against the light of the improvised torches, watching the wide shoulders belonging to the subject of his reverie. Was Itzcoatl right? Was this man capable of disposing of the Emperor and making it look like an accident, or better yet, the Tepanecs' doing? And how was the wily Adviser planning to force the Highlander into this action? He wouldn't do it willingly, not where the safety of the Empress was concerned. And the pretty woman was in a grave danger as well. Itzcoatl would not take her into his household, not this wild, dominant female; and he would not let her stay in the Palace, either. She was destined to die, too, and how would the Highlander deal with that challenge?

No, this man had better be kept away from any of it, scanning the Highlands and the Lowlands of the Acolhua people, instead. If the Texcocan was still alive, the Highlander was the best person to find him and keep him from harm. But was the adventurous Lowlander still alive?

CHAPTER 8

Dehe took a deep breath, fighting the urge to lean against the supportive poles of the gate.

"Would you like to come in, Honorable Second Assistant?" she asked, pleased to hear her voice firm and steady. Her heart pounded wildly against her ribs.

The man measured her with the glance of a person whose path had been crossed by a small, unimportant insect.

"Where is the Master of the House?" he asked curtly.

She took another deep breath. "The Master of the House is not in Tenochtitlan," she answered as curtly, her anger rising. "He is on a mission. He is escorting the Chief Warlord on his way to Tlacopan."

"Oh, I see." The man frowned and lost some of his haughtiness. "Well, the Chief Warlord was expected to return on the day before this. I hope he encountered no troubles. In such foul times, no one knows what could happen."

"With my husband leading the Chief Warlord's warriors, there will be no trouble," said Dehe as stonily as before. "Our Chief Warlord, the Emperor's half brother, is in no danger as long as my husband guards him."

The man blinked. "Well, as soon as he comes back, let your husband know that he is to visit the staff of the Imperial Court."

She knew it would come to that, she knew it as soon as the pudgy man appeared at the far end of the alley, proceeding hastily, clumsy, clearly not a person used to much walking, his servants and scribes trailing behind, his cloak displaying the embroidered symbol of the royal court. Still, the man's words hit her like a punch in her stomach.

"Why?" she asked before being able to stop herself. "Why is he required to visit the court?"

"He will be informed, of course, Honorable Lady." The man lifted his eyebrows. "You surely do not expect me to inform you of the Imperial Court's intentions. He is to report to the Palace as soon as he comes back. That is enough for you to know."

She watched the sweaty, round face, wishing to hack it with her sharp, polished nails, to wipe the smug expression off of it with this or that painful action.

"I will let him know," she said. "As soon as he returns."

"Good." The dark eyes of the man bore into her, glittering with what seemed like a genuine pity. It made her yet angrier. He was not finished, not yet. He had many powerful friends who would not let the court hurt him. Even the vile Empress. Oh yes, even that filthy woman would do anything to keep him from harm.

"You have our gratitude, Honorable Lady," said the man, tilting his head politely. "Please, make sure he understands that the matter is urgent and should be attended to with no delay." Giving her another look filled with open compassion, he turned away, gesturing to his entourage.

She watched them heading down the alley, her back straight, head still high. The light breeze brushed against her bare shoulders, making her shiver with cold. So the fears of the annoying Empress were not as unfounded as she had assumed they were?

Since the previous day, since that hideous meeting with the vile woman, she had spent so much time convincing herself that it was nothing, that the jealousy-filled Acolhua she-wolf had just used this excuse to summon her, Dehe, to the Palace, to scare her, or maybe to try to actually kill her.

Shuddering she remembered that feeling, coming up the perfectly swept path, seeing the beauty of the trees and the flowerbeds, understanding the danger but unable to avoid going into the trap, in some corner of her mind welcoming the confrontation, wishing to face her rival at long last. Well, it came to the confrontation, oh yes. She had definitely gone too far, threatening the mighty Empress, but that woman was so aggressive, so provoking, so hate-filled, still strikingly beautiful, still unbearably haughty, as though seven summers hadn't passed at all.

"Mistress, is everything well?" The voice of her maid tore Dehe from her reverie.

"Yes, of course." Turning around, she pretended a confidence she didn't feel. "Where are the other servants? Did they come back from the marketplace?"

The woman frowned. "No, of course not, Mistress. It's only mid-morning. I wouldn't expect them to return before noon. You gave them special instructions."

"Yes, of course. The evening meal should contain all of the Master's favorite foods. He is expected to return today. The official from the courts just confirmed that." She felt her stomach tightening and shook her head to banish the new wave of latent fear. "Make sure the house is clean, and also, take care of Mixtli for now. Is she still asleep?"

"Yes, Mistress. The sweet little thing is still having her morning nap."

"Well, I have to go out, so be there when she awakes and reassure her. I'll come back as soon as I can, and I don't care what it takes, but if I see her face all red and puffy from crying, your afternoon will be anything but pleasant."

The woman's face twisted. "But Mixtli never wants anyone but her mother," she protested. "She will cry if she can't find you."

Dehe bit her lower lip. "I know, I know! But I have to go, and I can't take her with me this time. So do your best to make her feel better." She took a deep breath. "I'm not telling you that I'll punish you if she cries. But I don't want to find out she cried all the time." The sunlit road glittered merrily against her measuring gaze. "Where are the boys?"

The maid's troubled face cleared. "Only the gods know," she said with a smile. "Up with the birds and away with their usual mischief. As always."

"Well, when they come back, tell them I want them to stay. No more going out, not today." She narrowed her eyes. "Make sure they understand that it comes from me and that they had better obey."

"Of course, Mistress." The dark cloud crossed the woman's face again. "You will want an escort, I suppose. I'll send for—"

"No, I don't need an escort." Turning back toward the house, Dehe shook her head. "Just bring me a bowl of water for washing and the turquoise blouse and matching bracelets." She frowned. "And the obsidian pins. And the yellow cream. I need to take care of my appearance."

In the master's set of rooms, and alone for a moment, she ran her palms through her hair, fighting the tangles. How had she not thought of this before? His uncle was still an influential man, and he cared for his nephew, no one better. He should hear about the trouble, and he might know what to do.

The walk through the sunlit alleys refreshed her, calming her worries. Since the meeting with the Empress she hadn't been able to sleep, fearful and oh-so-alone. She missed him and longed for him to come back, but at the same time, she feared his return, knowing that now it was safer for him to be away.

Oh, why didn't he leave with the Lowlander or on the planned raid against the Chalcoans? At the time, she had been so happy when both plans did not bear fruit, but now she wished he had been anywhere but near Tenochtitlan.

Imperial Court? Oh, gods! The Empress had not been exaggerating. He was in grave trouble, trouble caused by his carelessness, probably, by his easy confidence, by his disrespect for politics and danger; and also by his tendency to drink *octli* through all parts of the day, maybe.

Sighing, she recalled the way he would drain his cup in one powerful gulp, hurrying to fill it again with more of the spicy beverage. Why was he so fond of this thing? Was it the taste or the aftereffect?

Well, the spicy drink did not have much effect on him. She had seen people turning talkative, filling with mirth or anger, losing all restraint after just a few cups. But he could drink whole flasks of it and nothing would happen, aside from the mischievous glint to his eyes and the unsteady gait to his movements. He wouldn't turn silly or aggressive, nor would he behave any differently. But then why? Why didn't he drink water, instead?

The former Warlord's mansion loomed ahead, brightly colored and highly impressive, two-stories high, sprawling between the carefully planned rows of trees, its gates carved and guarded. She remembered seeing this dwelling for the first time, upon their arrival in Tenochtitlan, more than seven summers ago, just a dust-covered trio, apprehensive, tired and not belonging, coming from the mainland. The servant guarding the entrance didn't even want to let them in, making the Lowlander frustrated and Kuini outright angry. Oh, she remembered how she had wished they would leave the unfriendly island at once, never to come back. Yet, now the arrogant *altepetl* was her home. Or was it?

She shrugged, pushing the silly thoughts away. She belonged where he belonged. She had no other home. So if he chose to live here, leading warriors and mingling in their politics, then that was that.

"I wish to pay my respects to the Honorable First Chief Warlord," she said firmly, answering the careful glance of the sturdy man that was guarding the entrance, holding his gaze.

"Of course, Lady," said the man after a slight hesitation. "I will send a servant to make sure the Master is willing to receive visitors. Who is inquiring?"

"His favorite nephew's Chief Wife that has a matter of urgency to discuss."

She didn't let her smile show, but inside she felt the familiar glow, like she always did when using this title. She was his Chief Wife, his First Wife, his only wife. The Empress was just a lover, an insignificant form of life, lower than a concubine even.

Enjoying the walk up the perfectly groomed alley, she followed another servant, appreciating the symmetrical designs of the bordering stones and the mosaics adorning the flowerbeds. She hadn't been to this place since the turbulent events of her first moon in Tenochtitlan, and then she had been too busy and too miserable to appreciate the beauty of the gardens.

"Please, wait here, Noble Lady," said the servant, mounting the wide, polished stairs, passing the main hall and diving into the coolness of the smaller adjacent room. "You will be notified soon if the Master will see you."

"Please, let him know it's a matter of importance," she said, suddenly nervous. *What if the influential man did not wish to see her?* "It concerns the safety of his nephew, and—"

"Of course, Lady," said the man, heading back to the doorway and not turning his head. "Please, be patient."

Arrogant descendant of a rat, thought Dehe, seething. Please to be patient? As though she would come here had it not been something truly important.

To calm herself, she looked around. The sun flowing through the rectangular opening painted friendly pictures upon the bright, plastered walls. She watched the pretty arrangement of mats beside two low tables, the patterns upon the polished wood fascinating in their complexity. Squatting upon one of them, she studied the carvings, rectangles inside rectangles in a pattern that resembled the twists of a serpent's body. Sure enough, a likeness of a serpent's head crowned with feathers, or maybe maize leaves, squirmed free of the rectangles somewhere in the middle of the table. Quetzalcoatl, the Feathered Serpent. She touched the carvings with her fingers.

"This is a beautiful carving. I love it the best."

Startled, Dehe turned around, her heart beating fast. The woman at the doorway was tall and slender, not young but strikingly beautiful, her eyes large, her perfectly Toltec cheekbones high, glimmering with yellowish cream. Her hair was pulled in elaborately woven multitudes of tresses, and her generous mouth curved slightly, in a warm, amused half a grin.

"It invites you to feel it out, to make sure the serpent is real, doesn't it?" The woman came in, her paces light, her smile widening. "No, no, don't get up," she added, when Dehe attempted to jump onto her feet. "You are with child. One can see that." Her smile lost its previous glint of irony. "It is always the most challenging to get up after sitting. When I was carrying my children, I remember fearing to sit down, because at some point you will be required to get up. So I would prefer to remain upright whenever I could." The large, slanted eyes brushed over

Dehe's belly. "How far along are you?"

"I suppose about half of my time," muttered Dehe, at a loss and uncomfortable under the open scrutiny of the amused gaze.

The woman laughed. "Oh, then you have all the joys still ahead of you. Is that your first child?"

"No, it is not." Dehe frowned, trying to make her mind work. *Who was this woman?*

Picking up the hem of her long, richly decorated skirt, the woman squatted on the opposite mat, doing this with the elegance of an exquisite creature.

"So why do you think the Master of the House will grant you this interview?" she asked, her eyes friendly, smile not wavering.

Dehe took a deep breath, clenching her sweaty palms tight. "I came to inform him of a matter of urgency." She swallowed. "I came to seek his advice. I know the fate of his favorite nephew is of an interest to him, and I know he would wish to know what I want to tell him."

"His favorite nephew?" The woman frowned as though attempting to collect her thoughts, then her face brightened. "Oh, the young savage with the tattoos and the famous sword! Oh, you are his woman. I should have guessed."

Her breath caught, Dehe stared at the woman, wordless.

"What happened to him?" The woman went on, unabashed.

"He is not a savage," said Dehe when able to talk again. "He is a great warrior. He is a leader of the warriors."

The beautiful face crinkled with laughter. "Yes, of course. He is all that, too." Brushing a tendril of shiny hair off her forehead – clearly it had been washed with indigo only this morning – the woman smiled again. "My husband, indeed, is very fond of this young man. I think what he appreciates is his wildness. I think it appeals to him, being anything but an ordinary person himself."

"Your husband?" repeated Dehe, puzzled, then wanted to bite off her tongue. But, of course! The powerful uncle had many wives and a whole army of concubines, as the rumor had it. But he was so old, and the woman in front of her seemed hardly half twenty summers older than Dehe herself.

"Oh, I'm sorry. I should have introduced myself properly,"

said the woman, her gaze filling with more amusement. "It's just that I thought you were only a girl who came to seek favor with the powerful man. Or maybe the one who already enjoyed his favor and needed help to cope with the consequences." The large eyes twinkled, brushing over Dehe's bulging belly once again. "Don't look so scandalized. He is a vigorous man despite his advanced age, and you look so young and so innocent. How old are you?"

"I've seen more than twenty summers," muttered Dehe. She licked her lips. "I... I'm sorry that I gave you the wrong impression. I... I had better..." She began getting up again.

"Sit down, girl." Although still good natured, the woman's voice held a clear order this time. Oh, this one obviously was used to being obeyed. "He won't see you in a hurry. He is taking his bath now, and he will need to eat his special food afterward, and to rest. He may agree to see you through his meal, but you will still have to wait until it happens."

Shrugging, the woman clapped her hands. "Serve us drink and refreshment," she ordered the maid that appeared at the doorway before the sound of the clapping had died away. "And be quick about it."

The thought of the drink made Dehe dizzy with thirst.

"Well, now let me introduce myself properly. I am Cuicatl, the Second Daughter of Acolmiztli, the noblemen of the Culhuacan's royal family. And, of course, I am the Third Wife of the First Warlord of Tenochtitlan." The woman's eyes twinkled. "The favorite wife. Just like this favorite nephew of his, eh?"

Dehe swallowed. "I'm honored to meet you, Revered Lady," she said, overwhelmed by so many titles.

"Oh, and I'm honored to meet you, Little Wife of the Favorite Nephew." The woman's laughter trilled again, reminding Dehe that the word *cuicatl* meant song. "So what happened to the oh-so-highly-civilized young man with foreign tattoos, foreign name and the most mysterious sword anyone has ever seen?"

"Oh, well," Dehe cleared her throat. "I should talk to the Warlord about it. I think he would wish to know first, and..." She heard her voice trailing off under the glimmering gaze.

"Got himself in trouble this husband of yours, didn't he?" The woman frowned. "Why didn't he come himself? He is quite welcome in this house and, indeed, he visits here often. Almost as often as those noble-born, highly ambitious friends of his."

"He is not in Tenochtitlan at the present," said Dehe, thinking about the times he would spend his evenings here, or gods know where, instead of at his home, with her and the children.

"Then where is he? There are no campaigns that I've heard of, with both the previous Warlord and the current one busy with the turmoil in the Tepanec royal house." The large eyes sparkled triumphantly. "Oh, he went away escorting one of them. Tlatelolco or Tlacopan?"

"Tlacopan."

"Then our current Warlord is in good hands and safe, I suppose." Her eyes sparkled again, challenging. "So what happened in his absence?"

"I don't know," said Dehe, clenching her teeth in desperation. "I wish I knew. I hoped his Honorable Uncle would know what the trouble is and how to cope with it."

To her relief, the maids interrupted, coming in, carrying trays laden with plates and flasks, making her nausea worse with the heavy aroma of a chocolate drink.

"Help yourself, pretty girl," said the woman, when the maids arranged the table and melted away, as efficient and as soundless as the night's spirits. She picked up her cup. "When I was heavy with each of my children, I used to drink chocolate day and night. It made me restless, and I grew so fat I could use none of my gowns for moons afterward, but I couldn't help it. I needed chocolate drink badly, with the foam and all." She chuckled. "I still like it better than before, but I have to keep count these days, so I won't lose my pretty curves again." A wink. "The Warlord wasn't happy. They like us all curvy and soft, but not shapeless, don't they?"

"Yes, I suppose so," said Dehe politely, nauseated by the smell of the foamy drink, but forcing herself to sip some of it. There were no such expensive beverages in her household, and she never liked the spicy, slightly bitter taste of the chocolate, anyway.

"Was it easy for you to carry your children?" she asked, feeling obliged to respond with more than an empty politeness.

"Oh, yes," said the woman, draining her cup in one gulp. "Although, the girls were easier than the boys." She winked. "Boys are always so big, so pushy, yet so slow. They take their time, and they tear you apart on their way out. But girls? Oh, the girls are swift. They are just slipping out of you, pretty, elegant little things." The woman shook her head, deep in her thoughts for a moment.

"How many children do you have?"

"Four. Two girls, two boys, but they are grown up now. My girls are married, and only one of my boys is still in *calmecac*."

"But how?" Embarrassed by her own agitated reaction, Dehe stared at the woman, wide-eyed.

"Easily, girl." The pretty noblewoman laughed again. "I'm not as young as you might think. The Warlord took me when I was quite young, but it happened more than twenty summers ago." The smile playing on the full lips was dreamy as the large eyes clouded, wandering the mists of the past. "It was the New Fire ceremony, the first New Fire ceremony Tenochtitlan was celebrating. We'd been living in Tenochtitlan for some summers by then, and I was not missing Culhuacan as badly as in the beginning. I was fifteen, and my father wanted me to attend this ceremony as it was the biggest celebration this *altepetl* would have for another fifty-two summers. And who knew if I would live long enough to attend the next one. So, in spite of my mother's protests, he let me come, and was I excited!" Her favorite drink forgotten, the woman shook her head. "Oh, it was such a beautiful day. You should have seen it, girl! The music, the crowds, the colorful processions, the ceremonies in the temple atop the Great Pyramid. So many sacrificial offerings! I haven't seen so many offerings ever since." The gaze of the woman focused, as though remembering her audience. "We were invited to join the royal family upon their dais. The First Emperor had been dead for some summers, and his successor, Revered Huitzilihuitl, was very young and very nice. My father hoped that I would catch his eye. We were of a royal family ourselves, even if Culhuacan was subdued by then, defiled by the vile Tepanecs. However, a Toltec princess is always a welcome addition to any emperor's household. She makes it shine brighter. And I was held to be a beauty, too." The woman straightened up, filling her cup. "Well, Huitzilihuitl was attracted, of course. I could see that, and I was flattered. He was just a little older than me and very nice looking. But then, as the priests were offering the last heart, and the last body came tumbling down the stairs of the pyramid, the Chief Warlord came up the dais, to talk to the Emperor." The dreamy grin widened, became mischievous. "Oh, girl, you should have seen him back then, the way he came up, ignoring the stairs, mounting the dais in one powerful leap, a mighty jaguar, his spotted cloak swirling. My heart stopped, slid down my chest, to flutter somewhere in my stomach. All I wanted was to be seated urgently. I was afraid I might faint. My legs had no strength in them. But do you know what the most beautiful thing about all this was?" The dark eyes bore into Dehe, shining triumphantly. "He took one look at me, and he almost fell off the dais. I'm telling you, girl! He was about to talk to the Emperor, but all he did was stare. He just stood there, peering at me, as though he had seen a ghost, enthralled but scared too, his eyes wide and his mouth gaping." The woman laughed. "Oh, girl, it made me feel powerful. The famous First Chief Warlord, the conqueror of so many places, the closest adviser and the most trusted man of the First Emperor, Revered Acamapichtli, the most influential, dangerous, powerful person in Tenochtitlan was afraid of me. Oh, gods! But I still needed to sit down, because my legs were shaking."

"And then what happened?" asked Dehe, fascinated, when the woman fell silent, lost in her memories.

"Oh, then some time passed. Only a few moons, but it felt like a long time, ten, twenty seasons maybe. My father still wanted to give me to Huitzilihuitl, but then our Emperor acquired his Tepanec Chief Wife, so my father agreed to give me to the Warlord." She shrugged. "You see, the Warlord was a noble-born Tepanec himself. Otherwise, his multitude of titles and achievements would not have been enough. Culhuacan princesses are a treasure not to be distributed lightly. After the New Fire ceremony half of the noble-born in Tenochtitlan were besieging my father with requests on my behalf." Shaking her head, the woman grinned. "Oh, how worried I was that he would give me to someone else."

"But he is so old!" exclaimed Dehe, unable to hold her tongue.

The woman's laughter rang out, full of mirth, unconcerned. "Oh, he is old *now*, girl. But it happened more than twenty summers ago. He had seen about two times of twenty summers by that time, and he was so incredibly handsome! I promise you that half of the female population of Tenochtitlan would have loved to see me drop dead on the day I was given to him. They all wanted to be in my place. Even his other wives and concubines were jealous, because to them he gave very little – some pleasure so they could bear him his children and run his household, and give it more glamor, as all his other wives were also noblewomen, of course. But me? Oh, he wanted me badly. Me, and not my birthright. Sometimes I think I reminded him of someone, some long lost love of his youth. Something in his behavior, in the way he looked at me from time to time, in the way he was excited about the children I gave him, brought me this thought. There must have been this kind of a Toltec princess in his mysterious past. But I don't mind. He loved and cherished me and not this mysterious princess." The smile playing on the full lips was beautiful. "Oh, we made so much love, and he was happy when I gave him so many children. We were happy, and he still loves me, I can tell you this. He is an old man now, but his mind is keen." The slanted eyes sparkled mischievously. "And his body can still be of a great use." Leaning forward, the woman poured the last of the foamy chocolate into her cup. "I don't know why I'm telling you all this. I hope so much history did not bore you to tears. And you didn't drink your chocolate even. Don't you like this drink?"

"It was a beautiful story," said Dehe, feeling as though awakening from a dream. "I'm honored and grateful that you shared it with me. It was beautiful!"

"Oh, girl, I'm sure your story with your highly civilized leader of the warriors is as lovely. With no restraints of noble birth, you two must have been in each other's arms faster that it would take you to say 'Azcapotzalco.'"

She felt the familiar tightening in her chest. "No, it was not as lovely. He likes me; he treats me well. But the way your Warlord feels about you, he feels about someone else." She clenched her teeth tight. "He gives me what the Warlord gave to his other wives."

The plucked eyebrows climbed high, meeting each other across the beautiful forehead. "But how is that possible? You are such a beautiful, vital, obviously loyal little thing. It can't be true, girl! You must be needlessly jealous because he is busy making his way into the leading circles of the warriors' force." The woman smiled widely, slightly condescending now, like a grown up person talking to a child. "Warriors have a demanding life, especially promising leaders. You can't expect him to be there for you. My Warlord was also not there most of the time. You should have chosen an engineer or a peasant to live with, if you wanted that much attention." The large eyes bore into her, their amusement spilling. "Don't be a spoiled little brat. Your man may turn into a great leader one day. My husband certainly thinks he will. But it won't happen if he spends all his time pampering you."

Oh, had it only been the way this woman thought it was! Dehe bit her lips hard, fighting the rising wave of sadness.

Blinking forcefully, she cleared her vision. "No, I'm not a spoiled brat. But you are right, of course. I'm very lucky, and I should be happy with what I have." She paused so as not to let her voice break, studying the carvings upon the table. The serpent's head peeking from under the small bowl with honey kept blurring, and she blinked again, trying to make it focus.

"Who is she?" The woman's voice held none of its previous amusement.

Dehe clutched onto her cup, afraid to say anything, desperate to control her voice.

"Come, girl. Spill it out. We, women, do to talk to each other. It helps. And you are in a bad need of such talk, one can see that." The groomed palm came out, touching Dehe's chin gently, pushing it up. "You should not hold it inside. You will harm your child if you keep feeling bad." The large eyes glimmered with compassion. "Did he take a new concubine? Another wife?"

"No," whispered Dehe. "I… I'm sorry for making this mess. I don't know what came over me. It's all the worry about the trouble and…"

The narrowing eyes made her stop muttering. "Who is she?" repeated the woman, forceful now.

"The Empress."

"What?" The beautiful face turned into a mask of astonishment.

Dehe felt like clasping her mouth with both hands, trying to shove the words back in. "I'm not… I didn't mean it that way…"

A maid appeared in the doorway.

"Honorable Mistress," she said timidly, sensing the tension. "The Revered Master, he'll see your guest now."

Cuicatl exhaled loudly, as her eyebrows climbed high. The usual twinkle came back, glimmering in the large oval eyes.

"Well, girl, you had better go and talk to my husband. It is very kind of him. I didn't expect him to grant you this audience on such a short notice unless he is also aware of the trouble." The generous lips twisted in a suggestive kind of a smile. "It's been a pleasant, interesting, not to say fascinating, meal, and I thank you for that. I will not be put out if you come to visit me again. You are anything but an ordinary sort of a woman, Little Wife of the Favorite Nephew. Come and visit me anytime you need to talk to a friendly person."

CHAPTER 9

"What do you mean, our delegation was not received?" Chimal nearly sprang to his feet, staring at his Main Adviser, genuinely surprised. "They couldn't do that!"

From her small, woven chair, Iztac watched him, troubled as well. How could the Tepanecs refuse to receive Tenochtitlan's delegation? How could they just tell them off? And what did it mean? A war?

She felt her excitement welling along with her fear. Now Tenochtitlan would have to commit itself, would have to support her brother with more than just wonderful hospitality and vaguely given promises. But would the alliance between the not-yet-strong-enough Mexica and the defeated Acolhua be enough to hold their ground against the mighty Empire?

"Yes, they refused to let our delegation enter the Palace," repeated Itzcoatl impartially, his face – a mask made out of stone.

Chimal inhaled loudly, clutching his fists tight. He didn't look well, reflected Iztac, watching his pale, haggard face. Dark rings surrounded his eyes, and he had thinned visibly. Biting her lips, she knew that not only the Tepanecs and their unheard of rudeness were to blame. In part, it was her fault, too. Since that row about the Highlander, when she had lost her temper in the ugliest of ways, Chimal had been genuinely downcast. He had kept away from her through the rest of that day, but later on he tried to behave normally, as though nothing had happened, inviting her to attend his morning meetings as usual and coming to visit her set of rooms once or twice. He didn't try to instigate any intimacy, but he had clearly hoped she would do so.

However, she was still sick with worry, still angry with what she saw as his petty vengefulness, so nothing happened, and in both cases he went away after a meaningless conversation, doing his best to look as though he had come for nothing else.

Seeing him like this made her heart twist with pity, but she reasoned that maybe this treatment would bring him back to his senses, would make him abandon the idea of hauling the Highlander before the Imperial Court. She was planning to return to their usual pleasant, well familiar intimacy the moment it happened. He was not being fair, and he needed to be shown the error of his ways.

Shifting her gaze from her husband's haunted face to the stony, unreadable features of his main adviser, she shuddered. Oh, this one had changed, too, in some subtle, but quite noticeable, way. As formidable, as intimidating as ever, Itzcoatl looked more of his name now. Obsidian Serpent, oh yes, a dangerous snake, placid and sure of himself, so unreadable one never knew if he was before or after his meal. And somehow Iztac felt that now he was not full, not satisfied, that he had yet to swallow his next prey. She felt it in her bones, in the upper corner of her stomach, and it would twist uneasily, making her uncomfortable in this man's presence, for he had began looking at her differently now, too. He used to be annoyed with her and her interference, but through the last few days he would look at her with what seemed to be a cold, passionless regret. He was not annoyed with her anymore, and this, if nothing else, should have frightened her, she knew, should have shown her that something had changed.

That, and the fact that for more than a few days, since despised Maxtla came to rule the Tepanec Empire, Itzcoatl offered no advice, reporting as the Main Adviser was expected to do, listening impartially, indifferent and unmoved, as though it was none of his business. Why, recently the man did not even frequent the Palace the way he used to, reflected Iztac, a wave of anxiety washing through her being once again.

"So what do you say, Adviser? Does it mean war?" she heard Chimal asking, his tone demanding and firm, the tone of an emperor. She hid her smile, proud of him.

"Yes, I think it means war, although they sent us neither *tizatl* nor the appropriate offering of weapons and arms, yet."

"Well, we are ready to repulse their initial attack." Chimal straightened up in his woven chair. Pressing his lips, he looked at his uncle resolutely, serene and very determined. "I shall tour our wharves and both causeways tomorrow, to see if the earthworks could be erected on short notice." He frowned. "And I shall visit our temples and public places. This will reassure our people, will let them know that we are not afraid, that we will weather this storm, and we will come out of it stronger and more powerful than before."

Itzcoatl nodded thoughtfully, but something flickered in the depths of his dark eyes, something that made Iztac's stomach twist uneasily once again.

"Yes, you should tour the city, Revered Nephew. I'll tell your Chief Warlord to organize this tour for you."

Chimal brightened visibly. "Did Tlacaelel come back at last?"

"Yes, he came not very long ago." A mirthless grin brought the stone mask to life for a heartbeat. "Apparently, he had to deal with adventures of his own."

"What happened?"

"There was an attempt on his life."

"In Tlacopan?" gasped Chimal.

"Yes."

Iztac felt her heart missing a beat.

"Oh, the Tepanecs have no honor at all!"

"No, they have none. Apparently, they think many of the cities and *altepetl*s should change their rulers along with their policies." The thickset man shrugged. "I shall double the amount of warriors guarding the Palace."

This time Chimal jumped to his feet, unable to remain seated anymore. "They would never dare!" he cried out. "It would make the war inevitable, and they would never succeed in removing a lawful ruler of an independent *altepetl*, never. We are not a village!"

Itzcoatl shrugged once again. "Maxtla has no honor. He can try anything, and I don't want to see him succeeding, even if it won't achieve the results he might wish to achieve. Tlacateotl, the ruler of Tlatelolco, was also a lawful ruler of an independent city. Nezahualcoyotl is also not an outlaw for them to try to hunt him down the way the despicable Tepanec tried. Tayatzin was a lawfully appointed successor to the Tepanec throne, but he is dead now, and no one dares to ask questions. I don't want it happening here in Tenochtitlan. I don't want to see you dead, Nephew, even if your death would not make Tenochtitlan into a tributary of the Tepanec Empire."

Not daring to breathe, Iztac listened, her heart beating fast. Oh no, they would never dare. Never! And yet, Itzcoatl might be right. Dirty Maxtla had dared to do many things no one assumed he would do. What was there to stop him from trying to murder Chimal, whom he hated openly, whose delegation he had just refused to receive? Oh, gods!

She watched the impartial face, a stone mask once again. Did this man have Chimal's interests in his heart, after all? Were her suspicions, her unexplained dislike of this man, wrong and unfounded?

"I appreciate your concern for my safety, oh Honorable Uncle," she heard Chimal saying, his voice warm and heartfelt. "But I would give my life away gladly if I were required to do so for the benefit of Tenochtitlan."

"I believe you, Nephew. Yet, my mission is to ensure your safety for the greater benefit of Tenochtitlan." But again, the man's eyes flickered darkly, making Iztac shiver. He knew something Chimal did not, she realized suddenly. Something ominous and dark. Something that would scare her beyond any reason.

She shut her eyes, wishing the ominous feeling to go away. It must be her imagination. Recently, she'd had too many things to worry about, too much danger to cope with. People she loved were in trouble, all of them – Coyotl, the Highlander, and now Chimal. No, she should calm her nerves and should not let the stupid sensation of knowing the future ruin her life. She would not be of help to any of them if she turned into a quivering shouter of doom.

No, she decided. Today she would not worry, and she'd do

nothing but spend a quiet day with Citlalli, her daughter, the way she sometimes liked to do. They would draw pictures and chat and laugh, and they would gorge on sweetmeats, as well. Citlalli might have seen only six summers, but she was already a worthy companion, funny and willful, and smart; a delightful person. A friend.

She opened her eyes in time to see Tlacaelel coming in, tall and imposing, his paces wide, his face sunburned, his cloak creased, his whole being radiating purposeful energy, smelling of lake, campfires, and adventure.

"I beg to forgive me my neglected appearances," he said nearing the throne, not paying attention to the slaves who hurriedly prostrated themselves. "I came as soon as I could, as soon as I heard you wished to see me, Revered Brother."

"I'm so glad to see you back, well and unharmed!" exclaimed Chimal, jumping off his throne once again. "What happened?"

"Oh, filthy manure eating Maxtla was up to his tricks again!" Tlacaelel's nostril's widened as he took a deep breath. "This man is the most despicable half person that has ever been born."

"You should be flattered, Warlord," said Itzcoatl grimly. "He seems to be concerned mainly with rulers or would-be rulers."

But Tlacaelel just shrugged, unperturbed. "He didn't try to dispose of me for being me. He wanted to create a problem between Tenochtitlan and Tlacopan, so that city would be the first to join the war against us."

"Oh." This time Itzcoatl frowned, losing his usual composure. "How did you come to this conclusion?"

Tlacaelel shrugged. "It was an easy conclusion to arrive once I knew it was not the idea of Tlacopan's ruler."

"How did you discover the plot?" Chimal still stared at his Chief Warlord, wide eyed.

"My leader of the warriors is a resourceful man. His vigilance and sharpness of mind are to be commended."

Both Itzcoatl's and Chimal's faces darkened, and Iztac would have been amused to see them sharing a mutual feeling at long last, had it not been for the wild pounding of her heart. *He* had done something commendable once again. *He* had saved the

Warlord. Oh, he was the best of warriors and the best of men!

"I came here in such a hurry because of the news from our delegation in Azcapotzalco," she heard Tlacaelel saying, as though not noticing the tension.

Chimal's face clouded once again. "Yes! The despicable low-life is girding for war."

"So, is Tlacopan in this war or not?" asked Itzcoatl curtly, paying no attention to the exchange.

"Not yet." Tlacaelel pursed his lips. "But if the war goes badly I cannot predict when the temptation to join will be too high." He shrugged. "For now, they will stay neutral."

"They will not join our cause?"

"No, I wouldn't count on that."

"So, we are alone in this," stated Chimal quietly. "With Tlatelolco distraught and afraid, we have no allies."

Tlacaelel nodded thoughtfully. "We better make sure the Acolhua people are prepared to join our war in a hurry. I'm sure our Texcocan friend has completed the needed preparations, or at least almost done so. He didn't spend his time in vain while visiting his former lands through the last three summers; he wasn't staying in Texcoco to indulge his yearning for the past." Another causal lift of the wide shoulders. "We should also hope he has enlisted enough support from his untamed neighbors to the east."

"But he is on the run now," said Chimal. "We don't even know if he is alive."

"I'm sending a trusted person to look for him."

"The same resourceful leader, I presume," said Itzcoatl icily.

Tlacaelel's expression didn't change. "Yes, of course. Do you have a better person for this mission, Honorable Uncle?"

A dark glance and pursed lips were Tlacaelel's answer, but Iztac could hardly listen, her heart pounding, thoughts swirling around. He would be away, but also safe from danger. And if her brother was still alive, he would find him, and he would keep him safe.

Then her eyes rested on Chimal's set face, and her heart fell. The Emperor watched his advisers coldly, his lips pressed, eyes narrowed. He didn't say a word, didn't try to join their exchange. He just watched them, and in the depths of his eyes she could see that he had already taken some sort of an action.

Dehe hurried down the familiar alley, anxious to reach home. It was already well into the afternoon, and she had never spent so much time away from her home and her children. Almost half a day, but what a fascinating half a day it was. And also so reassuring.

Kuini's uncle had turned out to be a wonderful man, friendly and easygoing, not arrogant, and not dangerous, the way she remembered him from that day, seven summers ago, when she had overheard him plotting with the scary warlord how to use the Lowlander and the haughty young Aztec to the best of their, the warlords, interests. Back then she had also been different, she knew, frustrated and scared and sick with jealousy, so maybe she had judged this man wrongly once upon a time.

And not that he had detained her for a long conversation. The impressive old man understood immediately what the trouble was. Not spending his time on unnecessary deliberations or clarifications, he nibbled on the greenish *nopal* sticks of his salad, then told her to send Kuini here at once, the moment he came back.

Smiling kindly, he brushed aside her misgivings, promising to take care of the matter. It might come to her husband going away for a while, he told her, but she was not to worry. She and her children would be taken care of and protected the entire time her man would have to stay away. She had thanked him profusely, and knew that everything would be well.

Breathing the cool afternoon air with enjoyment, she went on, paying no attention to her tiredness. She would be home soon, and she would rest while waiting for Kuini to come home. Would it take him long to arrive? The fat official from the Imperial Court seemed to think the delegation from Tlacopan should have come back soon.

She shivered. The court! Taking a deep breath, she forced her thoughts off the morning's visit. He would be all right. His uncle would take care of this trouble.

Her smile widening, she recalled the fascinating noon, spent in the company of the formidable uncle's wife; the third wife – the beautiful, sparkling, talkative, oh-so-very-noble-born lady. What a woman! No wonder the mighty Warlord had fallen in love with her and had loved her ever since. Who wouldn't be enthralled with so much spark, so much liveliness, so much cleverness, such a highborn person, and yet, so down to earth. Oh, it would be wonderful to talk to this woman again, to receive more of her advice, to listen to her stories. Tenochtitlan must have been a very different city back in those times.

The alleys in her neighborhood were bursting with life at this time of the day, and she wondered if the twins were anywhere among the children dashing all around. She had left the instruction to keep them in the house, but she had not intended to stay away for half the day, and even she doubted the ability of anyone to keep them in for so long.

Yet, they were at home, crouching outside, on the patio, peering at the elaborately drawn sketch of a bean game. For a moment she caught her breath, staring at her husband's wide shoulders as he sprawled beside the boys, leaning forward, watching one of them reaching for a stone figurine upon the squares of the drawing.

"Are you sure you want to move this one? Did you check the rest of your figurines?"

"That's not fair, Father!" cried out the other boy. "You are helping him now."

"No, I'm not," protested Kuini. "I just want him to check all his possibilities."

Ocelotl, the other twin, whirled at his brother, pushing his hair out of his face.

"Yes, and he helped you before, too! You would have ended up in the middle squares if Father didn't tell you not to."

"Oh, yes, and that's why I'm always winning, eh?"

"Shut up, you stupid piece of rotten meat!"

"You both shut up," said Kuini good-naturedly. "Either you play or you fight. You can't do both." He motioned to Coatl, the first boy, clearly anxious to divert their attention before the twins dove into one of their endless arguments, this time, probably, pondering their possibilities of fighting and playing at the same time. "Choose your move now."

Her chest swelling with pride, she watched him patting the boy on his shoulder, signaling to him that he was satisfied with his choice, while passing the beans to the other one with a wink.

They were a good team, those boys of hers, she thought, walking the path, nearing them soundlessly, the way she always walked. Coatl was smarter, while Ocelotl was fiercer, but their coalition would always break whenever their father was around. Their competition for his attention was unrelenting and desperate.

He noticed her approach before the boys did, his warrior's senses making him turn his head.

"Oh, now we are truly honored." He beamed at her from the ground, not attempting to get up. "A beautiful woman just walked up the path. Tell me, boys, where did you find such a good-looking woman for a mother?"

The boys grunted something, not especially pleased with her interruption.

"So what have you been up to, woman?" he went on, his eyes glittering, teasing. "The warrior comes home and finds his fire off, his house abandoned, with only poor servants to take care of his needs. Luckily, these two rascals were around, offering a good pastime. Otherwise, I might have gone away, in search of a new woman."

She could not fight her smile anymore. "This new woman would run off, terrified, after spending just one day with you and this pair."

"Oh, well, then we would have to make do all by ourselves, wouldn't we boys?" He pushed his elbow into the nearest twin's ribs. "What do you say? With no women around, it could be good, eh?"

"Oh, yes," said Coatl happily. "No one would tell us what to do."

"Oh, yes?" asked Dehe, her hands on her hips. "And who would prepare your meals, and clean this free-of-orders house of yours?"

"The slaves," suggested Ocelotl. "That's what the slaves are for."

Kuini's eyes twinkled. "You are growing two perfect Lowlander noblemen, Lady. Good work."

"Take us back into the Highlands, and you'll have your perfect Highlanders." Shifting her accumulating weight from one foot to the other, Dehe frowned, aware of her tiredness now. "I need to talk to you."

"What about?"

"Well, it's urgent and... Would you come with me?"

He peered at her for another heartbeat, then began to get up, but both boys grabbed his arm, trying to pull him back.

"Father, you promised," they shouted, united for a change. "You promised!"

Kuini laughed and allowed himself to be pulled back.

"Listen, pretty woman," he said, flashing one of those smiles at her, those wide, unguarded smiles of his that made her heart melt in her chest. "I'll finish this game, then I'll be with you."

She watched him sprawling between the boys, so large and brown and weathered against their young, innocent freshness. A man, and yet just a boy like them, trustful and naive, and full of mischief. She wanted to argue, to tell him how urgent and important the matter was. Yet, she wanted him to stay where he was, too. They enjoyed him so rarely, she and the boys. They should be able to have him all for themselves for just a little longer.

"I'll see about the meal," she said, turning toward the house.

"While you're at it, send me a flask of a decent drink, would you?" he called after her, but she went on, pretending that she didn't hear. No, he should drink no *octli* this evening. He would need his wits sharp tonight.

The servants were in the adjacent structure that served as a kitchen area. Taking in the confused, cluttered activity, she organized them briskly, then rushed back into the house to find her daughter puffy from crying and sticky with sweetmeats, clinging to Dehe's legs, demanding to be picked up. A sweet little thing. Her heart twisted, thinking of her girl crying, looking for her mother and not finding her for such a long time. She pressed Mixtli tight, pushing the girl's sticky hair out of her face. It beamed at her, as round as a sunflower with two shiny jades for the eyes.

"How much honey did you gorge on, you sweet little thing?" she asked, shaking her head. This afternoon, she could forget the idea of feeding the girl properly. The maids had obviously tried to make her stop crying by using the oldest trick in human history. "We need to wash you up, you sticky honeycomb."

But she knew the girl wouldn't agree to climb off her hip, not for a while, so she turned around and headed back toward the patio, where the game progressed nicely with all three of the players absorbed in their figurines, agitated and full of life.

"It's not fair. He is cheating!" cried out Ocelotl. "He can't have five marks twice in a row. It's not fair."

As she bent above a bowl of water, washing Mixtli's sticky mouth against the desperate protests of the girl, she heard Kuini laughing.

"I know, I know. Your brother is a damn lucky bastard." He took a swig from his flask, and she wanted to curse the servants for bringing him *octli* anyway.

Coatl smirked. "It's not me, it's the beans. They just roll the way they roll." Deliberately slow, he took his time choosing between his figurines, moving one of them up with a showy push. "Almost there," he purred.

"Who cares, you stupid piece of rotten meat!" cried out Ocelotl, shoving forward and bringing his arms up, but whether to grab the beans or to strike his brother was not clear.

"Get the beans, boy," said Kuini calmly, not impressed. "Go on with the game. It's not over yet, and one has to know how to lose with dignity, too."

With Mixtli wriggling in her arms, trying to make her walk closer to the source of the action, Dehe lingered by the head of the path, enjoying watching them together. Oh, but for more of such evenings. She shook her head. If only she could take them all somewhere, away from this huge *altepetl* and its politics and wars, back to the Highlands, where he would hunt, and she would cook and take care of the family. She didn't need all those cocoa beans and the slaves. They were just a nuisance, another matter to take care of, to organize and to supervise. And he was such a good father, not like his highborn friends at all, teaching his boys and playing with them. Other men took no interest in their children. She had seen it all around her. But he was different. He loved his boys, and not only because they were his sons, to carry on his name and his family's traditions.

"The next game, I'm playing against Father," declared Coatl.

"No, you are not!" This time Ocelotl actually sprang to his feet. "Before this game is over you are getting punched in your ugly face."

Kuini laughed, reaching for the angry boy's arm, pulling sharply enough to make his son topple on top of him.

"The next game I'm going to talk to your mother. But when I get back, and if you two haven't killed each other in the meanwhile, I'll play a game against each of you."

Turning around to walk back toward the house, Dehe glanced over the road, and her heart stopped. Struggling to take a breath, she knew it would not come, as her eyes took in the group of men coming up the alley, the clumsy gait of the pudgy official in the lead painfully familiar, remembered well from this very morning. Surrounded by warriors, he looked even more cumbersome, panting his way up the slope.

She felt her heart making a strange leap, as though trying to slide up her throat. As if in a dream, she turned around, unbearably slow.

"Kuini!" she said, but it came out more of a whisper, and he didn't even hear her, gulping from his flask, laughing, busy dealing with another violent exchange between the twins.

The men were very close now. She could feel them nearing, could hear the gravel cracking under their feet. She had to run toward him, to warn him, but her legs were suddenly too heavy to move.

Mixtli began wriggling again, trying to pull her back toward the boys, but as the warriors approached them she went still, fascinated by the new attraction.

"Greetings, Honorable Lady," said the official stiffly, his tension obvious.

She just stared at him, unable to say a thing. Her eyes counted the warriors, seeking their leader, a tall, broad man with a badly scarred face.

"We are here to talk to the Master of the House." The official pushed his way past her, but the warriors stayed where they were, frigid and tense.

"What's this?" She heard Kuini's voice, calm and amused, and she knew he didn't even bother to get up, probably still sprawling by the boys, unconcerned. "What do you want?"

"We are here to invite you to the Imperial Court, Honorable Warrior," said the official hastily, obviously not as sure of himself as before.

She took a few steps up the path, but whether to come nearer to her husband or to put more distance between her and the warriors she didn't know.

"What?" Kuini's eyes widened, still amused, still unconcerned. Yet, the half grin playing upon his lips was anything but pleasant now.

"I am Tlacuilo, the Second Scribe of the Imperial Court," repeated the man, licking his lips and shooting a quick glance at the warriors. "Please, come with us."

Kuini rose to his feet slowly, not sparing a glance for the warriors, as it seemed.

"Go away," he said, deliberately rude. "I've been to the Palace this morning, and if I were needed in the Palace again my leader would have sent a messenger."

"This matter has nothing to do with your duties, warrior." The voice of the official had a strained tone to it now.

"Then what is this all about?"

"You are to be tried at the Imperial Court."

Kuini's unpleasant, one sided grin widened as his eyebrows

climbed up to his shaven hairline. "For what offense?"

The pudgy man shot another worried glance at his escorts. "You will be told in due time."

"Will I?" The Highlander's hand slipped over his girdle lightly, caressing the smoothness of his sword's hilt.

Beads of sweat glittered upon the scribe's forehead. "Yes, you will be informed. Please come."

"I don't think so, Scribe," said Kuini, shrugging. "I'm not used to being fetched in this way, with no message beforehand, and with a whole bunch of the Palace's guards ready to make me come should I refuse." Another shrug. "Go away. I'll stay here with my family, and you can send me a polite message tomorrow morning, when the court is convened. Maybe I'll come then." The mirthless grin disappeared. "Better still, apply to my leader. Honorable Chief Warlord is the person to deal with the troubles concerning his warriors. He will punish me, if necessary. He is my leader, and no one else."

"The Emperor is your leader!" exclaimed the scribe, appalled. "If you refuse to accompany me, his official messenger, you are refusing your Emperor, your lawful ruler and the leader of your land." The pudgy man frowned, his anger evidently giving him more courage. "You'll be adding another unforgivable crime against your Emperor if those warriors have to disarm you and drag you into the court by force."

Kuini's laughter rolled over the patio. "Oh, you don't really think that this pitiful amount of spoiled, pampered Palace's guards can disarm me and drag me anywhere. Stop talking nonsense and go away. You are disturbing the harmony of my house, and I don't want to dirty my patio with the guts of all those would-be warriors of yours."

She felt the movement behind her back, and her instincts told her to leap aside. But for Mixtli in her arms and the weight of the child inside her, she might have been successful in avoiding the warrior. Yet, as it was, she was not swift enough, and the powerful arm grabbed her shoulder, pulling her roughly, making her sway. If not for the warrior's other arm, that caught her across her chest, she might have lost her balance and fallen.

It all went so fast she didn't understand what had happened. One moment, she was standing there, terrified, watching her husband dealing with those men, so calm, so sure of himself. The next, the world was swaying, with her back pressed against an unfamiliar body, a strong arm pinning her to it, making it hard to hold onto Mixtli, who clutched her desperately, too terrified to start crying just yet. She struggled not to let the girl slip off, the obsidian blade pressing against her throat the last of her worries, for a moment.

"Come, warrior," hissed the low voice beside her ear, and somehow she knew it belonged to the man with the scarred face. "Just come with us quiet and nice. Or your patio will be full of the woman and the girl's guts."

Busy fighting for breath, her vision blurred, her throat hurt, she saw Kuini leaping forward, his sword out and ready. Yet, the obsidian pressed harder and it stopped his attack in midair, as she gagged and coughed, and still tried to hold onto Mixtli, who was now screaming and slipping out of her grip.

"Let her go!" she heard someone growling, and she wasn't sure it was Kuini, so low, so unnatural his voice sounded.

"Put your sword down. Now!" thundered the voice beside her ear, echoing strangely, like in a closed room.

The obsidian pressed harder, and she felt the world spinning around her, wondering how the warrior could still clutch her so tightly, when nothing was stable anymore. The sounds began to recede, and it was a mercy, but before she could let go, escaping the pain and the terror, and the screams of her child, there was the sound of something hitting the ground, and the pressure of the knife lessened.

Fighting for breath, the air seeping through her tortured throat with difficulty, she blinked, ridiculously grateful for the support of the hand clutching her across her chest. Even the knife still pressing lightly against her throat was a means to stay upright, to concentrate on her attempts to hold onto Mixtli.

Her gaze focused, taking in his wide shoulders, not very far from her, standing there with his fists clenched but without his sword, his teeth bared, eyes blazing, enormously large, lacking their usual spark, as dark as a moonless night.

"Let her go, *now!*" he half growled half hissed, his teeth clenched, his eyes wild and not completely sane. The sword was there, thrown carelessly beside his feet, displaying the wonderful carvings.

"Take the sword away from him," ordered the voice beside her ear, and there was a swift movement in the corner of her eye. "You go with us with no trouble, yes." The man made it a statement.

"I'll go with you. Take your knife away. *Now!*"

With the support of the knife and the strangling arm across her chest gone, she fought to keep her balance, while trying to improve her grip on the screaming child. The insistent little thing hung onto her with her whole body, tearing her hair, scratching her skin. Swaying, she knew she could not make it, but then his arms were around her, pressing her close, steadying her, giving her strength. There were other sounds, someone was crying somewhere, and the warriors were talking loudly, agitatedly.

"I'm coming, you filthy, stinking manure-eaters," she heard him hissing. "And I swear, you will pay for this. All of you, one by one!"

He was still pressing her hard, too hard, and it was again difficult to keep Mixtli from slipping, but she didn't mind, wishing to hide inside his reassuring warmth and this familiar scent of his, his smell that she loved so much, mixed with some sweat and the spicy aroma of *octli*.

"You stupid frog-eaters, what are you staring at? Come and help her," he shouted, obviously addressing the slaves now.

His grip eased, letting her breathe more freely, but leaving her disappointed. She didn't want to leave the safety of his arms.

"Can you hold on?" he whispered into her hair. "Are you hurt?"

She shook her head. "I tried to warn... I'm sorry." She coughed, trying to clear her mouth. "I should have... It's my fault."

He lifted her head gently, his fingers brushing against her throat, light but still hurting.

"It's nothing," he murmured. "Just a flesh wound." She saw the relief in his eyes, and it made her chest swell, making it difficult to keep the sobs at bay.

"Listen, I have to go now. When you can, send a word to Tlacaelel. Let him know what happened." He frowned. "I would rather have you put under his protection. If only Coyotl were here..."

"Come, warrior. Let us move." Now it was the scribe talking.

"I'll go to your uncle's house," she whispered, holding the tears back, but unable to control her trembling. Her whole body shook, and her throat hurt more and more with each passing moment. Mixtli stopped screaming, but to have her sagging there, so quiet and lacking in life, was more alarming. "He will protect us, he promised."

"Yes, do that!" He pressed her to him again, now lightly and hurriedly. "Hold on, fighting girl. You haven't changed, and I'm proud of you. Always." Pushing her toward the slaves, who now stood next to them, ready to support her, he eased away. "I'll be back before the next dawn." The last sentence he said loudly, challenging his persecutors.

She watched him going up the path, pushing his way past the warriors, not prepared to be led anywhere, even to the Imperial Court. Her nausea growing, eyes blurry, she leaned against the supportive hands of the maids, seeing him turning his head, waving at the twins, who stood beside the drawing of the bean game, transfixed, two frozen statues, their mouths gaping, eyes enormous in the paleness of their faces.

"Don't make any trouble until I come back," he shouted lightly, and she knew what effort it must have cost him, to be so light in the middle of such monumental rage. "If I hear you gave your mother a trouble, you are done for, you two rascals."

Only when they were out of sight, disappearing behind the slope, did she stop fighting the dizziness, stopped trying to banish the sparkling mist from the corner of her eyes.

"Take Mixtli," she whispered, unable to hold on against the swaying of the world anymore.

The darkness spread, but without her daughter in her arms she dove into it gratefully, because it was a place with no trembling, no nausea, no pain, and most of all, no desperate worry for him.

CHAPTER 10

The setting sun made it impossible to look in the direction of the mainland, which spread beyond the water and the narrow pass of the causeway. Tlacaelel shielded his eyes, trying to make out the silhouettes of the hills and other landmarks surrounding distant Tlacopan.

He had just walked this causeway once again, more than half of its length, inspecting it thoroughly, studying the earthworks, making sure the artificial pass of land could be blocked on the shortest notice, preventing potential invaders from storming Tenochtitlan. The wall and the fortified gates guarded the city well, blocking any immediate access to the uninvited visitors, yet he didn't want it coming to this. His warriors wouldn't be fighting on the streets of his beloved *altepetl*. It wouldn't come to this. Not if he could help it.

So its war, he thought, clenching his teeth, his stomach heavy, chest hurting. Well, they all knew it would come; that one day it would happen, but, nevertheless, it had happened too soon. They weren't ready, not yet. They were alone, facing the mighty Empire. Just like the Acolhua people, less than a decade before – forsaken, surrounded by enemies or bystanders, with no allies worth mentioning, and no real friends, with many fence-sitters watching and waiting, contemplating their next move, ready to join the winning side.

He ground his teeth. Well, it was different back then. Tenochtitlan had no choice but to wait and see, and it could not be blamed for joining the winning side. Or could it? *Stop wasting your time on stupid thoughts*, he admonished himself, turning around and heading back toward the city gates. The Acolhua had handled their war foolishly, making all the wrong moves. Tenochtitlan did a sensible thing in joining the winning Tepanecs. The stupid Acolhua Emperor, Coyotl's father, was to blame. And yet, would Tenochtitlan handle its war against the Tepanecs any better? Or would the fence-sitters, like Tlacopan, join their enemies in the end, assisting in delivering the final blow, thinking the way he was thinking just now?

"Double the amount of warriors touring both causeways," he said to one of the minor leaders. "And summon the engineers to inspect the earthworks first thing in the morning. If those things will not hold up against twenty times of twenty attacks, I will execute them personally, one by one. Tell them that."

"What about the wharves, Honorable Warlord?" asked the man, frowning.

"The areas surrounding the wharves are protected well enough for now. When the war begins, we will see what places the Tepanecs will concentrate on the most. Then, we'll act accordingly."

Oh, thank all the gods that we are an island city, he thought. *There are only so many directions to attack us from, and none of them by surprise.* Even a siege could not be put on Tenochtitlan directly. The most the enemy could do would be to block the causeways. An inconvenience, surely, but one that would not put Tenochtitlan into a desperate position. No, Tenochtitlan would weather this storm. It would not end up like Texcoco.

"Send a few groups of scouts, to monitor the happenings on the mainland," he grunted.

And speaking of Acolhua, he thought, it was time for the Highlander to head over there, to see what was happening and to speed the events up.

"Run a word to the leader of the group that accompanied me to Tlacopan," he said to another of his assistants. "Tell him to come to my quarters in the Palace." He hesitated. No. The Highlander had better stay away from the Palace and Itzcoatl. "On the other hand, we are done here, so just send for my palanquin. I will detour by the Plaza and the temples, and then by the dwellings of some of my warriors. An escort of half twenty men should be enough. Take your men back to their quarters, in the meanwhile."

He didn't close the curtains of his litter, watching the roads and the alleys sweeping by, proud of his *altepetl*. People rushed around, all sorts of people, young and old, traders and peasants, men and women, they all moved out of his way, but they did so calmly, matter-of-fact, as efficient, as purposeful as always. The prospect of the war had obviously not bothered them that much. Well, no more than the prospect of a natural disaster. It was something to prepare for, but not something to fret about, to lose one's sleep over. Oh, how could they lose with such people? His Mexica-Aztecs were truly a chosen nation to rule the world.

By the last of the daylight, he finished touring the Plaza, pleased with his day, interviewing engineers, traders, and builders, talking to people happening on his way, asking questions, striking up conversations, reassuring, informing them what was expected from them. Satisfied with what he saw, he made his scribes take notes, writing down the amount of needed materials, talking to the heads of the traders' guild, discussing the quantity of perishable goods that were already in the city and how much more should be brought in and stored. Yes, Tenochtitlan was ready to withstand a siege, so now he could busy himself with the grander strategy of planning how to shift the war into the enemy's lands.

The alleys of the neighborhoods adjacent to the Plaza were usually busy in this time of the evening, with their dwellers preparing for the evening. People moved out the way of his palanquin, but not as hastily as in other places. Important persons were not a novelty in this part of the city. Yet, the alley leading to his friend's house was quiet, strangely lifeless, as though abandoned, cleared by some ominous magic. No people moved around, and no torches lightened the patio or the path leading to the house.

Stepping out of his litter, Tlacaelel looked around, puzzled. The house was inhabited, as he could hear people's voices, could see the silhouettes moving inside, but it didn't look like a place greeting the Master of the House upon his return. In fact, it looked like Tenochtitlan might look if the Tepanecs were more successful than he expected. The sight of an overturned low table near the patio made his nerves prickle.

"Wait for me here," he said to his warriors, heading toward the wooden gate.

A woman he did not recognize came out of the house. Gasping, she stared at the warriors, terrified. After a heartbeat of hesitation, she charged up the path, as though trying to flee.

"What is going on?" he demanded, blocking her way.

"Nothing, Honorable Leader. Nothing at all."

"Who are you? What were you doing in this house?" He moved closer, making sure the woman could not brush past him. She seemed as though pondering this possibility.

"I just came to check on the mistress of this house, Honorable Leader. I'm seeking no trouble." The woman's face grimaced fearfully. "Please, I came in all innocence."

"What happened to the mistress of this house?"

The woman's gaze dropped. "She is not well. She was wounded when the master was taken."

"Taken? Taken where?" Surprised by his own agitation, he tried to moderate his tone. "What happened?"

The woman shifted uneasily, and he wanted to shake her into spilling her story out.

"Tell me in a hurry!" Staring at her sternly, he used his commander's voice, not caring if he scared her any further. He would beat the news out of her if he had to.

Something of it, probably, reflected in his gaze, as the woman's face twisted with fear, and her voice shook. "It happened some time ago. The leader who lives here was taken to the court."

"To the court? At this time of the day? You are talking nonsense. The courts are conducted through the mornings."

"Yes, Honorable Leader, yes, of course. But the warrior wasn't here when the official came for him the first time. So the official returned later, in the early afternoon, and he was accompanied by many warriors. But the Master of the House wouldn't come. And he was rude, and there was a violent exchange..." The woman's voice trailed off as her eyes dropped once again.

"Who got hurt?" asked Tlacaelel, clenching his teeth against the bad feeling. They couldn't have taken him, unless he was dead, or wounded very badly.

"Only the mistress."

"What?" Tired from the fragmented story that didn't make any sense, he grabbed his informer's shoulder, shaking her violently. "Tell me what happened. Now!" He could hear the warriors behind his back holding their breath.

The woman cried out. "I'm telling you everything, Honorable Leader. The warrior wouldn't come, and he wasn't afraid, either. They were arguing loudly, and the whole alley gathered to watch. He said they should go before he spilled the Palace's guards' guts on his patio. Then one of the guards grabbed the mistress." The woman bit her lips. "She was standing right here, where we were standing, and the guards were right there." She pointed at his warriors. "And one grabbed her and the little girl, and he said he would slash her throat. And when the warrior tried to attack him, he pressed it, and we were sure she was going to die. Her throat was bleeding, and she was about to fall."

"And then?"

"Well, then the warrior said he would come, but he promised to avenge himself on every one of them, and the way he said it made us all shiver with fear. Then he went away, and she fainted, and there was a terrible mess, so we, who were friendly with her, came to help. But the others just rushed away. No one wanted any trouble with the Imperial Court."

"The Imperial Court, eh?"

Now the pieces of the mosaic began falling together. Oh, yes, Chimal hated the Highlander, trying to make Itzcoatl get rid of him. But why now? And how was Itzcoatl connected to all this?

"Well, you may go for now." He frowned. "You did a good thing when you came to help her. Come again after I'm gone. Make sure she is all right."

The woman stared at him, puzzled. Then her face crinkled in a careful grin. "Of course, Honorable Leader. I'm always happy to help. My name is..."

But he had already charged up the path, not sparing her

another thought. Bursting through the open door, he glanced at the main room, which was quiet, barely lit, messy, not pretty anymore. He remembered visiting here maybe a market interval ago, enjoying this cozy place and the hospitality of the mistress of this house, everything so warm and pleasant about the house and the woman alike.

Diving into the depths of the rooms, he passed by two terrified maids, bursting into what seemed to be the master's suite – a spacious space of invitingly arranged mats and podiums and chests.

Two unfamiliar women, clearly more neighbors, sprang to their feet, but he ignored them as his eyes drew to the figure on the mat, half sitting half laying, curled into a ball, hugging her knees, so small and fragile, his stomach twisted. Her eyes, enormous in the paleness of her heart-shaped face, now drawn and covered with sweat, leaped toward him. He saw them widening, filling with life.

"Don't," he said, stopping her with a commanding gesture as she made a movement, trying to get up. The little girl, curled up beside her, in a deep sleep but still sobbing, shivered. He neared her hurriedly. "Tell me what happened."

"He was taken by the people of the Imperial Court," she said gruffly, her voice breaking. She cleared her throat, but the motion made her face twist with pain. "Please, you have to help him."

He tore his gaze off her swollen neck and the crusted blood upon it. The side of her cheek was cut, too. "Did they say for what offense?"

She pressed her lips tight, then shook her head. "No, but I know it has something to do with the Emperor and the priests over the incident in the marketplace." She licked her lips. "And it has to do with the Main Adviser, too. He could have prevented it, but he didn't."

The pieces of the mosaic kept falling together, arranging themselves into a very alarming picture. He frowned. But if it was so, then why did the Highlander come back into the city as though nothing happened? If he had known all this, he should be charging for the Acolhua lands without so much as kissing the shores of Tenochtitlan wharves with the tip of his boat.

"How do you know all that? He told you?"

She shook her head, the light in her eyes dying rapidly.

"How then?"

Her gaze, now closed and full of pain, didn't waver. "The Empress told me."

"What?" He stared at her, taken aback. "When did you meet the Empress?"

"Two dawns ago."

"And she told you all that?"

"Yes."

"Why?"

"She wanted me to warn him when he came back." Her face was now a mask chiseled out of lifeless stone, and yet it managed to grow stonier with every word uttered.

"And did you?"

"No."

"Why?"

Her lips quivered, and she pressed them tight, her nostrils widening with every convulsive breath.

"It was my fault," she whispered finally, her voice breaking. "I am to blame."

Taken with compassion, he dropped beside her, pressing her shoulders between his palms carefully, trying to reassure. She was so fragile and forlorn, so brave in her attempts to dominate her fear and her pain, so honest in admitting it all to him. Used to dealing with lies and half-truths, he found her surprisingly refreshing, so utterly different, so unlike the people he had known. Even her husband lacked this sort of straightforwardness and honesty.

"No," he said, pressing her between his palms, but lightly. One wasn't supposed to touch one's warriors' women. "You are not to blame. You did everything you could. I know you did. You must have had a good reason for not telling him. You are the most loyal woman I've ever met. You are not to blame."

Her face did not move. The bottomless eyes, glued to his, did not blink, yet the tears rolled down now, silent and huge, not belonging, as though having a life of their own.

"I tried to do things, stupid things." Her voice trembled so badly, he had a difficult time understanding her words. "I went to his uncle. I spent a whole day there. So stupid. I thought it would solve the problem. And I let that warrior catch me. Like the stupidest marketplace rat, standing there, fat and clumsy, inviting them to use me." She swallowed. "I should have stayed home and waited for him, so I could have told him right away. And I should have been quicker, should have helped him instead of just being there, for them to use, to make him go tamely." Her words gushed out now, like a wild current, trembling, breaking.

He fought the urge to embrace her, to hide her from all this, to spare her as much pain as he could. But an embrace would be utterly inappropriate. He shouldn't have been touching her at all. Even reassuring hands on her shoulders were wrong, a troublesome situation or not. One doesn't touch the wives of one's friends, neither chief nor minor.

"Listen to me," he said, taking his hands away, but picking up a cushion to prop it behind her back, to make her more comfortable. "You are not to blame. Of all people, you are the last person to be at fault. He did stupid things. More than a few. But he is a lucky bastard, and you are a part of his luck. So, for now, put him out of your head and take care of yourself. Were you hurt badly?"

She shrugged.

"Where is that healer woman, that friend of yours? Did you send for her?"

Her eyes widened while her eyebrows met each other across her sweaty forehead, making her look like a very young girl. "Oh, I forgot... I didn't think... Yes, I will send for her. Yes, of course, that was stupid of me."

"Do that." He frowned. "I will send my warriors to fetch her, in case she makes trouble because it's so late."

"No, no! Please don't." She straightened up abruptly as though trying to physically stop him from doing that, but her face twisted and she let out a gasp, clutching her stomach. "Please, don't," she repeated quietly, leaning back against the wall, her face glistening with sweat. "She is a friend. She will come."

He looked up. The women were still there, huddled near the doorway, watching them, consumed with curiosity. His look sent them scattering.

"Send her maids to that healer from the marketplace," he called after them. "Or do it yourself. And hurry!" He turned back to her. "I'll make sure he is all right. You can trust me. Just take care of yourself for now."

Her eyes filled with tears once again, and it made his heart twist. She wasn't concerned with herself in the least. She was just worried about her man, regretting that she hadn't done more to save him, not bothered with the fact that she was the one who had been hurt. Did the Highlander deserve to be loved in this way?

"He will be taken to the Palace, I suppose." He began to get up.

There was a rustling outside, and a round face appeared at the opening in the wall. With the nimbleness and grace of a small animal, the boy pulled himself up, throwing his body over the windowsill, landing on the floor lightly. A jaguar cub. Was that the one called Ocelotl, the Jaguar?

She came to life all at once. "Coatl, where have you been?" she called out, stretching her arm toward him. "Where is your brother? Why did you come in this way?"

The boy hesitated. "There are warriors outside the gate," he said, not taking his eyes off Tlacaelel, wary and ready to flee.

"They are my warriors, boy. Answer your mother. Where have you been?"

The large eyes studied him carefully, clearly pondering the possibilities. "Just around," said the boy finally.

"Where is your brother?" Her voice had a ring of panic to it now.

"He is around, too."

"You are not telling the truth, boy," said Tlacaelel, very put out. It was not the time for silly children's tricks.

"The Honorable Warlord is going to help your father. He is with us," she pleaded, making Tlacaelel angrier yet. Those boys needed to be disciplined. "Please go and fetch your brother."

The boy bit his lips, a frown not sitting well with his fine, delicate features.

"They put Father in the temple, near the Plaza. The temple of Huitzilopochtli," he said in the end.

"What?"

"Not in the temple itself. But there was this stupid thing under the stairs, outside. Like a cabin or something." The boy's eyes measured them carefully, still wary and obviously ready to bolt for the window.

"That's where they put people after the trials, to await their execution," said Tlacaelel, then wanted to push the words back, hearing her gasp. "It doesn't mean anything," he added, glancing at her before turning back to the boy. "How do you know that?"

"We followed them." The boy returned his gaze, his eyes large and slanted like these of his mother's, glimmering darkly in the paleness of his face, holding none of their usual sparkling mischief. Oh, this family had been put through much this afternoon, he realized.

"And where is your brother?"

"He stayed to watch, in case they try to take Father somewhere else. I just came to tell Mother. I'm going back now."

"No," she pleaded, but her voice held none of her usual brisk determination. She dropped her gaze, hugging her knees tightly. "How is he?" she whispered. "Did he try to do something? Did they hurt him?"

"No!" The boy's eyes sparkled proudly. "He just kept telling them what he will do to them. All the way to the Plaza. He was so angry. And scary. He told awful things." His lips twisted. "They were scared, too. I could see that. They were afraid of him. He had no sword, and they were still afraid of him. They locked him in this place, and they stayed to guard him, all of them." He shrugged. "Then Ocelotl stayed to watch, and I came here, to see if you... if you were well." He glanced at his mother from under his brow, and suddenly looked just like the little boy he was.

Her lips quivered. "You are a good boy, Coatl. You and your brother. You are the best boys ever!" She looked at him imploringly. "But now that the Honorable Warlord is taking care of this trouble, please, go and fetch your brother and come back here. We may need to go to another place to stay, and... and we should be together..."

"No!" exclaimed Coatl, backing away toward the window. "We are going to stay there until they leave, then we will let Father free."

"They won't go anywhere, boy," said Tlacaelel, suppressing a grin. What a funny plan! "But you did a sensible thing. Your mother is right. I will make sure no one does any harm to your father. So just take me there now. But then you both are coming back here, and it's an order. I'm not your father; I will punish you hard if you don't obey."

The boy tried to stand his glare bravely, but in no time his eyes were back upon the floor. Lips pursed, eyebrows forming a straight line beneath his forehead, he stood there stubbornly, his whole posture radiating his resentment.

"Is that clear, boy?"

"Yes." The word came out muffled, having difficulty seeping through the clenched teeth.

"Good." He turned back to her. "And you, stop worrying about him. Make sure you are well and ready to receive him back. I would rather have you moved to another place, though. If only Coyotl were here... I don't want you to stay here all alone, not after what happened. Especially if he'll have to flee." He pursed his lips. "I'll leave a few of my warriors to guard you, in the meanwhile."

But he knew it was a bad idea. If the Highlander had to flee, or worse yet, if he did what Itzcoatl was clearly trying to push him to do, his warriors wouldn't help her. They would be the ones required to do the imperial bidding, should the Emperor wish to make an example out of this man's family.

"As soon as I'm better I will take the children and go to his uncle's house," she said quietly.

"To the old Tepanec?" He hesitated. It could have been a good idea, but would the old nobleman agree to help her? Did he approve of his nephew's family? The First Warlord of Tenochtitlan was a highborn aristocrat, brought up in Azcapotzalco itself. He had clearly forgiven his nephew some of the more common blood flowing through his veins, but he might not be as tolerant toward this woman's humble origins. "Well, it could be a good idea. I'll talk to him tomorrow and will let you know."

She smiled guiltily. "I talked to him already. Well, before it happened. I hoped he would be able to help Kuini, and he promised to help. He said Kuini might have to go away, but that he will protect us in the meanwhile." She looked at him searchingly. "Do you think it will cause too much trouble for him?"

"No. If he suggested it, then it is perfectly all right."

So much like her, he thought, slightly amused, admiring her once again. To take care of all the small details. She would have made a good wife – a Chief Wife – even for such a household as his. Pity that she belonged to the Highlander and had no noble blood whatsoever.

"If you are certain that he will receive you, then I'll send you and the child there now in my palanquin. The twins I'll send later, after they have shown me the place." He gave the boy a direful look. "Tied and dragged all the way, if need be."

The rebellious gaze and the ready-to-flee posture were his answer.

"Thank you," she said, her voice breaking once again. "I'm grateful, so grateful. You are so good to us! I wish I could express my gratitude properly. I wish I could do something wonderful for you. If one day I am able to repay you your kindness, I'll die a happy person."

Watching her bottomless eyes, so innocent and open, so trusting, he swallowed the knot in his throat. "You have no cause to feel grateful. He saved my life many times. And I know he will do it more in the future. I owe him this. As for you..." He shrugged and signaled the boy. "Come. Take me to that temple of yours, and remember, one word of argument, one gesture of disobedience..." He tried to keep his grin from showing, watching this small replica of his friend, standing there, legs wide apart, as though readying to withstand the attack. Another unruly, resourceful spirit, but this time a double version of the same thing.

Oh, gods, he thought. *I pity their future leaders, and the teachers of their calmecac, too.* And yet, what those boys had done tonight was a useful, sensible, very brave thing to do. Why, not every pair of children only six summers old would do this, not after their mother was nearly slain before their very eyes by those same warriors they chose to follow, devising a naive plan of rescuing their father. Were they that fond of the Highlander, too? Oh, this man enjoyed too much loyalty and love, that much was obvious.

"My palanquin bearers will wait outside, and I'll leave some warriors to escort you to the old Tepanec's place as well. They are waiting by the gate. When you are ready, send your maids, and they'll come and fetch you." He held her gaze, trying to relate to her a calmness he didn't feel. "Remember, I'm taking care of it now. So put it out of your head, and take care of yourself."

CHAPTER 11

Iztac stretched lazily, watching the sun flowing in through the open shutters. For a heartbeat she hesitated, contemplating calling her maids and demanding they close the shades.

She liked to sleep late, but recently, with all the hectic activity, with the turmoil in the gods accursed Azcapotzalco, she had to wake up early. Not with the sunrise like the warriors, but early enough. Chimal used to start his days way before midmorning meals, busy meeting his subjects, besieged with advisers, engineers, leaders of districts, and traders' guilds. And then, after the first meal, it was off to the courts, and more meetings, discussions, deliberations, many of them apprehensive and troubled since the death of the legal Tepanecs ruler.

She buried her head under the blanket, but the sleep wouldn't come. There would be no meetings today, as Chimal was supposed to go out and tour the city, to show himself, to reassure people, to let them know that their Emperor was confident and not afraid. The looming war with the Tepanecs preyed on everyone's mind, and if Tenochtitlan was to withstand a siege, its citizens should be kept as calm and as positively inclined as possible.

Turning again, she curled around one of the cushions. The damn Tepanecs, she thought. They were warring on her again. Conquering her former people, her beautiful Texcoco, was not enough. Now they coveted Tenochtitlan, and just as she had begun regarding this place as her home. Cursing softly, she listened to the careful footsteps. The maids were bringing in trays, carrying her favorite chocolate drink. The clinking of cup against flask had told her that.

Iztac sat up abruptly, defeated.

"How did you know I was awake?" she asked Chiko, her main maid.

"I didn't, Revered Empress," said the woman, smiling. "I just guessed. You've been moving around for some time." Her smile widening, the woman put the tray down. "It's not very early, anyway."

"Well, it's early enough," complained Iztac, feeling ridiculous. It was not their fault. They did not wake her up. The Tepanecs were to blame. And also her nagging worry.

The day before, the moment she had seen Tlacaelel returning, she had fought the temptation to send her trusted girl with the message. The Highlander needed to be warned. Chimal seemed to be determined, and Tlacaelel might have been too busy to interfere. And yet, she had fought the temptation and did not send word to him. His so-called chief wife had been warned.

Pursing her lips, she remembered their meeting. Oh, what gall! This woman had no shame. To threaten the Empress of Tenochtitlan, to tell her to stay away from the insignificant *cihua*'s path? Oh, what cheek, and coming from such a small, fragile, innocent-looking creature. Unbelievable! But at least it meant that the filthy *cihua* was strong and determined, and so should have been able to properly relate her, Iztac's, message. Therefore, today she could send for him safely.

She took a deep breath, fighting to keep her smile from showing. Today, she'd arrange a nice, private place for their meeting, to warn him, and also to spend some time with him. A better time than in that temple more than a market interval ago. Picking up her cup, she found herself grinning openly now. Yes, he should be allowed to worship his goddess properly. He owed her that, too. He had said it himself.

"Here you are," said the maid, chuckling. "All smiling now. Such a quick change. But now, let us take care of your hair and your clothes—"

"I want it washed with indigo this morning!" declared Iztac. "And my eyebrows need to be taken care of, too." She hesitated.

"The Emperor has no morning meetings, does he?"

Another maid peeked in, signaling with her eyes.

"What is it now?" grunted Chiko, hurrying for the doorway.

Where should she organize their meeting? thought Iztac, sipping her chocolate. Some place with light. He needed to see her properly, and she would wear her favorite topaz bracelets and anklets that would sparkle off her skin, which she would oil just a little...

"Revered Mistress, the Noble Lady, the Third Wife of the First Chief Warlord, is wishing to pay her respects to you," said Chiko, returning.

"At this time of the morning?"

"It's not that early, Revered Mistress. The sun has been in the sky for some time."

"Well, maybe for you and the other commoners, but for a Toltec princess?" Iztac snorted. "By the time such a lady would leave her sleeping quarters and be done with her appearances, the sun would be on its way back to its resting place." She frowned. "I don't want to receive anyone. I'm all tussled, and I want to drink my chocolate in peace. It is the first morning with no Emperor's meetings and no politics. I want to enjoy one morning of quiet!"

But the maid's face twisted with regret. "Of course! Of course, you deserve a quiet morning. But you can't refuse to see such a noble lady."

"I know that!" Putting her cup back, Iztac banged it pointedly against the tray. "Well, if the noble lady has trouble sleeping this morning, then she will have to do with the Empress all tussled and untidy. I hope her haughty Toltec eyes will not pop out in disgust. Send her in."

"But, Revered Mistress—"

"Send her in!"

She made herself more comfortable upon the mat, tucking a cushion under her elbow, reclining in what she thought was a royal posture. She was the Empress, and it was still early in the morning.

Nibbling on a slice of avocado, she frowned, wondering what the haughty noblewoman might want from her. They had met on many official occasions, but never in private. The Toltec princess was old, at least ten summers older than Iztac or more, and she had been a friend of the previous Empress, the awful Tepanec woman. Iztac snorted. No, they had nothing in common.

She watched the tall woman coming in, nearing with graceful paces, walking the invisible straight line, light and delicate. In the sunlight, her hair shone like perfectly polished obsidian, clearly having already been washed with indigo. When did this one wake up in the morning?

"Greetings, pretty Empress," she said in her melodious, slightly accented voice, not bothering with proper titles. "It is such a delight to see a face as beautiful as yours so early in the morning."

Oh, yes, it is early, thought Iztac. *Nice of you to notice that.*

"Greetings, Noble Lady," she answered as sweetly. "The delight is all mine. I'm honored and pleased with your visit. I wish we could meet more often."

"Maybe we should." The woman's large, pleasantly slanted eyes measured Iztac with an amused appreciation, as though not having seen her before, not properly. Gracefully, she knelt upon the opposite mat and allowed the maids to pad her seat with cushions, making sure the rims of her flame-colored skirt encircled her legs in a perfect half circle.

"Well, Noble Empress," she said when the maids served the refreshments and both their cups were filled with more foamy chocolate. "I'm glad to see you so beautiful and well, not a heartbeat older since the day you became an empress."

"Oh, thank you, but I'm none of that this morning," said Iztac, forcing another wide, exaggeratedly polite smile. "I feel the weight of the trouble our *altepetl* is facing along with the weight of my years today."

"Oh, yes, the treacherous policies of the Tepanec royal house are troubling everyone's sleep these days," agreed the woman. She was held to be a great beauty, but in the daylight and the close proximity she looked more her age, noticed Iztac, studying the lines running alongside the generous mouth.

"Your husband was the First Warlord of Tenochtitlan. He must be worried over the possibility of the Tepanec attack."

"Oh, he worries. Of course, he does." The woman's smile turned amused once again. "But both the current and the former Chief Warlords are honoring his house with their visits, coming for good conversation and good advice. It makes him feel involved and, therefore, satisfied. He thinks we will be able to weather this storm." The large eyes twinkled. "You know how the men are."

"Well, *my* husband is worried," said Iztac, a little put out with this chattiness. They were not friends. This woman was a friend of the previous empress. Had they gossiped with each other this way, too?

The woman's plucked eyebrows climbed high, letting Iztac know that she should control her temper better.

"Your husband is a very able young man, and he has good advisers. He should trust their opinions more, though, if you ask me. Some of them are wise and very capable, having long summers of experience behind them." A cold smile twisted the full lips. "You are a wise woman yourself, so I hear. You should think more like a ruler and less like a woman."

Having a hard time coping with the suddenness of her rage, Iztac clutched her cup tight.

"You think too highly of me, Noble Lady. I think neither like a ruler, nor like a woman. And if, sometimes, the Emperor finds my advice to be of value to him, I'm honored. Yet, I do not presume to sound my opinions often. I'm just the First Wife of the Emperor. I'm nothing like the previous Empress of Tenochtitlan."

Here, have this, she thought, glaring at her uninvited visitor. *Your friend was a pushy good-for-nothing. But I'm not her. You won't come here to advise me on how to run an empire.*

The woman's smile widened, turned genuine, surprisingly so.

"Oh, I'm sure you are all that and more, pretty Empress. I should not presume to advise you, should I?" She picked up her cup and studied the foam before bringing it to her lips. "Oh, this chocolate is good. The Palace's kitchen slaves know how to prepare it, don't they?"

Still seething, Iztac finished her drink. "I love chocolate," she said, appreciating the obvious attempt to lighten the conversation. "I had to switch quite a few slaves before they served me my drink as I like it."

"Oh, yes, not every kitchen slave would know how to prepare a proper chocolate drink. I had to change quite a few slaves myself."

What do you want? thought Iztac, puzzled. *Why are we having this meaningless conversation?* She watched the beautiful face, refusing to contribute yet another empty phrase to the silly dialogue. Who cared for the troubles of maintaining and organizing the slaves? Didn't this woman have better things to do with her morning?

"Your husband seems to have a busy day ahead of him," said the woman, as chatty as before. "He intended to tour the city, didn't he?"

"You are well informed."

"Oh, this information is no secret. The whole of Tenochtitlan is talking about it, expecting to see their Emperor, expecting to be reassured. His Chief Warlord does this same thing. The vigorous leader of the warriors was seen all around the city yesterday, checking the causeways and the gates, talking to people, making sure Tenochtitlan is ready and not afraid. A very impressive young man. My husband thinks highly of him."

"My husband appreciates his half brother's efforts and abilities very much, too. He made this man his Chief Warlord for a reason. He doesn't need to be reminded of this man's virtues." Iztac concentrated, suddenly on guard. There was something about this light, gossipy conversation. The woman was trying to get somewhere.

"Oh, yes, I'm sure he does. Tlacaelel is the person to make sure Tenochtitlan withstands any attack or invasion." The large eyes rested on Iztac, their expression light. "So the Emperor just needs to encourage the people some more." A shrug. "And yet, he spends his time judging in Imperial Court. Why would he try people during war time? Let alone warriors."

"Well, there are matters the judges of the districts cannot deal with," began Iztac, finding it difficult to follow the constantly changing conversation. From her involvement in the imperial matters, to Tlacaelel, to Tenochtitlan's readiness for war, to the imperial courts, what was this woman trying to say? "The Imperial Court has to be convened from time to time."

"But in war time?" The woman shook her head. "Why try warriors, let alone leaders of warriors, when Tenochtitlan is about to be invaded?"

"Well, I suppose, if the warriors committed some offense against the royal house..." And then it dawned on her, and she caught her breath, staring at the woman, unable to think. "Is there... is there a trial? This morning?"

"Yes, there is a trial this morning." Something lurked in the depths of her guest's eyes, and the gaze resting on Iztac grew piercing before turning back into its typical, haughtily amused lightness. "A minor leader of the warriors, mind you. Not anyone of importance. The man must be guilty of a serious crime against the royal house, to justify the convention of the Imperial Court at such difficult times."

She tried to get a grip of her senses, then felt the cup slipping from her fingers. It fell with a bang, rolling over the floor, splashing the last of the chocolate. They both watched it come to a stop, fascinated.

"When? When is the trial?" She was hardly able to recognize her own voice, so strangled, unnaturally high it sounded.

The woman watched her, frowning, her smile gone.

"This morning," she said finally, her face softening, filling with compassion. "Maybe now."

Now? In these very moments?

"I... I don't understand. How? Why was I not told?"

But, of course! Of course, she hadn't been told. Chimal promised not to discuss this matter with her again, not after she screamed at him and accused him of all sorts of unfounded charges. And now he was in the court, and she needed to do something urgently. Or maybe it was too late. She clasped her palms tight and felt the pain as her nails sank into her flesh.

"I'm sorry," she heard the woman saying, and it helped her a little, forced her to concentrate on something tangible. She needed to get rid of her guest first.

"I... I'm sorry. What were you saying?" She stared at the beautiful face, seeing none of the previous arrogance but only a genuine concern.

"We can ride in my palanquin if you want to. It's spacious, and my bearers know their trade. We won't be tossed more than necessary."

Iztac blinked, painfully aware that she still had not been able to understand this woman, not fully. "To ride in your palanquin? Where?"

"To see the trial, of course. Where else?"

"But I need to see Chimal first. I need to talk to him. I have to..." She bit her lips until it hurt. *Why was she saying this aloud?* "Please, I need to do things. I'm sorry. I will be honored if you visit me again..." Her voice trailed off under the mirthless smile of her visitor.

"The Emperor must already be on the Plaza. It's nearing midmorning. But you will be able to talk to him after that. Maybe you could join him on his tour around the city. The people of Tenochtitlan will be delighted to see their beautiful Empress as cheerful and as unafraid as their ruler. While riding with him, you may have a chance to talk to him about this warrior, to make him postpone any degree of punishment he may have decided upon." The woman hesitated. "I'm sorry I came so late. I wish I had been able to warn you in time."

Iztac just stared. Somehow she was on her feet now, but she didn't remember herself getting up. "Why do you do this? How does any of this concern you?"

The woman's lips stretched. "It concerns me, believe me, it does. I've been sheltering this warrior's family since they arrived at the warlord's house last night. It wasn't pretty, what happened." Shaking her head, the woman pursed her lips. "Sometimes the officials and their guards can be quite brutal, when not obeyed."

She clasped her mouth with her palm, feeling as though she were wandering through a horrible maze, like that of the Underworld, where every turn, every path was worse than the previous one. But, of course! Of course, he didn't go tamely. Not him, never him!

"Was he hurt?" she whispered and was hardly able to understand her own words, the way they came out through her palm, muffled and blurred.

The woman's eyes sparkled with what seemed to be a hint of anger.

"No," she said impatiently. "He was made to go tamely while someone else got hurt."

"Who?" Her relief was too vast, impossible to conceal.

The frown upon the beautiful face deepened. "No one that would concern you." It came out hostile, almost an accusation.

"What do you mean? Did he kill any of the guards? The officials?"

"He didn't kill anyone," said the woman impatiently. "He went with no trouble because they threatened to cut his woman's throat. They almost did it, too. She is in a bad shape now, poor girl." The almond-shaped eyes narrowed. "But I'm sure it will not make you sick with worry."

"They did this?" Oh, yes, this would make him go tamely. Or would it? She thought about the cheeky *cihua*. So she was almost cut and in a bad shape. How bad? "What happened to her?"

The woman shrugged and rose to her feet, as graceful as before. "I'm sure you don't care to know. So let us go and make sure you do everything you can to save this warrior."

But Iztac refused to move, facing the woman, about the same height as she was. Something was not right in this story; something was missing.

"Why are you concerned with his safety?" Then she remembered. "Oh, he is the warlord's nephew. That's why you are willing to help."

The beautiful eyes sparkled angrily. "No, this is not why I'm willing to help. My husband has his own ways of saving his nephew, and believe me, he is doing his best in these very moments. However, he wouldn't try to solve this problem through me, or you, or any other woman for that matter. He doesn't think that highly of women." The generous lips pressed into a thin line. "He is not aware of my humble attempts to help. And I'm not doing this for your, or for your warrior's, sake, either. I'm doing it for *her*. The poor girl is too concerned with his safety to take care of herself, and she needs all her strength now. That's why I want you to save him. For her. Only for her!"

Speechless, Iztac stared at the furious face, seeing the high, perfectly Toltec cheekbones, the oval eyes narrow and blazing, the generous curve of the mouth pressed tightly. She had seen enough of this woman over the summers, and she had heard about her, too. Such a perfect, aristocratic lady, always in control, always unreadable, concealed behind her haughty, good-natured mask. Well, now the mask was off, revealing the person inside the perfect statue.

"Was she hurt badly?" she asked.

The woman raised her eyebrows, and her cold eyes held Iztac's gaze for a heartbeat.

"She will not die from her wounds. But she may lose her child, and in this stage, it could be quite dangerous."

The sun was already high in the sky, promising yet another hot day. Pressing her palms tight, Iztac huddled in the cozy palanquin, half hidden by the colorful curtain. She didn't want to be seen, neither by Chimal, nor by anyone else, as, of course, empresses didn't sneak to watch imperial trials uninvited. They had better things to do.

Luckily, Cuicatl's palanquin bearers did, indeed, know their trade. Not only had they made the litter sway steadily, almost pleasantly, but they also had enough sense to place it on the higher ground near one of the temples, so the two noblewomen could watch the happenings without the need to get up or clear the way through the crowds.

"Here, we can watch with no fear of being seen," said Cuicatl, satisfied. She brushed a leaf off her richly embroidered skirt, then accepted a small cloth from the hands of her maid. "It's starting to become hot already," she said, wiping her delicate brow.

Iztac didn't bother to answer, her eyes on the crowds surrounding the imperial dais. It seemed as if many onlookers had gathered to see the trial. From their vantage point she could see Chimal clearly, sitting on his reed chair, his face pale, serene, closed, frowning but not direfully, his usual pleasant, serious self.

The Highlander stood before the dais, half hidden by the surrounding guards, probably all twenty of them, or maybe more, alerted and tense. She strained her eyes, willing them to move away, as all she could see were his wide shoulders and the back of his head, high and proud, his warriors' lock swaying in the slight breeze. By the way he stood there, she guessed that his hands were probably tied behind his back.

"He reminds me of my husband," whispered Cuicatl, making herself comfortable upon her cushioned seat. "Same height, same width, same proud bearing. The Warlord was never too obedient or deferential, either. Not even with the Emperor. They say he respected Acamapichtli, but when I was given to him, Acamapichtli was already dead, and the Warlord never paid the proper respect to his successor, Huitzilihuitl."

"When I was given to Huitzilihuitl, the Warlord had already left his position to Itzcoatl," said Iztac absently, watching the priests and the officials talking to the Emperor at length, each in his turn. Presenting their case, she assumed, not bothering to try to listen, wishing all of them dead. How dare they persecute him?

"Oh, yes, of course. You were given to Revered Huitzilihuitl much later, when our *altepetl* had changed its policies toward your, Acolhua, people." There was a smile in the woman's voice. "Oh, how my husband resented that. Tepanec himself, he hated to see Tenochtitlan falling under the Tepanec rule. Curious, isn't it?"

"Well, yes, maybe," muttered Iztac, watching Chimal nodding, listening to the officials. She tried to listen to what they said, but their voices were carried the other way, muffled by the breeze.

"The Emperor is about to speak."

I can see that, she thought, enraged. Couldn't the annoying *cihua* just shut up for a few heartbeats?

"I hear the accusations, and I find this man guilty of murder," said Chimal, not getting up, his voice clear, carrying above the crowds. He had learned the technique of oratory diligently, Iztac knew, practicing the ability to pitch his voice higher when talking to the crowds. "What do you have to say to justify your deeds, warrior?"

The Highlander's shoulders straightened up even more, although they were anything but sagging before.

"I've heard what I'm accused of, and I say that those accusations are as wild as they are unfounded." His voice carried over the Plaza as clearly as Chimal's had, loud and powerful, a voice of a man used to giving orders on the battlefield. Iztac caught her breath, her heart squeezing with pride. "The murdered adviser was the one guilty of treason. Not me. But what's the use of me saying that? You are set on finding me guilty, Emperor. You are eager to execute me, and we both know it has nothing to do with the filthy adviser."

Chimal's face paled visibly as he drew in a sharp breath. "You are accused of murdering the adviser and two of the foreign traders and visitors of my *altepetl*. Are you guilty of that or not?"

"The adviser was plotting against you and some of the noble guests of your Palace, with those same foreign traders or visitors. There is a scroll to prove that. Ask your Chief Warlord. But why would you bother investigating this case? You are too anxious to have me executed to bother with proper procedures. Why spend your time on this farce?"

She could see Chimal's knuckles whitening as he clutched onto his chair, his lips pressing tight, eyes blazing. "This is the proper way to conduct a court case, foreigner! You did murder this man, didn't you? That is all I wish to know."

"I've killed hundreds of men through the long summers I've been a warrior." The Highlander's voice rolled over the crowded Plaza, resounding against the temples' walls. "And I captured a few alive, too. Many of those while fighting for the glory of your *altepetl*." He turned his head, and now Iztac could see his eagle-like profile, and the way his nostril widened angrily with every breath. "Most of those people were brave, courageous, worthy adversaries. They are in the warrior's paradise now, enjoying their well deserved stay in this wonderful place. But the adviser? The adviser was nothing but a slimy, detestable lowlife with no honor and no dignity. To execute me for his murder is to spit on the memory of the fallen warriors, each and every one of them!"

The Plaza went so silent that they could hear the buzzing of the insects and the distant clamor coming from the wharves.

"I've heard enough!" cried out Chimal. "I've found this man guilty of murder—"

"Of course, you do!" The Highlander's voice thundered, still controlled and not contorted in any way. "But even with me dead, you will never get what you really want, Emperor. I was there first, long before you came along. You may think I was taking what was yours, but it was the other way around. You had taken what was mine! And my death will not change anything for you. Remember my words. You will always be chasing what you can't have."

Chimal leaped to his feet so forcefully, his chair went flying. "Silence, you insolent foreigner! You will be stoned here on the Plaza before the sun will run its course today. Because of your insolence, you will receive the worst punishment, reserved only for the lowest of criminals. No honorable death for you, you savage. Take him away!"

The salty taste in her mouth brought Iztac to her senses. Head reeling, she tried to unclench her teeth, her lips bleeding, limbs numbed, turned into stone.

A gentle palm brushed against her arm.

"Are you all right, girl?"

She tried to concentrate. "Yes, yes, I'm all right."

Unable to tear her eyes off the Plaza, she watched the guards surrounding him coming to life, peering at him, ready for trouble. But, of course, he was too proud to resist when they began clearing their way through the crowds, away from the Plaza, away from the enraged Emperor upon the dais. She saw people murmuring, beginning to move about.

"That was quite a show." The melodious voice startled her once again. "A fascinating young man. I can see what you two see in him."

"I... I should go back," muttered Iztac, unclenching her fists with an effort. "I need to... to talk to him, probably." She moved her fingers, trying to recover the feeling in her numb palms.

"To talk to the Emperor?" Cuicatl's eyes narrowed dubiously. "I don't think it'll help. Your glorious hero made sure the Emperor won't be able to forgive."

"Itzcoatl," said Iztac firmly, getting a grip on her senses. "I'll talk to him. And Tlacaelel, too. They may not know what is happening. One of them may be able to help."

"The Adviser knows. My husband talked to him this morning." The woman shrugged, then signaled the palanquin bearers. "But yes, talk to the Chief Warlord. And anyone else who might be able to help. I wouldn't bet many cocoa beans on this young man's life now, but who knows? With so many highborn friends and sympathizers, he may be able to escape the Emperor's wrath yet. Somehow." The full lips quivered, turning into an inverted sort of a smile. "It was about you, wasn't it? This last exchange. Was he really there before the Emperor?" The large eyes sparkled against Iztac's furious gaze, unafraid. "Oh, girl, don't give me those furious looks. I have discovered too many secrets over the past few days, and, like your warrior, I'm not afraid of the royal wrath."

CHAPTER 12

Watching the queue of canoes forming a line before the closing wooden partition of a bridge yet again, Tlacaelel sighed. He would rather have sailed all the way up to the Plaza, but with the excessive traffic of too many canoes, this journey was taking too much of his time. On the dry land everyone would be scattering, anxious to clear his way, but the long, narrow canal and its regulated traffic made it impossible for the people to pay him the proper respect.

"Get closer to the shore," he said to his rower curtly, not bothering with explanations.

As the boat kissed wooden planks, Tlacaelel leaped out of it, scrambling up the incline, loving the solidness of the dry land. His warriors left the boat as promptly, not requiring an explanation as well.

Wiping his brow, he narrowed his eyes, measuring the sun. It was still very high, but he frowned nevertheless. When he had sailed for Tlatelolco this morning, he hadn't planned on spending half a day there. He just needed to ensure the loyalty of this nearby island, as the thought had occurred to him during the night that someone of importance must visit it. After the untimely death of its ruler, Tlatelolco might have fallen prey to all sorts of silly ideas, like siding with the powerful Tepanecs, for one.

So, before the dawn broke, he had left Tenochtitlan, having no opportunity to talk to either Chimal or Itzcoatl. The trouble with the Highlander would have to wait. More serious matters were at stake. Yet now, he began feeling bad, because he didn't keep his promise to *her*. Last night, when the boy had shown him the temple, he had wanted to enter, but the warriors guarding the entrance were apologetic but firm. Their orders were to keep the prisoner alone, with no visitors, unless authorized by the Emperor himself. Although uncomfortable in denying entrance to the Chief Warlord, they held their ground, so he went back to the Palace, seething. What was Chimal's game?

"Shall I send for your palanquin, Honorable Warlord?" asked the leader of his warriors, tearing him out of his reverie.

"No. We will head straight for the Palace." Tlacaelel looked around, squinting against the glow of the midday sun. "We'll go by the way of the causeway. The engineers will be there now, and I need to talk to their headman."

What in the name of the Underworld? he wondered, nearing the Plaza, which burst upon them, teeming with life. He watched people rushing about, chattering, agitated, more lively than its typical hubbub. By the wide base of the Great Pyramid, he saw the engineers' cloaks sweeping by.

"Bring them here," he ordered one of his warriors, eyeing the crowds, puzzled. Something was out of the ordinary, something was amiss. What? Had the Tepanecs made a move? Sent the customary *tizatl* and the armor? What had he missed spending his morning in Tlatelolco?

"Honorable Warlord?" The main engineer rushed toward him, out of breath.

"What are you doing here? Aren't you and your men supposed to be taking care of the earthworks?"

"Yes, of course, Honorable Warlord. We were on our way there now."

"What were you doing on the Plaza?"

The man hesitated, dropping his gaze. "We were just passing by. There was a trial, and we stopped to watch. The Plaza was impossible to cross anyway, it was crowded so badly." The man looked up, imploring, clutching onto his scrolls. "But I promise you, Honorable Warlord, the last embankment will be ready before sunset. I promise you that personally, Honorable Leader. You won't be disappointed."

Tlacaelel narrowed his eyes, put out with the man's obvious

fear.

"Before sunset, engineer! It had better be ready before sunset. Remember, you are not here to take strolls around the Plaza and watch trials."

He shook his head. People must be truly upset with the impending war, out of their usual busy selves, to crowd the Plaza for a petty trial.

Then it hit him.

"Was there a trial this morning?"

The tall man nodded readily. "The Revered Emperor sentenced a warrior to be stoned on the Plaza this evening, so the people are expectant."

"What?" Embarrassed by his own agitated reaction, Tlacaelel struggled to keep his voice calm. "When?"

"Today, before sunset."

He tried to organize his thoughts. "Tell me about that trial. All of it!"

The engineer's forehead broke out with beads of sweat. "Well, Honorable Leader, the Emperor judged a warrior, for that murder on the marketplace. The one that happened some time ago." Struggling to keep his scrolls from falling, the man wiped his face. "The warrior was very insolent, and kept saying strange things that made the Emperor furious. So he was sentenced to stoning, today, before the sun runs its course. That is all, Honorable Leader."

Tlacaelel made an effort to control himself, seeing the man looking as though he were about to take a step back, shrinking under his gaze.

"Well, engineer, take your men and go back to your causeway. Work by torches at night if you must, but make sure the last earthwork is ready for tomorrow." He turned to the leader of his warriors. "Take ten men to the guard house. The other ten are coming with me."

Not bothering to make sure his orders were followed, he turned around and stormed the Plaza, heading toward the temple of Huitzilopochtli, his thoughts whirling, not well organized. So Chimal had taken it personally, and the Highlander was enraged enough to abandon any caution and normal sort of behavior. If ever the wild man had behaved normally. He cursed aloud. The damn stupid, unruly foreigner! Why, why did he always live as though there were no rules but his own?

The temple's walls shone brilliantly against the strong, midday sun, peaceful and tranquil. No warriors guarded the entrance, and only a young priest crouched inside, organizing baskets of thorns for a private self sacrifice.

"Where is the warrior who was held here through the night?" asked Tlacaelel curtly, not bothering with polite pleasantries.

"He was taken away, Honorable Warlord," answered the priest composedly, getting to his feet.

"When?"

"Not very long ago."

"By whom?"

"By the people of the Honorable Adviser." The priest hesitated. "The warriors didn't want to let them have their prisoner. There was an argument." A slight grin lit the man's tired face. "A heated argument. Then the Adviser's men took the warrior away."

"Did he make any trouble?"

"No. The foreigner seemed to be relieved, actually."

"Well, thank you. Soon you will have worthy offerings for the great god to enjoy."

"I thank you, Revered Warlord. May you have many glorious battles ahead of you."

Once outside, Tlacaelel hesitated, wanting to curse again. It seemed that he could not do much for his friend now. Between the Emperor, thirsty for his blood, and the Adviser, thirsty for his abilities to shed the Emperor's blood, the Highlander was caught, firmly and hopelessly. Oh, he still may have succeeded in wriggling out of this situation – the man's ability to survive was remarkable – but there was nothing he, Tlacaelel, could do to help him anymore. And yet…

Slowly, he went up the road, deep in thought. And yet, he had promised. He remembered her bottomless eyes, so trusting and innocent, and in pain. He had promised her that he would save her man, and she had trusted him, relieved, ridiculously grateful, still beautiful and appealing even through her suffering.

He pressed his lips tight. He should not be thinking about any of this. He had the troubles of Tenochtitlan upon his shoulders. The Highlander and his woman were just two people, two of the many he had to take care of. The boy burst upon him out of the bushes lining the road, startling him. Dust smeared and scratched, his loincloth torn, his muddied hair covering his face, he looked strikingly wild, a vision from one of the forest tales.

"Go away, you filthy piece of dung," shouted one of the warriors, trying to kick the boy away.

"I need to talk to you!" cried the boy out, avoiding the grabbing hand of the other warrior with the light ease of a catlike creature. He rushed toward Tlacaelel, but another warrior caught him by his long, uncut hair, pulling hard, making the twin cry out. Struggling to keep his balance, the wild thing turned to face his attacker, evading renewed attempt to grab him, but as the palm of the first warrior landed across his head, he wavered and lost his balance.

"Leave him alone," said Tlacaelel. "What do you want, boy?"

Landing on his hands and knees, the twin scrambled to his feet nimbly, avoiding the kick of the warrior's sandal. The round, dirty face turned to him, frightened, furious, ready to flee. The large eyes studied Tlacaelel, offended and undecided. No innocent trustfulness about those eyes, although they looked so much like hers.

"I need to tell you something," said the boy finally, wiping his face with the back of his hand, smearing more dust upon it.

"What?"

"I..." He sucked the blood off his upper lip, glancing at the warriors. "I can't with them listening."

Tlacaelel hid his grin, amused against his will. "Those are my warriors, boy. So just spill it out, or go back to your mother. You shouldn't be here anyway, and I don't have time for this."

He watched the round face darkening, the small lips pursing tightly.

"You promised," the boy muttered finally. "You told Mother you would help."

He felt it in his stomach, like a blow, squeezing his entrails. For a moment, he wanted to order his men to take the wild thing away, to tie and drag him home, if need be. He had better things to do than to make little children feel better, even if their fathers were taken away, to be executed in the most humiliating, painful of ways.

"Oh, you dirty troublemaker, come with me and spill it out." He turned to his warriors. "Follow me, but keep some distance. Will that arrangement suit you, oh-honorable-petitioner?"

The boy watched him suspiciously, clearly not understanding the last question at all. Tlacaelel turned to go.

"Come," he said curtly, beginning to walk up the road.

The boy had fallen in step with him easily.

"Which one of the twins are you? Coatl from last night?"

"Yes," said the boy readily.

"What happened?"

"My brother. The warriors caught him."

"What?"

The boy watched the ground below their feet.

"How? When?" *And most importantly "why,"* he thought, dumfounded.

"We were on the roof of that place, and they saw us. So we ran, but Ocelotl jumped badly." The boy hesitated. "It was not high at all, but they were throwing stones, and we had to jump. And he couldn't run, and they caught him." Pressing his lips, he blinked, clearly trying to hold the tears back, but his eyes glittered, reminding Tlacaelel that, with all the high-spirited resourcefulness, this child had seen barely six summers.

"So you came looking for me?"

The boy studied the ground.

"Oh well." Halting abruptly, Tlacaelel caught the thin shoulder, holding it tightly against the attempts to break free. "Look at me, boy. Now!" The glistening gaze rose reluctantly, stormy and afraid. "Listen to me, and listen carefully. We are going to sit there, on that stone, and you are going to tell it all to me. All of it, boy! Down to the last tiny detail. You are going to answer my questions, and you are not going to lie to me, not even about the smallest insignificant thing. Is that clear?" He pressed his palm tighter. "One lie, one small lie, and I won't help your family anymore, and your father will die, and maybe your brother, too." He saw the tears and the panic flooding in, and regretted his last words, remembering again that this wild thing was just a child. "Is that clear? If you want me to save them both, you will have to tell it all to me."

Not releasing his grip, he steered the boy toward the row of stones beside the road, gesturing to his warriors to keep away.

"Now tell me from the beginning. Were you there on the Plaza, watching the trial?"

The boy nodded, studying the ground once again.

"What happened?"

The troubled gaze flew to him. "I don't know. It was strange. And we couldn't see because there were so many people. The Emperor was talking. We climbed the temple's roof, and then we saw better. And then the Emperor was yelling at Father, and Father was yelling at the Emperor. And they were so angry. But the Emperor was afraid, too. I could see that." The large eyes sparkled proudly. "He was on this high thing, and Father was down there and tied, and still the Emperor was afraid of him, and of the things he said."

"What did he say?"

"I don't know. I didn't understand. Something about taking things. Like the Emperor took things from him and he from the Emperor. He said he was there first. Somewhere there." The old mischievous grin flashed. "It made the Emperor so angry!"

Oh, gods, stupid, stupid, stupid! How could such a smart man be so stupid? Why would he let his arrogant anger rule his mind? What a waste!

"And then what happened?"

The smile disappeared. "The Emperor said he'd die horribly, and they took him back to the temple. It was easy to see from that roof, so we stayed."

"So you saw the Adviser's warriors coming to take him?"

"What?"

"The warriors," said Tlacaelel impatiently. "Did you see who came to take him?"

The boy shrugged. "Other warriors."

"And you, two wild things, followed them, of course." He shook his head. "Where did they take him?"

"There was this small house, by the shore. Where they put things."

"Warehouse. Go on."

"He asked questions, but they just pushed him in, and he was really angry again. He was running back and forth, from wall to wall. Like really angry."

"How do you know that?"

The boy said nothing, eyes again drilling holes in the ground.

"You climbed that roof, eh?" Tlacaelel suppressed a grin. "Was it difficult?"

"No." The boy scowled. "It was low, with twenty or more things to stand on."

"Is he still there?"

"No, the scary man who came to talk to him let him out."

"What scary man? What did he look like?"

"I don't know. Big, scary."

"Did he wear a special cloak, a headdress?"

A blank gaze was his only answer.

"You know, the thing with feathers. Around his head."

The boy's face lit up. "Oh, yes, he did. It looked huge. You wouldn't—"

"Did you hear what they said?"

"Yes, it was easy. There was this opening near the roof—"

"What did they say?"

Another frown twisted the childish features. "I don't really remember. It was difficult to understand. He told Father that he would need to run away." The boy snorted. "Like Father didn't know that himself."

"And then?"

"And then they talked and talked. Well, the man talked, and Father was really quiet. It was like he just froze. He just stood and he listened to the other man and he didn't move at all."

Tlacaelel made an effort to curb his impatience. "Listen, you have to try to remember. It's important. " He leaned forward, putting his face closer to the child's, holding the wary gaze. "If you want me to save your father, you have to remember. You have to tell me everything you heard, even the things you did not understand. Then I will be able to save your father, to help him run away and take all of you with him."

The small lips quivered as the boy's eyes filled with tears. "And my brother?"

"Yes, of course. But first, tell me what the scary man told your father. Everything you heard. Even if it sounded strange or stupid."

"Well, he said that Father had to run away, like I told you. And then he was talking and talking, about the Emperor and other people. Those who want to war on us."

"The Tepanecs?"

"Yes."

"Did he talk about certain people? You know, did he use names?"

"Oh, yes, a lot."

"Maxtla? Tlacopan? Nezahualcoyotl?"

"Yes, yes, all of these!" The large eyes widened, peering at him in wonder. "How did you know?"

"I know many things, boy. Go on. What did your father say to all this?"

"Father just listened. He was really quiet. He didn't even move. He just stood there and listened."

"And then?"

"And then the man said something that made Father jump. He grew so angry, he would have smashed something. But his hands were tied."

"What did he say?"

"Father? He cursed, a lot."

Tlacaelel felt like smashing something, too. "Not your father! What did this man say? What made your father so angry?"

The boy shifted as though preparing to run. "I don't remember. We were busy looking at Father." He shut his eyes as though trying to show how hard he was trying to remember. "He was talking about the Emperor again, I think." The eyes opened, sparkling triumphantly. "Yes, now I remember. He was talking about how the Emperor was angry with father. And also, he told him that the Emperor was angry with someone else, too. Because of Father. He said she was in danger too, like Father. It was a woman, because he said 'she,' I remember this now. He said the Emperor would kill her, too. And then Father was cursing and demanding to be untied."

A woman in danger of the Emperor's wrath? Tlacaelel frowned. What woman? Whom was Chimal incensed with? Not the Empress surely. He would know if Chimal was accusing her of something. Or would he?

"Oh, Father was so angry again!" The boy's voice vibrated with excitement. "He was spitting with anger. He demanded to be set free, and he said that he would do the dirty work for the dirty Tepanecs, or whoever else needed to use his skills. No problem, he said. He'd do anyone's dirty work. That's what he said. And the other man was staring at him, also angry now. But smiling, too. Then he took his knife out, and Ocelotl turned his head, because he thought he was going to kill Father. But I knew he wouldn't. He was smiling like he'd won in a bean game, and he cut Father's ties and told him to remember that he didn't have much time. It had to be done tonight, he said."

And then he understood it all, marveling at the neatness of Itzcoatl's solution. The pieces of mosaic fell together, beautifully arranged. Of course, he didn't know about Chimal being angry with the Empress. Because he wasn't. The Empress was safe, as always. Chimal would never harm the woman he worshipped. But make the Highlander think she was in danger, make him believe that the Emperor was now avenging himself against both of the lovers, and that was that – Chimal could be considered a dead man. Oh, how deviously beautiful!

He held his breath. No, he wouldn't be betting too many cocoa beans on Chimal's life now. Not with the Highlander free and anxious to save his woman, with Itzcoatl masterminding this game.

The boy watched him, full of curiosity.

"Well," he eyed his unexpected source of information, pondering. Clearly Itzcoatl wished to keep him, Tlacaelel, out of this. Why? Because of his friendship with the Highlander? Or was there more to it? "Well, first of all, we get you back to your mother..."

But his informant backed away, aghast. "But my brother! You promised!" Fists clenched, lips pressed tight but quivering, eyes glistening with new tears, the boy stood there, obviously set on fighting for his rights.

Tlacaelel wanted to curse, forgetting all about the other twin. He didn't need a children's crisis on his hands now. And these weren't even his own sons.

"Wait, don't give me those crying fits. Where did you see your wild brother last?"

The boy swallowed, making an obvious effort to banish the tears. "We were on that roof, and the warriors saw us. They laughed, then started to throw stones at us."

"Was it when that man and your father were still inside?"

"No, they were gone already."

"Together?"

"No. First the man left."

"With the warriors?"

"Yes. Some of the warriors, but not all of them."

"And then?"

"And then Father left. He just climbed out of that same opening under the roof, and we got scared he was going up. Because he would be angry with us for not staying at home with Mother." The large eyes sparkled, then dropped. "We ran to the other side of the roof, but he didn't get up at all. We didn't hear anything, and when we went to look, he was gone. I think he just jumped down and ran away. But he made no sound, I swear. He can move like a real jaguar. I swear he can."

"I know that," said Tlacaelel, amused against his will, remembering their adventures seven summers ago, when the Highlander had made him climb the Palace's terrace. He still remembered how silly, but also worthless, it had made him feel. And how his leg had hurt when they had to jump down with no preparations beforehand. He had twisted his ankle and also got scratched and hurt, while his wild companion displayed no signs of discomfort, damn his wild, Tepanec eyes.

"Then we started to argue," he heard the boy saying. "Ocelotl wanted to try and follow him, but we didn't know where he had gone. So I told him we should go home. Because he might be looking for us, but we wouldn't be there, with Mother staying in that huge house." He shrugged. "And then the warriors saw us, and started to throw stones. So we jumped from the other side, but Ocelotl landed badly. He couldn't stand on his leg. And the warriors came, and they were still laughing, but the other ones got inside the building, and they were screaming angrily from the inside." The boy's voice shook, and he blinked again and again, but his eyes were full of tears now. "We tried to run away, but Ocelotl couldn't run, and the warriors caught him easily. And the ones from the inside came out, cursing and screaming. They forgot all about me and didn't try to catch me, but they took Ocelotl with them. They said the boy might know something. The warrior just dropped him over his shoulder and carried him this way. And he slapped him hard to stop him from fighting." The tears were streaming now, leaving dirty strips over the round, muddied face. "You have to find him! You have to take him away from them. You have to!" The word poured out loudly, shaking, choking with tears.

Tlacaelel caught his shoulder.

"Stop it," he said. "Stop yelling. Nothing will happen to your brother. Knowing you two, I bet he probably got away from them already. But I'll make sure he is all right." He peered into the tearful eyes, fighting the sudden wave of compassion. "I'll find your brother, and I'll send him home. But I'm sending you home first. No more running around, trying to save everyone on your own. If I see you on the streets again, I won't help you anymore. Is that clear?"

The boy nodded, sniffing loudly.

Tlacaelel gestured to one of his warriors. "Take him to the First Warlord's house. And don't just dump him there. Make sure he gets to his mother."

CHAPTER 13

The sun was beginning to tilt toward the other side of the sky, and Iztac cursed aloud once again. She had been pacing her terrace for what seemed like days, since Cuicatl's palanquin bearers had delivered her back to the Palace, around midday.

Still in panic, she had sent all her maids to look out for Tlacaelel or Itzcoatl. The ever-busy Tlacaelel was reported to spend his morning in Tlatelolco, making sure Tenochtitlan was not about to be betrayed by its closest neighbors, while Itzcoatl was out there, touring the city with the Emperor, probably, or doing something as useless. The impending war with the Tepanecs was preying on everyone's mind, but for Iztac it was now just one more thing to curse about. She had so little time, and no one to turn to for help.

"Did you hear anything?" she asked Chiko as the maid peeked in carefully.

"No, Revered Mistress." The woman's round face reflected her troubled mood. "Why don't you come in and take a rest? You will make yourself sick, pacing this way."

"Send someone to the city. Make them search for the Chief Warlord or the Main Adviser. They could not have just disappeared from our Fifth World, could they?" She stomped her foot. "I need to see them, and the matter cannot wait!"

"All your servants are watching every entrance, ready to alert you of their arrival, Mistress," said the woman, sighing. "Please, at least let me bring you a good cup of sweetened chocolate."

Under the terrace, raising voices made Iztac peek out, her hope piquing. But it was only Citlalli, the yellow-eyed princess, arguing with her maids.

"Stop following me!" shouted the girl, waving her hands in the air angrily. "I want to go to the pond all by myself." She tossed her head high, and the waterfall of her black shiny hair cascaded over her thin shoulders. "I can do it!"

"Where do you want to go all alone, you wild thing?" called out Iztac, her desperation lifting for a heartbeat, as it always did upon seeing her daughter.

The girl looked up, startled.

"Nowhere," she said, clutching the pieces of paper she held close to her chest.

"Nowhere? Then what was this all about, you yelling and shouting in the middle of the day. You should be resting now. Go back to your rooms."

The slender face twisted. "I don't want to rest."

Behind her back, Iztac could hear her maid chuckling. *Not funny,* she thought, her worry returning. *I wish I could rest now and worry only about the stupid war with the stupid Tepanecs.*

"Come up here," she said in a voice that brooked no argument, then turned back to Chiko. "Bring her here. And then, well, send more servants to watch the gates, and one or two into the city. Or I'll just go there myself," she added, narrowing her eyes.

And don't you think I won't be able to do this, she thought, seething, remembering the days when she would climb those terraces whenever she needed to go somewhere on her own. She still could do that; that, as well as anything else required in order to save him. She had saved him once; she had killed a warrior to save him, and she might very well do this again, if need be.

The girl came out onto the terrace, light and sure-footed, her shoulders straight, her bright, yellowish eyes squinting against the glow of the early afternoon sun, challenging, the pieces of expensive *amate*-paper clutched in her hands, fluttering with the slight breeze.

"Why aren't you in your rooms, resting?" asked Iztac, coming closer to brush wandering tendrils out of the small lovely face.

"I don't want to rest," said the girl. "I want to go back to the pond, and I don't want them all running after me."

"You are the First Daughter of the Emperor, Citlalli. You can't go to the pond all alone."

"Of course, I can. I've been going there a lot. I was there just now, too. All alone, Mother!" The bright gaze stood Iztac's frown.

She was hardly six summers old, this daughter of hers, but she was already a handful. Not a natural troublemaker, reflected Iztac, knowing all about being a troublemaker. No, her daughter was not like her in that aspect. She was a quiet, self-contained little thing, preferring to spend her time drawing or studying scrolls, fascinated with calendars, ceremonies, gods, and temples. And yet, with all her seeming niceness, the girl could be incredibly stubborn, standing the wrath of her elders and betters with her strange eyes glowing, and her small legs planted wide apart, not intimidated by the worst of the threats or punishments.

"What would you do all alone at the pond, little one?" asked Iztac, amused as always. While pretending a sternness she didn't feel, she liked her daughter just the way she was. "It's hot out there, and boring. And you have no comfortable place to put your drawings upon. What would you do by the pond now?"

A surprisingly open smile lit the girl's face. "Nothing," she said, her eyes sparkling, disclosing her excitement.

Iztac wanted to laugh. "Come, you can tell me. You know I never punish you for real. What have you been up to, little rascal?"

The girl bit her lip, her face squeezing with an effort to decide.

"I may let you go there if you tell me," whispered Iztac temptingly. "I'll tell the maids to leave you alone. They will listen to me, you know that."

Citlalli came closer. "There is a funny looking boy there," she breathed, almost trembling with excitement. "He can't walk. His knee is broken or something. He is hiding there from the warriors. He is funny and we talked."

Iztac let out her breath, disappointed. Somehow she had expected to hear something wonderful, not ordinary. Not a tale of imaginary boys.

"Citlalli, stop making things up," she said, unable to stop herself. "There are no strange boys hiding in the pond. I thought you stopped making things up. We talked about it, didn't we? "

She watched the lively face falling, losing its spark. The girl's eyes blinked, glittered with tears, but she pressed her lips tight, determined to hold them back.

"I'm not making it up, Mother," she cried out, her small fists clenched and trembling. "This boy, he was there, and I promised to show him my drawings. I came back because—"

The running footsteps made then both look up in time to see one of the maids bursting into the terrace.

"Revered Empress, the Chief Warlord just arrived. He was heading for the guard house and—"

Iztac's heart missed a beat. "Send a maid to inform him that I need to see him on a matter of urgency." Running her hands through her hair, she glanced at the sun. "No, there is no time. I'll go and see him now. This matter cannot wait."

"But, Mistress," cried out the woman, appalled. "You can't just go to the guards' house. You need to—"

"I can and I will!" Rushing toward the entrance and forgetting all about the girl, Iztac was startled to meet the offended yellow gaze. "Go to your rooms, little one, and rest. Get her maids to take care of the princess," she added, brushing past Chiko.

The heat was still heavy, and she wiped her forehead, racing up the abandoned paths. Would Tlacaelel be able to help? Had he heard about the trial? Her sandals made rustling sounds against the dry earth, and her thoughts bounced around like mad squirrels. Maybe she would have done better spending her time out there, trying to find the way to set him free. The time was running out, and if Tlacaelel would not be able, or willing, to help, then she may not be able to save him, after all. He would be stoned, right there on the Plaza, dying in pain, a difficult death, with people looking and cheering, expecting him to present them with a remarkable memory, such a proud, foreigner with his impressive height and width and those alien tattoos of his, the owner of the famous sword.

She shut her eyes against the terrible pictures her mind was painting too vividly. No, it would not come to that. Not if she could help it.

Nearer the gates, the Palace's gardens became livelier. Servants rushed about, and warriors strolled by. They all stared at her, reminding her of that time, seven summers ago, when she had stormed the main wing of the Palace in order to confront the Empress, acting on an impulse, not giving much thought neither to her actions nor to her appearances. Well, back then she had been yelled at and locked in a small, airless room, threatened with all sorts of punishments. But now? Oh, now she *was* the Empress, and she could do whatever she liked.

"I wish to see the Warlord," she said to the nearest warrior, a tall, widely built man with an impressive turquoise plug adorning his lower lip.

The man hesitated. "Of course, Revered Empress," he said finally. "Let me find him and let him know."

She allowed them to escort her to the shadow of a wide tree, her stomach turning, twisting uneasily. The sun was moving down its path with an unseemly speed, and she knew there was not much time left.

"Revered Empress." Tlacaelel neared her with his wide, confident paces, his face a friendly mask, but his eyes reserved and unreadable, as always.

"Honorable Chief Warlord." She returned his gaze, striving to appear as calm as he was.

"What a rare pleasure," he said, a light, indifferent smile stretching his lips. His eyes measured her, neither friendly nor hostile, returning her gaze, avoiding the obvious question. Oh, no, this man was not about to make it easy for her.

"Has your visit in Tlatelolco brought the results you expected to achieve?" she asked, feeling compelled to break the awkward silence. She had nothing to do around the guards' house, that much was obvious, but the annoying man was letting her feel that as well.

"Oh, it was an interesting visit. Our neighbors needed to be reminded where their loyalties should be."

"I daresay you reminded them of all that and more."

"I did my best, yes."

Another spell of awkward silence. She wanted to hit

something. "While you were away, there was a trial in the Imperial Court."

"Yes, I have heard about that."

More silence.

"Well, is there anything you may want to do about it?" she asked in desperation, unable to cope with the meaningless talk anymore.

He raised his eyebrows, unbearably haughty all of a sudden. "What can I do about it? The Emperor is the one to judge in the Imperial Court."

She bit her lips hard. "He is your friend. You may try to save him, somehow. Friends do those things for each other."

The deeply set eyes turned colder, not wavering, not turning away from her accusation.

"People in my position have no friends, Noble Lady," he said, his lips twisting in a one-sided, somewhat contemptuous grin. "He is one of my warriors." A shrug. "A highly praised warrior. A promising leader."

She felt it like a punch in her stomach. It made her insides shrink, but whether from fear or from rage she didn't know.

"He considered you his friend. He always spoke highly of you. He did many things for you. I know he did. Not as just another of your warriors, or a promising leader." She clasped her teeth, trying to control her voice. It trembled in the most annoying of ways. "But he was wrong, wasn't he? One can never trust nobles. There is no friendship and no loyalty in the royal house; not when it comes to one's interests."

She saw a flicker of rage flashing through the dark eyes, as his face froze, turning into a stone mask.

"I know you know all about the interests of Tenochtitlan's royal house, oh Revered Empress," he said coldly. "After all, you have been in this Palace for much longer than you have been an Empress. It's been a long way, has it not?" The cold eyes held her gaze, flickering darkly.

"I betrayed no friends," she said, making an effort not to avert her gaze, her stomach hollow and fluttering. "I was loyal to those I loved or respected."

"Oh, but it's not always that simple, is it? You choose, you decide to remain loyal, or to step away. To betray, the way you put it. According to circumstances, according to your needs, according to your feelings, sometimes." The pointed eyebrows lifted suggestively. "And those choices are not always approved by other people, are they? Some of your actions can be seen as betrayal, too, not by you but by other people."

"What are you saying?" she asked, her throat dry.

"I am saying that before your accuse anyone else of betrayal, remember that you may be as guilty of this accusation." He paused. "I might have kept to myself, but I was here in the Palace all the time. I saw the emperors changing. And the empresses."

She felt a need to take a deep breath, or maybe to lean against something, fighting the memories. Yes, of course, this man was there all the time. He was the previous emperor's first son, but she barely remembered him, a reserved, very able, very promising youth, busy training to be a warrior. Where was he seven summers ago, when this *altepetl* was in such turmoil? Here in the Palace, of course. Serving Itzcoatl, most probably. Involved in the schemes of the devious Warlord, and therefore growing friendly with her brother, and the Highlander.

The Highlander! How close to death he had come back then. And how close to death he was now! And she hadn't been able to help him, no more now than then. She bit her lips until they hurt, then made an effort to concentrate, meeting the piercing gaze of the haughty royal offspring.

"I may be guilty of betrayals," she said tiredly, wishing to go back now, to return to her set of rooms, to crawl into the farthest corner and to curl up there, with no curious or accusing eyes upon her. "Yes, I suppose you are right. I'm guilty of all that and more. I... I should be going. I'm sorry for wasting your time. I shouldn't have..." She paused, desperate to control her voice, his face blurry, swimming before her eyes.

"He is not going to die," she heard him saying, as she began turning away. "He won't be executed."

She clenched her teeth tight, fighting the urge to turn back, unwilling to let him see the tears.

"Don't worry about him. He will be fine. Isn't he always?" There was a thread of amusement in his voice now, and it sounded warmer and not stony or cutting anymore. "You know he won't die that easily. Not him."

"How do you know?" she whispered, refusing to look back.

"I know. Trust me to know. But of course I would appreciate if you kept it to yourself for a while. Let your husband discover it on his own."

Now she truly needed to lean against something. "Yes, of course, I will," she said, meeting his gaze, seeing the light smile and the compassion in his eyes. "Thank you. I will not forget it. If I could ever repay you—"

He shook his head vigorously, openly amused now. "It was not my doing. Believe me, I did nothing. I was in Tlatelolco, as there are more important matters than the safety of one crazy warrior." He shrugged. "I may not be a good friend. You might have been right about that. Still, you can put your worries to rest." His face darkened. "Some of your worries."

"What else should I worry about?" she asked, shivering, not liking the ominous note to his voice and the way his eyes turned back to their usual unreadable state.

"Many things, Revered Empress. Many things." He straightened up abruptly. "But I have matters of importance to take care of. So, if there is nothing else..." He gestured to his warriors, then began turning away. "Oh, but you can help in one matter, if you wish it so." Halfway on the path now, he turned his head, his eyes sparkling, alive again, almost mischievous. "One of his boys may be loose somewhere here in the Palace. Don't ask me how he got here. This wild pair is something out of the ordinary. The stupid boys tried to help and got into trouble, and one is now missing and may be somewhere around, hurt probably. If you can put your maids to work, it would help our mutual friend greatly. He won't be pleased to discover that one of his sons has died in the Palace. He is not in a forgiving mood at the present."

She stared at him, speechless. "The twins? They are here?"

"Only one, and he might be in trouble," repeated Tlacaelel, turning away. "If you find him, send him to the First Warlord's house."

She watched his cloak as it swayed confidently, exposing his well muscled shoulders and calves. He was already talking to his warriors, brisk and purposeful. They squinted against the glow of the afternoon sun, and she measured it too, her stomach twisting.

Then the realization struck. She had no need to worry about the sun anymore. *He* wouldn't be executed at sunset. Lightheaded, she began walking the path, struggling to keep her elation at bay. He wouldn't die tonight. He had escaped the danger. As usual, he had challenged the death and had managed to survive. The Underworld journey was not awaiting him. And not the warriors' paradise. Not yet.

She gestured to her maids, seeing them lingering nearby, watching her from a safe distance. "Send a slave to prepare the baths. I'm going to rest now, but make everything ready. The clothes and the creams. And I want my hair washed with indigo."

Nearing the main wing's polished stairs, she mounted them briskly, wishing to tear her clothes off now, the seat-soaked cotton clinging to her body, unpleasantly so. She had spent the whole day in this same blouse that she had picked hastily when Cuicatl, the First Warlord's Third Wife, had come visiting, turning her whole world upside down. Had it happened only this morning? It seemed that a whole market interval had passed, a market interval saturated with agony and worry. But it was in the past now. She had nothing to worry about, the remark of Tlacaelel about her other worries notwithstanding.

"Revered Mistress!" Chiko sprang toward her outside the doorway of her suite of rooms, her round face troubled, glistening with sweat.

"What now?" asked Iztac, pushing herself past the maid, bursting into the familiar cozy mess, halting abruptly.

Chimal squatted on the pile of mats, staring into space, his eyes empty, shoulders sagging, hands laying listlessly in his lap. Her stomach twisted, with fear, then with pity. He looked so desolate, so lost, so *resigned*, as a person who had been struck would look.

"Chimal!" She came closer, forgetting their quarrel and their troubles, overwhelmed by the familiar urge to protect him. She hadn't seen him this way since the death of his mother, or even earlier, since he was a child, the cute little boy she had come to like through her first summers in this Palace. Her only friend.

He said nothing, did not even raise his head, so she knelt beside him, placing her palms upon his shoulders.

"Chimal, what happened?"

His eyes shifted, and his gaze did not light as it always had when looking at her. It remained dead, distant and empty.

"Was it true what he said?" he asked quietly.

"What?" she peered at him, genuinely bewildered.

"Was it true what he said?" he repeated, his gaze growing more intense. "Was he there first? Did I take what was his?"

She stood his gaze, her stomach growing empty, filling with ice. "What do you mean?"

"You know what I mean, Iztac Ayotl. *Did I take what was his?*"

Numb and suddenly cold, she took her hands away, then rose to her feet. A gust of wind burst through the open shutters, rustling in the covers, bringing slight relief in the afternoon heat. She looked at the shafts of light lying across the floor and once again felt the wave of excitement that the sunset meant nothing to her, not anymore.

"Why do you want to know that?" she asked finally, unable to stand the silence.

His gaze burned her skin. "Because I need to know."

"It will change nothing, Chimal. It has nothing to do with us."

"It has everything to do with us."

She looked at the open shutters. "I have known this man since I was a princess in the Texcoco Palace. Since before I was given to your father."

She heard him letting out a held breath and looked back in time to see the light going out of his eyes. Just like that. One moment alive, the next gone. There was no anger, no resentment, no rage. He just blew out, like a torch in a strong gust of wind. Her heart squeezed, and she rushed toward him, kneeling again, but this time grabbing his sagging shoulders forcefully.

"It means nothing. Chimal, listen to me. It means nothing, like I told you before. I love you, too. I do!"

His lips twisted. "You love me, *too*? That is nice."

"But it's true. I do love you. You were my only friend, and you were always so good to me. I loved you from the moment I saw you for the first time. Remember? Around that pond with the mosaic. When you ran away from that man who had taught you oratory." She smiled at the memory. "You were so scared, but excited too, and we talked."

He shrugged.

"I've loved you ever since, Chimal."

"Like a brother. Not like a man." He shifted, freeing his shoulders from her grip.

"Yes, like a brother back then. But now, I love you like a man. I let you make love to me, don't I?"

He refused to look at her. "Yes, you *let* me make love to you. Any woman can *let* the man have her. It means nothing."

"Well, I'm not any woman. I wouldn't let you if I didn't love you."

"Did you love my father, your first husband?"

She took a deep breath. "Well yes, you are right. Any woman can let the man have her. But I was given to your father. I had no choice." Putting her palm on his arm, she leaned closer. "I was not given to you. I came to you of my own free will."

"What choice did you have?" he muttered, but she could see a flicker of hope brightening his gaze.

"I had choices, Chimal. Believe me, I had. I didn't have to stay in Tenochtitlan."

"Where would you go? You could not return to Texcoco." Now his eyes were upon her, openly hopeful.

"No, but my brother came to Tenochtitlan already back then. And also..." She took another deep breath. "I could have gone with *him*."

That served to darken his gaze all over again. "Where to?"

She shrugged.

"To the savage Highlands?" His lips quivered, stretching into a mirthless grin. "The noble Acolhua-Tepanec princess?"

She sprang to her feet. "Yes, Chimal!" she said, suddenly furious. "If not for the war with the Tepanecs, I would have been there for ten summers by now. I was supposed to leave with him before I was given to your father."

He peered at her in disbelief, his eyes wide open and bewildered, the hurt in them so obvious it twisted her heart.

"It's all in the past now, Chimal. An old story. I do belong to you now, and it was of my choosing. I came to you of my free will." She squatted again beside him. "I never wanted to be an empress. I stayed here only because of you. And I'm not here now because I love being an empress. I can leave if you want me to."

He shifted his gaze, studying the wooden tiles of the floor once again. "To the Highlands?"

"Yes."

A mirthless chuckle escaped his clasped lips. "So you love us both." He made it a statement.

"Yes." She sighed. "I know it's strange, and it's not supposed to be this way, but that's how it is."

He glanced at her darkly. "He won't die tonight. He escaped my warriors. Did you know that?"

"Yes."

"Were you a part of it?"

"No, but I tried to do everything I could."

"He won't be allowed to enter Tenochtitlan. Never! If he does, he dies." He paused, then glanced at her again. "You will never see him again, Iztac Ayotl."

She winced, having had no time to think about that. But, of course. He wouldn't be able to live in Tenochtitlan anymore.

"Will it make it difficult for you to keep loving me?" he asked, peering at her.

She moved away, leaning against the wall and hugging her knees. The tears were threatening, but she held them back, determined not to let it spoil the rest of this horrible day, not when it had just gotten better. She would think about it later, when it would be easier to cope with.

"Yes, I will love you still," she whispered, then clenched her teeth against the trembling of her voice. Shutting her eyes, she tried to push the tears back, but they kept squeezing through her eyelids, insistent and warm.

And then his arms were around her, enveloping her gently, considerate as always, but somehow protective, pulling her into his warmth and this clean, delicate smell of his. So she clung to him and let the tears flow, sobbing and letting him rock her softly into calmness.

"It will all be well, Iztac Ayotl," he murmured, caressing her hair. "It will be all right. You'll see."

She heard the footsteps and wanted to curse the servants for not leaving them alone.

"Revered Emperor."

"What do you want?" asked Chimal curtly, clearly as put out.

"The Honorable Adviser is waiting in the main hall. And the engineers you summoned. And the Chief Warlord."

She felt him sighing. "I have to go," he said. "I'm sorry. Will you be all right?"

"Come here tonight," she whispered into his chest, refusing to look up, unwilling to let him see her so ugly, smeared with dust and puffy with tears. "I will be waiting for you, and I will not let you go until the dawn breaks."

He pressed her to him tightly, and she felt more than saw his smile, breaking through the depths of his gloom.

"I love you, Iztac Ayotl. I always will."

His paces were light, resounding confidently against the plastered walls, his positive, cheerful self once again. She took a deep breath, fighting the ominous feeling. He was so open, so trustful, so easily cheered up. Was his life in danger, too?

She thought about Itzcoatl and his strange indifference of the past market interval, since the dirty Tepanec ruler had disposed of his own brother, the lawful ruler of Azcapotzalco. Was Chimal safe from the dirty tricks of this man? And how was Itzcoatl connected to all this?

"Bring me a bowl of fresh water and clean cloths," she said to her maids. "I want to wash my face and to change my clothes before I go to the baths."

"Tomorrow there will be a ceremony held in Revered Tezcatlipoca's temple," said Chiko, supervising the maids, who came in carrying the requested water and a flask with a sweetened drink.

"What ceremony?"

"The priests announced it today. They wish to appease the great god. Before the war, of course."

"Will they have anything worthwhile to offer?" asked Iztac, wiping her face with the wet cloth, enjoying the feeling. She took her blouse off and brushed the soft cotton against her shoulders and breasts. "Well, I suppose they might still have a few prisoners. Since the last raid against the Chalcoans."

Chiko picked a turquoise blouse out of the pile of garments.

"This is a pretty color," she said, smiling. "You wear it so rarely, but it might go well with the gold of your skin." She chuckled against Iztac's scowl. "Or maybe you can give it to your daughter. The princess would look stunning in turquoise."

"Citlalli? Oh, yes. She is bright. She might look pretty in turquoise."

"And it'll set off the princess's eyes most nicely," said Chiko, pouring her a drink.

But Iztac winced, unsettled when people mentioned her daughter's eyes ever since the meeting with the filthy *cihua*, Kuini's wife. Was his mother truly an important priestess of some barbarian goddess? Had she had the same yellow, ocelot eyes? Frowning, she banished the unwelcome thoughts.

"Send Citlalli to me. I want to tell her about the ceremony. She would love to attend it. I'll take her there with me."

As another maid rushed away to summon the princess, Iztac let the women help her into a turquoise blouse and a matching skirt, then leaned back and closed her eyes for a moment, allowing them to tie up her sandals. The unusual color of her daughter's eyes drew attention, but not overly so. She was a princess, the Emperor's First Daughter by his exalted, impeccably noble Acolhua Chief Wife. The girl's strange eyes were assumed to be the part of the magic, allowed in such high nobility. So what if some barbarian priestess had the same eye color? thought Iztac uneasily. No one would make any connection. It was too farfetched.

No one but the filthy *cihua*. Oh, this one knew it all, and she was not afraid to threaten her, Iztac, with this knowledge. She had said that should she or her children feel threatened... As though Iztac would think of harming *his* children. The wild twins or any other of this *cihua*'s brood.

The wild twins!

She jumped to her feet, gasping, the memory of what Tlacaelel had said springing into her mind, making her fight for breath. One of the twins was lost somewhere in the Palace, probably hurt, or maybe dying. Oh, gods! She clasped her mouth with her palm. She had to send her maids out to look for the child.

The women stared at her.

"Listen," she frowned, trying to collect her thoughts. "I need you to do something..."

And then another thought hit her, and she turned around and rushed out and down the corridor, heading for her daughter's set of rooms. Citlalli! Citlalli had seen a boy, a wild boy who could not walk. Not imaginary but real! That's why the girl wanted to go to the pond alone, with no maids trailing after her. She wanted to show him her drawings. And when this girl wanted something...

Bursting into the neatly arranged space, which smelled of sweetmeats and incense, she half expected to find it empty and so wasn't surprised.

"Where is the princess?" she asked the troubled maid.

"Sneaked out again, Revered Mistress. I'll go and find her."

"Don't." Iztac turned around. The little rascal was by the pond now, surely. "I know where she is, and I don't want you to follow me. Is that clear?" She glared at the woman. "If I see you, or anyone else, following, I'll have you punished and sold away. Do you understand that?"

Not waiting for the frightened woman to answer, she stormed down the corridor and out into the sunlit world, yet again enjoying the thought that the sun, and the way it was about to kiss the top of the trees, meant nothing to her.

Nearing the pond, she slowed her steps, careful to make as little sound as she could. She knew this place by heart, could draw its likeness with her eyes shut, every tree, every cluster of bushes.

Since arriving at the Palace, ten summers ago, she had found this pond wonderfully secluded, sneaking here every now and then, to enjoy peace and quiet, to spend time with her memories and her thoughts. And then, when she had become friendly with Chimal, they would come here together, to play and to laugh. This pond was so nicely hidden, unlike the other one – the large, beautiful affair of artificial waterfalls and elegant bridges. Here was where she had brought the Highlander when he had reappeared at the height of the turbulent events seven summers ago. Here Citlalli had been created, she realized suddenly, not having thought about it before.

Guessing the spot her daughter would pick for drawing, or for holding clandestine meetings, she made her way soundlessly between the trees, sneaking around the bushes adorning the western side of the pond. Indeed, they crouched between the greenish branches. She could see Citlalli's slender back, bent above a spread piece of paper, outlining something with her finger and talking. Oh, the little rascal looked so pleased with herself! The boy crouched beside her, listening with what seemed like a genuine interest. He was a mess of disheveled hair and scratched, muddied limbs.

Absorbed and oblivious of their surroundings, they didn't notice her approach until she was near the edge of the bushes. Then the boy straightened. As tense as a small animal, he looked up, his eyes large and dark, glittering alertly. Their gazes met, and he jumped to his feet, but wavered and almost fell back, his face twisting with pain.

"What are you doing?" cried out Citlalli, while the boy waved his arms, trying to stabilize himself. She looked up. "Oh, Mother," she said, meeting Iztac's gaze, not afraid in the least.

Steady at last, the boy looked up, putting his weight on one leg and holding the other one strangely.

"Don't worry," said Citlalli matter-of-fact. "Mother won't tell on you."

Of course, this did not reassure the wild thing, who still seemed to be pondering his possibilities. But for his damaged leg, he would be running away and fast, realized Iztac, strangely amused.

"What are you doing here?" she asked, addressing her daughter, trying to sound stern.

"I told you I was going to show him my drawings." The yellow eyes stood her gaze, calm and sure of themselves.

"And I told you to stay in your rooms." Iztac shrugged, not prolonging the staring contest. It was of no use, anyway.

She eyed the boy once again, liking the gentle, round face almost against her will. He looked nothing like Kuini, but she could imagine the Highlander behaving the same way.

"Let me see your knee," she said.

The boy narrowed his eyes, his forehead creasing with the effort to decide.

She came closer. "You can't run anyway, so you have no choice but to trust me."

He bit his lips, still hesitating, but as Citlalli got up, putting a possessive arm upon his shoulder, he relaxed visibly.

"Sit down," said Iztac. She squatted beside them, then studied his knee, which was swollen badly, caked with dried blood. "Does it hurt to bend it?"

The boy shrugged.

"Yes, it does," said Citlalli in his stead. "He can't bend it at all when he walks."

"But I can when I'm not walking," said the boy, clearly not liking to be bossed around. "I can bend it if I'm not standing on it." Supporting himself with his hands, he lifted the damaged leg and bent it slightly, his face twisting, lips pressing tight.

"Of course, that hurts, too," called out Citlalli triumphantly. "I can see that!"

"You need to be seen by a healer," said Iztac, getting onto her feet. "So what we do now is, we pack you into my palanquin and send you home to your mother." She eyed the boy sternly. "And you stay there. You have no business running around the Palace. Do you understand that?"

The boy's eyes flashed. "I was not running around the Palace. The warriors brought me here. But I got away."

She remembered what Tlacaelel had said. "Well, they didn't

take you from your home, did they? If you had stayed with your mother, no one would be able to drag you anywhere."

The dark gaze was her answer.

"Anyway, I'm going to summon my palanquin bearers. You stay here, and don't move. If you are not here by the time I'm back, you will be truly sorry, boy. Do you hear me? I promised to get you back home safely, but if you try to make trouble, I will be very angry with you."

"I'll stay with him until you are back," said Citlalli importantly.

"No, you will not. You are coming with me, and you are staying in your rooms. No more running away for you, either."

"But Mother!" The girl stood there, legs wide apart, eyes stormy. "I did not run away. I told you why I was going to the pond. You didn't believe me, but I told you the truth!" The glare of the bright eyes was amusing in its intensity. "I want to help!"

She felt like laughing. This whole day was a terrible mess of unusual happenings.

"Oh well, if you want to help, run now, as fast as you can. Find Chiko, and tell her I want her here at once. Tell her I need my palanquin ready, too, but if she doesn't believe you, then just tell her I need her here."

The girl hesitated for a heartbeat, eyeing Iztac suspiciously, then she turned around and burst into a run without another word.

"And try not to get caught by your own maids. They are looking for you, you know," called Iztac after the flying garment, watching the funny gait of the thin legs, openly amused. Her daughter was anything but a runner.

Turning back, she met another suspicious gaze, this time oval and dark brown.

"Does it hurt?" she asked nodding toward his leg.

He shrugged.

"You and your brother should know better than to run around the warriors."

"We are not running around the warriors. Not usually." The direful frown made the boy look funny, like a small version of a grownup man. "We never get caught. I just jumped badly."

"Were you trying to help your father?"

Another shrug.

"He'll be all right, you know? He got away." Involuntarily, she glanced around, making sure they were alone.

"Yes, I know that."

Now it was her turn to open her eyes wide. "How? Did you see him running away?"

The boy's face lit up. "Oh, yes, we saw him. He just climbed the wall, and jumped out of that opening under the roof. He made no sound. He just climbed, jumped, and disappeared. He is like a jaguar. He can do those things."

She watched the sparkling eyes, fascinated, knowing all about the way he could move, yes, like a jaguar, as soundless and as lethal.

"If he'd had his sword with him, he would have cut all the warriors, and he wouldn't have been wounded at all," the boy went on, almost shining now. "Because his sword is magical. It gives him power, and it keeps him safe."

She grinned. "What keeps him safe is his own abilities and skills. It's not the sword."

"Yes, it is! Ask anyone. They are talking about his sword on the marketplace and everywhere. Everyone knows it's magical. It is!" His face darkened against her widening smile. "I touched it once, when he didn't see me. It feels magical. It has carvings, and some are frightening and alive. You didn't see it, so you don't know!"

"I saw it and I touched it, boy. I even saved it for him once. Ask him about that. He didn't want to fight without his sword. He wanted to leave Tenochtitlan. But because I saved it, he stayed." She smiled against those memories, remembering how elated he had grown, and how he had told her that she was the bravest, the strongest, the most wonderful girl alive.

The dark eyes watched her, openly doubtful. "Father let you touch his sword?"

"I told you, I saved it for him. I kept it hidden in my room for ten dawns."

"When?"

"Before you were born." Laughing, she watched the various

expressions chasing each other across the round, dirtied face. "But enough of history. Tell me more about how he got away. Who helped him?"

"No one. I told you he doesn't need anyone. He just climbed—"

"Yes, but before. Anyone came to see him?"

"Oh, yes. There was the scary man with feathers."

"What scary man? What did he look like?"

The boy shrugged. "I don't know. He came in, and he talked to Father for so long. It was boring."

"Was he tall? Did he look like a warrior?"

"I don't know. He was big and wide and scary."

"Did he wear a cloak and a headdress like this?" She tried to describe the Adviser's headpiece with her hands.

"Yes, yes, with lots of feathers. It looked pretty, but funny, too."

Itzcoatl! She bit her lips.

"And don't you remember what he said to your father? Nothing at all?"

"No, but in the end Father was really angry. He was cursing a lot. Then the man took out his knife, and I thought he was going to kill Father. So I looked away. But my brother told me that he just cut the ties and looked at Father very hard, then went out. Then Father was gone, too."

She felt like cursing herself. "You must remember something. Were they talking about the war? The Tepanecs? The Highlands?"

"I don't know. Yes, there was something about the Tepanecs. When Father was really angry he said he would do the Tepanecs' dirty work. Or something like that." The boy giggled. "What dirty work those Tepanecs do? Do they clean dirty places?"

He went on, bringing up more ideas, pleased with himself, but Iztac stopped listening, her thoughts in a jumble. The dirty work of the Tepanecs? What work? And what was the sneaky Adviser up to? Oh, Itzcoatl would not save the Highlander for nothing. He had been the one to betray him in the first place, and now he was saving him. But for what devious purpose?

She saw Chiko heading up the path, followed by Citlalli, who still ran, waving her hands in the air. She was such a girl, reflected Iztac. She didn't know how to run at all.

"We'll get you home in the palanquin," she said to the boy, who now straightened up again, alerted and tense. "And you stay with your mother until your father comes home. Is that clear?"

"Mother is not in our home now," said the boy, unsure of himself. He studied the ground with exaggerated interest. "She is sick."

She remembered the haughty Toltec woman, the First Warlord's wife. "Yes, I know. But the house she is staying in is even better. No warriors will come to bother your family there, and your mother will get better soon."

He looked at her searchingly. "She will?"

"Yes, of course. Why not?"

"I don't know. She looked really sick and Kaay was angry all the time."

"Who is Kaay?"

"The healer woman."

"What did she say?"

"I don't know. She said nothing. She just started bringing in things. And then she threw us out." He frowned. "She is always smiling and bringing us sweetmeats, but this morning she was just angry."

"Oh, healers are always like that when they have to care for a sick person. It means nothing. Your mother will be well."

"She brought scary things." His gaze was firm upon the ground now, his fingers crushing dry leaves. "Knives, sticks and spoons. Like she was going to cut her, or to eat her, maybe."

She winced at the terrible memories. Yes, there were incredibly bitter brews and terrifying looking things that, indeed, were used to cut her, to make it possible to pull the child out of her. She clenched her sweaty palms, her stomach twisting, constricting painfully. She had survived, and she was gifted with Citlalli, while this boy's mother…

"Your mother will be well. I'm sure she will," she said, getting to her feet and waving at Chiko. "She gave birth to you two, and some more children, didn't she? She'll be all right. You'll see." But her stomach felt cold, full of ice, remembering the pain and the feeling of dying.

His eyes lifted, wide open and expectant, battling tears. "Will you come and make sure she is all right?"

She felt like laughing hysterically. "No, I can't come. I can't leave the Palace."

But as she said that she suddenly knew that she would, at least, take him back home herself. Only to the Warlord's house. Just to make sure this child got there safely. The noble lady, the Warlord's wife, paid her a visit this morning. Why couldn't she pay a visit back?

She measured the sun, knowing it was not the time for social visits. Not so near sunset.

"I'll take you back myself," she said. "But only to the house of the Warlord. We'll ride in the palanquin together."

CHAPTER 14

Tlacaelel stared at the warrior, enraged.

"What Tepanecs?" he asked. "Where? How many?"

The man shifted uneasily, quailing under the stern gaze. "Honorable Leader," he said, apologetic. "I don't know if any of this is true. Coming from the servants, such information is highly doubtful. Still, I thought I should inform you."

"Bring the servant who told you this."

"Yes, Honorable Warlord."

Watching the man's retreating back, Tlacaelel frowned. He'd need to alert all the guards if there were wandering Tepanecs loose inside the Palace. However, on this particular night it was the last thing he wanted to do. Too many people were involved, too many bets put on this particular game. The beans were cast, and there was nothing he, or anyone else, could do to stop this.

He shrugged. Were the wandering Tepanec intruders a part of this game?

He thought about the earlier meeting in the main hall, when Chimal had come in, back to his cheerful, bright, positive self. He remembered the wondering look upon Itzcoatl's face, reflecting his own puzzlement. The young Emperor was changing fast. Only this afternoon impatient and irritated, talking rapidly, curtly, avoiding his closest advisers' gazes, Chimal had toured the city, deep in his gloomy thoughts. Yet, now he smiled and looked as though he didn't have a single worry in the whole world. Puzzling.

Watching the young, pleasant-looking face, Tlacaelel found himself feeling sorry that this half brother of his was destined to die. He was a good man and not a bad ruler. He was thorough and thoughtful, and he tried very hard. In other times he might have been a satisfactory emperor, but not now, not with Tenochtitlan facing the worst crisis in its history.

Shaking his head, Tlacaelel remembered the argument that had broken in the main hall, when Itzcoatl maintained that it was a mistake to wait for the Tepanecs' offensive. The Adviser had wanted to gather Tenochtitlan's warriors and lead them out, to camp on the mainland, to await the Tepanecs there, displaying the Aztec's readiness to fight, and their lack of fear. Warrior and leader of many summers, Itzcoatl had surely known better. Yet, Chimal argued that the Tepanecs' superiority in numbers made it wise to keep to their island, to withstand the siege.

"It's not only about the numbers," growled Itzcoatl, hanging onto his temper, but barely. "The warrior's forces can be deployed wisely, can ambush the enemy and render their numbers useless." The Adviser paused, trying visibly to calm down. "But it's not about that even. Maxtla is a coward. Such a display of our determination might deter him from taking any action at all, giving time for the Acolhua heir to organize his uprising. This strategy would not have worked against Tezozomoc. It might not have even worked against late Tayatzin, but with cowardly Maxtla... The dirty lowlife is beneath contempt. He'll grow afraid, and he'll call his warriors back. To their immense resentment and disappointment, which will harm their fighting spirit even further."

Listening avidly, Tlacaelel tended to agree with his former commander. However, Chimal argued that such an action would most surely provoke the Tepanecs, while more careful politics might prevent any war at all. They still had a good chance to solve the problem peacefully. Oh, how angry Itzcoatl had grown!

"Honorable Warlord." The voice of the warrior tore Tlacaelel out of his reverie, bringing him back to the deepening dusk. "Here is the slave who saw the Tepanecs."

Watching the frightened servant – a young man, thin and haunted, dressed in a loincloth only – Tlacaelel scowled.

"Tell me everything you saw," he said curtly, repulsed by the open fear of the youth. "And do it quickly."

The silence prevailed.

"Do what the Honorable Warlord asks, you useless piece of meat," growled the warrior, pushing the slave forward so hard that the man almost went sprawling. "On your knees!"

Tlacaelel gestured for the warrior to step away. Passed out or hurt, the slave will be useless, he knew, fighting the urge to beat the story of out of the stupid servant himself.

"You are not in trouble, slave," he said, moderating his tone, watching the terrified face in front of him. "You did well by reporting to my warriors. But I wish to hear your story myself." He peered at the man sternly. "So hurry up before you do get into trouble."

The youth fell to his knees, trembling. "Revered Warlord," he mumbled. "I did nothing wrong. Please, believe me. I was sent to bring the clothes... the laundry slaves sent me... I was told to detour by the ponds because we were supposed to look for—"

"Stop mumbling!" Tlacaelel cut him off, his sandaled feet itching to kick the man. "Tell me about the Tepanecs. Where did you see them?"

"Behind the secondary kitchen houses," whimpered the youth. "Near the farthest gates."

"How many?"

"Four warriors."

"Why do you think they were Tepanecs?"

The man winced. "I... I heard them talking." He looked up, pleading. "With this dreadful accent of theirs."

"What did they say?"

"I didn't understand, Revered Master. They were whispering. Oh, please forgive me, please."

"I said you did nothing wrong!" growled Tlacaelel, losing the last of his patience. "Where did they go?"

"I don't know, Revered Master. I didn't dare to stay."

"What did they wear?"

"Strange garbs, Revered Master. Dark clothes and no cloaks."

"Did you see their weapons?"

"No, Revered Master." The man hesitated. "Well, one held out a strange knife. He was the one who talked, whispering and gesturing with his hands."

"How strange?"

"It was bright, glittering."

"Were there swords on their girdles?"

"I don't know, Revered Master. I didn't see."

"Anything else?"

The man shook his head, still on the ground, trembling.

"Well, slave, you did good by reporting to my warriors. If you remember anything else, come and report to me directly." He turned to the warrior. "Let him go for now, but make sure he manages to reach me if he reappears."

"Yes, Honorable Leader," answered the warrior, clearly perturbed. "Go away," he said to the youth, kicking him. He glanced at Tlacaelel. "Do we—"

"We do nothing for the moment. Keep this information to yourself until I talk to the Adviser. Is that clear?"

"Yes, Honorable Leader."

Alone at last, Tlacaelel frowned. It would have been easy to send his warriors combing through the Palace's grounds, looking for strange Tepanec killers, who must still be hiding by the back gates. It was the sensible thing to do.

He shrugged. The thorough search of the Palace's grounds would probably reveal more than he would care to find, with the Highlander most certainly lurking somewhere around, too. And somehow, he felt it would all connect to Itzcoatl in the end. Had the devious adviser had a backup plan, in case the Highlander did not make it?

Greatly perturbed, he turned on his heels, heading back toward the Palace. If only he could find a way to contact this wild friend of his, to send him away to Acolhua lands with no delay. Away from this Palace, away from trouble.

"Those tortillas are very good," said Iztac, picking another pastry from the large, round plate. "I didn't notice how hungry I was."

"Well, it's been an eventful day." The Toltec woman's smile was polite and reserved, as she sat opposite to Iztac, tall and impeccably groomed, as always. Yet, no ironic smile stretched the generous lips, and there were shadows in the large, almond-shaped eyes.

The woman clapped her hands. "Bring us another plate of tortillas, and a bowl of honey. Also, make sure they put enough vanilla into our chocolate," she said to the maid, who arrived with admirable swiftness.

Iztac frowned. "Please, I don't want to put you to this trouble. I must go back, anyway. I can't stay."

"Oh, please, Noble Empress," said the woman, grinning and finally looking her typical amused, slightly derisive self again. "It's not every day my house is honored to such a degree. You must let me enjoy your exalted company for a little longer." The grin widened. "Also, you do look famished. I can see that you have not stopped to eat during this day. But now that you can put some of your worries to rest..." The woman shrugged, her smile disappearing. "You did a wonderful thing, pretty Empress. And frankly, you surprised me."

"I did nothing," said Iztac, uncomfortable under her hostess's measuring gaze. "Everyone would do the same in my place. He is just a child. He could not be held responsible for the actions of his father. I was lucky the princess found him."

"Well, he was the lucky one, to run into both of you and not other inhabitants of the Palace. Not everyone would be as understanding or as forgiving." The large eyes narrowed. "But it's not what surprised me about you. You could have sent him here, but you chose to accompany him, to bring him back here yourself."

"Yes, of course. I could have sent the boy here, but he was wounded and frightened, and, well, I wanted to pay you a visit, to thank you for honoring me with your company this morning."

She stood the openly amused gaze, irritated. Yes, she had been stupid to bring the boy here herself. Yes, she was stupid to let her daughter accompany them. She had been exhausted and confused by the long demanding, unsettling day, and her judgment was flawed. Still, she didn't have to justify her actions, did she? And it was none of this woman's business, anyway.

Seething, she stared back, holding her ground. *You may be so wise and so noble, and oh-so-very-pleased-with-yourself,* she thought, *but you can't tell me what to do, you arrogant cihua. I am the empress, and you are just the third wife of the man who used to be the warlord once upon a time.*

The large eyes watched her, glimmering now with open laughter. "Oh, this is so very kind of you, Noble Empress. I'm truly honored."

"I should be going," said Iztac firmly. "Please, send someone to fetch the princess and tell your servants to summon my palanquin."

The woman shook her head, still laughing. "Oh, you take offense too easily, pretty Empress. But let me apologize. I didn't mean to imply you were acting wrongly or stupidly. On the contrary. I didn't think you had so much kindness in you." The smile disappeared as the shadows returned to the darkening eyes. "What you did was very kind. His poor mother was worried so, but now that the child is back and relatively unharmed..." A shrug. "It might make it easier for her."

Iztac felt the tortilla sticking halfway down her throat. "Is she dying?" she asked, swallowing hard.

The dark gaze did not waver. "Yes."

"I want to see her."

Surprised by her own words, Iztac stared into the beautiful face, seeing nothing, her limbs numb, stomach twisting painfully. The memories were back, disturbingly vivid. It had happened so long ago. More than six summers had passed, and she thought she'd forgotten all about it. After all, she was safe, she could not have any more children. Yet, suddenly it was all back, her bottomless fear, and the pain, and the loneliness, the horrible, hopeless sensation of being alone and forgotten.

"No!" The woman's voice burst through the thickening fog, bringing her back from the nightmare, thankful. It was all in the past. She was safe; it could not happen to her again. She watched the beautiful face in front of her losing any trace of its usual amused superiority, turning into a stone mask. "No, you can't see her. She doesn't need that."

Iztac clenched her palms tight. "I know what she is going through. I... I've been there. She needs to see a familiar face, even if it's the one she hates." She shrugged, seeing the widening eyes, knowing that under different circumstances it would amuse her to watch the haughty woman losing her perpetual composure. "If he would come, it would be wonderful for her."

"Oh, that would be too much to expect from the wild warrior, wouldn't it?" said Cuicatl bitterly. She hesitated. "Come with me."

The walk through the beautiful gardens of the Warlord's house refreshed her, but her heart fluttered inside her chest, and she welcomed the woman's unusually silent presence. She needed to collect her thoughts. Why had she insisted? What was she going to say to her dying rival?

The other wing of the impressive house was smaller but just as richly decorated, its corridors wide, statues glittering. Torches glimmered in the deepening dusk, held by the servants who had lowered their gazes before their nearing mistress, yet, their curiosity was obvious, tangible in the thickening darkness.

Regretting her impulse to come, Iztac found it difficult to follow, her legs heavy, heart beating fast. The smell hit her nostrils as she entered the small set of rooms, and she gasped, clutching onto the supportive pole of the doorway. It was there before, too, creeping down the corridor, but here it was present in force, this well familiar, stomach-twisting odor of blood, and discharges, and smelly potions.

Cuicatl was talking to a strange looking woman, clearly a Mayan, judging by the crossed, grim, unreadable eyes, but Iztac paid them no attention, her gaze drawing toward the next room as though against her will. From where she stood, she could see the small figure surrounded by cushions, curled under the blanket, tiny, fragile, ethereal.

Oblivious of the women, she crossed the room, went through

the doorway firmly, determined now. As the thin, lifeless face turned to her, she studied the stark features, taking in the protruding cheekbones where it previously had been just a pleasant roundness, like that of the boy from the pond.

The dark eyes glittered with recognition, and she saw the thin shoulders tensing. "What do you want?" asked the woman hoarsely, clutching onto her blanket.

Iztac just shrugged and knelt beside the mats. The smell became heavier, and she tried not to wince. She must have been smelling as badly back then. "Your son was worried about you. He asked me to come."

The gaunt face twisted, turned yet paler. "Yes, I'm sorry. I thank you for finding him... for bringing him back." The woman's chest rose and fell rapidly, laboring for breath. "I wish I could tell you... how grateful... I am."

"You don't have to thank me. I did nothing," said Iztac, wishing to be anywhere but here. She watched the woman clenching her teeth, waiting for another bout of pain to pass. "Why won't your healer make something to take away the pain?" she asked, clenching her own teeth against the vivid memories.

"I don't want her to," whispered the woman, her face now covered with sheen of perspiration.

"Why?"

"It's none of your business!"

Oh, now it was more like the cheeky *cihua*. Iztac felt something close to relief.

"You have to fight on. You may feel like dying, but you don't have to."

The woman clasped her lips tight and said nothing.

"Your son, he was afraid you would not heal. He was scared, and he doesn't look like a boy who gets scared easily."

"Which one?"

"I don't know. One of them."

The feverish eyes narrowed. "You presume to act on his behalf, but you don't even know who he is." Sinking deeper into the cushions, the young woman closed her eyes, exhausted.

"Listen," said Iztac, astounded by her own lack of

appropriately angry reaction. "I know you are tired and in pain. And I know you've given up." She made herself more comfortable by taking one of the cushions. "You think you are dying, but you don't have to die. You can heal if you decide it to be so."

The dark eyes were now peering at her, narrowed and hostile. "I can't heal. I'm bleeding, and my body is burning, and it's not because of the child anymore. The child is gone." The cracked lips stretched into a mirthless grin. "Can't you feel the smell? It's the smell of death. I know that much." She coughed, and her face twisted again, teeth sinking into the dry, colorless lips.

"I'll call for your healer," said Iztac, shivering.

"Don't," whispered the woman, leaning heavily against the cushions, her breath coming in gasps. "She can't help."

"Yes, she can." Surprised by her own agitation, Iztac caught the thin arm, feeling it warm and dry, burning against her palm. "Listen to me. I know what you are going through. I've been in your place." She leaned closer, and the smell hit her nostrils, but she didn't move back, holding the woman's gaze. "I almost died giving birth to my daughter. I know how you feel. You grow weary of the pain, and you don't care anymore. Yes, I didn't want the healers around me either after some time. They didn't help. They just hurt me. And I didn't care anymore, because the people I wanted to see weren't near, and I was surrounded by strangers, and I just wanted some time with no pain and no fear." She pressed the fragile hand lightly, afraid of hurting it. "But you do have people who love you, people who need you. The twins. And the other child. And him, too. He needs you. He won't be happy with you gone."

The woman didn't make an attempt to sit up, clearly too exhausted even to try. She just peered at Iztac, her eyes huge, glittering with fever, domineering the thin, bloodless face. Yet at Iztac's last words, her face darkened.

"He won't even notice," she whispered. "Or maybe he will be relieved. He never wanted me. He just accepted me, because I forced... forced myself on him." She swallowed. "From the very first time, he told me that he could not make love to me. He said he had many reasons. He said I would understand when I was older." The glittering eyes closed, but the breaking voice went on hurriedly, as though anxious to say what needed to be said. "I didn't accept that. I insisted and then... then he made love to me, and it was wonderful. It was nothing, nothing like... like the warriors before..." Her voice broke, and she opened her eyes, blinking the tears away. "But he was right, you know? I'm older now, and I understand. He shouldn't have agreed. He was right to refuse me on that riverbank. He was thinking about you. He was planning to go to Tenochtitlan. He is a wonderful man, and he deserves better. You should leave your Palace. You should go with him." She took a convulsive breath. "When I'm dead, you should do this. Take good care of him"

Shivering, Iztac felt the slim arm trying to pull out of her grip as the woman turned her face away, closing her eyes once again, drained of the last of her strength. Her head reeled, and she wanted to let the arm go. It was hot and dry and unpleasant to touch, and the smell enveloped her, making the urge to run away stronger.

"No, I won't take care of him," she said, forcing herself to lean closer, her grip on the woman's arm tightening. "You keep forgetting that again and again. You keep forgetting that I'm not just another woman. I'm the Empress of this *altepetl*. I have better things to do than to care for a wild warrior."

She didn't back away, although she wanted to, as the feverish gaze leaped to her, coming to life, flashing with rage. The effort coated the pale face with beads of sweat, and she could feel the wasted body tensing under the blanket.

She stood the intensity of the dark gaze. "I won't leave Tenochtitlan, and I won't leave my husband, the Emperor. But the Highlander? He will have to leave now. He will have to flee this city, and he may not even make it, because he will be alone, and because he will have to take care of his children. Alone, woman! Think about it. With no one to help and no one to trust, because he will lose both of his women." She saw the fear creeping into the wide-open eyes, and her heart twisted with compassion, but she went on, hardening her voice even more. "And even if he does make it to the Highlands, with his children alive and unharmed, what will happen to them, do you think? He'll dump them on his family, if he has any family left, and he will go and join my brother in his war. And the wild twins will grow up with strange people, yelled at and punished all the time. Won't they?" Taking a deep breath, she marveled at her own cruelty, seeing the large eyes filling with tears. "And all this because you decided that you'd had enough. Think about it. Do they deserve this? Your children and your man." She shrugged. "You are right, he is a wonderful man. I know this, believe me I know. He is different, and there is no one like him in the whole World of the Fifth Sun. But you are wrong about the rest. He needs you. Yes, he loves me. We have loved each other since we were stupid children, hardly fifteen summers old. I gave him my virginity, and we planned to run away together. But, of course, we didn't make it. Real life interfered. And then he came to Tenochtitlan. With you." She peered into the burning eyes, holding their gaze, afraid it would cloud and go away. "He brought you here, and he made you his woman, his Chief Wife. Do you think it was your doing? Do you think you forced him into any of this? Oh, how little you know your man. He can't be forced into anything. He is a law unto himself. No one can force him. Even the Chief Warlord of Tenochtitlan understands this, you silly woman. Even the Emperor. Everyone in Tenochtitlan knows that the Highlander can't be tamed. Everyone, but you, his woman. Think about it."

The burning gaze clung to her, making her shiver.

"Why do you think I hated you so much? Because he took you? How silly. Warriors take women all the time. Some they dump, some they keep. You know that I told him to take more women into his household? Oh, I kept telling him this many times. And you know why? Because I knew how he loved you, and I didn't want him feeling this way. I wanted him to love me and me alone. But he just laughed, and he refused to let me talk bad about you." She shook her head. "He even had the gall to accuse me of being jealous. He was that insolent. He told me how wonderful and good you are. He told me that he is jealous because his friends, my brother and the Chief Warlord, are too appreciative of you. He wouldn't let me say bad things about you, so I hated you even worse. I wished you would die. But now I know better. You can't die because he needs you. He needs you badly. You can't leave him alone now. He doesn't deserve this."

She watched the cracked lips quivering, pressing against each other.

"It's too late," whispered the woman. "I'm dying. I can't change it. I wish I could. I wish I had been more careful. I wish I hadn't let that warrior catch me. So stupid." Her voice broke, and she closed her eyes once again, her chest rising and falling, fighting for breath.

Iztac felt like fighting for breath herself. Helplessly, she reached out, brushing a damp tendril off the burning forehead.

"I know how you feel," she whispered, her voice also difficult to control now. "I felt the same, when Citlalli was born. I was so weak in the end, I didn't feel the pain anymore. Didn't even notice when they pulled Citlalli out of me. I didn't care. It was even nice to be like that, weightless and floating. That's how you feel now, don't you?"

The woman nodded, not opening her eyes.

"Well, I know how it is. But then you know what happened? I heard Citlalli crying, somewhere in the other room. The women were fussing around her, I could hear that, too. Nursemaids and others, they tried to make her shut up, but she would not. The insistent little thing just kept screaming. And then I knew that she wanted me. She wanted her mother. But her mother was dying, she was going away, leaving her all alone." She clenched her teeth against the memories. "And then I grew angry when I thought about these women who couldn't even make her stop crying. They tried very hard, but they didn't care enough. And I knew they would not take good care of her. So I just yelled at the maids to bring the baby to me. And when I saw her, I knew I had to stay around. To take care of her. The maids were just not good enough."

The large eyes were upon her, clinging to her, hanging on every word.

"You don't have this baby, but you have your other children, and you can't leave them. The twins will not prosper without you.

They will grow wilder and more unruly, and they will not be happy. And your other child... Is it a boy or a girl?"

"A girl." The woman's voice was so low it was difficult to understand her words. "Was she crying a lot?"

Iztac took a deep breath. "I didn't hear crying babies on my way here, but maybe she just fell asleep. Maybe she cried herself to sleep. It's late now."

She winced, thinking about the darkness outside. She shouldn't be here. She should be in the Palace, in her rooms, waiting for Chimal. It would take him some time to finish his meetings and activities, but long before midnight, he'd be hurrying toward her rooms, and she had better be there by that time.

Focusing on the young woman's haunted face, she forced a smile.

"Your girl, does she need you a lot?"

"All the time"

"Then you can't leave her."

She felt the dry hand moving, tightening around her palm. "What did you... what did you do... when you decided not to die?" The wide-open eyes bore into her, burning, painfully intense.

Iztac smiled. "I don't know. I think I told the healers to prepare everything they could think of. And then I drank it all, every smelly, disgusting brew. I drank all they gave me, and I asked for more. And I insisted on keeping Citlalli in my rooms, to remind me, you know?" She patted the thin shoulder, then began easing away in order to get up. "Shall I tell your famous healer to start working? This one will surely be able to fill you with potions and brews to bursting."

A smile twisted the woman's dry lips. "Yes, she can do that. But..." She frowned painfully, and her gaze grew troubled and intense. "Can you just call her from here? You don't have to go out to fetch her. You can just shout..." The dry fingers pressed into Iztac's palm. "Could you stay? Just for a little while? Just to make sure... To remind me, if I forgot. Please?" The burning gaze clung to her, pleading and forceful at the same time, full of so much fear and hope, Iztac's heart twisted. "Please..."

"Yes, I'll stay." She pulled another cushion up. "I'll just make myself comfortable, and then we'll make sure you fight on. How old is your girl?"

"She has seen close to two summers."

"Oh, then we can't drag her here now. Citlalli was a helpless baby. She could not object to all the mess and the smell, and the people running around. But your girl might make trouble. So I'll be here in her stead." She smiled. "But now let us call for your healer and get her to pour her most disgusting brews into you, one by one until you cry for mercy." She grinned again. "I'm telling you, those healers just love making you suffer. What would happen if they put some honey into their medicine, eh? Would it hurt them?"

She saw the cracked lips twisting. "I'm a healer too… and no, you can put no honey into your medicine. It could spoil the whole thing."

"Then you are as bad as they are," declared Iztac, pleased with the way the woman's face changed, growing more lively, yet more peaceful, too. "And anyway, I know you are a healer, but I won't be drinking any of your brews, you can be sure of that. Even if you fill it with honey and vanilla to bursting." Grinning, she put her arm on the thin shoulder. "But now, let us make sure you are alive and well, before I grow angry again about what happened upon our first meeting."

CHAPTER 15

Kuini felt his tiredness welling, and he shook his head, forcing himself to concentrate, watching the moonlight bouncing off the Palace's wall, dangerously bright. It was not a good night to sneak around the Palace uninvited, he knew. He glanced at the sky, wishing for an occasional cloud to obscure it.

Shaking his head resolutely, he headed toward the open patch of ground, to cross it hurriedly, diving into the shadow under the terrace. He had been watching this part of the Palace since sunset, counting the openings in the wall, calculating and recalculating. He had never been to the Emperor's quarters. Aside from that incident, seven summers ago, when he had forced Tlacaelel to scale the nearby wall, he hadn't been to this side of the Palace at all. He grinned at the memory, as always, wondering if Tlacaelel remembered it, too.

The light breeze rustled in the nearby bushes, and he pitted his face against it, enjoying its touch. Taking a deep breath, he tried to banish the tiredness, knowing it wouldn't go. He hadn't eaten or slept since the day before, since before the warriors had come to his house. Filthy lowlifes! Fighting the new wave of rage, he forced his body into calmness, studying the wall, seeking protrusions.

His head ached, and his feet slipped more than once, his fingers barely able to hold his weight, his cramped muscles refusing to react properly, the sword hindering his progress up the wall. He would have liked to leave it somewhere – his knife was more than enough for what he was about to do – yet, he had made sure to go to his house the moment Itzcoatl had made his escape possible. He *needed* his sword. Not to use it, but to be there, to keep him safe, to give him strength and a bit of good luck.

He frowned, remembering how empty and abandoned his house appeared when he had come there, sneaking along the back alleys carefully, unwilling to be detected. He knew that Dehe, being her practical, efficient self, would have taken the children and left for his uncle's dwelling, the way she had promised to do. Still, he had probably half hoped to find her there, maybe lingering, packing something, leaving instructions for the slaves. He wanted to see her, to let her know he was well, to make sure she was feeling better. She hadn't been in a good shape when he left.

A twinge of anxiety passed through his stomach, but he pushed the thoughts about her away. This, and the memory of the overturned, untidy house he had found. This was so not like her to leave in such a hurry. But maybe she was just afraid.

Panting, he reached the upper story of the wall and clung to the railing, regaining his breath. The clubs pounding inside his skull redoubled their efforts, and his stomach twisted once again, the way it had since the morning trial. Before that he had just been angry, incredibly angry, but since his exchange with the Emperor, the fear dominated him. Fear for *her*. He had lost his temper in the most disturbing of ways, saying so many stupid, unnecessary things that it hurt even to think about it.

Oh but he just couldn't help it. The moment he saw the Emperor on the podium, this slender, gentle-looking slip of a man, he just wanted to put his arms around the skinny neck and strangle the annoying son of a rat to death. Who did this slim piece of excrement think he was to order his warriors and officials to drag him, Kuini, out of his house, to accuse him of the silliest charge possible? Enough that the young piece of dirt was pissing everyone off, not listening to Tlacaelel or Itzcoatl, doing all the wrong things; enough that he clung to Iztac Ayotl, making it impossible for her to leave Tenochtitlan. But to behave this way with a warrior of his caliber? No, it was beyond any acceptance.

Yet, back in the temple, he had found himself shivering with fear, his thoughts rushing about in panic, impossible to control.

He was not afraid of death, not even by stoning, but he was afraid for her. Oh, he must have implicated her badly. At the time, he had enjoyed watching the ever-pleasant expression leaving the Emperor's face, twisting it with frustration and rage. Oh, he had humiliated his rival, and he had made sure the slimy bastard would not enjoy a moment of peace, even after the execution, would not enjoy *her* without the nagging thought in the back of his head. But then the realization struck, and if not for his tied hands he would have punched himself, understanding that he had ruined it for her, too. The Emperor would ask questions, and she would not lie about it. She would tell him the truth, and then she would be in grave danger.

He had paced his small prison until his legs could not hold him anymore. And then, when they had come to take him and he recognized Itzcoatl's warriors, some of them familiar and old friends, he breathed with relief and waited for the former Warlord to make his move. He didn't expect the Adviser to come and set him free personally, but the man had come, and they talked, and when he had heard that the filthy Emperor was about to make an example out of her, he knew that his worst fears had come true. So, when Itzcoatl cut his ties, he was ready to do what had to be done, reading in the broad face of his rescuer that this was the main reason why he had been saved. However, he didn't mind. Whichever were Itzcoatl's goals, he had his own reasons for doing the deed.

Clinging to the cold, stony railing, he peered inside the opening, seeing podiums and reed stools and clusters of mats, dotted with statues and darkly glimmering mosaics. Anxious to see if there were people in any of these rooms, he strained his eyes, unable to arrive at the decisive conclusion. Finally, tired of clinging to the cold stones, he threw his body over the windowsill. Whether the Emperor was guarded or not, he was going to kill him, even if he had to die doing this.

Holding his breath, afraid to move, he listened, but no sound broke the silence of the night. The room was empty. He scanned the rich settings with his gaze, taking in the neatly arranged covers and mats. No, no one slept here tonight.

Moving carefully along the wall, he slipped into another smaller room, then another. It was eerily empty, but not abandoned. Not like *his* house. The owner of those beautiful rooms was living here, but he wasn't around just now. Where was he? he asked himself, tired beyond measure. In the main hall, meeting with scribes and advisers? Because of the impending war? Well, he could just wait here, for the Emperor to come back and settle in and send his servants away. Or maybe...

He clutched his sword with so much force that it made his fingers lose feeling. What of the Emperor had gone to her set of rooms, if she was still there, held there against her will, maybe, imprisoned. Rigid with fury, he slipped back toward the first room, and then froze, listening. A scratching against the wall outside was too distinct to miss.

Holding his breath, he moved closer to the open shutters, his fingers untying his sword. Another sound, this time as though someone slipped, then regained his balance, but from a different direction. More than one person?

Sword clutched tightly, he slipped behind a golden statue of a serpent, his fingers caressing the carvings, calming his taut nerves. The silence was nerve wracking, but he didn't dare to move, not even when the silhouette slipped into the room. Ready to pounce, he waited, wishing to see better before deciding on any action.

The dark form of a man, clearly a warrior, judging by a prominent topknot, darted to the shadows of the wall, away from the brightness of the opening, freezing and listening too, while another silhouette slipped in. The first man gestured, reminding Kuini of the killers from the Texcoco Palace, the ones who were sent against the Aztec Warlord, his uncle. The way these men had gestured, talking in some obscure sign language, looked familiar.

The first man moved closer, heading for another room, clearly perturbed now. Like him, they too did not expect to find those rooms empty, he realized.

He waited patiently, the opportunity to dispose of the man neatly and quietly the moment he came nearer too good to miss. Yet, a few paces away the warrior hesitated, tensing visibly, turning his head, scanning his surroundings in the darkness, suspicious. Not waiting for the intruder to explore any further, Kuini pounced, his sword hitting from below, saving him a movement.

The man darted aside, his reactions admirable, still, the sword cut through his upper leg, slicing deeply, making the dark figure waver and then crumble onto the floor. Not checking on his wounded rival and not waiting to be attacked by his companion, Kuini launched forward, trying to catch the other silhouette off guard.

It didn't work. The man leaped aside, and he heard the knife swishing, cutting the air. Surprised, he threw his own body sideways, losing his balance but avoiding the lethal touch of the razor-sharp obsidian. Struggling to get to his feet, he felt the man landing upon him, pressing him with his weight, another knife ready in his hand.

His senses in panic, Kuini squirmed, trying to free his hands, his knife useless, still tied to his girdle. The man's dagger glittered strangely, close to his eyes now, not like obsidian, but more brightly, strikingly smooth. Having never seen a knife like that before, he knew it should be as sharp and as dangerous.

With the last of his strength, he kicked at the intruder's groin in time to move out of the knife's path. It cut his cheek, but not deeply, slipping harmlessly toward the floor.

Pushing with everything he had, he rolled over his rival, his hand catching the bright blade, oblivious of the pain in his palm where it cut into his flesh, determined not to let it pounce again. His other palm sank into the man's neck, his fingers claws, digging as though trying to break through the skin.

His rival gurgled, still clutching the knife, but not trying to use it anymore. His other hand shot up, hitting Kuini, but weakening from blow to blow. Panting, his senses still in panic, Kuini pressed on for a long time after the man went still.

When he crawled from under the man, reeling and dizzy, his palm bleeding, his cut cheek on fire, the other warrior was already still upon the floor where he had left him. The glossy dark pool told Kuini his cut in the man's thigh was good.

Picking up the strangely bright knife, he stumbled toward the window, anxious to get away before the Palace's guards should appear. He didn't want to explain anything. He was a runaway outlaw, in a worse position than those killers even.

Breathing the fresh air with relief, he went over the windowsill, and hung there for a moment, gathering his strength. A nearby terrace cut into the silvery darkness, indifferent, abandoned. Yet something was wrong there, too. Breath caught, he watched two more silhouettes materializing out of the dark entrance, moving nimbly and purposefully, going over the railing.

Puzzled, he watched them working their way down the wall, as nimble as two lizards. When they jumped down and disappeared in the nearby bushes, he gasped, suddenly terrified, eyeing *her* terrace in disbelief, his dread welling.

Unable to breathe, he rushed in the same direction, clumsy, his senses all amok, clinging to the wall with his whole body, miraculously not falling off, his hands slippery, smeared with fresh blood, his and that of the other man, his heart thumping. Panting, he leaped over the parapet, charging through the doorway, oblivious to the possibility of running into more killers. Or the Palace's guards.

Having never been to her rooms, he knew that the cluttered mess of the place could belong to no one but her, with pretty items, clothes, and cushions scattered upon the floor, forcing the visitor to pick his pace. Treading on carelessly, hearing the things crushing under his feet, he rushed toward the crumbled form upon the cluster of mats, his heart pumping, the ice in his stomach making it difficult to breathe.

Grabbing the man's shoulder, he wavered and almost fell, the vastness of his relief making it difficult to stay on his feet. He wanted to laugh hysterically. How could one mistake a man for a woman? She was so slender, so delicately built, and although the Emperor was not a broad, well muscled man in himself, he looked nothing like her.

Still anxious, he dropped the body, and rushed through the rest of the rooms, scanning them thoroughly. Nothing. She wasn't there. But then, where was she?

His fears returning, he headed back toward the main room.

Where could the Empress spend her night if not in the Palace? Had the dirty son of a rat locked her away, to await her trial, the way he had done with him, Kuini? The thought made him dizzy with rage.

Coming back, he squatted beside the body, studying the slain man once again. The young Emperor's face looked grim but peaceful, not surprised and not terrified. He must have been killed in an instant, realized Kuini, studying the deep cut in the man's upper back. A beautiful blow. One that was sure to silence the victim right away.

He got to his feet, somewhat at a loss. The Emperor was dead, but who had done this, and why? Watching the young, pleasant face, so peaceful and serene, he felt none of his hatred, none of his previous rage. Tenochtitlan's Third Emperor was no more, slain in the prime of his life, by unknown killers and for no apparent reason. A pity. It was all right to die as a warrior, but this youth was not a warrior. He was just a young man who had tried very hard to be a good ruler.

Curiously glad he was not the one to kill this youth, Kuini shrugged, then straightened up. He had better get out of here in a hurry.

Back on the terrace, he hesitated, not knowing how he should go about looking for her. He took a deep breath. There was only one man who would surely know more than anyone else about the happenings, *any* happenings.

Clenching his teeth against his exhaustion, he went over the railing, the way the two killers had gone a very short time ago. But while those men had probably headed toward the back gates, trying to escape the Palace, their mission completed, he knew he was going to climb another wall. The quarters of Tlacaelel were familiar, and he knew everything about the way those were guarded.

CHAPTER 16

The sun was coming up, unusually red, the color of fresh blood. Iztac watched it, numbed, huddled in the corner of the small terrace, curled into a ball. Hugging her knees, she rocked back and forth, afraid to stop the movement, afraid of the stillness and the silence. It was very quiet out there on her terrace, and very bright now that the moon had faded, before the sun rushed out to dominate the sky.

She watched it quietly, willing it to go away. She didn't want any light now, and she definitely didn't want the new day to be born. Not now, not after the terrible news. Hugging her knees tightly, she shivered in the chilly breeze, listening to the bushes rustling beneath the terrace, hoping to hear… what? Something reassuring. Something that would tell her that this night hadn't truly happened.

The night and the previous day. Oh, yes, it had gone from bad to worse from the moment she was awoken too early, unable to go back to sleep. First, the Toltec princess coming to ruin her morning, then the trial, followed by her bottomless worry, and her attempts to help.

She ground her teeth until they screeched. Such an ugly sound. She should have stayed in the Palace. She should have sent the boy with her palanquin bearers and stayed. Then maybe she could have saved Chimal. Maybe, somehow. But then Kuini's woman would have died, probably. So it came to this. She had saved one person, and let the other one die. Her husband, the man that she loved.

She thought about their last conversation, the way he had

hugged her and promised that everything would be well, telling her that he loved her, that he would always love her. So much like him! To always be there, to love her no matter what, even after everything that had happened. No one loved her like that. No one. Not even the Highlander.

Shutting her eyes tight, she tried to hold the tears back. She had cried so much that she thought nothing was left, but the warm trickling was back, wet upon her cheeks, threatening to go out of control again, to rack her body in the hopeless, most frightening of ways. Since she had heard about Chimal's death it had been like this, coming in waves, triggered by a wandering thought, by a passing memory. Since Kuini had appeared, so terribly looking, dirty and smeared with blood, and oh-so-very-exhausted, his face thin and haggard, his eyes wild.

It had been well past midnight, but she had still been there, sitting beside Dehe – by then she had learned this woman's name, so strange, so foreign sounding, as small and as delicate as the woman herself – holding her hand or keeping the wet cloth pressed against the burning forehead, the way the healer had instructed her to do.

She needed to get up, to stretch her limbs, and also to relieve herself. She needed to go back to the Palace, too, to explain it all to Chimal. But every time she tried to move away, thinking her patient had fallen asleep, the grip on her arm would tighten and the huge eyes would open in panic, pleading, full of fear. So, she would press the thin arm, would caress the lank hair, would talk some more, saying silly things that would make the cracked lips stretch into a faint smile.

"Please, don't go yet," the woman would plead weakly. "Not yet. In a little while. But not now."

And she would feel her stomach twisting, remembering how frightened she had been when it was her time to battle the spirits of the Underworld.

"You fight on," she would say every time. "Don't worry. I'm here. I'm making sure you won't give up. I'm keeping a close eye on you. You won't go anywhere as long as I'm here. So just rest and get ready for another potion. Your healer will bring it here shortly. I can hear her stirring things in the other room. Disgusting, horribly smelling things. I'm so glad you are the one to drink it and not me."

Satisfied with yet another faint smile, she would caress the damp forehead, pondering whether to put another wet cloth upon it. And then she would sink back into her thoughts. Calm, happy thoughts. She would go back in the morning, she had reasoned, and she would explain it all to Chimal. And he would understand. Like always.

And then, when it was well past midnight and Dehe was truly asleep and much cooler after yet another brew she had managed not to throw up, there were voices in the corridor, loud agitated voices, and then Cuicatl was there, disheveled, her eyes wide.

"Come," she said, gesturing to Iztac.

"I can't," whispered Iztac. "I promised not to leave her. She could wake up any moment."

"Come," insisted the tall woman in a voice that brooked no argument.

Iztac measured her with a wondering glance, astounded. But there was something in the woman's face, something that made her blood freeze, so she brushed past the healer, who stood there just as untypically upset. *What had come over everyone?*

And there, in the dimly lit corridor, her knees almost gave way when she saw *him*, half naked, with his cloak missing, his body scratched and dirty, his face haunted and thin, his eyes wild, the warrior's lock askew.

He stood there and just stared at her in disbelief, and something had held her back from rushing toward him, the way she would have under regular circumstances. And no, it was not the presence of Cuicatl, or his uncle and the servants. Something in his face, in the way his eyes stared at her, relieved and afraid at the same time, made her wish to clutch the nearby pole for support.

"Go to the terrace," said Cuicatl, assuming command. She glanced at her husband, and the old Warlord nodded solemnly, his impressive, still handsome face closed and foreboding.

And then they were on the terrace and alone, and she touched his shoulder shyly, wishing to make sure it was truly him and not the fruit of her imagination. She had worried about him so much through the last day and night! So when he caught her in his arms, pressing her to his chest forcefully, reeking of sweat and blood, but still welcoming and reassuring, she clung to him, and let her fears go away.

"I can't believe you are here," he whispered. "I would never imagine. Of all places. I worried about you so much."

She clung to him desperately, marveling at the miracle of his being here, and alive, and unharmed, relatively.

"Why would you worry about me?" she whispered into his chest, unwilling to break free from the safety of his embrace. "It was you we were worried about. All of us. So many people running around, trying to make sure you wouldn't die."

She felt him tensing against her body. "Who? Who was running around?"

"All of us, even your twins, even your uncle's haughty Toltec wife." She wriggled, nestling more snugly in his arms.

He kept silent for a long moment. "She was the one to bring you here?"

"No." This time she squirmed free, leaning against his arm, trying to see his face in the darkness. "It's a strange story, too long to explain just now. But I shouldn't be here. With sunrise, I'll go back to the Palace, and I hope I'll be able to explain. You see—"

"You can't go back to the Palace, Iztac Ayotl!" he breathed, visibly aghast.

"What do you mean?" She peered at him through the darkness. "Of course, I can. Chimal will be angry, but I'll explain, and he will understand. He always understands." He seemed to stop breathing, but she paid it no attention, rushing on, afraid to stop talking, afraid of his revelations. Something was wrong, terribly wrong. "Don't worry, he won't be angry with me. I will explain everything to him. I just came to pay the Warlord's wife a visit, and then, you see, I had to stay, because..." She paused. "You see, your wife, she was very sick and—"

"How sick? What happened?"

"She lost the child, and she was suffering a lot, and—"

"She lost the child?"

She nodded.

"Oh, gods, I have to see her!" He released her at once. "Listen, stay here. I'll be back shortly. Don't go anywhere. I'll be back with you in a matter of heartbeats. Stay—"

"She is asleep now, but, of course, you should go to her. But I won't stay. I can't. I should hurry back to the Palace. Maybe if I come now and not in the morning no one will notice..." She brought her palms to her forehead, suddenly aware of the sweat and the reeking of her clothes. "Maybe under the cover of the darkness... I need to call for my palanquin bearers—"

He caught her shoulders once again. "You can't go to the Palace, Iztac Ayotl. Not anymore."

"What? What do you mean?" She found it difficult to breathe, as though the night air had just emptied or lost its magical qualities. "I told you, he'll understand."

"He is dead."

"What?" She felt his arms rigid around her shoulders, like those of a stone statue. Struggling to stay calm, to make sense out of it, she slipped from his grasp. "That is the silliest thing to say. The most stupid thing I've ever heard."

He didn't move to catch her. He just stood there frozen, a part of the darkness, but she wished she could see his eyes. It was so quiet on the terrace and below, so quiet and empty.

"That is stupid nonsense," she repeated. "You can't say such things."

But he kept silent, as though afraid to move.

"Say something!" she demanded, her stomach turning. "Tell me it's not true."

"It is." It came out so quietly, she wasn't sure he had said the words.

She clasped her palms tight. "No, it's impossible. It can't happen! You are mistaken." She heard herself shouting and was glad that something at least broke the suffocating silence. It kept rising like water in the lake, surrounding, threatening to drown her. "I'll go back now, and I'll show you that it is not true." His silent presence there in the darkness made her want to break something. It was a vicious labyrinth with no way out. "If no one calls for my palanquin bearers, then I'll walk. I'll get there, and then you will know it is not true."

Suddenly, he came back to life. "No, Iztac Ayotl. You can't go there. Not now, not ever." He took a step forward, catching her shoulders in his arms, holding her tightly as she struggled to break free. "You can't. You will be dead too if you do."

"Let go of me!" she hissed, hitting his chest with her clenched fists. "You can't hold me here against my will. I have to go there, I have to make sure... I have to see him. I have to!"

He didn't move, didn't try to avoid her blows. He just stood there, holding her, making it impossible to break free.

She kicked him wildly. "Let me go! You can't hold me against my will. Who do you think you are to touch me at all?" But her voice broke, turning into sobs, making it more difficult to breathe, and to fight him. She felt his arms around her, but this time they brought no reassurance, because she knew it would not help, would not make his words disappear.

"How did it happen?" she asked after a while, when able to talk once again, her tears smeared upon his chest, mixing with the dust and the sweat, and the dried blood upon it.

He shrugged, not moving, as though afraid that should he lower his guard, she'd use the opportunity to run away.

"Did you see it happening?"

"No."

Suddenly, the thought hit her, and she made a desperate effort to break free. To no avail, but it didn't matter. *He was somewhere around the city since the early afternoon, free and very, very angry with Chimal.*

"You did this?" she whispered, her throat dry, voice trembling.

"No," he said, but there was a slight hesitation in his voice.

"Tell me the truth!" she demanded. "Tell me now, or I swear I'll—"

"I didn't do it, but I wanted to," he said firmly. "I was about to do it."

She felt the strength leaving her body at once, draining off like water from a broken pottery. Her legs gave way, but his arms still encircled her shoulders, so she didn't fall.

"Who did this?"

"The Tepanecs."

"Impossible. No Tepanecs would get into the Palace."

"These did." He shrugged again. "I killed two of them. Tlacaelel said... well, he said they were Tepanecs."

"So the Chief Warlord knew about it?"

He said nothing.

"And Itzcoatl?"

More silence.

She felt her anger welling, its intensity hurting her chest, but also giving her her strength back. "I will not rest," she hissed. "I will not rest until I have avenged his death on both of them!"

"Tlacaelel had nothing to do with it," he said finally. "He did nothing against his half-brother."

"But he did nothing to prevent it either, eh?" Free at last, she stood before him, challenging. "How else did he know they were Tepanecs?"

"I don't know," he said tiredly.

She cleared her throat. "Why were you going to kill him? Because of the trial?"

Not standing next to him, she could still feel his tension, and his rising anger.

"Was that not enough?" He paused. "He was angry with you, too, and I wasn't sure you would have enough sense to leave the Palace. But clearly you did."

Glad for the cover of ever-concealing darkness, she stared at him, her mouth agape.

"I didn't leave the Palace because of that. I... Chimal was angry with me, but he understood."

The sound of his name made her remember, and she felt her stomach shrinking again, her insides collapsing against each other. Taking a step back, she leaned against the stone parapet, because her legs began to tremble.

"That's not what Itzcoatl said," she heard him saying. "And the Adviser would know. Your husband did not understand, and he did not take it kindly." She saw the silhouette of his shoulders lifting in a shrug. "You were lucky to be here instead of there."

Itzcoatl! Her rage was so sudden, so overwhelming, she gasped for breath. But it helped to stop the trembling.

"What did Itzcoatl say?" she breathed, in half a whisper half a shriek.

He stepped forward and again was standing next to her, ready to catch her, she realized, should she fall, or maybe try to run away.

"It doesn't matter now," he said quietly. "It happened, and it's in the past. You didn't get hurt. That's what matters." Another shrug. "Well, to me."

"I need to know what he said." She heard her own voice, shrill and high, ugly, but she didn't care. The trembling was back, and she clenched her teeth tight, trying to make it go away.

"He said the Emperor was going to execute his Chief Wife for infidelity." He swallowed. "After all the stupid things I said in the trial, it was easy to believe that."

Oh, gods! She slipped down the railing and sat upon the floor, powerless even to pull her legs closer to her chest. It was good not to have to spend one's energy on standing upright. But the picture was there, vivid and clear. Itzcoatl's behavior over the past market interval made perfect sense.

"But you didn't kill him?" she whispered, feeling him squatting beside her, as drained as she was.

"No. He was already dead when I found him."

"Who killed him?"

He shook his head. "I don't know. They wore dark clothes, and they carried knives. Probably to be able to sneak around undetected. Strange knives. I took one such with me." A mirthless chuckle. "The Palace's guards should have caught them, if you ask me. Tlacaelel says they were Tepanecs."

"Maxtla?"

"Probably." But the way he said that made her look up, trying to see his face in the darkness.

"Was Tlacaelel in on this, too?"

"No, he was not."

"Then how did he know all this?"

He sighed. "Listen, it doesn't matter. Tlacaelel is Tlacaelel. He knows everything. But the main thing is that you are not safe in the Palace, not anymore. Itzcoatl cannot let you live. He will be the next Emperor. He will fight the Tepanecs, and he has a fair chance of making the best out of this mess." He paused. "But none of us will be here to see it."

"What do you mean?" she whispered, shivering at the thought of Itzcoatl there in the Palace, ruling Tenochtitlan. Yes, he would not let her live, not after what had happened. That's why he had been looking at her strangely through the last few days, she realized. With that sort of a mirthless regret she had found so odd and alarming. Oh, gods. Had she known what he was planning…

"It's time we do what we always planned to do," he was saying in that same quiet, expressionless voice of this evening. "It's time I kept my promise to you."

She leaned against the wall, hugging her knees. It felt cold and hard behind her back. She didn't care. Eyes shut, she tried to think. Yes, of course. It was the perfect solution. She felt neither joy nor sorrow. Empty, drained of feelings. Had she craved for him to take her away once upon a time? It seemed strange, like a long-forgotten dream.

His arms squeezed her shoulders, but hesitantly, not as forceful or as demanding as always. They were trembling too, she could feel that.

"Your daughter, I will make sure to smuggle her out of the Palace. Tlacaelel will help," she heard him saying.

"She is here, somewhere around."

"What? How?"

"It's a long story." She was so tired.

There were voices outside the terrace, and she remembered her promise.

"I have to go back to her," she said, the effort to talk making her dizzy. "I promised not to leave her."

"Whom?"

"Your wife. She needs me there."

She could feel him peering at her through the darkness.

"I'll go to her," he said finally. "You need to rest. I'll take you back inside the house."

But she shook her head so vigorously it bumped against the stone railing, the effort taking the last of her strength.

"I'll stay here," she whispered, knowing that it would break any moment. "Please. Let me stay here. Please. I need to be alone now. I can't see any of them. Not now. Please."

She felt his arms tightening, enveloping her, his body warm, sheltering against the coldness of the pre-dawn wind. And, suddenly, it all came back, the familiar feeling of being safe with him, inside his arms.

So she let the tears flow, let them rack her body, drain it of the last energy, lose all control. As long as he was there, keeping her safe, she could do this and not be afraid anymore. He wasn't there on both previous occasions that she had broken down this way, neither ten summers ago, when he didn't come to Texcoco Plaza, nor four summers later when she was dying giving birth to Citlalli, but he was here now, and it was wonderful to have his support. Enveloped in his warmth and his scent, she could finally let go.

However, later on, she had made him go back to Dehe, having insured that should the poor woman demand her presence, she would be called upon immediately. And so she had stayed on the terrace, to await the sun. And to think.

Alone and relatively calm, she allowed herself to think of Chimal, remembering it all, the boy and the young man, his sweet, cheerful, loyal presence. A wonderful man, her only friend.

The tears were flowing again, but she let them out uninterrupted this time, not struggling, not afraid anymore. Chimal deserved all this grief and more, and the Highlander was there, just a few rooms down the corridor, and he would not leave her alone anymore.

Dehe watched the sun coming up, too. From where she lay she could not see it appearing in the sky, but the open shutters allowed the flaming rays in, covering the bright walls with pretty patterns. She studied them, liking the pictures they drew, happy to lay there and think of nothing, exhausted and sweat covered but not in pain anymore. Not freezing or burning. *Not dying.*

Well, the lack of pain was most likely due to the medicine, she knew. And maybe the lack of fever, too. But it didn't matter. Her body needed time to recover, and the medicine would help it to do that.

Shifting her gaze back to the side of her bed, she watched him as he curled there, asleep. He looked funny, crouching beside her mat, leaning against the wall, his arms tucked against his sides, his face peaceful, as it always was when he slept, not sitting well with all the dust and the dry blood smeared upon it, his blood and someone else's.

She smiled, remembering watching him when she had first met him and he had fallen asleep in her improvised home in Huexotzinco's woods. She had been startled by the change back then too – one moment a dangerous warrior, the other just a peacefully sleeping boy.

Well, some things never change, she thought, her smile widening. All the dirt, and the blood, and the killings, and here he was, curled into a ball like one of his sons, falling asleep without bothering to lie down.

She shivered, remembering waking up in the deep of the night, seeking the hand of the Tenochtitlan's Empress, her unexpected savior, and not finding it. She had panicked immediately, because only as long as this woman was beside her did she know that she would not die.

But then she felt his presence. Even before opening her eyes, she knew he was there, and that reassured her, too, although she still needed that woman to be near. He was leaning close to her, holding her shoulders, talking to her, whispering things, the fear in his voice obvious. He needed her strength and her reassurance, she realized, struggling to make her eyes focus, and to smile, too.

Well, it worked. His face calmed, and he hugged her tightly and promised not to leave her for any reason. Just like the woman before. But the woman was gone. Still, she agreed to drink yet another potion and closed her eyes, making sure his hand was clasped firmly in hers.

And now it was bright and warm, and he was still here, curled beside her legs like a large animal. A dirt-covered, battered male jaguar, after it had fought a whole pack of hungry winter wolves. And come out victorious. As always.

She smiled and tried to reach for his face, to caress it lightly, but for that she would need to rise, and she couldn't do that. Not yet. But she would, she promised herself. In a day or two, with plenty of medicine and plenty of rest, she would be up and about, as strong as before. Just like the woman had promised.

Where was she, the mighty Empress? she wondered, wishing to see the beautiful face once again. Had she gone back to the Palace? Well, most probably she had. It was a wonder she had been able to stay for so long. It was a wonder she had come at all. But she had, she had come, and she had saved her, Dehe, as spicy, as annoyingly haughty as always, but good, incredibly good and wise. Oh, gods. She, Dehe, was such a bad, selfish person. How could she have thought of leaving her children alone? And him, too. How selfish!

She smiled again, thinking about the twins. Oh, no, no one would get to raise her children, to yell at them, and to punish them. No one! The woman was right. This was exactly what would have happened. The wild pair wouldn't get along, not even with their own grandmother, the yellow-eyed witch. She shivered at the thought. No, she would get better, and she would take care of her children, whether they stayed in Tenochtitlan or left.

Frowning, she let her thoughts wander. Would they have to flee the island-city? The woman said he would have to leave now, and she was right about many things. Oh, it would be good to leave the busy *altepetl* behind, good to return to the Highlands. And if the woman was right about that, maybe she was right about the other thing, too.

She studied his face once again, frowning now. Did he love her, Dehe, as much as he loved his Empress? Could a man truly love two women at the same time? Men took women into their households, wives and concubines and just occasional females while away on campaigns. But it has nothing to do with love. It was a necessity. Yet, not with him. With him it was different. She wanted his love, and the Empress wanted it, too. That's why they hated each other, the woman had said, and she was right. Not because he made love to both of them, but because he may have loved each one.

The troubled thoughts were back, nagging. She would have to make sure she met with this woman before leaving. To thank her, and maybe to talk some more. But how? She wouldn't be allowed into the Palace with no invitation, and she could not send notes to the haughty Empress.

She shifted uneasily. Well, then she would have to sneak into the Palace, maybe disguised. The way Kaay had smuggled her in seven summers ago. She fought her smile from showing, remembering the basket of rotting avocados. Yes, she would have to make sure to put something less delicate into her basket this time. Chili peppers, maybe?

He stirred, and she watched him as he opened his eyes, abruptly like always – one moment asleep, the next wide awake and ready to pounce. Stretching, he peered at her, a broad smile lighting his pale, muddied face.

"You look better," he said, moving closer in a long graceful movement. A jaguar! Still battered, but now ready for his next hunt.

She smiled. "I feel better. I will not die now."

"Oh no, you won't!" He reached for her cheek, caressing it gently, lovingly. "You had us all worried. Don't do this again, woman."

She chuckled, although the effort left her breathless, covered with sweat. "You were not the one worried. You were away." Seeing his face darkening, she made an effort to rise, reaching for his hand. "I didn't mean it as an accusation. I was glad you didn't see it. The child... There was so much blood, and... It was horrible. I'm glad you didn't see it."

She closed her eyes against the welling tears, desperate to hide them. Tears were a private matter. Yet, when he gathered her into his arms, she felt them flowing anyway, warm and salty upon her cheeks.

"It will never happen again, never," he was whispering, pressing her close. "I'll make sure of that. I should have been more careful. I should never have endangered my family like that. When I saw this man pressing his knife to your throat..." His voice broke, and she felt him swallowing, trying to control himself. "I... I would cut my own throat if that would prevent him from cutting yours, I swear. I could not lose you, not you!"

Snug in his embrace, although uncomfortable with the way he pressed her too tightly, she felt the tears bursting unrestrained. But they were not tears of grief anymore. He loved her, he did love her! The woman had been right about that, too.

"Will we leave Tenochtitlan?" she asked after they both had calmed down and he put her back, making her comfortable upon the cushions.

"In a few dawns, yes. The moment you feel better. When you can travel."

"Can we wait? Is it not dangerous for you in Tenochtitlan now?"

He shrugged.

"Maybe you should go away now, before the Emperor sends his warriors after you. We will join you the moment I can travel. I can manage—"

"The Emperor is dead."

She studied his darkening face, searching for signs of him teasing her.

"How?" she asked finally, appalled.

He pressed his lips tight and said nothing, staring ahead, into unknown depths.

"You did this?" she whispered.

That brought him back from his reverie. "No," he said in a cutting voice that invited no more questions. Now it was the warriors' leader speaking.

She tried to think clearly. If the Emperor was dead, then Kuini was in no danger anymore. Or was he? She thought about what Tlacaelel had said. No, it was not that simple!

"Tell me what happened."

He frowned. "Leave it, Dehe. Leave this *altepetl* and its politics alone. We are going away, and that what matters."

"What will happen to the Empress?" she asked, suddenly worried. *When had the woman left? Was it before the Emperor was killed?*

His eyes softened, took on an amused glint. "What do you think?"

"I don't know," she said, on guard now. "Will she marry the next Emperor?"

Now he laughed outright. "Itzcoatl? Oh, no, he will have her killed the moment she catches his eye."

"Then you have to help her. You have to save her. She saved my life and..."

His eyes glimmered. "She will leave with us."

"Oh!"

"Yes, oh." His grin was broad and unbearably smug. "I hope you two will find a way to get along. Just like my uncle's or my brother's wives. I wouldn't like to see you two going for each other's hair."

She glared at him, forgetting her exhaustion. "She won't like it in the Highlands, you know. Not the haughty Empress."

He shrugged. "Who knows? She may get along. And anyway, she will be able to move back to Texcoco the moment we take this *altepetl* from the Tepanecs. With a brother for an emperor, she will be well settled."

"And you?"

He shrugged again. "We'll see about me. I may move to Texcoco, too, depends on what that same Emperor will offer." His grin was one-sided and suggestively crooked. "Long ago, when we were mere youths, he said he would make me his Chief Warlord when he became an emperor. So if he keeps this particular promise, you may need to grow used to managing a house like this one. Lots of rooms, lots of gardens, plenty of things, an army of slaves. Are you up to this challenge, oh Honorable Lady?"

She still glared at him. "With Tenochtitlan's former Empress for your Chief Wife, I won't have to work that hard, I'm sure."

"Oh!" He frowned, then shrugged again. "Well, we'll see how we go about that when Texcoco is ours, won't we? No need to get all indignant just now." Leaning closer, he cupped her face between his palms. "I love you, woman. I will never put you aside or make you unhappy in any other way. You can trust me on that." He peered at her, his eyes losing their amused spark. "I cannot lose you. Not you. I was so close to it, and I didn't like it in the least. You mean too much to me, wife. Don't you ever endanger yourself again."

She felt her chest tightening and wondered if she could cope with so much happiness in her exhausted condition. The tears were back, but she blinked them away resolutely. She wouldn't be caught weeping like a silly *cihua*, and she wouldn't make him repeat himself. What he'd said was enough.

"I will not make you lose me," she said, when able to control her voice. "I will always be there for you." She tried to squirm free from his cupping hands as he kept peering at her, studying her face, his smile flickering. "Don't look at me like that. Not now, not when I'm ugly and sweaty, and smelling bad."

He laughed, then leaned forward, parting her dry lips with a forceful kiss. "You are not ugly. You never are. And I'll be busy filling you with a new baby the moment I can show you my love. So just get better soon."

He sprang to his feet, light and nimble, as though after a good night's sleep, and not after running about and fighting and doing gods-know-what for the most of the night.

"I need to see to our Empress and then to the baths," he declared, stretching and greeting the entering Kaay with a short nod. "So glad my uncle's house has those beautiful baths right in the middle of his gardens. I'm going to stay there for half a day." He grinned. "When I'm Coyotl's Warlord, I'm going to have a house just like that. Between the Plaza and the Palace. You haven't been to Texcoco, but you'll love this *altepetl*. It's nothing like Tenochtitlan. It's beautiful, and full of magic. You'll fall in love with that city, you just wait and see." Winking at her, he headed for the doorway. "You'll have the serious task of making that future huge house of ours as perfect as our previous home. Iztac

Ayotl will just make a mess out of it, so it will be up to you, woman, to turn it into something presentable."

She watched him walking away with those long, forceful paces of his, in peace with his world, for a change. Oh, yes, he'd make a fine Chief Warlord, she thought. Just like Coyotl would make a great Emperor.

Smiling, she looked at Kaay. "Come with us," she said to the old woman, liking her greatly. "What do you have in Tenochtitlan to stay for?"

"Oh, how very generous of you, girl," laughed Kaay, putting her tray on the floor and squatting beside it with an effort, fatter than ever. "I'll think about it, when you are the most important noble lady of Texcoco."

And why not? thought Dehe, accepting a cup of a smelly brew and drinking it obediently, just like the Acolhua Empress had told her to do. She would make a fine Chief Wife for the Honorable Chief Warlord. Even as the Second Wife she'd have great chances to matter. Cuicatl was the Third Wife, and no one had thought to dismiss her as unimportant.

She took a deep breath, fighting the nausea. Oh, yes, she thought. She would be just like that noble Toltec lady, as wise and as confident, as derisively amused, but as generous and kind.

"I will bring you to Texcoco the moment we take it back from the Tepanecs," she declared, relieved that she had managed to keep yet another potion down. "You just wait and see."

CHAPTER 17

Tlacaelel eased his shoulders, shifting his weight from one foot to the other, eyeing the Plaza far below his feet, enjoying the sight of it packed with hundreds of people. The excited crowds were spilling into the nearby alleys, watching and talking, and gesturing, their spirits high. Oh, his Mexica people were not fearful, not afraid of the approaching Tepanecs. No, the current Masters of the Valley would not intimidate them anymore.

His chest swelled with pride. The Tepanecs could not win, not this time. Tenochtitlan was not ready, stunned by the death of its Emperor and still alone, with no worthwhile allies; yet now, watching the Plaza from the height of the Great Pyramid, he knew that they would win, eventually. And not in the too distant future. The siege would be short, and it would not harm his beloved *altepetl*.

Easing his shoulders once again, he made sure his posture was straight and proud, reflecting his mood. This ceremony was being held for his sake. Today at the high noon he had been made *Cihuacoatl*, the Head Adviser, achieving the most exalted position, next only to *Tlatoani*, the Revered Speaker, the Emperor. Itzcoatl, the new Emperor, had made sure to hold this ceremony before throwing all of his energy into the nearing war. He had needed to ensure his Chief Warlord's absolute loyalty, reflected Tlacaelel, slightly amused. Hence, the ceremony and the second most exalted position in the land.

Hiding his grin – oh yes, he had nothing to complain about – he glanced at Itzcoatl, standing beside him, tall and broad, imposing, a perfect leader, a perfect Emperor. The ideal man to stand up to the mighty Tepanecs. Yes, Tenochtitlan could have asked for no better leader in such difficult times. Despite his relatively humble origins, this man was the right person for this difficult mission.

As though sensing his companion's scrutiny, Itzcoatl turned his ᵢead. "Not a small gathering."

"No. And they did not come here only to watch the ceremony. ᵉy have come here to show us their trust. They are letting us know that they are not afraid."

"An interesting observation, Nephew." Itzcoatl nodded, his lips twisting into an untypically amused grin.

"Too bad we cannot lead our warriors out right away. I should love to spare us the humiliation of a siege."

"It will be a short siege, Nephew. Never fear."

"I don't."

On the podiums below the stairs, he saw many familiar faces, Itzcoatl's Chief Wife, a very reserved and not especially good looking noble lady of Tlatelolco, his own wives, other members of the royal family, too numerous to count.

His eyes picked out the serious, fresh face of Moctezuma, a very promising youth, another half brother of his. At the age of seventeen, and already finished with his *calmecac* training, this youth showed a knack for leading and organizing, displaying much bravery. It was said that five dawns ago, upon hearing the news of Chimalpopoca's death, young Moctezuma, who was returning from a short mission on the mainland, refused to sail back to Tenochtitlan, organizing his companions and followers instead in a sort of a battle formation, taking out his bow and preparing to fight the approaching invaders. The incident had earned him a new nickname that was beginning to catch, *Moctezuma Ilhuicamina – the Sky Shooter*.

Tlacaelel grinned, liking the youth. He would take him along when they headed for Azcapotzalco. This young half-brother of his might do well with the proper guidance.

"The old Tepanec is finally happy," he heard Itzcoatl murmuring, still amused and in the best of moods. "The canning bastard has got it all according to his dirty scheming. Just the way he had planned it for the past half twenty of summers or more."

Searching out the broad, wrinkled, impressively dignified face in the crowds, Tlacaelel found it difficult to fight his grin this time. Oh, yes, the First Warlord of Tenochtitlan was happy. The hard work of Revered Acamapichtli was beginning to bear fruit, and with Tenochtitlan free from the Tepanec yoke, it would blossom with no restraints.

"He deserves this," he said, admiring the man greatly. "He is the last reminder of the old times, when everything was wild and dangerous and out of the ordinary. Revered Acamapichtli was this sort of a ruler, an exceptional man who didn't go with the rules and wasn't afraid of a challenge. It was so much like him to pick this man, this Tepanec, to entrust with more responsibility than his status warranted." He shrugged. "There are no people like him anymore. I'll be sorry to see this man embarking on the Underworld journey."

"It won't happen any time soon." Grinning, Itzcoatl turned to watch the priests as the matted, dark clothed figures brought forward their utensils and tools. "This man enjoys his life too much. He won't leave our Fifth World in a hurry."

Shielding his eyes, Tlacaelel watched the priests, too. "His nephew left on the day before this one."

"To join his Acolhua friend." Itzcoatl made it a statement, seemingly immersed in what the priests were doing. "I heard there had been word from our Texcocan. He seemed to be gathering quite a force up there in the Highlands."

"Yes, Nezahualcoyotl's warriors came back, very worried. Apparently, he chose to go to Huexotzinco all alone, trusting the highlanders. Which was not a wise thing to do, according to his leading escort. But a few days after Chimalpopoca's death, a messenger came, bearing good news, to lighten the tragedy of this day. The Acolhua heir is alive and well, and the Highland's leaders agreed to supply him with a considerable amount of warriors." Tlacaelel shrugged. "I wish they would organize faster, but the Highlander thinks it will take a few moons, or more. They will need to organize the Acolhua people, as well."

The lifted eyebrows were Tlacaelel's answer. "He won't be

coming back, you know that, don't you?"

Tlacaelel squinted his eyes against the glow of the high-noon sun. "He will join our attack on Azcapotzalco all the same. Leading his Highlanders or the Acolhua people, instead."

"I wish well to his future leaders," said the new Emperor, shrugging good-naturedly. "Don't mistake me, Nephew. I don't wish him harm. And I don't mind his joining our war. I just don't want him among my warriors. I want my people obeying my orders."

"He has his merits. He is a great warrior, and there is no better man to have by one's side in dangerous situations."

"Oh, yes. A perfect man for special missions. But as a regular warrior or regular leader? I'm happy to let the Texcocans handle this basket of troubles."

Tlacaelel said nothing, annoyed with himself. Why did he feel obliged to defend the Highlander's good name? The man was a friend, there was no argument about that. A sort of a friend that even a highborn exalted aristocrat like himself needed from time to time. He meant what he'd said to the haughty Empress. A man in his position had no friends, and yet the Highlander came closer than anyone to this particular status. Still, friend or not, the fierce, proud foreigner needed neither help, nor protection. He would laugh and would say that the manure-eating new emperor was right, that he was all of what they said about him and more. The smug, cheeky bastard was that sure of himself.

And then he knew what was wrong. He had missed him, this unruly savage and his baiting, insolent, disrespectful presence. This man was the only person whom he could trust entirely, to be there when needed, to guard his, Tlacaelel's, back. Too honest and often rude, but loyal, always loyal. Oh, the Highlander was loyal to the people he loved and respected. He was loyal to Nezahualcoyotl, guarding the Acolhua heir's interests with his life, if need be. He was loyal to him, Tlacaelel, too, he realized. Unruly and short tempered, but more dependable than anyone else in the whole of Tenochtitlan. And in his, Tlacaelel's, position, it was a rare thing, people who would do something for you out of a pure friendship, rarer than a chocolate drink in a peasant's household.

"Did he take the late Emperor's wife with him?"

The question brought Tlacaelel back from his reverie, making him struggle to keep his face aloof and indifferent.

"I don't know."

"I'm sure you don't." Itzcoatl chuckled, pleased with himself. "Mind you, I don't want to see this woman dead, either. I just want her and her troublesome presence away from me and my *altepetl* and its provinces." He yawned, covering his mouth with the back of his hand. "On the other side of the Great Lake, the wild barbarian can keep enjoying her, as far as I'm concerned. Just like he had, probably, been enjoying her here for summers upon summers."

The priests' voices rose, and their chanting took a different tone as the first offering was brought forward.

"The princess, the First Daughter of Chimalpopoca has disappeared, too," said Itzcoatl, turning back to the altar, not shielding his eyes and not even blinking against the strong sun. "Which makes one wonder..."

Could it be? thought Tlacaelel, taken aback, trying to remember the little girl and what she looked like.

"She looked outlandish enough," commented the new Emperor, echoing his thoughts. He chuckled. "And to think of our beautiful empress among the savages..."

Tlacaelel shrugged. "The willful Acolhua woman will be the most important lady of Texcoco as soon as Nezahualcoyotl gets his *altepetl* back, I predict. But she'll miss her Empress's status. She liked being that."

"She'll be busy telling our Acolhua friend what to do. This one will not stay out of politics, trust me on that. An interesting woman. If not for her foul temper and her unruliness, I would have taken her into my household, would have made her an empress again." Itzcoatl rolled his eyes. "So much beauty, so much nobility, so much temper. It would have been interesting to sample her. They all kept losing their heads, abandoning any reasonable thinking, the moment it would come to her – Chimalpopoca and the Highlander, and even her brother. There was something about this woman." The wide shoulders lifted in a shrug. "But I'm glad she is gone. Tenochtitlan is better off without dominant empresses. The future capital of the Great Lake shall be ruled by its lawful rulers, and no one else."

Yes, thought Tlacaelel, turning his eyes to the priests and the man spread upon the stone altar. Tenochtitlan would win this time, and it would rule the lands around the Great Lake, and far beyond them. It would be the greatest city in the whole World of the Fifth Sun, and it would be governed by their lawful emperors alone.

He took a deep breath, finding it difficult to contain his welling excitement. Oh, yes, it would happen, and he would be the one to make it possible. He would not be the emperor, but he would be remembered.

AUTHOR'S AFTERWORD

In 1428 a short siege had, indeed, been launched on Tenochtitlan, then lifted hurriedly when the Acolhua people, under Nezahualcoyotl's leadership, and reinforced by the Highlanders of Huexotzinco, and even the more distant Tlaxcala and Xaltocan, crossed the Great Lake toward Azcapotzalco.

Alarmed, Maxtla had abandoned the blockade of Tenochtitlan, rushing back to defend his capital, with the Aztecs hot on his heels. While Nezahualcoyotl advanced from the north, the main Mexica forces attacked the eastern Tepanec provinces, taking semi-neutral Tlacopan on their way.

Some sources said that the siege upon Azcapotzalco lasted for 114 days, with Nezahualcoyotl and the Highlanders keeping the western watch, and the Mexica forces sealing the other roads leading to the great city. Other sources claim it was a shorter affair.

In the end, after many sorties and one large battle with the suddenly appearing Tepanec relief force, Azcapotzalco fell to the hands of its former tributaries and subjected nations, and the history of the Lake Texcoco changed.

Following the great victory, Tenochtitlan, Texcoco, and Tlacopan formed the Triple Alliance, or what we came to know as the famous Aztec Empire. Many sources state that the future empire, which had, indeed, stretched almost from coast to coast, encompassing much of the modern-day Mexico, while reaching far south into Mesoamerica, was the fruit of Tlacaelel's work. Many hold this man to be "the architect of the Aztec Empire", although he had never been an emperor.

Both Tlacaelel and Nezahualcoyotl lived long, fruitful lives, ruling their corners of the empire differently, but with much success.

What happened next is presented in the fifth book of the series, **"The Fall of the Empire"**.

ABOUT THE AUTHOR

Zoe Saadia is the author of several novels on pre-Columbian Americas. From the architects of the Aztec Empire to the founders of the Iroquois Great League, from the towering pyramids of Tenochtitlan to the longhouses of the Great Lakes, her novels bring long-forgotten history, cultures and people to life, tracing pivotal events that brought about the greatness of North and Mesoamerica.

To learn more about Zoe Saadia and her work, please visit
www.zoesaadia.com

Made in the USA
San Bernardino, CA
09 December 2017